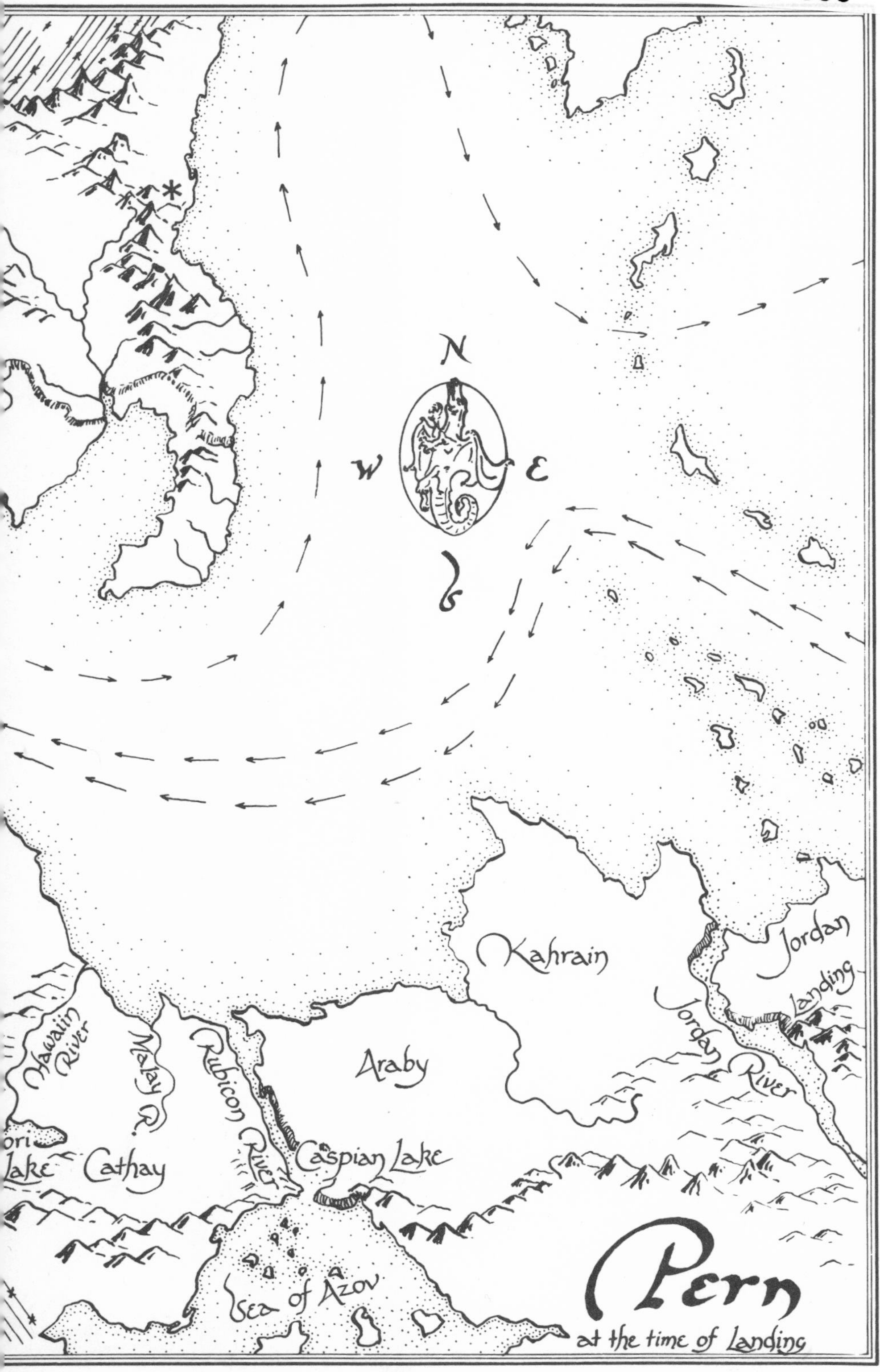
N
W
E
Kahrain
Jordan
Landing
Jordan River
Araby
Hawaiin River
Malay R.
Rubicon River
Caspian Lake
Lake
Cathay
Sea of Azov
Pern
at the time of Landing

DRAGONSDAWN

BY ANNE MCCAFFREY
Published by Ballantine Books:

Decision at Doona
Dinosaur Planet
Dinosaur Planet Survivors
Get off the Unicorn
The Lady
Restoree
The Ship Who Sang
To Ride Pegasus

THE DRAGONRIDERS OF PERN®
Dragonflight
Dragonquest
The White Dragon
Moreta: Dragonlady of Pern
Nerilka's Story

THE CRYSTAL SINGER BOOKS
Crystal Singer
Killashandra

Edited by Anne McCaffrey:
Alchemy and Academe

Dragonsdawn

Anne McCaffrey

A Del Rey Book
BALLANTINE BOOKS ▸ NEW YORK

A Del Rey Book
Published by Ballantine Books

Library of Congress Cataloging-in-Publication Data
McCaffrey, Anne.
Dragonsdawn.
"A Del Rey book."
I. Title.
PS3563.A255D76 1988 813′.54 88-47806

ISBN: 0-345-33160-5
Text design by Ann Gold
Manufactured in the United States of America
First Edition: November 1988

10 9 8 7 6 5 4 3 2 1

THIS BOOK WAS ALWAYS FOR

Judy-Lynn Benjamin del Rey

CONTENTS

PROFOUND ACKNOWLEDGMENTS

This book could not have been written without the advice, assistance, and aid of Dr. Jack Cohen, D.Sc., lately Senior Lecturer of Reproductive Biology at Birmingham University, England, whose expertise and enthusiasm helped me *create* the dragons of Pern, and attendant botany/biology/ecology. Jack made fact out of myth, and science out of legend. I am not the only writer of his acquaintance who owes him a tremendous debt of gratitude.

I am also indebted to Harry Alm, Naval Engineer of New Orleans, Louisiana, for his configuration of the Thread Fall Patterns, based on only casual remarks in various of my books. To his wife, Marilyn, I owe the patient and correct transmission by Compuserve of this incredible technical data.

PART ONE
Landing

"Probe reports coming through, sir," Sallah Telgar announced without taking her eyes from the flickering lights on her terminal.

"On the screen, please, Mister Telgar," Admiral Paul Benden replied. Beside him, leaning against his command chair, Emily Boll kept her eyes steadily on the sunlit planet, scarcely aware of the activity around her.

The Pern Colonial Expedition had reached the most exciting moment of its fifteen-year voyage: the three colony ships, the *Yokohama*, the *Bahrain*, and the *Buenos Aires* were finally approaching their destination. In offices below the bridge deck, specialists eagerly awaited updates on the reports of the long-dead Exploration and Evaluation team that, 200 years earlier, had recommended Rukbat's third planet for colonization.

The long journey to the Sagittarian Sector had gone without a hitch, the only excitement being the surprise when the Oort cloud encircling the Rukbat system had been sighted. That phenomenon had continued to engross some of the space and scientific personnel, but Paul Benden had lost interest when Ezra Keroon, captain of the *Bahrain* and the expedition's astronomer, had assured him that the nebulous mass of deep-frozen meteorites was no more than an astronomical curiosity. They would keep an eye on it, Ezra had said, but although some comets might form and spin from its depths, he doubted that they would pose a serious threat to either the three colony ships or the planet the ships were fast approaching. After all, the Exploration and Evaluation team had not mentioned any unusual incidence of meteor strikes on the surface of Pern.

"Screening probe reports, sir," Sallah confirmed, "on two and five." Out of the corner of her eye, she saw Admiral Benden smile slightly.

"This is sort of anticlimactic, isn't it?" Paul murmured to Emily Boll as the latest reports flashed onto the screens.

Arms folded across her chest, she hadn't moved since the probes had been launched, except for an occasional twiddling of fingers along her upper arms. She lifted her right eyebrow in a cynical twitch and kept her eyes on the screen.

"Oh, I don't know. It's one more procedure which gets us nearer to the surface. Of course," she added dryly, "we're sort of stuck with whatever's reported, but I expect we can cope."

"We'll have to, won't we?" Paul Benden replied a trifle grimly.

The trip was one-way—it had to be, considering the cost of getting over six thousand colonists and supplies to such an out-of-the-way sector of the galaxy. Once they reached Pern the fuel left in the great transport ships would be enough only to achieve and maintain a synchronous orbit above their destination while people and cargo were shuttled down to the surface. To be sure, they had homing capsules that would reach the headquarters of the Federated Sentient Planets in a mere five years, but to a retired naval tactician like Paul Benden, a fragile homing capsule did not offer much in the way of an effective backup. The Pern expedition was composed of committed and resourceful people who had chosen to eschew the high-tech societies of the Federated Sentient Planets. They expected to manage on their own. And though their destination in the Rukbat system was rich enough in ores and minerals to support an agriculturally based society, it was poor enough and far enough from the center of the galaxy that it should escape the greed of the technocrats.

"Only a little while longer, Paul," Emily murmured, her

voice reaching his ears alone, "and we'll both be able to lay down the weary load."

He grinned up at her, knowing that it had been as difficult for her as it had been for him to escape the blandishments of technocrats who had not wished to lose two such charismatic war heroes: the admiral who had prevailed in the Cygni Space Battle, and the governor-heroine of First Centauri. But no one could deny that the two were the ideal leaders for the Pern expedition.

"Speaking of loads," she went on more loudly, "I'd better be there to referee my team now the reports are coming in. I suppose specialists *have* to consider their own disciplines the most important ones, but such contentiousness!" She stifled a groan, then grinned, her blue eyes twinkling in her rather homely face. "Just a few more days of talking, and it'll be action stations, Admiral."

She knew him well. He hated the interminable debate over minor points that seemed to obsess those in charge of the landing operation. He preferred to make quick decisions and implement them immediately, instead of talking them to death.

"You're more patient with your teams than I am," the admiral said quietly. The last two months, as the three ships had decelerated into the Rukbat system, had been made tedious with meetings and discussions which seemed to Paul to be nitpicking over procedures that had been thoroughly thrashed out seventeen years before in the planning stages of the venture.

Most of the 2900 colonists on the *Yokohama* had passed the entire journey in deep sleep. Personnel essential to the operation and maintenance of the three great ships had stood five-year watches. Paul Benden had elected to stand the first and last five-year periods. Emily Boll had been revived shortly before the rest of the environmental specialists, who had spent their time railing at the superficiality of the Exploration and Evaluation Corps report. She saw no point in reminding them of their enthusiasm for the same words when they had signed up for the Pern expedition.

Paul continued to absorb the display information, eyes flicking from one screen to another, absently rubbing the thumb of his left hand across three fingers. Though not the sort of man Emily was attracted to, Paul Benden was undeniably handsome, and Emily much preferred him with his hair grown out of the spaceman's crop that had been his trademark. She thought that the thick blond mass softened the strong features: the blunt nose, the forceful jaw, and the wide thin-lipped mouth, just then pulled slightly to the left in a little smile.

The trip had done him good: he looked fit and well able to face the rigors of their next few months. Emily remembered how terribly thin he had been at the official ceremony commemorating his brilliant victory at Cygnus, where he and the Purple Sector Fleet had turned the tide of war against the Nathis. Legend said that he had remained awake and on duty for the entire seventy hours of the crucial battle. Emily believed it. She had done something of the sort herself during the height of the Nathis attack on her planet. There were many things a person could do if pushed, she knew from experience. She expected that one paid for such physical abuses later on in life, but Benden, well into his sixth decade, looked vigorously healthy. And she certainly felt no diminution of her own energies. Fourteen years of deep sleep seemed to have cured the terrible fatigue that had been the inevitable result of her defense of First Centauri.

And what a world they were now approaching! Emily sighed, still unable to look away from the main screen for more than a second. She knew that all those on duty on the bridge, along with those of the previous watch who had not left, were totally bemused by the magnificent sight of their destination.

Who had named it Pern, she did not recall—quite probably the single letters blazoned across the published report had stood for something else entirely—but it was Pern officially, and it was theirs. They were on an equatorial heading; as she watched, the planet's lazy rotation hid the northern continent and the spine of mountains up its coast, while the western desert of the southern landmass was revealed. The dominant topographical feature was the wide expanse of ocean, slightly greener than that of old Earth, with a ring of islands splattered across it. The atmosphere was currently decorated with the swirling cloud curl of a low-pressure area moving rapidly northeast. What a beautiful, beautiful world! She sighed again and caught Paul's quick glance. She smiled back at him without really taking her eyes from the screen.

A beautiful world! And theirs! By all the Holies, this time we won't botch it! she assured herself fervently. With all that magnificent, productive land, the old imperatives don't apply. No, she added in private cynicism, people are already discovering new ones. She thought of the friction she had sensed between the charterers, who had raised the staggering credits needed to finance the Pern expedition, and the contractors, the specialists hired to round out the basic skills required for the undertaking. Each could end up with a largeous amount of land or mineral rights on this new world, but the fact that the charterers would get first choice was a bone of contention.

Differences! Why did there always have to be distinctions, arrogantly displayed as superiorities, or derided as inferiorities? Everyone would have the same opportunity, no matter how many stake acres they could claim as charterer or had been granted as contractor. On Pern, it would truly be up to the individual to succeed, to prove his claim and to manage as much land as he and his cared for. That would be the catholic distinction. Once we've landed, everyone will be too bloody busy to fret over "differences," she consoled herself, and watched in fascination as a second low-pressure area began to spin down from the hidden north across the sea. If the two weather systems melded, there would be a tremendous storm over the eastern curve of the oceanic islands.

"Looking good," Commander Ongola murmured in his

deep, sad bass voice. Emily had not seen him smile once in the six months she had been awake. Paul had told her that Ongola's wife, children, and entire family had been vaporized when the Nathi had attacked their service colony; Paul had specifically requested him to join the expedition. Stationed at the science desk, Ongola was monitoring the meteorology and atmospherics displays. "Atmospheric content as expected. Southern continent temperatures appear to be normal for this late winter season. Northern continent enjoying considerable precipitation due to low-pressure air masses. Analyses and temperatures consistent with EEC report."

The first probe was doing a high-altitude circumnavigation in a pattern that would allow it to photograph the entire planet. The second, taking a low-level course, could reexamine any portion required. The third probe was programmed for topographical features.

"Probes four and six have landed, sir. Five is on hold," Sallah went on, as she interpreted the new lights that had begun to flash. "Scuttlebugs deployed."

"Show them on the screens, Mister Telgar," the admiral said. She transferred the displays to screens three, four, and six.

Pern's image continued to dominate the main screen as the planet rotated slowly to the east, from night to day. The southern continent's coastline was day-lit; the spinal range of mountains and the tracks of several rivers were visible. The thermal scan was showing the effect of daylight on the late winter season of the southern continent.

Probe scuttlebugs had been landed at three not-yet-visible specific points in the southern hemisphere and were relaying updates on current conditions and terrain. The southern continent had always been favored as the landing site: the survey-team report mentioned the more clement weather patterns on the high plateaus; a wider variety of plant life, some of it edible by humans; eminently suitable farmland; and good harbors for the tough siliplex fishing vessels that existed as numbered pieces in the holds of the *Buenos Aires* and the *Bahrain*. The seas of Pern teemed with aquatic life, and at least a few of the species could be safely consumed by humans. The marine biologists had high hopes of populating the bays and estuaries with Terran piscine types without harming the present ecological balance. The deep-freeze tanks of the *Bahrain* contained twenty-five dolphins who had volunteered to come along. Pern's seas were eminently suitable for the support of the intelligent mammals, who enjoyed sea-shepherding as well as the opportunity to see new worlds.

Soil analyses had indicated that Terran cereals and legumes, which had already adapted well to Centauran soil, should flourish on Pern, a necessity as the native grasses were unsuitable for Terran animals. One of the first tasks facing the agronomists would be to plant fodder crops to sustain the variety of herbivores and ruminants that had been brought as fertilized ova from the Animal Reproduction Banks of Terra.

In order that the colonists could ensure the adaptability of Terran animals to Pern, permission to use certain of the advanced biogenetic techniques of the Eridanis—mainly mentasynth, gene paring, and chromosome enhancements—had been grudgingly granted. Even though Pern was in an isolated area of the galaxy, the Federated Sentient Planets wanted no further disasters like the bio-alts, which had aroused the strong Pure Human Life Group.

Emily Boll repressed a shudder. Those memories belonged to the past. Displayed on the screen in front of her was the future—and she had best get down and help the specialists organize it. "I've dallied long enough," she murmured to Paul Benden, touching his shoulder in farewell.

Paul pulled his gaze from the screen and smiled at her, giving her hand a friendly pat. "Eat first!" He waggled a stern finger at her. "You keep forgetting we're not rationed on board the *Yoko*." She gave him a startled look. "I will. I promise."

"The next few weeks are going to be rough."

"Hmm, but so stimulating!" Her blue eyes twinkled. Then her stomach audibly rumbled. "Gotcha, Admiral." She winked again and left.

He watched her as she walked to the nearest exit off the bridge, a lean, almost bony woman, with gray and naturally wavy hair which she wore shoulder length. What Paul liked most about her was her wiry strength, both moral and physical, which was combined with a ruthlessness that sometimes startled him. She had tremendous personal vitality—just being in her presence gave one's spirits a lift. Together they would make something of their new world.

He looked back to the main screen and the enthralling vista of Pern.

The large lounge had been set up as an office for the heads of the various teams of exobiology, agronomy, botany, and ecology, along with six representatives of the professional farmers, who were still a bit groggy from their term in deep sleep. The room was ringed by multiple screens displaying a constantly altering range of microbiology reports, statistics, comparisons, and analyses. There was much debate going on. Those hunched over desk monitors, busily collating reports, tried to ignore the tension emanating from the departmental heads who occupied the very center of the room in a tight knot, each one with an eye out for the screens displaying reports on his or her specialty.

Mar Dook, head agronomist, was a small man whose Earth Asiatic ancestry was evident in features, skin tone, and physiology: he was wiry, lean, and slightly bowed in the shoulders, but his black eyes gleamed with eager intelligence and the excitement of the challenge.

"The schedule has long been decided, my dear colleagues. We're in the first wave down. The probes do not contradict any of the information we already have. The dirt and vegetation samples match. There's the same sort of red and green algae reported along the shoreline. Marine life has been sighted by the sea probe. One of the low probes has caught a comforting variety of insects, which the EEC also found. The aerial fax that came up with that flyer reported—what did the team call them?—wherries."

"Why 'wherries'?" Phas Radamanth asked. He scrolled through the report searching for that particular annotation. "Ah," he said when he found it. "Because they resemble airborne barges—squat, fat, and full." He allowed himself a little smile for the whimsy of that long-dead team.

"Yeah, but I don't see mention of any other predators," Kwan Marceau said, his rather high forehead creased, as usual, with a frown.

"There's sure to be something that eats them," Phas replied confidently.

"Or they eat each other," Mar Dook suggested. He received a stern frown from Kwan. Suddenly Mar Dook pointed excitedly to a new fax coming up on one screen. "Ah, look! The scuttlebug got a reptiloid. Rather a large specimen, ten centimeters thick and seven meters long. There's your wherry eater, Kwan."

"Another scuttle has just run through a puddle of excretal matter, semiliquid, which contains intestinal parasites and bacteria," Pol Nietro said, hurriedly tagging the report for later reference. "There do seem to be plenty of wormlike soil dwellers, too. Rather a significant variety, if you ask me. Worms like nematodes, insectoids, mites that really wouldn't be out of place in a Terran compost heap. Ted, here's something for you: plants like our mycorrhizas—tree fungi. Speaking of that, I wonder where the EEC team found that luminous mycelium."

Ted Tubberman, one of the colony botanists, gave a contemptuous snort. He was a big man, not carrying any extra flesh after nearly fifteen years in deep sleep, who tended to be overbearing. "Luminous organisms are usually found in deep caves, Nietro, as they use their light to attract their victims, generally insects. The mycelium reported by that team was in a cave system on that large island south of the northern continent. This planet seems to have a considerable number of cave systems. Why weren't any scuttles scheduled for subterranean investigations?" he asked in an aggrieved tone.

"There were only so many available, Ted," Mar Dook said placatingly.

"Ah, look! Now, this is what I've been waiting for," Kwan said, his usually solemn face lighting up as he bent until his nose almost touched the small screen before him. "There are reef systems. And yes, a balanced if fragile marine ecology along the ring islands. I'm much encouraged. Possibly those polka dots they saw are from a meteorite storm."

Ted dismissed that instantly. "No. No impact, and the formation of new growth does not parallel that sort of phenomenon. I intend looking into that problem the first moment I can."

"What we have to do first," Mar Dook said, his tone gently reproving, "is select the appropriate sites, plow, test, and, where necessary, introduce the symbiotic bacteria and fungi, even beetles, needed for pastureland."

"But we still don't know *which* landing site will be chosen." Ted's face was flushed with irritation.

"The three that are now being surveyed are much of a muchness," Mar Dook replied with a tolerant smile. He found Tubberman's petulant restlessness tedious. "All three give us ample scope for experimental and control fields. Our basic tasks will be the same no matter where we land. The essential point is not to miss this first vital growing season."

"The brood animals must be revived as soon as possible," Pol Neitro said. The head zoologist was as eager as everyone else to plunge into the practical work ahead. "And reliance on the alfalfa trays for fodder is not going to adjust their digestions to a new environment. We must begin as we mean to go on, and let Pern supply our needs."

There was a murmur of assent to his statement.

"The only new factor in these reports," Phas Radamanth, the xenobiologist, said encouragingly, without turning his eyes from his screens, "is the density of vegetation. We may have to clear more than we thought in the forty-five south eleven site. See here—" He gestured to the disparate images. "Where the EEC pic showed sparse ground cover, we now have heavy vegetation, some of it of respectable size."

"There should be at least that, after two-hundred-odd years," Ted Tubberman said irritably. "I never was happy about the barrenness. Smacked of a depauperate ecology. Hey, most of those circular features are overgrown. Felicia, run up the EEC pics that correspond." He bent his big frame to peer over her shoulder at the double screen below the probe broadcast. "See, those circles are barely discernible now. The team was right about botanical succession. And that isn't a grassoid. If that's mutant vegetation . . ." He trailed off, shaking his head and jutting his chin out. He had loudly and frequently insisted that the success of Pern as a colony would depend on botanical health.

"I, too, am happier to see succession, but according to the EEC reports, it's—" Mar Dook began.

"Shove the EEC reports. They didn't tell us the half of what we really need to know," Ted exclaimed. "Survey, they called it. Quick dip at the trot. No depth to it at all. The most superficial survey I've ever read."

"I quite agree," said the calm voice of Emily Boll, who had entered while the botanist was ranting. "The initial EEC report does seem to have been less than complete now that we can compare it to our new home. But the most crucial, salient points were covered for us. We know what we needed to know, and the FSP was quite happy to turn the planet over to us because it certainly doesn't have anything to interest them. And it's not a planet that the syndicates would fight over. Which is why *we* were allowed to have it. I think we have to be grateful to that team, not critical." Her smile swept everyone in the crowded room. "The important elements—atmosphere, water, arable soil, ores, minerals, bacteria, insects, marine life—are all present, and Pern is eminently suitable for human habitation. The gaps, the in-depth investigations that report did not contain, are what we shall spend a lifetime filling in. A challenge for each and every one of us, and our children!" Her low-pitched voice rang in the crowded room. "Let's not worry at this very late date about what we weren't told. We'll find the answers soon enough. Let's concentrate now on the great work we have to begin in just two days' time. We're ready for any surprises Pern might have for us. Now, Mar Dook, have you seen anything in the updates to suggest we must alter the schedule?"

"Nothing," Mar Dook replied, warily glancing at Ted Tubberman, who was frowning at Emily Boll. "But those soil and vegetable matter samples would occupy us usefully."

"I'm sure they would." Emily grinned broadly at him. "We'll be busy enough—ah, here's the information you need. And what a bumper crop to digest."

"We still don't know *where* we're landing," Ted complained.

"The admiral is discussing that right now, Ted," Emily replied equably. "We'll be among the first to know."

Agronomists were to be in the first shuttleloads to reach the surface, for it was vital to the colony's future to break land for crops as soon as possible. Even while the engineers were setting up the landing grids, agronomists would be plowing fields, and Ted Tubberman and his group would be setting up sheds and seeding the precious soil brought from Earth. Pat Hempenstall would set up a control shed using indigenous dirt, to see if Earth or colonial variants would thrive unassisted in an alien soil. Sufficient packaged organisms had also been brought to introduce symbiotic bacteria.

"I will be very glad," Pol Nietro murmured, "if the reports confirm those insectoids, winged and subterranean, reported by the EEC team. If they should prove sufficient to do the work of dung beetles and flies on our Terran-style detritus, agronomy will be off to a good start. We've got to get nutrients back into the soil and introduce the rumen bacteria, protozoans, and yeasts for our cows, sheep, goats, and horses so they'll thrive."

"If not, Pol," Emily replied, "we can ask Kitti to work a bit of her micro-magic and rearrange innards that can deal with what Pern has to offer." She smiled with great deference at the tiny lady seated in the center of the little cluster.

"Soil samples coming up," Ju Adjai said into the pause. "And here's vegetable mash for you, Ted. Get your teeth in that."

Tubberman launched himself to the position next to Felicia, his big fingers nimble and accurate over the keyboard.

In moments the rattling of keys, punctuated by assorted mutters and other monosyllables of concentration, filled the room. Emily and Kit Ping exchanged glances tinged with amused condescension for the vagaries of their younger colleagues. Kit Ping then turned her eyes back to the main screen and continued her contemplation of the world they were rapidly approaching.

As Emily sat down at her workspace, she wondered how under the suns the expedition had lucked out enough to include the most eminent geneticist in the Federated Sentient Planets—the only human who had ever been trained by the Eridanis. Emily had only seen pics of the altered humans who had made the first abortive mission to Eridani. She suppressed a shudder. Pern wouldn't ever require that kind of abominable tinkering. Maybe that's why Kit Ping was willing to come to the edge of the galaxy—to end what had already been a long and incredible life in a quiet backwater where she, too, could practice selective amnesia. There were many on the colony's roll who had come to forget what they had seen and done.

"The grassoid on that eastern landing site is going to be hell to cut through," Ted Tubberman said, scowling. "High boron content. It'll dull cutting edges and foul gear."

"It'd cushion the landing," Pat Hempenstall said with a chuckle.

"Our landing craft have landed safely on far more inhospitable terrain than that," Emily reminded the others.

"Felicia, run a comparison on the botanical succession around those crazy polka dots," Ted Tubberman went on, staring at his own screens. "There's something about that configuration that still bothers me. The phenomenon is all over the planet. And I'd be happier if we could get an opinion from that geologist whiz, Tarzan—" He paused.

"Tarvi Andiyar," Felicia supplied, accustomed to Ted's memory lapses.

"Well, memo him to meet me when he's revived. Damn it, Mar, how can we function with only half the specialists awake?"

"We're doing fine, Ted. Pern is coming up roses for us. Not a joggle off the report data."

"That's almost worrying," Pol Nietro said blandly.

Tubberman snorted, Mar Dook shrugged, and Kitti Ping smiled.

Admiral Benden's chrono tingled against his wrist, reminding him that it was time for his own meeting.

"Commander Ongola, take the conn." Reluctantly, his eyes focusing on the main screen until the access panel of the exit closed, Paul left the bridge.

The corridors of the great colony ship were becoming more crowded by the hour, Paul noticed as he made his way to the wardroom. Newly revived people, clutching the handrails, were jerkily exercising stiff limbs and trying to focus body and mind on the suddenly hazardous task of remaining upright. The old *Yoko* would be packed tighter than reserve rations while colonists awaited their turns to reach the surface. But with the promise of the freedom of a whole new world as the reward of patience, the crowding could be endured.

Having paid close attention to the various probe reports, Paul had already decided which of the three recommended landing sites he would choose. Naturally he would accord his staff and the other two captains the courtesy of a hearing, but the obvious choice was the vast plateau below a group of strato volcanoes. The current weather there was clement, and the nearly level expanse was adequate to accommodate all six shuttles. The updates had only confirmed a tentative preference made seventeen years ago when he had first studied the EEC reports. He had never anticipated much difficulty with landing; it was a smooth and accident-free debarkation that caused him anxiety. There was no rescue backup hovering solicitously in the skies of Pern, nor disaster teams on its surface.

In organizing the debarkation, Paul had chosen as flight officer Fulmar Stone, a man who had served with him throughout the Cygnus campaign. For the past two weeks, Fulmar's crews had been all over the *Yoko*'s three shuttle vehicles and the admiral's gig, ensuring that there would be no malfunction after fifteen years in the cold storage of the flight deck. The *Yoko*'s twelve pilots, under Kenjo Fusaiyuki, had gone through rigorous simulator drills well spiced with the most bizarre landing emergencies. Most of the pilots had been combat fighters, and were fit and fully experienced at extricating themselves from tricky situations, but none had quite the record of Kenjo Fusaiyuki. Some of the less experienced shuttle pilots had complained about Kenjo's methods; Paul Benden had courteously listened to the complaints—and ignored them.

Paul had been surprised and flattered when Kenjo had signed up with the expedition. Somehow, he had thought the man would have signed on to an exploratory unit where he could continue to fly as long as his reflexes lasted. Then Paul remembered that Kenjo was a cyborg, with a prosthetic left leg. After the war, the Exploration and Evaluation Corps had had their choice of experienced, whole personnel, and cyborgs had been shunted into administrative positions. Automatically, Paul made his left hand into a fist, his thumb rubbing against the knuckles of the three replacement fingers which had always worked as well as his natural ones. But there was still no feeling in the pseudoflesh. Consciously, he relaxed the hand, certain once again that he could hear a subtle plastic squeak in the joints and the wrist.

He turned his mind to real problems, like the debarkation ahead, knowing that unforeseeable delays or foul-ups could stall the entire operation as cargo and passengers began to flow from the orbiting ships. He had appointed good men as supercargoes: Joel Lilienkamp as surface coordinator, and Desi Arthied on the *Yoko*. Ezra and Jim, of *Bahrain* and *Buenos Aires*, were equally confident in their own debarkation personnel, but one minor hitch could cause endless rescheduling. The trick would be to keep everything moving.

The admiral turned starboard off the main corridor and reached the wardroom. Once again, he hoped that the meeting would not drag on. As he raised his hand to brush the access panel, he could see that he had arrived with two minutes to spare before the other two captains screened in. First there would be the brief formality of Ezra Keroon, as fleet astrogator, confirming the exact ETA at their parking orbit, and then the landing site would be chosen.

"The betting's eleven to four now, Lili," Paul heard Drake Bonneau saying to Joel as the access panel to his wardroom *whoosh*ed open.

"For or against?" Paul asked, grinning as he entered. Those present, led by Kenjo's example, shot to their feet, despite Paul's dismissing gesture. He took in the two blank screens which in precisely ninety-five seconds would reveal the faces of Ezra Keroon and Jim Tillek, and to the center one where Pern swam tranquilly in the black ocean of space.

"There're some civilians don't think Desi and me can make the deadline, Paul," Joel answered with a smug wink at Arthied, who nodded solemnly. Not a tall man, Lilienkamp was chunkily built; he had an engaging monkey face, framed with graying dark hair that curled tightly against his skull. His personality was ebullient, volatile, and could be caustic. His quick wits included an eidetic memory that allowed him to keep track of not only any bet he made, for how much and with whom and what odds, but every parcel, package, crate, and canister in his keeping. Desi Arthied, his second-in-command, often found his superior's levity a trial, but he respected Lilienkamp's abilities. It would be Desi's job to shift the cargo that Joel designated to the loading decks and on board the shuttles.

"Civilians? Who don't know you very well, do they?" Paul asked dryly, taking his seat and smiling noncommittally at Avril Bitra, who had been in charge of the simulation exercises. Ambition had hardened her. He wished that he had not spent so much of his waking time during the voyage involved with the sultry brunette, but she *was* stunning. Soon they would all be too busy for personal relationships. More and more attractive young women were appearing in the corridors. He wanted one of them to want to marry Paul Benden, not "the admiral." Just then, the two screens lit up, the right-hand one displaying Ezra Keroon's saturnine countenance, with his distinctive fringe of gray hair, and the left showing Jim Keroon, his square face wearing his usual cheerful expression.

"G'day, Paul," he said, just ahead of Ezra's more formal salute.

"Admiral," Ezra said solemnly. "I beg to report that we have maintained our programmed course to the minute. Estimated arrival to parking orbit is now forty-six hours, thirty-three minutes, and twenty seconds. No deviations anticipated at this point in time."

"Very good, Captain," Paul said, returning the salute. "Any problems?"

Both captains reported that their revival programs were continuing without incident and that their shuttles were ready for launch once orbit had been achieved.

"Now that we know when, the matter of where is open for discussion," Paul said, leaning back in his chair to signal that comment was invited.

"So, tell us, Paul," Joel Lilienkamp said with his usual disregard for protocol, "where're we landing?" All through the Nathi War, Joel's impertinence had amused Paul Benden at a time when amusement was scarce, and he had consistently proved himself a near miraculous scavenger. His impudence caused Ezra Keroon to frown, but Jim Tillek chuckled.

"What are the odds, Lili?" he asked, his expression sly.

"Let us discuss the matter without prejudice," Paul suggested wryly. "The three sites recommended by the EEC team have now all been probed. If you will refer to the chart, the sites are at thirty south by thirteen point thirty, forty-five south by eleven, and forty-seven south by four point seven five."

"There's really only one, Admiral, from my point of view," Drake Bonneau interrupted excitedly, jabbing his finger at Paul's own choice, the strato site. "Scuttlebug scans say it's almost as level as if it had been graded for us, and broad enough to accommodate all six shuttles. The site at forty-five south eleven is waterlogged right now, and the western one is too far from the ocean. Temperature readings are near freezing."

Paul saw Kenjo's nod of agreement. He glanced at the two screens. Ezra's growing bald spot was evident as he bent to consult his notes; unconsciously, Paul smoothed back his own thick hair.

"That thirty south is nearer sea for me," Jim Keroon remarked amiably. "Good harbor about fifty klicks away. River's navigable, too." Keroon's interest in sailing vessels was exceeded only by his love of dolphins. Accessibility to open water would be a high factor in his choice.

"Good heights for observatory and met stations all right," Ezra replied, "though we've no real criterion from those reports about climatology. Don't fancy settling that close to volcanoes myself."

"A point, Ezra, but—" Paul paused to screen the relevant

data for a quick scan. "No seismic readings were recorded, so I don't see volcanic activity as an immediate problem. We can have Patrice de Broglie do a survey. Ah, yes, no seismic readings from the EEC, so even the one that has erupted has been dormant for well over two hundred years. And the weather and general conditions on the other two sites do mitigate against them."

"Hmm, so they do. Doesn't look from a met point of view as if the conditions at either will improve in two days," Ezra conceded.

"Hell, we don't have to *stay* where we land," Drake exclaimed.

"Unless there's some freak weather brewing up," Jim Keroon said, "which I'm sure the met boys will be able to spot, let's settle on the thirty-south site. That's the one the EEC team favored, anyhow. Besides, the scuttlebugs say it's got a thick ground cover. That should cushion the shock when you bounce, Drake."

"Bounce?" Drake's gray eyes widened at the mild jibe. "Captain Keroon, I haven't bounced a landing since my first solo."

"Very well, then, gentlemen, have we settled on our landing site?" Paul asked. Ezra and Jim nodded. "Relevant updates and detailed charts will be in your hands by 2200 hours."

"Well, Joel," Jim Keroon said, his sly grin broadening, "didja win?"

"Me, Captain?" Joel's expression was that of injured innocence. "I never bet on a sure thing."

"Any other problems to raise at this point, Captains?" Paul paused courteously, looking from one screen to the other.

"All ahead go, Paul, now I know I'll land this bucket in her parking space on time," Jim said, "and where to send my shuttle." He waved a casual salute toward Ezra and then his screen blacked out.

"Good evening, Admiral," Ezra said more formally. His image faded.

"Is that all now, Paul?" Joel asked.

"We've got the time and the place," Paul replied, "but that's a tough timetable you've set, Joel. Can you keep it?"

"There's a lot of money says he will, Admiral," Drake Bonneau quipped.

"Why do you think it took me so long to load the *Yoko*, Admiral?" Joel Lilienkamp replied with a wide grin. "I knew I'd have to unload it all fifteen years later. You'll see." He winked at Desi, whose expression showed the faintest hint of skepticism.

"Then, gentlemen," the admiral said, standing up, "I'll be in my cabin if any problems do arise."

As he swung out of the wardroom, Paul heard Joel asking for bets on how soon knowledge of the landing site would circulate the *Yoko*.

Arvil's throaty voice replied. "Those odds, Lili." Then the door panel *whoosh*ed shut.

Morale was high. Paul hoped that Emily's meeting had been as satisfactory. Seventeen years of planning and organization were about to be put to the test.

On the deep-sleep decks of all three colony ships, the medics were working double shifts to arouse the fifty-five hundred or so colonists. Technicians and specialists were being revived in order of their usefulness to the landing operation, but Admiral Benden and Governor Boll had been insistent that everyone be awake by the time the three ships achieved their temporarily programmed parking position in a stable Lagrangian orbit, sixty degrees ahead of the larger moon, in the L–5 spot. Once the three great ships had been cleared of passsengers and cargo, there would be no more chance to view Pern from outer space.

Sallah Telgar, coming off duty from her watch on the bridge, decided that she had had quite enough space travel for one lifetime. As the only surviving dependent of serving officers, she had spent her childhood being shunted from one service post to another. When she had lost both parents, she had been eligible to sign on as a charter member of the colony. War compensations had permitted her to acquire a substantial number of stake acres on Pern, which she could claim once the colony had become solidly established. Above all other considerations, Sallah yearned to set herself down in one place and stay there for the rest of her natural life. She was quite content that that place be Pern.

As she exited bridge territory for the main corridors, she was surprised to see so many people about. For nearly five years she had had a cabin to herself. The cabin was not spacious even for single-occupancy, and with three sharing, it offered no privacy at all. Not eager to return, Sallah made for the off-duty lounge, where she could get something to eat and continue planet-gazing, courtesy of the lounge's large screen.

At the lounge entrance, Sallah hauled up sharp, surprised at how few seats were available. In the brief moments it took her to collect food from the dispensers, her options were narrowed down to one: a wall-counter seat well to the port side of the big room, with a slightly distorted view of Pern.

Sallah shrugged diffidently. Like an addict, she would take any view she could get of Pern. However, as she slipped into the seat, she realized that her nearest neighbors were also the people she least liked on board the *Yokohama:* Avril Bitra, Bart Lemos, and Nabhi Nabol. They were seated with three men she did not know, whose collar tabs identified them as mason, mechanical engineer, and miner. The six were also about the only people in the room not avidly watching the screen. The three specialists were listening to Avril and Bart, their faces carefully expressionless, though the oldest man, the engineer, occasionally glanced around to check on the attention of those nearby. Avril had her elbows on the table, her handsome face marred by the arrogant, supercilious sneer she affected, her black eyes glinting as she leaned forward toward homely Bart Lemos, who was enthusiastically punching his right fist into his left palm to emphasize his quick low words. Nabhi was wearing his perpetual expression of hauteur, an expression not far removed from Avril's sneer, as he watched the geologist.

Their attitudes were enough to spoil anyone's appetite, Sallah thought. She craned her neck to see Pern.

Gossip had it that Avril had spent a good deal of the last five years in Admiral Paul Benden's bed. Candidly, Sallah could see why a virile man like the admiral would be sexually attracted by the astrogator's dark and flashing beauty. A mixture of ethnic ancestors had given her the best of all possible features. She was tall, neither willowy nor overripe, with luxuriant black hair that she often wore loose in silky ripples. Her slightly sallow complexion was flawless and her movements gracefully studied, but her eyes, snapping with black fire, indicated a highly intelligent and volatile personality. Avril was not a woman to cross, and Sallah had carefully maintained her distance from Paul Benden, or anyone else seen more than three times in Avril's company. If the unkind pointed out Paul Benden's recent marked absence from Avril's side, the charitable said that he was needed for long conferences with his staff, and the time for dalliance was over. Those who had been victims of Avril's sharp tongue said that she had lost her bid to be the admiral's lady.

However, Sallah had other matters on her mind than Avril Bitra's ploys. She was waiting to hear which site had been chosen for landing. She knew that a decision had been made, and that it was to be kept secret until the admiral's formal announcement. But she knew, too, that the news was bound to leak. Bets had been surreptitiously made about how soon the rest of the ship would know. The news should percolate through the lounge real soon now, Sallah thought.

"This is where," a man suddenly exclaimed. He strode to the screen, jabbing his forefinger at a point that had just become visible. He wore the agronomy plow tab on his collar. "Right—" He paused as the screen image moved fractionally. "Here!" He planted his forefinger at the base of a volcano, discernible only as a pinpoint but nevertheless recognizable as a landmark.

"How much did Lili win on that one?" someone demanded.

"Don't care about him," the agronomist shouted. "I've just won an acre off Hempenstall!"

There was a ripple of applause and good-natured joking, infectious enough to make Sallah grin, until her gaze happened to spot the contemptuous smile of superiority on Avril's face. Seeing the astrogator's expression, Sallah knew that Avril had known the secret and withheld the information from her table companions. Bart Lemos and Nabhi Nabol leaned closer to exchange terse sentences.

Avril shrugged. "The landing site is immaterial." Her sultry voice, though low, carried to Sallah's ears. "The gig's equipped to do the job, believe me." She glanced away and caught Sallah's eyes. Instantly her body tensed and her eyes narrowed. With a conscious effort she relaxed and leaned indolently back in her chair, maintaining eye contact with an insolence that Sallah found aggravating.

Sallah looked away, feeling slightly soiled. She drank the last gulp of coffee, grimacing at the bitter aftertaste. The ship's coffee was lousy, but she would miss even that facsimile when the supply was exhausted. Coffee had failed on all the colony planets so far, for reasons no one had yet discerned. The survey team had discovered and recommended a Pernese shrub bark as a coffee substitute, but Sallah did not have much faith in that.

After the identification of the landing site, the noise level in the lounge had risen to an almost intolerable pitch. With a sigh, Sallah ditched her rubbish in the disposer, passed her tray under the cleanser, and stacked it neatly with others. She permitted herself one last long look at Pern. We won't spoil this planet, she thought. I personally won't let anyone spoil it.

As she turned to leave, her glance fell on Avril's dark head. Now there's an odd one to be a colonist, Sallah thought, not for the first time. Avril was listed as a contractor, with a handsome stake as a professional fee, but she scarcely seemed the sort who would be comfortable in a rural environment. She had all the sophisticated manners of the citified. The Pern expedition had attracted some first-rate talents, but most of those to whom Sallah had talked had been motivated to leave behind the syndicate-ridden technocracy and its ever-spiraling need for resources.

Sallah liked the notion of joining a self-reliant society so far from Earth and her other colonies. From the moment she had read the Pern prospectus she had been eager to be part of the venture. At sixteen, with service compulsory at that point in the bitterly fought Nathi War, she had chosen pilot training, with additional studies in probe and surveillance techniques. She had completed her training just as the war ended and then used her skills to map devastated areas on one planet and two moons. When the Pern expedition was put together, she had not only been eligible to be a charterer, but had the experience and skills that would make her a valuable addition to the professional complement.

She left the off-duty lounge to return to her quarters, but she was not sure she would be able to sleep. In two days, they would reach their long-awaited goal. Then life would get interesting!

Just as Sallah turned into the main corridor, a little girl with burnished deep red hair lurched into her, tried to regain her balance, and fell heavily at Sallah's feet. Bursting into loud sobs, more from frustration than from hurt, the child clung to Sallah's leg in a grip astonishingly strong for one so young.

"There now, not to cry. You'll get your balance back, pet," Sallah said soothingly, reaching down to stroke the child's silky hair and then to loosen her frantic grip.

"Sorka! Sorka!" An equally redheaded man holding a little boy by one hand, and a very pretty brunette woman by the other, moved unsteadily toward Sallah. The woman had all the signs of someone only just awake: her eyes didn't quite focus, and while she was trying to respond to the situation, she was unable to concentrate.

The man's eyes flicked to Sallah's collar emblem. "I do apologize, Pilot," the redheaded man said, grinning apologetically. "We're really not awake yet."

He was trying to disencumber one hand to come to Sallah's assistance, but the woman refused to relinquish her grasp, and plainly he could not let go of the tottering boy.

"You need help," Sallah said pleasantly, wondering which medic had let the totally unstable quartet out on their own.

"Our quarters are only a few steps along." He nodded toward the splinter aisle behind Sallah. "Or so I was told. But I never appreciated how far a few steps could be."

"What's the number? I'm off duty."

"B–8851."

Sallah looked at the plates on the corridor corners and nodded. "It *is* just the next aisle. Here, I'll help. There now, Sorka—is that your name? Here, I'll just—"

"Excuse me," the man interrupted as Sallah moved to lift the child into her arms. "They kept telling us we'd be better off walking. Trying to walk, that is."

"I can't walk," Sorka cried. "I'm lopsided." She clung more fiercely to Sallah's legs.

"Sorka! Behave yourself!" The redhead frowned at his daughter.

"Got an idea!" Sallah said in a brisk friendly tone. "You take both my hands—" She peeled Sorka's fingers from her leg and grasped each little hand firmly in her own. "—and walk in front of me. I'll keep you on an even keel."

Even with Sallah's help, the family made slow progress, impeded by the more agile walkers rushing by on private errands, and by the uncertainty of their own steps.

"I'm Red Hanrahan," the man said when their progress improved.

"Sallah Telgar."

"Never thought I'd need help from a pilot before we

reached Pern," he said with a wide grin. "This is my wife, Mairi, my son, Brian, and you've got Sorka."

"Here we are," Sallah said, reaching their compartment and throwing open the door. She grimaced at the size of the accommodation and then reminded herself that their occupancy would only be for a short time. Even though the bunks were strapped up against the walls in their daytime position, the remaining floor space allowed for little movement.

"Not much larger than the quarters we just vacated," Red remarked equably.

"How are we supposed to exercise in here?" his wife demanded, a rather shrill note in her voice as she rolled her body around the doorjamb and got a good look at the size of their cabin.

"One by one, I guess," Red said. "It's only for a few days, pet, and then we'll have a whole planet to range. In you go, Brian, Sorka. We've kept Pilot Telgar long enough. You really saved us, Telgar. Thanks."

Sorka, who had propped herself against the inside wall of their cabin as her father encouraged the rest of his family to enter, slid to a sitting position on the floor, her little knees against her chest. Then she cocked her head to peer up at Sallah. "Thanks from me, too," she said, sounding more self-possessed. "It's really silly not knowing up from down, and side from side."

"I agree, but the effect will disappear very quickly. We all had to go through it when we woke up."

"You did?" Sorka's incredulous expression turned into the most radiant smile Sallah had ever seen, and she found herself grinning, too.

"We did. Even Admiral Benden," she said mendaciously. She ruffled the child's silky, magnificently titian hair. "I'll see you around. Okay?"

"While you're in that position, Sorka, do those exercises we were shown. Then it'll be Brian's turn," Red Hanrahan was saying as Sallah closed the door behind her.

She reached her own quarters without further incident, though the corridors were filled with recent sleepers lurching about, their expressions ranging from intense concentration to horrified dismay. The moment Sallah opened her door, she was aware of the occupants asleep inside. She grimaced. Very carefully she slid the panel back and leaned against it, wondering what to do. She was too keyed up to sleep yet; she had to wind down somehow. She decided to go to the pilots' ready room for some stimulating simulator practice. The moment of truth for her abilities as a shuttle pilot was rapidly approaching.

Her route was impeded by another recently awakened colonist whose coordination suffered from prolonged disuse. He was so rake-thin that Sallah feared he would break a bone as he lurched from side to side.

"Tarvi Andiyar, geologist," he said, courteously introducing himself as soon as she had supported him to a vertical stance. "Are we really orbiting Pern?" His eyes crossed as he looked at her, and Sallah managed to suppress the grin that his comical expression evoked. She told him their position. "And you have seen with your own bright and pretty eyes this marvelous planet?"

"I have and it's every bit as lovely as forecast," Sallah assured him warmly. He smiled broadly in relief, showing her very white and even teeth. Then he gave a shake of his head, which seemed to correct the aberrant focus of his eyes. He had one of the most beautiful faces she had ever seen on a man—not Benden's rugged, warrior features, but a sophisticated and subtle arrangement, almost sculpted, like some of the ancient Indic and Cambodian princes on ruined stone murals. She flushed as she remembered what those princes had been doing in the murals.

"Would you know if there are any updated probe reports? I am exceedingly eager to get to work."

Sallah laughed, amusement easing the sensual jolt his face had given her. "You can't even walk and you want to get to work?"

"Isn't fifteen years' holiday long enough for anyone?" His expression was mildly chiding. "Is that not cabin C–8411?"

"It is indeed," she said, guiding him across the corridor.

"You are as beautiful as you are kind," he said, one hand on the panel for support as he tried to make a very courtly bow. She had to grab at his shoulders as he overbalanced. "And quick." With a more judicious inclination of his head, and with considerable dignity under the circumstances, he opened his door.

"Sallah!" Drake Bonneau exclaimed, striding down the corridor toward her. "Anybody told you where we're landing?" He had the eager expression of someone about to confer a favor on a friend.

"It took no more than nine minutes for the scuttlebutt to circulate," she said coolly.

"That long?" He pretended disdain and then produced one of the smiles that he assumed would charm anyone. "Let's drink to it. Not much longer to enjoy our leisure, eh? Just you and me, huh?"

She suppressed her distrust of his flattery. He was probably not even conscious of the triteness of his glib phrases. She had heard him trot out the same smooth lines for any reasonably attractive female, and at the moment, his casual insincerity irritated her. Yet he was not a bad sort, and certainly he had had courage enough to spare during the war. Then she realized that her uncharacteristic annoyance was a reaction to the sudden bustle, noise, and proximity of so many people after the last few years of quiet. Relax, she told herself sternly, it's only for a few days and then you'll be too busy flying to worry about crowds and noise.

"Thanks, Drake, but Kenjo has me down for simulator practice in—" She glanced at her wrist. "—five minutes. Getcha another time."

To avoid the crowded corridors, she took the emergency tube down to the flight deck, then made her way past the variety of cargo secured there to the admiral's gig, the *Mariposa*. It was a compact little craft, with its delta wing and its perky, pointed nacelle, but it would be full of quiet and unoccupied space. Sallah punched the hatch release.

Sallah shared her next watch, the dogwatch, with Kenjo Fusaiyuki. There was little for either of them to do, bar reacting if a glitch halted the programs. Sallah was hacking around, trying to find something interesting enough to keep her awake, when she noticed that Kenjo had activated one of the smaller screens on his position.

"What have you got there?" she asked before she remembered Kenjo was not generally outgoing and might resent her interruption.

"I was decoding the gen on that eccentric wanderer," he replied, without looking up from the screen.

"Oh, the one that had the astronomers all excited?" Sallah asked. She grinned, remembering the unusual spectacle of the rather staid, pedantic astronomer, Xi Chi Yuen, flushed with excitement and dancing about the bridge.

"Quite likely," Kenjo said. "It does seem to have an enormously eccentric orbit, more cometary than planetary, though its mass indicates its planetary size. Look." He tapped out a sequence that brought up the satellites of Pern's star system in relation to their primary and to one another. "It computes to come in farther than the usual fourth planet position and actually intrudes on the Oort cloud at aphelion. This is supposed to be an old system, or so the EEC report leads one to believe, and that planet ought to have a more conventional orbit."

"There was talk that it could be a stray that the Rukbat sun attracted."

Kenjo shook his head. "That has been ruled out." He typed

out another sequence and the diagram on the screen shifted to another projection. In a few seconds, equations overlaid the system diagram. "Look at the odds against that." He pointed to the blinking nine-figure probability. "It would have to be a cometary-type orbit, right into the system. But it's not." His long, bony fingers reset the screen. "I can't find a harmonic with the other planets. Ah, Captain Keroon registers the opinion that it might have been captured by Rukbat about ten of its cycles ago."

"No, I think Xi Chi Yuen ruled that out. He computed it to be just after aphelion right now," Sallah said. "What did he say? Ah . . ." She tried to remember.

Kenjo was already accessing that file. "His report actually says that the eccentric planetoid had just exited the Oort cloud, pulling some of the cloud matter with it."

"He also said, and I remember that distinctly, that in about eight years' time, we'll have a rather spectacular meteorite show as our new world goes through the wisps of Oort material."

Kenjo snorted. "I'd rather we didn't. I don't have much faith in that EEC report now that it's being compared with what's there. Those polka dots may be meteor damage after all."

"I'm not going to lose any sleep over it."

"Nor I." Kenjo crossed his arms over his chest as the report continued to scroll up the screen. "Yuen apparently believes that with such an eccentric, almost parabolic orbit, this Pluto body may exit the star system again, or fall into the sun."

"Which wouldn't much notice, would it?"

Kenjo shook his head, his eyes still scanning the report. "Frozen solid. Much too far from Rukbat to get any warmth during most of its orbit. There's a possibility of a cometary tail visible when it's close in." He exited that program and tapped out a new sequence. "Pern's two moons are much more interesting."

"Why? We're not colonizing *them.* Anyway, fuel consumption allows for only the one trip to the moons, to set up the relay disks."

Kenjo shrugged. "You *always* leave yourself an escape route."

"To a moon?" Sallah was openly skeptical. "C'mon, Kenjo, we're not at war with anyone or anything this far from the Hub. Give over." She spoke kindly, knowing that Kenjo had had several very narrow escapes in the Nathi War.

"Old habits die hard," he murmured in such a low voice that she almost missed it.

"Yeah, they do. But we're all going to be able to start fresh."

Kenjo merely grunted, signaling an end to his talkative mood.

As the colony ships slowed, they were filled with constant activity as sleepers continued to be awakened, and the immense cargo pods were opened and their contents transferred to decks, spilling into access corridors. When the shuttles had been secured for the long voyage, they had already been loaded with the grid components and other necessities to build a safe landing field for the mass of matériel and people to be discharged from the colony ships. The urgency was to have the next shipment—agricultural tools and supplies—ready to be hustled on board as soon as the shuttles returned. The agronomists had promised to break ground before the next shuttle flight could reach the planet.

There were six shuttles between the three ships: three in the *Yoko,* two in the *Buenos Aires,* and one in the *Bahrain,* the latter equipped with special fittings for transporting livestock. Once the vessels had achieved their Lagrangian orbit, debarkation would commence.

Twelve hours before that event, all the sleepers had been revived. There was a fair amount of grumbling about the crowding. Many felt that the unessential people, especially young children, should have slept on until planetside accommodations were completed. But despite the inconvenience, Sallah agreed with the governor's announcement that no one should be denied the chance to witness the end of the long journey and the incredible vision of their new world spinning in black space. Sallah could not keep her eyes off Pern and watched on whatever screen was available, even the tiny one in her quarters. She had also managed to get on the duty roster for the most important watch of the entire trip.

Afterward, Sallah always stoutly averred that she had known the instant the *Yokohama* reached its orbital position. The great ship had been slowing for days; the slight puff of the retros as they reduced the forward motion to a match with the planet below was infinitesimal. Suddenly they were turning with the planet, in position over a real point on Pern, seeming to come to a halt in relation to the geography below them. Somehow Sallah sensed that moment. She actually looked up from her console just as the helmsman, with suppressed excitement, turned to salute the commander.

"We have arrived, sir," the helmsman announced.

At the same instant, a similar report came in from the *Bahrain* and the *Buenos Aires,* and those on the bridge erupted into cheers and undisciplined expressions of relief and exultation. Commander Ongola immediately informed the admiral of the completion of the maneuver and received formal thanks. Then he ordered all screens to focus on the planet spread out below them, curving away into night on the one side, and into brilliant day on the other.

Sallah joined in the hullabaloo until she noticed a break in the chatter from the probe and checked the monitor. The probe was merely switching its site as programmed. As she looked up, she caught a very sad, oddly pensive expression on Commander Ongola's face. Aware of her scrutiny, he arched one eyebrow in query.

Sallah smiled back in sympathy. The end of his last voyage, she thought. Who wouldn't be sad?

Both of Ongola's heavy eyebrows went up, and with great

dignity he turned his head away, giving the order for the shuttle-bay doors to be opened. The crew and the initial landing party were already strapped into their seats aboard the shuttles, awaiting the history-making order. Under her breath, Sallah murmured a good luck to Kenjo, Drake, and Nabol, who were piloting the *Yoko*'s three shuttles.

Klaxons announced the imminent departure, and immediatedly the main screen turned its eye to the landing site. The watch officers sat alert at their stations. Smaller screens showed the opened shuttle-bay doors from several angles, so that the bridge personnel could watch the shuttles begin to drift from their mother ship, dropping quickly on puffs of their jets before the main engines were ignited. They would spiral down across the planet, entering Pern's atmosphere on the western edge of the northern continent, and braking as they continued on down and around the globe until they reached their landing site on the eastern end of the southern continent. Exterior cameras picked up the other three shuttles, which took their positions in the flotilla. Gracefully, all six arrowed down and then out of sight over the curve of the planet.

Sallah's watch ended before the estimated time of arrival on Pern, but she made herself small against the side wall, along with everyone else from her watch, in order to have the best view possible. She knew that every screen on the ship was broadcasting the same information, and that the visual of the actual landing would flash simultaneously on all three colony vessels—but somehow it seemed more official to see it all from the bridge. So she stayed, reminding herself to breathe from time to time and shifting from one tired swollen leg to another. She would be relieved when the spin went down in order to facilitate the moving of cargo—but soon she would be planetside, with no convenient spin to turn off to reduce the effects of gravity.

"Got rid of your mates?" Stev Kimmer asked, stepping quickly into Avril's room after a quick glance over his shoulder. He closed the door behind him.

Avril turned to face him, arms extended; she flicked her fingers to indicate unoccupied space, and smiled in smug satisfaction. "Rank has privileges. I used mine. Lock it. Occasionally that oaf Lensdale tries to foist someone off on me, but I added three names below mine, and he may have given up."

Kimmer, due shortly at the loading bay to take his place in one of the *Yoko*'s shuttles, got straight to the point. "So where is this incontrovertible proof of yours?"

Still smiling, Avril opened a drawer and took out a dark wood box with no apparent seam. She handed it to him, and he shook his head.

"I told you I've no time for puzzles. If this is a ploy to get a man into your bed, Avril, your timing's way off."

She grimaced, annoyed by his phrasing as well as the fact that changed circumstances forced her to seek assistance from others. But her first plan had run aground on the reef of Paul Benden's sudden and totally unexpected indifference to her. Smiling away her distaste, she repositioned the box on her left palm, made a pass at the side facing her, then effortlessly lifted the top. As she had predicted, Stev Kimmer inhaled in surprise, the sparkle in his eyes fleetingly reflecting the rich glow of the ruby that sat nestled in the box. His hands made a movement toward it, and she tilted the box ever so slightly, causing the gem to twinkle wickedly in the light.

"Magnificent, isn't it?" Avril's voice was soft with affectionate possession as she turned her hand, letting him see the brilliance in the heart of the rose-cut gem. Abruptly, she took the jewel from its bed and handed it to him. "Feel it. Look at it through the light. Flawless."

"How did you get it?" He shot her an accusing glance, his features set with a combination of envy, greed, and admiration.

The latter was all for the magnificent jewel as he held it up to the lighting strip and examined its perfection.

"Believe it or not, I inherited it." At his suspicious expression, she leaned gracefully against the small table, arms folded across her well-formed breasts, and grinned. "My grandmother at seven removes was a member of the EEC team that explored this mudball. Shavva bint Faroud, to give her her maiden name."

"Fardles!" Stev Kimmer was genuinely astounded.

"Furthermore," Avril went on, enjoying his reaction, "I have her original notes."

"How did your family manage to keep this all those years? Why, it's priceless."

Avril raised her lovely arched eyebrows. "Great-grandmother was no fool. That bauble was not the only thing she brought back from here, or the other planets she explored."

"But to bring this with you?" It was all Kimmer could do not to clench his fingers around the beautiful gem.

"I'm the last of my line."

"You mean, you can claim part of this planet as a direct descendant of the EEC team?" Stev was beginning to warm to such possibilities.

She shook her head angrily at his misconstruction. "The EEC takes bloody good care that doesn't happen. Shavva knew that. She also knew that sooner or later the planet would be opened for colonization. The ruby and her notes—"Avril paused dramatically. "—were handed down to me. And I—and her notes—are now in orbit around Pern."

Stev Kimmer regarded her for a long moment. Then she reached over and took the ruby from him, negligently tossing it in one hand while Kimmer nervously watched.

"Now, do you want in on my scheme?" she asked. "Like my beloved and far-seeing predecessor, I have no wish to remain at the end of the galaxy on a seventh-rate world."

Stev Kimmer narrowed his eyes and shrugged. "Have the others seen the ruby?"

"Not yet." She smiled slowly with sly malice. "If you'll help me, they may never need to."

By the time Stev Kimmer made a hurried departure to the loading dock, Avril was sure of his participation. She glanced at the chrono and was pleased to see that her timing was perfect. She smoothed her hair, dabbed on a bit more of the heavy musk scent she preferred, and burnished her nails for a few moments before she heard a discreet knock on the door.

Nabhi Nabol entered. "Are your roommates out?"

Kenjo Fusaiyuko tensed at the first shudder as the shuttle hit atmosphere. The admiral, seated between Kenjo and Jiro Akamoto, the copilot, leaned forward eagerly, straining at his safety harness and smiling in anticipation. Kenjo permitted himself to smile, too. Then he carefully blanked his expression. Things were going far too well. There had been no problems with the countdown checklist. For all its fifteen years of inactivity, the shuttle *Eujisan* handled perfectly. They had achieved an excellent angle of entry and should make a perfect landing on a site that, according to probe report, was as level as a natural area could be.

Kenjo had always worried about possible contingencies, a habit that had made him one of the best transport pilots in Cygnus Sector Fleet in spite of the fact that the few emergencies he had faced had never been ones that he could have foreseen. He had survived because, in planning for foul-ups, he had been ready for anything.

But the Pern landing was different. No one, apart from the long-dead Exploration and Evaluation team, had set foot on Pern. And, in Kenjo's estimation, the EEC team had not spent enough time on the planet to have made a proper assessment.

Beside him, Jiro murmured reassuring readings from his instrumentation, and then both pilots felt the resistance as the shuttle dug deeper into the atmospheric layer. Kenjo tightened his fingers around the control yoke, setting his feet and his seat deep for steadiness. He wished the admiral would lean back—it was unnerving to have someone breathing down his neck at a time like this. How had the man managed to find so much slack in his safety harness?

The exterior of the shuttle was heating up, but the internal temperature remained steady. Kenjo shot a glance at the small screen. The passengers were riding well, too, and none of the cargo had shifted under its straps. His eyes flicked from one dial to the next, noting the performance and health of his vehicle. The vibration grew more violent, but that was to be expected. Had he not pierced the protective gases of a hundred worlds in just the same way, slipping like a penknife under the flap of an envelope, like a man into the body of his beloved?

They were on the nightside now, one moon casting a brilliant full light on the dark landmass. They were racing toward day over the immense sea of Pern. He checked the shuttle's altitude. They were right on target. The first landing on Pern simply could not be perfect. Something would have to go amiss, or his faith in probability would be shattered. Kenjo searched his control panel for any telltale red, of any blinking yellow malfunction light. Yet the shuttle continued its slanting plunge as the sweat of apprehension ran down Kenjo's spine, and moisture beaded his brow under his helmet.

Beside Kenjo, Jiro looked outwardly calm, but then he bit nervously at the corner of his lower lip. Seeing that, Kenjo turned his head away, careful not to let his expression betray the satisfaction he felt at the revelation that his copilot, too, was experiencing tension. Between them Admiral Benden's breath was becoming more rapid.

Would the old man expire in joy beside him? Kenjo felt a sudden stab of alarm. Yes, that could be it. The shuttle would land safely, but Admiral Benden would die on the point of arrival at his promised land. Yes, that would be the flaw in the trip. A human error, not a mechanical failure.

As Kenjo's mind played with the ramifications of that disaster, resistance on the skin of the shuttle decreased as it dropped below the speed of sound. Skin heat was okay, the shuttle was responding smoothly to the helm, and they were at the correct altitude, dropping as programmed.

Remember, Kenjo, use as little fuel in retro as possible. The more fuel saved, the more trips can be made. And then—Kenjo cut off that line of thinking. There would still be the atmosphere planes to drive for many years to come. Power packs lasted for decades if carefully recharged. And if he could scrounge the right parts . . . His spirit would not be grounded for a long time yet.

He took quick altitude readings, checked his compass, trimmed the flaps, did a quick calculation on his speed, and squinted ahead toward the shoreline, which was coming up in plain sight ahead of him. His screens told him that the other shuttles were following at the prescribed safe intervals. The shuttle *Eujisan,* with Kenjo at the helm and both Admiral Benden and Governor Boll aboard, would be the first to touch down on Pern.

The shuttle was hurtling over the eastern ocean, its shadow preceding it on the water as it overpassed the lumps of islets and larger masses in the archipelago that extended northeastward from their landing site. As he spotted a perfect strato volcano rising above the water, Kenjo nearly lost his concentration: its resemblance to the famed Mount Fuji was incredible. Surely that volcano was a good sign.

Kenjo could see surf boiling at the base of the rocky promontory that signaled their approach to the chosen landing site.

"Retro-rockets, two-second blast," he said, pleased to hear his voice steady and calm, almost bored. Jiro acknowledged, and the shuttle tugged back slightly but evenly as the retros broke its forward speed. Kenjo lifted the nose, slightly bleeding airspeed. "Landing gear down."

Jiro nodded. As Kenjo watched, hand hovering over the retros in case the landing gear failed to emerge, the green lights came on unwinkingly, and then he felt the pull of air against the great wheels as they locked into position. The shuttle's speed was a shade too high for landing. The vast field was coming up under them, a field that undulated like the sea. Kenjo fought down the panic. He checked drag, windspeed, and, wincing at the necessity, fired the retros again briefly and pulled the nose up as he persuaded the shuttle to settle to the surface of Pern.

Once the big wheels touched, the shuttle bounced a bit over the uneven ground. Braking judiciously and making full use of his flaps, Kenjo swung the shuttle in a wide circle so that it faced the way it had just come and rolled to a complete stop.

Kenjo permitted himself a small smile of satisfaction, then returned his attention to the control panel, to begin the landing checklist. Noting the fuel expended, he gave a grunt of pleasure at his economy. Liters under the allowance.

"Fine landing, Kenjo! Jiro! My compliments," the admiral exclaimed. Kenjo decided that he would forgive him that enthusiastic clout on the shoulder. Then suddenly he and Jiro were startled by unexpected sounds: the snapping of metal clasps, and the sudden noise of air rapidly evacuating.

Alarmed, Kenjo turned just in time to see the admiral and the governor disappearing down the cabin's escape hatch. Kenjo glanced frantically at his console, certain that the expedition's leaders must be reacting to an emergency of some sort, but only the red brake light was on. Smells of burning grass and oil and rocket fuel wafted up to the two pilots through the open hatch. Simultaneously they were aware of the shouts from the passenger cabin—shouts of joy, not cries of panic. A glance in the screens proved to Kenjo that their passengers were releasing their safety harnesses. A few had risen and were tentatively stretching legs and arms, talking excitedly in anticipation of stepping out on the surface of their new home. But why had the admiral and the governor left the shuttle so precipitously—and through the escape hatch instead of the main exit?

Jiro eyed him questioningly. All Kenjo could think to do was shrug. Then, as the cheering subsided into a silence punctuated by nervous whispers, Kenjo realized that, as pilot, it fell to him to take charge. He activated the cargo-hold release mechanism, then switched the sensors to exterior, setting the cameras to record the historic moment. Above all, he must pretend that everything was in order, despite the strange behavior of the admiral and the governor.

Kenjo unstrapped himself, motioning for Jiro to do the same. He stooped, briefly, to activate the hatch closure. Then he took the three steps to the panel between the two cabins and palmed it open.

Cheers greeted him and, modestly, he dropped his head and eyes. The cheers subsided expectantly as he reached the rear of the payload cabin and undogged the passenger hatch. With an unnecessary but satisfying force, he pushed open the door. As the aperture widened and the ramp extended, the fresh air of the new world poured in. He was not the only one to take a deep breath of the oxygen-rich, aromatic air. Kenjo was debating with himself the protocol of such an occasion, since the logical candidates had already evacuated the vehicle, but Jiro, beside him, began to point excitedly. Kenjo peered around the slowly opening hatch and blinked in astonishment.

There, visible not only to him but to the other five shuttles which had landed in due order behind him, were two brilliant banners. One was the gold and blue of the Federated Sentient Planets. The other was the brand-new standard for the planet Pern: blue, white, and yellow, with the design of sickle and plow in the upper left-hand corner, signifying the pastoral nature of the colony. Occasionally hidden by the flapping of the banners in the steady breeze over the meadow were the triumphant figures of Admiral Benden and Governor Boll. The pair of them were grinning like idiots, Kenjo saw, as they enthusiastically beckoned the passengers to emerge.

"Let us welcome you, my friends, to the planet Pern," the admiral cried in a stentorian voice.

"Welcome to Pern!" the governor shouted. "Welcome! Welcome!"

They looked at each other and then began the formal words in an obviously well rehearsed unison.

"By the power vested in us by the Federated Sentient Planets, we hereby claim this planet and name it Pern!"

The engineers, the power-resource group, the jacks-of-all-trades, and every able-bodied man and woman who knew which end of a hammer to grip were set to work putting down the landing-strip grids. A second work force erected the prefabricated sections of the landing control and meteorology tower, in which Ongola and the other meteorologists would be based.

The tower was three stories high, two square sections supported by a wider and longer rectangular base. Initially the ground level would serve as headquarters for the admiral, the governor, and the informal council. When the proper administrative square had been built later on, the entire installation would be turned over to meteorology and communications.

The third and smallest group—all eight of Mar Dook's agronomists, plus a dozen able-bodieds, Pol Nietro from zoology, Phas Radamanth and A. C. Sopers of xenobiology and Ted Tubberman and his crew—had the task of choosing the site for the experimental farm. Others were detailed to scout for varieties of vegetation that might be efficiently converted into various plastics which the colony would need for building. On the one minisled brought along, Emily Boll flew between the agronomy survey and the control tower, correlating data. Once the emergency infirmary was set up, medics were kept busy patching bruises and scrapes, and peremptorily ordering rest periods for the older workers who were overextending themselves in enthusiasm.

By midday, those in orbit had a nonstop show of the disciplined but constant activities on the surface.

"It keeps people home," Sallah remarked to Barr Hamil, her copilot, as they traversed nearly empty corridors on their way back from the main hangar where they had been checking cargo manifests for their first trip down.

"It's fascinating, Sal. And *we'll* be there tomorrow!" Barr's eyes were shining, and she wore a silly grin. "I really can't believe we're here, and will be there!" She pointed downward. "It's like a dream. I keep being afraid I'll wake up suddenly."

They had reached their own quarters and both had eyes only for the vid screen in the corner.

"Good," Barr said with a relieved sigh. "They've got the donks assembled."

Sallah chuckled. "Our job is to get the shuttle down in one piece, Barr. Unloading is someone else's problem." But she, too, was relieved to see the sturdy load handlers lined up at the end of the almost completed landing strip. The donks would greatly facilitate unloading, and speed up the shuttles' return to their mother ships for the next run. Already there were informal competitions between the various units to bring their projects in faster and more efficiently than programmed time allowed.

Sallah and Barr watched, as everyone did, until the dark tropical moonless night rendered the broadcasts impossible to interpret. Broadcasts from the surface would be primitive until Drake Bonneau and Xi Chi Yuen, in the admiral's gig, had a chance to install the commsats on the two moons. Nonetheless, the last scene raised a nostalgic lump in Sallah's throat, reminding her of the hunting trips that she and her parents had enjoyed in the hills around First on Centauri.

The screen showed tired men and women seated around an immense campfire, eating an evening meal that had been prepared in a huge kettle from freeze-dried Terran vegetables and meats. In the failing light, the white strips of the runway grids and the wind sock having convulsions in the brisk breeze, were just barely visible. The planetary flag, so proudly displayed that morning, had wrapped itself around the pole above the control tower. Someone began to play softly on a harmonica, an old, old tune so familiar that Sallah couldn't name it. Someone else joined in with a recorder. Softly and hesitantly at first, then with more confidence, the tired colonists began to sing or hum along. Other voices added harmony, and Sallah remembered that the song was called "Home on the Range." There certainly had been no "discouraging words" that day. And the evening serenade did make the landing site seem a bit more like a home.

The next morning Sallah and Barr had been up long before the klaxon sounded, assembling their passengers and making last-minute weight calculations. The pilots had been given a very serious briefing from Lieutenant Commander Ongola on the necessity of conserving fuel.

"We have just enough liquid fuel to get every man, woman, and child, beast, parcel, package, and reusable section of the ships down to the surface. Waste not, want not. Fools waste fuel! We have none to waste. Nor," he added, with his sad wistful smile, "fools among us."

Watching on the loading-bay screens, Sallah and Barr could follow the six shuttles lifting from the planet's surface. Then the scene shifted to a panoramic view of the main landing site.

"It's breathtaking, Sal, breathtaking," Barr said. "I've never seen so much unoccupied, unused land at one time in my life."

"Get used to it," Sallah replied with a grin.

With the activities of the landing party to watch, it seemed like no time at all before the shuttles were locking on. The loading detail were trundling the first crates into the hold before Kenjo and Jiro could exit. Sallah was a little annoyed with Kenjo for his brusque dismissal of Barr's excited questions. Even Jiro looked abashed by his senior's truculence as Kenjo succinctly briefed Sallah on landing procedures, advice on handling the shuttle's idiosyncrasies, and the frequency for the tower meteorological control. He wished her a safe drop, saluted, and, turning on his heel, left the bay.

"Well, hail and farewell," Barr said, recovering from the snub.

"Let's do the preflight even if Fussy Fusi has made such a big deal of turnover," Sallah said, sliding into the lock of the *Eujisan* an inch ahead of the next big crate being loaded. They had finished their check by the time loading was complete. Barr did passenger inspection, making very certain that General Cherry Duff, the oldest charterer and the pro tem colony magistrate, was comfortable, and then they were cleared for the drop.

"We were barely there," Barr complained as Sallah taxied the *Eujisan* into takeoff position at the end of the runway eight hours later. "And now we're away again."

"Efficiency is our guide. Waste not, want not," Sallah told her, eyes on the instrumentation as she opened the throttle on the *Eujisan* for lift-off thrust. She grimaced, eyes flicking between fuel gauge and rev counter, not wanting to use a cc more of fuel than necessary. "Kenjo and the next eager set of colonists will be chewing hunks out of the cargo hatch. We must up, up, and away!"

"Kenjo never made an error in his life?" Barr asked of Sallah sometime later after the famous pilot had made a disparaging remark about the shuttle's consumption of fuel during the trips made by the two women.

"That's why he's alive today," Sallah replied. But his comment rankled. Though she knew that she had expended no more fuel than was absolutely necessary, she began keeping a private record of consumption on each of her trips. She noticed that Kenjo generally oversaw the *Eujisan*'s refueling and supervised its fifty-hour checks. She knew that she was a better than average pilot, in space or atmospheric craft, but she did not want to make waves with a hero pilot who had far more experience than she did—not unless she absolutely had to, and not without the ammunition of accurate records.

Patterns were quickly established. Those on the ground began each morning by erecting the housing and work areas for those due to arrive during the day. The agronomy teams handily cleared the designated fields. The infirmary had already dealt with its first clients; fortunately, all the accidents so far had been minor. And despite all the hard work, senses of humor prevailed. Some wit had put up street signs with estimated distances in light-years for Earth, First Centauri, and the homeworlds of the other members of the Federated Sentient Planets.

Like everyone else waiting to drop, Sorka Hanrahan spent a lot of time watching the progress of the settlement, which had been informally dubbed "Landing." To Sorka, watching was only a way to pass the time. She was not really interested, especially after her mother kept remarking that they were seeing history made. History was something one read about in books. Sorka had always been an active child, so the enforced idleness and the constriction of shipboard life quickly became frustrating. It was small comfort to know how important her father's profession of veterinary surgeon was going to be on Pern when all the kids she had met in the mess halls and corridors were getting down to Pern faster than she and her brother were.

Brian, however, was in no hurry. He had made friends with the Jepson twins, two aisles away. They had an older brother Sorka's age, but she did not like him. Her mother kept telling her that there would be girls her age on Pern whom she would meet once she got to school.

"I need a friend now," Sorka murmured to herself as she wandered through the corridors of the ship. Such freedom was a rare privilege for a girl who had always had to be on guard against strangers. Even home on the farm in Clonmel, she had not been allowed out of sight of an adult, even with old Chip's protective canine presence. On the *Yokohama,* not only did she not have to watch out, but the whole ship was open to her, provided she kept out of engineering or bridge territory and didn't interfere with crew. But at that moment she did not feel like exploring; she wanted comfort. So she headed for her favorite place, the garden.

On her first long excursion, she had discovered the section of the ship where great broad-leafed plants arched over the ceiling, their branches intertwining to make green caves below. She loved the marvelous aroma of moist earth and green things, and felt no inhibition about taking deep lungfuls of air that left a clean, fresh taste at the back of her mouth. Beneath the giant bushes were all sorts of herbs and smaller plants with tags on them, soon to be transported to the new world. She did not recognize most of the names, but she knew some of the herbs by their common names. Back at home her mother had kept an herb garden. Sorka knew which ones would leave their fragrances on her fingers and she daringly fingered the marjoram, then the tiny thyme leaves. Her eyes drank in the blues and pale yellows and pinks of the flowers that were in bloom, and she gazed curiously at the hundreds of racks of shoots in little tubes of water—nutrient fluids, her dad had told her—sprouted only a few months back, to be ready for planting once they reached Pern.

She had just bent to gently feel the surface of an unfamiliar hairy sort of silver-green leaf—she thought it had a nice smell—when she saw a pair of very blue eyes that no plant had ever sprouted. She swallowed, reminding herself that there were no strangers on the ship; she was safe. The eyes could belong only to another passenger who, like herself, was investigating the peaceful garden.

"Hello," she said in a tone between surprise and cordiality.

The blue eyes blinked. "Go 'way. You don't belong here," a young male voice growled at her.

"Why not? This is open to anyone, so long as you don't

damage the plants. And you really shouldn't be crouched down in there like that."

"Go 'way." A grubby hand emphasized the order.

"I don't have to. Who're you?"

Her eyes, adjusted to the shadows, clearly read the boy's resentful expression. She hunkered down, looking in at him. "What's your name?" she asked.

"I doan gotta tell nobody my name." He spoke with a familiar accent.

"Well, excuse me, I'm sure," she said in an affected tone. Then she realized that she recognized his accent. "Hey, you're Irish. Like me."

"I'm *not* like you."

"Well, deny you're Irish." When he didn't—because he couldn't, and they both knew it—she cocked her head at him, smiling agreeably. "I can see why you'd hide in here. It's quiet and it smells so fresh. Almost like home. I don't like the ship either; I feel—" Sorka hugged herself. "—sort of cramped and squashed all the time." She lengthened the words to make them express her feelings. "I come from Clonmel. Ever been there?"

"Sure." The boy's tone was scornful, but he brushed a strand of long orange hair from his eyes and shifted his position so that he could keep his eyes on her.

"I'm Sorka Hanrahan." She looked inquiringly at him.

"Sean Connell," he admitted truculently after considerable delay.

"My dad's a vet. The best in Clonmel."

Sean's expression cleared with approval. "He works with horses?"

She nodded. "With any sick animal. Did you have horses?"

"While we was still in Ballinasloe." His expression clouded with resentful grief. "We had good horses," he added with defensive pride.

"Did you have your own pony?"

The boy's eyes blinked, and he dropped his head.

"I miss my pony, too," Sorka said compassionately. "But I'm to get one on Pern, and my dad said that they'd put special ones in the banks for you." She wasn't at all sure of that, but it seemed the proper thing to say.

"We'd better. We was promised. We can't get anywhere 'thout horses 'cause this place isn't to have hovervans er nothing."

"And no more gardai." Sorka grinned mischievously at him. She had just figured out that he must be one of the traveling folk. Her father had mentioned that there were some among the colonists. "And no more farmers chasing you out of their fields, and no more move-on-in-twenty-four-hours, or lousy halts, and no roads but the ones you make yourself, and—oh, just lots of things you really want, and none of the bad things."

"Can't be all that good," Sean remarked cynically.

Suddenly the comm unit in the garden erupted into sound. "The boarding call has been issued for the morning drop. Passengers will assemble immediately in the loading bay on Deck Five."

Like a turtle, Sean drew back into the shadows.

"Hey, does he mean you?" Sorka tried to make out Sean's face in the darkness. She thought she saw a faint nod. "Boy, are you lucky, going so soon. Third day! What's the matter? Don't you *want* to go?" She got down on her hands and knees to peer in at him. Then slowly she drew back. She had seen real fear often enough to recognize it in Sean. "Gee, I'd trade places with you. I can't wait to get down. I mean, it's not that long a trip. And it'll be no different from getting to the *Yoko* from Earth," she went on, thinking to reassure him. "That wasn't so bad, was it?" She had been so excited, even knowing that she would be put in deep sleep almost as soon as they got on board, that she had been unaware of anything but the first pressure of take-off.

"We was shipped up asleep." His words were no more than a terrified mutter.

"Gee, you missed the best part. Of course, half the adults," she added condescendingly, "were weeping about their last view of old Terra. I pretended that I was Spacer Yvonne Yves, and my brother, Brian, he's much younger than we are, but he made like he was Spacer Tracey Train."

"Who're they?"

"C'mon, Sean. I know you all had vidscreens in your caravans. Didn't you ever see *Space Venturers?*"

He was openly scornful. "That's kid stuff."

"Well, you're a Space Venturer right now, and if it's only kid stuff, there's nothing to be afraid of, is there?"

"Who said I was afraid?"

"Well, aren't you? Hiding away in the garden."

"I just needed a decent breath of fresh air." Suddenly he pushed himself out.

"When you've a planet full of fresh air below you, only hours away?" Sorka grinned at him. "Just pretend you're a space hero."

The comm unit came alive, and she could hear the edge to the embarkation officer's voice. Desi Arthied had not had to remind any other load of passengers to assemble. "The shuttles drop in precisely twenty minutes. Passengers scheduled for this drop who default go to the end of the list."

"He's angry," Sorka told Sean. She gave him a little push toward the door. "You'd better git. Your parents'll skin you alive if you keep them from making their drop."

"That's all you know," he said savagely. He stomped out of the garden room.

"Scaredy-cat," she said softly, then sighed exaggeratedly. "Well, he can't help it."

Then she turned back to examine the fragrant plant.

By the sixth day all essential personnel were on the surface. Seating was removed from all but one of the shuttles and set about the bonfire square until needed again. Mountains of supplies were dropped, distributed, and stored. Delicate instruments packed in shockproof cocoons followed, along with sperm and the precious fertilized ova from Earth and First—Sallah was certain that Barr did not take a deep breath throughout those drops. Immediately fertilized eggs were implanted in those cows, goats, and sheep that had fully recovered from their deep sleep. Small sturdy types had been brought, not themselves the best genotypes available on Earth but suitable as surrogate dams; the embryos were different again, specially adapted for hardiness and resistance. The resultant progeny would, it was hoped, be able to digest Pern-grown fodder, which would have much more boron in it than the usual Terran produce, and a good variety of native weeds. If there were problems, Kitti Ping and her granddaughter, Wind Blossom, would use the Eridani techniques to alter the next generation appropriately. The plan was for at least some of the animals to be tailored to make the required enzymes in their own glands, instead of using symbiotic bacteria as their ancestors had on Earth.

Admiral Benden proudly remarked that by the time the ships were completely evacuated, the first chicken eggs were likely to hatch on Pern. He went on to announce that there was evidence that the planet harbored its own egg-layers, too, for broken shells had been found above the high-tide line on the beach where the harbor and the fish hatchery were being constructed. Zoologists were trying to figure out what sort of creature had laid the chickenlike eggs; they hoped it was the rather beautiful and unusual avaians mentioned by the EEC team, but so far, the reptiloid creatures mentioned in the survey report had not been observed. As the analysis of the shells showed a high level of boron, the team put egg and its inhabitant on the dubious list of indigenous inedibles.

The shuttles made only two trips a day for the next four, since the loading and unloading of all that matériel was time-consuming.

"I prefer a few passengers," Barr remarked as the off-duty

pilots were enjoying dinner in the mess hall, "as a leaven to crates and crates, big, little, medium. Or all those absolutely irreplaceable herbs and bushes. There's still plenty of people to go down." The mess hall, not nearly so crowded anymore, was still full of diners.

Looking about, Sallah noticed the redheaded family seated at the far left. She waved, smiling brightly because the youngsters looked so glum.

"Gorgeous red hair, isn't it?" Sallah said wistfully.

"Too unusual," Avril Bitra said derisively.

"I dunno," Drake remarked, staring at the party. "Makes a nice change."

"She's too young for you, Bonneau," Avril said.

"I'm a patient man," Drake countered, grinning because it was not often that he got a rise out of the sultry beauty. "I'll know where to find her when she grows up." He appeared to consider the prospect. "Of course, the boy is much too young for you, Avril. A full generation away."

Avril gave him a long, disgusted look and, grabbing the wine carafe, stalked to the dispensers. Sallah exchanged glances with Barr. Avril was scheduled first the next morning, and the wind factors provided sufficient danger even without alcohol-blurred reactions. They both looked toward Nabol, her copilot, but he shrugged indifferently. Sallah hadn't hoped for much support from the man. No one had much influence on Avril.

"Hey, Avril, hold off on the sauce," Drake began, rising to intercept her. "You did promise me a rematch in gravity ball. The court'll be empty now." His smile was challenging, and from where she sat, Sallah could see his hand slide caressingly up Avril's arm. The astrogator's mouth assumed a less discontented line. "We'd best use it while we may," he added, his smile deepening. Moving his arm up to her shoulders, he took the carafe from her hand and placed it on the nearest table as he guided her out of the mess hall without a backward look.

"Wow! Charm has its uses," Barr said.

"Shall we see if it's ball they're playing in the grav court?" Nabol suggested, an unsettling glitter in his eyes.

"There's ball games and ball games," Sallah said with a diffident shrug. "I've seen 'em all. Excuse me." She stood up and strode over to the Hanrahans' table. She knew she had left her friend stranded, but Barr could leave, too, if Nabol made her uncomfortable. "Hi, there. When do you drop?" she asked, as she reached the Hanrahans.

"Tomorrow," Red said with a welcoming grin. He pulled a chair over from the next table. "Join us? I think we're on your ship."

"We are." Sorka beamed at Sallah.

"You've had a long wait," Sallah remarked, sitting down.

"I'm vet, and Mairi's childcare," Red replied. "We aren't exactly essential personnel."

"Perhaps not now," Sallah replied with a wide grin that acknowledged the future importance of their specialties.

"Is it really as nice down there as it looks?" Sorka asked.

"I can't say I've had much time to find out," Sallah said with a rueful expression. "We drop, unload, and lift. But the air is like wine." She flared her nostrils in deprecation of the recycled atmosphere of the ship. "And a breeze, too." She laughed. "Sometimes a bit stiff." She pantomimed fighting with the control yoke of the shuttle. Mairi looked wistful, while her husband looked eager. Sallah turned to the kids. "And school's great. Outdoors! Teaching you all we know about our new home." The two children had groaned at her first phrase, but began to brighten as she went on. "Sometimes the teachers are just a skip ahead of the students."

"They didn't have bonfires last night," Brian said, disappointed.

"That's because they got light pylons up, but watch tonight. You aren't the only one who missed 'em. I heard they decided to have a bonfire square, and every night somone new gets a chance to light it, if they've worked very hard and earned the privilege."

"Wow!" Brian was elated. "Whaddya have to do to get to light it?"

"You'll think of something, Brian," his father assured him.

"See you all bright and early?" Sallah rose, giving Sorka's hair a ruffle.

"Be there before you," Red replied with a grin.

To Sallah's surprise, they were, for Mairi had insisted on reassuring herself that their precious personal baggage was safely stowed in the cargo hold. Mairi had worried and worried about her precious family heirlooms, especially the rosewood dower chest which had been in her family for generations. It had been carefully unglued and took up most of the weight allowed them, but Mairi had insisted that it accompany them to Pern. Indeed Sorka could not recall her parents' bedroom without the dower chest under the window. Sorka had been forced to reduce her treasured collection of toy horses to three of the smallest, and her book tapes to ten. Brian's ship models had been dismantled, and he, too, fretted about finding the proper glue.

That was his urgent question when Sallah and Barr greeted them.

"Glue?" Sallah repeated in surprise. "They've dropped everything else; why on earth would they leave glue out?" She winked at Red, who grinned. "Otherwise our local experts are sure to be able to whomp something up. Pern seems to be well supplied. On board with you now, Clan Hanrahan. We're only a skip ahead of today's horde."

As the first arrivals, the Hanrahans got their choice of seats, and Sorka suggested that they take the last row so they would be the first out. It was almost agonizing to have to wait until everyone else was strapped in and the drop begun. Excitement almost strangled Sorka. She was disappointed that the forward screen was malfunctioning, because then she did not know exactly when the shuttle left its bay. And a display would have given her something to distract her from the shuttle's vibrations. She looked anxiously at her parents, but they had their eyes closed. Brian looked as bug-eyed as she felt, but she would not give him the satisfaction of appearing scared. Then, suddenly, she remembered Sean Connell, hiding in the garden, and forced herself to imagine Spacer Yvonne Yves leading an exciting mission to a mysterious planet.

And then they were there. The retros pushed her back into her padded seat, nearly depriving her of breath, and the shuttle bumped lightly as its landing gear made contact.

"We've landed! We made it!" she cried.

"Don't sound so surprised, lovey!" her father said with a laugh, and reached over to give her knee a pat.

"Can we eat when we get out?" Brian asked petulantly. Someone up front chuckled.

Sorka heard the *whoosh* as the passenger hatch was cracked. Then the two pilots appeared at the top of the aisle and gave the order to disembark. A blast of sunlight and fresh air streamed into the spacecraft, and Sorka felt her heart give an extra thump of gladness.

Laughing, her father flipped open her safety belt and urged her to move. But a moment of nervousness held her back.

"Go on, you little goose," Red said, grinning to let her know that he understood her hesitation.

"Hey, Sorka, you can leave now," Sallah called.

Sorka's legs were a bit wobbly as she stood. "I'm heavy again," she exclaimed. Full weight was a new sensation after the half gravity of the *Yoko*. At the exit, she stopped, awed by her first glimpse of Pern, a vast panorama of the grassy plateau, with its knobs of funny bluish bushes and the green-blue sky.

"Don't block the exit, dear," said a woman who was standing outside by the ramp.

Sorka hastily obeyed, though how she got down the ramp with so much looking around to do, she never knew. The ground cover was subtly different from grass on the farm. The bushes were more blue than green, and had funny-shaped leaves, like the put-together geometric shapes of a toy she had played with as a toddler.

"Look, Daddy, clouds! Just like home!" she cried, excitedly pointing to the sky.

Her father laughed and, with an arm about her shoulders, moved her forward with him.

"Maybe they followed us, Sorka," he said kindly, smiling broadly. Sorka knew that he was just as excited as she was to be landing on Pern at last.

Sorka threw her head back to the fresh breeze which rippled across the plateau. It smelled of marvelous things, new and exciting. She wanted to dance, free once more under a sky, without ceiling or walls to constrict her.

"Are you Hanrahan or Jepson?" the woman asked, a recorder in her hand.

"Hanrahan," Red replied. "Mairi, Peter, Sorka, and Brian."

"Welcome to Pern," she said, smiling graciously before she made a tick on her sheet. "You're House Fourteen on Asian Square. Here's your map. All the important facilities are clearly marked. Now, if you'll just lend a hand to unload and clear the shuttle . . ." She handed him a sheet, gestured toward the float that was backing up to the open cargo hatch, then moved on to the Jepsons, who had just emerged.

"We made it, Mairi love," Red said, embracing his wife. Sorka was surprised to see tears in her parents' eyes.

There was more to be unloaded than just the personal luggage of the passengers. Cartons of stores still had to be checked off the supercargo's lists.

"Tell the dispatcher that more furnishings are required," Sallah was told once the shuttle's hold had been emptied. "Or some people won't have beds tonight."

"That's efficiency for you," Sallah remarked to Barr. She waved to the Hanrahans as she closed the hatch to prepare for the return flight. "Soon there won't be anyone above and precious little left of the ships but the hulls."

"I know," Barr replied. "I half expect to find our bunks already gone."

The two began their take-off check and Sallah grinned as she made her notations. She had the glide down to perfection, which meant that she was saving nearly twenty liters every journey. The wind was veering to stern, and she warned Barr to speed up her checklist.

"Want to take advantage of that tail wind. Saves fuel."

"Good God, Sal, you're as bad as Fussy Fusi." But Barr completed her list with a flourish. "What I want to know is why are we busting ass saving fuel? We can't go anyplace useful with what we'd be saving. And once the ships are gutted, there isn't any use for space shuttles, now is there?"

Sallah gave her a searching stare and then chuckled drolly. "A very good point, my friend. A very good point. I think," she added after a moment's thought, "I'll check the tanks while Fussy's dropping."

But when she had done that, she was not that much wiser. If they were saving so much fuel, then the level in the tanks should have been higher. Barr, who was enjoying a flirtation with one of the resource engineers, forgot her idle observation. But Sallah did not. During one of Kenjo's drops, she did a bit of checking in the mainframe's banks.

Fuel consumption was at acceptable levels in both of *Yoko*'s remaining tanks. Sallah computed in her average fuel consumption per trip, plus an estimate of Kenjo's, and came up with a total that should have left them with an extra two thousand liters of available fuel. She knocked off a percentage, based on consumption during her heavier trips, when drift and wind factors had required a higher expenditure of fuel. Once again she came up with a deficit figure, slightly lower than before but still higher than the amount available.

What good would it do anyone to hoard fuel? Avril? But Avril and Kenjo were not at all friendly. In fact, Avril had made snide remarks about Kenjo on several occasions, unacceptable ethnic-based slander.

"Of course, if you wanted to put someone off the track . . ." Sallah murmured to herself.

Checking the distance to the nearest system, which had been interdicted a century before by the EEC team, and the distance to the nearest habitable system, and computing in the cruising range and speed of the captain's gig, Sallah came up with the answer that the *Mariposa* could, even with the most careful management, make it only to the uninhabitable system. But what good would that do anyone? Disgusted by the waste of the afternoon, Sallah went in search of Barr. They had the evening run to make, and that meant that they would get to sleep planetside.

To Sorka's utter delight, school on Pern concentrated on adapting the students to their new home. Everyone was given safety instruction about common tools, and those over fourteen were taught how to operate some of the less dangerous equipment. They were shown specimens of the plants to be avoided and lectured on the botany so far catalogued: the varieties of fruit, leafy vegetables, and tubers that were innocuous and could be eaten in moderation. One of the jobs for the young colonists, they were told, would be to gather any edible plants they found to supplement the transported foodstuffs. They were also shown slides of native insectoids and herpetoids. Finally those under twelve gathered in the main classroom, while the older ones assembled outside to be assigned work with adult team leaders.

"During this settling-in period," Rudi Shwartz, the official headmaster, told the older children, "you will have a chance to work with a variety of specialists, learning what craft or profession you'd like to pursue within the context of the work force on Pern. We're going to revive an apprentice system here. It worked pretty well on old Earth, has been successful on First Centauri, and is particularly suitable to our pastoral colony. All of us will have to work hard to establish ourselves on Pern, but diligence will be rewarded."

"What with?" asked a boy at the back of the class. He sounded slightly contemptuous.

"A sense of achievement and," Mr. Shwartz added, raising his voice and grinning at the skeptic, "grants of land or material when you reach your maturity and want to strike out for yourself. All of us have the same opportunities here on Pern."

"My dad says the charterers will still end up with all the good land," a young male voice said from the anonymity of the group.

Surveying the children through slightly narrowed eyes, Rudolph Shwartz waited to answer until his audience began to move restlessly.

"The charter permits them first choice, it is true. This is a large planet with millions of acres of arable land. Even charterers have to prove the land they claim. There will be some left for your father, and for you. Now . . . how many of you already know how to manage the basic sled controls?"

Sorka had been sizing up her fellow students, and reluctantly concluded that there were no girls her age. The clutch of teenaged girls had already formed a group excluding her, and the other girls were all much younger than she was. Resigned, Sorka then looked in vain for Sean Connell. Wasn't it just like a tinker to skip school as soon as possible?

That initial morning session was concluded with instructions on how to apply to the commissary for their needs, from the carefully rationed candy and treats of Earth, to field boots or fresh clothing. Everyone, their headmaster insisted, had the right to certain luxury items. If an item was available, it would be issued. After a short lecture on moderation, the students were dismissed to enjoy a lunch served from the communal kitchens set up near Bonfire Square and told to report back to the school at 1300 hours for their afternoon duties.

After nearly two weeks of inactivity on the ship, Sorka welcomed the fetch-and-carry tasks. She was almost alone in her preference. The older girls in particular were appalled to be put to rough labor. Farmbred Sorka felt rather superior to those city lilies, and worked so diligently in helping to clear stones from the fields that her agronomist team leader cautioned her to take it easy.

"Not that we don't appreciate your vigor, Sorka," the

woman said with a wry grin, "but don't forget you were inactive for fifteen years. Work those muscles in gently."

"Well, at least I've got some," Sorka replied with a scornful glance at a team of girls who scowled sullenly as they held plastic poles in place for fencing.

"They'll get used to Pern. They're here to stay." The team leader gave a sort of snort. "We all are."

Sorka sighed with such contentment that the older woman reached out to ruffle her hair. "Ever consider a career as an agronomist?"

"Naw, I'm going to be a vet like my dad," Sorka replied cheerfully.

The agronomist team leader was the first of many adults who would have liked to have Sorka Hanrahan as an apprentice. She was only a few days on the rock-picking detail before she and five others were sent down to the harbor and the hatchery.

"You've proved you can work without supervision, Sorka." Headmaster Shwartz told her approvingly. "Just the attitude we need to get Pern going."

After a morning learning to recognize those marine specimens that had already been catalogued, she and the other five youngsters were split into two groups and sent in opposite directions along the immense sweep of the natural harbor to gather any unidentified types of seaweeds and grasses, or anything new that might have been trapped in tidal pools after the previous night's storm. Delighted, Sorka went off happily with Jacob Chernoff, who, as the oldest, was appointed leader and given a beeper for emergencies.

"This sand ought to be different, not just the same," the third member of the group complained as they set off.

"Chung, oceans grind stones on Pern the same way they do it on Earth and the result just has to be the same: sand," Jacob said amiably. "Where were you from?"

"Kansas," Chung replied. "Betcha don't know where that is." His mocking glance fell on Sorka.

"Bounded by the old states of Missouri on the east, Oklahoma on the south, Colorado in the west, and Nebraska on the north," Sorka replied with studied diffidence. "And you don't have sand out there. You got dirt!"

"Say, you know your geography," Jacob said to Sorka with a smile of admiration. "Where are you from?"

"Colorado?" Chung demanded sarcastically.

"Ireland."

"Oh, one of those European islands," Chung said dismissively.

Sorka pointed to a large purplish branch of weed just ahead of them. "Hey, do they have this one yet?"

"Don't touch," Jacob warned as they reached it. With tongs, he lifted the weed for a closer examination. It had thick leaves that branched irregularly from a central stem.

"Looks like it grew from the sea bottom," Sorka remarked, pointing to a clump of tendrils at the base that looked like roots.

"They didn't show us anything that big," Chung said. So they wrapped it in a specimen bag to bring back for study.

That was almost their only find that afternoon, though they sifted through many piles of already identified sea vegetation. Then they rounded an outcropping of the rough gray stone that punctuated the long crescent beach, and came upon a sizable pool in which were trapped a variety of marine life, things that scurried on multiple legs, a couple of purple bladderlike objects that Sorka was certain would be poisonous, and some finger-long transparent creatures that seemed almost like fish.

"How can they be almost fish?" Chung demanded when Sorka voiced her opinion. "They're in the water, aren't they? That makes them fish."

"Not necessarily," Jacob replied. "And they don't really look like fish. They look like . . . well, I don't know what they look like," he admitted. The life-form seemed to have layers of fins along its side, some of which were in constant motion. "Hairy, they look."

"All I know is we didn't see anything like 'em in the tanks at the hatchery," Chung said. Taking out a specimen bottle, he lowered himself to the edge of the pool to catch one.

Though Jacob was able to get one of the bladders into a jar, and three samples of the many-legged species almost leaped into captivity, the finger fish eluded both boys.

When Sorka's suggestions for capture were dismissed, she wandered farther down the beach. Around a second pile of boulders, she found a massive outcropping that resembled a man's heavy-featured head, complete with brow ridges, nose, lips, and chin, though part of the chin was buried in the sand and lashed by the waves. Delighted and awed, Sorka stood in rapt admiration. It was wonderful, and *she* had found it. One of the girls in her own Asian Square had fallen down a hole that turned out to be one of the many entrances to a series of caves to the south and west of Landing. They had been officially named the Catherine Caves after their inadvertent discoverer.

Sorka's Head? She murmured the title under her breath. No, people might think it was her head, and she didn't look like that at all. As she pondered the question she glanced above the splendidly imposing cliff. It was then that she saw the creature, seemingly suspended in the air. She gasped in wonder, for in that moment the sun caught and dazzled the creature into a golden statue. Abruptly it dove and swooped out of sight, behind the pate of the stone head.

No one had shown her anything that resembled that marvelous creature, and Sorka was filled with excitement. She would have something stupendous to report when she got back to the hatchery. She ran toward the vast head, which was beginning to lose its illusory resemblance. That no longer mattered to Sorka. She had discovered something far more important: a creature of Pern.

She had to scramble up a series of boulders to reach the summit. She paused just before she reached the top and peered over, hoping to catch a closer glimpse of the winged life-form. But she stood up in disappointment. There was nothing visible but naked rock, pitted here and there by faults and holes. She drew back hastily when the surf, beating against the cliff face, became a fountaining plume through one of the holes, showering her with cold seawater.

Disconsolate, she completed her climb onto the pate, keeping well away from the spume holes. The height gave her a splendid view of the crescent harbor. She could see Jacob and Chung sprawled by the tidal pool and even distinguish some activity at the hatchery and the first of the fishing ships riding at anchor. She looked to the west and saw a magnificent vista of small beaches bounded by more outcroppings of the same type of rock she stood on. Ahead of her was nothing but ocean, though she knew that the northern continent was somewhere over the curve of the planet.

She turned about, looking at the thick vegetation growing up to the edge of the cliff. She was thirsty suddenly. Seeing what she thought was a red fruit tree, she decided to pick one. She could cut a few to bring to the boys, too. They were probably ready for a break.

Two things happened at once: she nearly stepped into a large hollow that was occupied by a number of pale, mottled eggs, and something dove at her, its claws just missing her head.

Sorka dropped to the stone surface, peering anxiously about to see what had attacked her. It zoomed in on her again, talons extended, and she waited, as she had done once with an angry bull, to roll away at the last moment. A wave of anger and outrage swept over her, so intense that Sorka inadvertently called out.

Confused by the unexpected emotions but fully aware of her immediate danger, Sorka scrambled to her feet and ran, half-crouched, to the cliff edge. Screams of rage and frustration split the air and lent speed to Sorka's descent. She heard a *whoosh* of air and ducked instinctively to evade another attack, then edged under a rocky overhang. Flattening herself against the rock face, she had an all too vivid look at her assailant, something dominated by eyes that rippled with red and orange fire. The creature's body was gold; its almost translucent wings were a paler shade against the green-blue sky, their dark frames clearly outlined.

The creature screamed in confusion and surprise, and soared up, out of sight. Sorka wondered if it could not see her in the shadow under the ledge. She heard it calling again, the sound muted by, she hoped, distance and the noise of the waves.

Abruptly a wave broke over the rocks about her, soaking her thoroughly. Anxiously she realized that the slight Pernese tide was bringing waves higher on the shoreline, and she would be well advised to move. Soon.

Cautiously she looked about her, listening, but the creature's cries were still distant. A second wave added a certain urgency, and Sorka began to edge down and toward the bluff. Her feet slipped on the wet rocks, and the last meter was an uncontrollable fall. Arms thrashing for balance, she landed on the beach. Still young enough to cry when she was hurt, Sorka let out an anguished wail, as hands, chin, and knees were scraped in the bruising fall.

From overhead came such a replica of her sounds that she forgot her pain and stared above her to where the flying creature hovered.

"Are you making fun of me?" Sorka suddenly felt as irritated as if one of her peer group had taunted her. "Well, are you?" she demanded of the golden creature. Abruptly it disappeared.

"Wow!" Sorka blinked, then scanned the sky for the creature, amazed by the speed with which it had disappeared from sight. "Wow! Faster than light."

Rising slowly to her feet, Sorka turned a complete circle, certain that the flyer had to be visible somewhere. Then another wave crashed at her feet, and she hastily stepped back, though she was thoroughly soaked already. But her hands and knees were stinging from the salty water, and she had a long walk back to the hatchery ahead of her with really nothing to show for her scrapes. She had subconsciously decided not to mention the flyer to anyone yet.

She jumped in surpise when the bushes on the bluff above her parted and a blond head poked through.

"You fecking gobshite, you iggerant townie. You skeered her away!"

Sean Connell came slithering down the slope, his skin no longer white but red with sunburn, his blue eyes flashing. "I've been lying doggo since dawn, hoping she'd walk into my snare, and you, you blow it all on me. Fecking useless you are!"

"You'd snare her? That lovely creature? And keep her from her eggs?" Appalled, Sorka flung herself on Sean, her hands automatically flattening, her fingers tight as she sliced at the boy in hard blows. "Don't you dare! Don't you dare harm her!"

Sean ducked and managed to evade the full force of her blows.

"Not to harm! To tame!" he yelled, dodging with his hands up to deflect her jabs. "We don't kill nuthing. I want her. For me!"

In an unexpected lunge, Sean tackled Sorka, sending her sprawling onto the sand where he fell on top of her. His longer and slightly heavier frame effectively pinned her. Recovering her breath, she squirmed, trying to angle her legs to kick at him.

"Don't be so stupid, girl. I wouldn't harm her. I've been watching her for two days. An' I haven't told a soul about her."

Finally understanding what he was saying, Sorka lay quiescent, eyeing him suspiciously. "You mean that?"

"Yup."

"It'd still be wrong." Sorka heaved against him experimentally, but he pressed her harder into the sand. Stones were bruising her back. "Taking her from her eggs."

"I was gonna keep watch on 'em."

"But you don't know if her hatchlings need her or not. You can't take her."

Sean regarded Sorka with equally angry suspicion. "An' what were *you* going to do? There's a reward for such as her. An' we need the money a lot more than you do."

"There isn't any money on Pern! Who needs it?" Sorka regarded him with surprise and then sympathy for the dismay in his face. "You can get anything you need at Stores. Didn't they explain that to you when you went to school?" Sean regarded her warily. "Oh, you didn't even stay in school long enough to learn that, did you?" She gave a disgusted snort. "Let me up. I've got stones digging holes in my back. You really are the absolute end." She got to her feet and swatted at the worst of the sand on her clothes. She faced Sean again. "Did you at least wait to find out what was poisonous?" When he gave her a slow nod, she exhaled in relief. "School isn't all bad. At least, not here."

"No money?" Sean seemed unable to grasp that astonishing idea.

"Not unless someone brought some old coins for keepsake. I doubt it: coins'd be heavy. Look," she said quickly, catching his arm when he started to twist away. "You go to the Stores building at Landing. It's the biggest one. Tell them what you want, sign you name on a chit, and if they have it, they give it to you. That's called requisitioning, and every one of us, kids included, are entitled to requisition things from Stores. Well, reasonable things." She grinned, hoping to lighten his scowl. "What are you doing way out here?" She felt a twinge of annoyance as she realized that if he and his family were in that area, then she had not been the first person to see the headland, and she could not ask to have it named after her.

"Like you told me on the spaceship—" He grinned suddenly, a smile full of charm and mischief. "Once we got here, we could go where we please. Only we can't go really far yet until we get some horses."

"Don't tell me you brought your wagons with you?" Sorka was appalled at the weight those would take up in a cargo hold.

"Wagons were brought for us," he told her. "Only we've nothing to pull 'em with." He waved toward the thick underbrush. "But we are free again, and camping where we want until we get our animals."

"That's going to take a couple of years, you know," she said earnestly. Once again he nodded solemnly. "But we've started. My dad's a vet and he said they'd woken up some horse and donkey mares, cows, goats, and sheep and made 'em pregnant with our kinds of animals."

"Woken up?" Sean's eyes protruded.

"Sure, who could muck livestock out for fifteen years? But it'll still take eleven months for the horses to be born, if that's what you're waiting for."

"Horses, always. We were promised horses." Sean sounded wistful as well as emphatic, and she experienced a moment of kindliness toward him.

"You'll get them, too. My father said so," she added mendaciously. "He said that the ti—the traveling folk were first on the list."

"We'd better be." Sean glowered darkly. "Or there'll be trouble."

"You see me before you make any trouble here. My da always got on well with your people in Clonmel. Believe me, you'll get your horses." She could see that he was skeptical. "Now, mind, I hear that you've harmed our creature and I'll see you don't, Sean Connell!" She held up a warning hand, the flat edge in an offensive position. "Not that you could catch her. She's smart, that one. She understands what you're thinking."

Sean eyed her, more scornful than skeptical. "You know so much about her?"

"I'm good with animals." She paused, then grinned. "Just

like you are. See you 'round. And remember about requisitioning!"

She turned and started back down the beach to catch up with Jacob and Chung—just in time to help carry the samples back to the hatchery.

When Sallah Telgar heard the call for volunteers to make up a skeleton crew so that those who had not yet been down to the surface would have a weekend break on Pern, she hesitated until she saw the names of the first three volunteers: Avril, Bart, and Nabhi. That trio did nothing that did not further themselves. Why would *they* volunteer? Suspicious, she scrawled her name down immediately. Also, she was still curious about what Kenjo had been up to with his fuel economies. The *Eujisan* had drawn its quota regularly, yet her private calculations indicated a growing balance that had neither been burned up by the *Eujisan* nor was in the *Yoko*'s fuel tanks. Very strange. Soon there would be no place on the old *Yoko* to hide a thimbleful of fuel, much less the volume of the shortfall she had calculated. But Kenjo was not among the volunteers.

All six shuttles went up to relieve the ships' crews and to bring down more bits and pieces. Sallah flew the *Eujisan* up with the skeleton crew for the *Yoko*. Avril had a smile on her face, smug enough to satisfy Sallah that the woman had personal plans for her weekend. Bart Lemos looked apprehensive and fidgeted while Nabhi continued to look supercilious. They were up to something, Sallah was sure. But what it might be she couldn't imagine.

When Sallah sprang the hatch on the *Yoko*'s landing deck, she was nearly bowled over by the jubilant men and women waiting to board the *Eujisan* for their first trip to the surface of their new home. Sallah had never seen a faster loading. Shortly all that would remain of the *Yoko* would be bare hull and the corridors leading to the bridge, where the mainframe computer banks would remain intact. Most of the computer's vast memory had been duplicated for use on the surface, but not all—the bulk of the naval and military programs were protected and, in any case, irrelevant. Once passengers and crew left the three spaceships in their orbit, there would be no need to know how to fight space battles.

The volunteers were given their orders by the crew members they were replacing and then the shore-leave party merrily departed.

"Gawd, this place is eerie," Boris Pahlevi whispered as he and Sallah made their way to the bridge through the echoing corridors, which had been stripped of siding and were down to the central plank of flooring.

"Will the last man off roll the plank up behind him?" Sallah asked facetiously. She shuddered when she noticed that the safety hatches between sections had been removed. Lighting had been reduced to three units per corridor. She watched where she put her feet.

"It's rape, though," Boris remarked in a lugubrious tone, as he gazed around, "gutting the old girl this way."

"Ivan the Terrible," Sallah said. That was the pilots' nickname for the ship's quartermaster in charge of the removal process. "He's Alaskan, you know, and a real scrounger scrooge."

"Tut-tut," Boris said with a mock stern expression. "We're all Pernese now, Sal. But what's Alaskan?"

"Fardles, you is the most iggerant bastard, Boris, even for a second-generation Centauran. Alaska was a territory on Earth, not far from its arctic circle, and cold. Alaskans had a reputation for never throwing anything away. My father never did. Must have been a genetic trait because he was reared on First, although my grandparents were Alaskan." Sallah sighed with nostalgia. "Dad never threw anything away. I had to chuck the whole nine yards before we shipped out. Eighteen years of accumulated—well, it wasn't junk, because I got good prices on practically everything in the mountain, but it was some chore. Hercules and the Augean stables were clean in comparison."

"Hercules?"

"Never mind," Sallah said, wondering if Boris was teasing her by pretending ignorance of old Earth legends and peoples. Some people had wanted to throw everything out, literature, legend, language, all the things that had made people so interestingly different from each other. But wiser, more tolerant heads had prevailed. General Cherry Duff, the colony's official historian and librarian, had insisted that records of all ethnic written and visual cultures be taken to Pern. Those who had craved a completely fresh start consoled themselves with the fact that anything not valid in the new context would eventually fall into disuse as new traditions were established.

"You never know," Cherry Duff frequently admonished, "when old information becomes new, viable, and valuable. We keep the whole schmear!" The valiant lady defender of Cygnus III, a healthy woman in her eleventh decade with great-grandchildren making the trip with her on the *Buenos Aires*, affected idiomatic speech in order to make her points memorable. "Takes up no space at all on the chips we've got."

Sallah and Boris found the bridge territory reassuringly intact. Even the danger doors were still in place. Boris took the command chair and asked Sallah to confirm the stability of their orbit. He was an engineer who dabbled in computer programming, and as weekend duty officer, he would probably spend all his time on the mainframe. He was certainly competent to detect and deal with any untoward deviation from orbit. He had welcomed the respite from outdoor work, as he had forgotten to protect a fair skin against sunburn while he was helping to erect temporary power pylons for the hydroelectric unit. He was annoyed with himself for ignoring a simple precaution just because everyone around him had been shucking shirts to get planet-brown.

"Program's been left up," Sallah told him, sliding into the chair at the navigator's position. "The *Yoko*'s smack dab on orbit."

"The duty officer really should have remained here until I

officially took over," Boris muttered. Then he exhaled. "But I suppose she was afraid that they'd leave without her. No harm done, at any rate."

Boris began calling in the other manned stations, confirming the duty personnel from the roster he had been given. Avril Bitra and Bart Lemos were assigned to Life Support, and Nabhi Nabol was in Supply. While Boris was involved in roll call, Sallah began some discreet checking of her own from the big terminal. She initiated a program to discover who else had been accessing the mainframe. That sort of internal check was a function of the bridge terminal and not available on any of the others, except the one that had once been in the admiral's suite. By the time Sallah left the *Yoko,* she would know who had asked for what, if not why.

"D'you know if they've got all the library tapes down below yet?" Boris asked, relaxing in the command chair once the call had been completed and logged in.

"I think General Duff said they are, but why not get your own copies while there's tape left?"

"Well, I'll just do a few for private consumption. After all, my hide has been flayed to produce power to run 'em."

Sallah laughed, but she could not help but feel compassion. Poor Boris's face was raw with sunburn, and he wore the loosest possible clothing. She regarded him casually until he became absorbed in a perusal of the library; then she turned back to the computer.

Avril was asking for figures on the remaining fuel in the tanks of all three colony ships. Nabol was inquiring about machine parts and replacement units that had already been landed. He was accessing their exact locations in Stores. So he won't have to ask to get them, Sallah thought. More worrisome were Avril's programs, for she was the only fully qualified and experienced astrogator. If anyone could make use of available fuel, it was Avril. And where were the liters and liters that Kenjo had scrounged?

Avril requested the coordinates for the nearest planet capable of sustaining humanoids. Two had EEC reports that indicated developing sentient life. They were distant, but within the range of the admiral's gig. Just. Sallah could not quite see why Avril would be at all interested in those planets, even if they were within reach of the *Mariposa*. Granted Avril could calculate her way there, but it would be a long, harrowing trip even at the maximum speed the gig could achieve. Then Sallah remembered that the gig had two deep-sleep tanks: a last resort and not one she herself would undertake. If she were in deep sleep, she would prefer to have someone awake and checking the dials. The method was not as foolproof as all that. But there were two tanks. So who was the lucky one to go with Avril? If escape from Pern was what she planned. But why would anyone escape from Pern when she had just got there, Sallah wondered, mystified. A whole new sparkling world, and Avril was not going to wait until she had given it a chance? Or was she?

Sallah continued her surveillance throughout the three-day stint and took hard copy before she erased the file. By the time she boarded the shuttle to return planetside, she understood why the crews had needed shore leave. The poor old nearly gutted *Yoko* was a depressing place. The two smaller ships, *Buenos Aires* and *Bahrain,* would be claustrophobic. But the stripping was nearly complete, and soon the three colony ships would be abandoned to their lonely orbit, visible at dawn and dusk only as three points of light reflecting Rukbat's rays.

Despite her parents' tacit disapproval of Sean Connell as a friend for their daughter, Sorka found many reasons to continue seeing him, once he had relaxed his natural suspicions of her. Curiously enough, Sorka also noticed that his family was no keener on his friendship with her than her own was. That added a certain fillip.

They were bound together by their fascination with their creature and her clutch of eggs. Sorka was watching the nest with Sean, as much to be sure that he did not succeed in his efforts to snare her as to be present when the eggs hatched.

That morning—a rest day—Sorka had come prepared for a long vigil with sandwiches in her pack. She had brought enough to share with Sean. The two children had hidden, bellies down, in the underbrush that bordered the headland rock, in a spot where they could keep the nest in sight. The little gold animal sunned herself on the seaside; they could see her eyes glittering as she maintained her watch over her eggs.

"Just like a lizard," Sean murmured, his breath tickling Sorka's ear.

"Not at all," Sorka protested, recalling illustrations in a book of fairy tales. "More like a little dragon. A dragonet," she said almost aggressively. She did not think that "lizard" was at all appropriate for such a gorgeous being.

She carefully waved away another one of the many-legged bugs that was urgently trundling its three-sectioned body through the underbrush. Felicia Grant, the children's botany teacher, had called them a form of millipede and was happy to see them. She had explained their reproductive cycle to the class: the adult produced young, which remained attached to the parent until it reached the same size, whereupon it was dropped off. Two maturing offspring were often in tow.

Sean was idly building a dam of leaves to turn the bug away from him. "Snakes eat a lot of these, and wherries eat snakes."

"Wherries also eat wherries," Sorka said in a disgusted tone of voice, recalling the scavengers at work.

A subtle crooning alerted them as they sprawled, half-drowsing in the midday heat. The little golden dragonet spread her wings.

"Protecting them," Sorka said.

"Nope. Welcoming them."

Sean had a habit of taking exactly the opposite line in any discussions they had. Sorka had grown used to it, even expected it.

"It could be both," she suggested tolerantly.

Sean only snorted. "I'll bet that trundle-bug was running from snakes."

Sorka suppressed a shudder. She would not let Sean see how much she detested the slithery things. "You're right. She's welcoming them." Sorka's eyes widened. "She's singing!"

Sean smiled at the sound that was growing more lyrical. The little creature tilted her head so that they could see her throat vibrating.

Suddenly the air about the rock was busy with dragonets. Sean grasped Sorka's arm, as much in surprise as to command her to silence. Openmouthed in astonishment, Sorka could not have uttered a sound; she was too delighted with the assembly to do more than stare. Blue, brown, and bronze dragonets hovered in the air, blending their voices with that of the little gold.

"There must be hundreds of the dragonets, Sean." The way they were wheeling and darting about, the air seemed overladen with them.

"Only twelve lizards," Sean replied, impervious. "No, sixteen."

"Dragonets," Sorka said firmly.

Sean ignored her interruption. "I wonder why."

"Look!" She pointed to a new flight of dragonets that appeared suddenly, trailing large branches of dripping seaweeds. More arrived, each with something wiggling in its mouth, the burden deposited on the seaweeds that made an uneven circle about the nest. "Like a dam," Sorka murmured wonderingly. More avians, or perhaps the same ones on a return trip, brought trundle-bugs and sandworms, which flopped or burrowed in the weeds.

Then, as they saw the first of the eggs crack and a little wet head poke through, Sorka and Sean clung to each other in order to contain their excitement. Pausing in their harvesting, the airborne creatures warbled an intricate pattern of sound.

"See, it is welcome!" Sean knew that he had been right all along.

"No! Protection!" Sorka pointed to the blunt snouts of two huge mottled snakes at the far side of the underbrush.

The intruders were spotted by the flyers, and half a dozen dove at the protruding heads. Four of the dragonets sustained the attack right into the vegetation, and there was considerable agitation of branches until the attackers emerged, chittering loudly. In that brief interval, four more eggs had cracked open. The adult avians were a living chain of supply as the first arrival shed its shell and staggered about, keening woefully. Its dam herded it, with wing motion and encouraging chirps, toward a nearby dragonet that was holding a flopping fishling for the hatchling to devour.

A bolder snake, emerging from the sand where it had hidden itself, attempted a rush up the rock face toward another hatchling. It braced its middle limbs as it raised its head, its turtlelike mouth agape, to grab its prey. Instantly the snake was attacked by the airborne dragonets. With a good sense of preservation, the hatchling lurched over the damlike ramparts of seaweed, toward the bush under which Sorka and Sean hid.

"Go away," Sean muttered between clenched teeth. He waved his hand at the keening juvenile, shooing it away from them. He had no wish to be attacked by its adult kin.

"It's starving, Sean," Sorka said, fumbling for the packet of sandwiches. "Can't you *feel* the hunger in it?"

"Don't you dare mother it!" he muttered, though he, too, sensed the little thing's craving. But he had seen the flyers rend fish with their sharp talons. He would prefer not to be their next victim.

Before he could stop her, Sorka tossed a corner of her sandwich out onto the rock. It landed right in front of the weaving, crying hatchling, who pounced and seemed to inhale the bit. Its cry became urgently demanding, and it hobbled more purposefully toward the source. Two more of the little creatures raised their heads and turned in that direction, despite their dam's efforts to shoo them to the adults holding out succulent marine life.

Sean groaned, "Now you've done it."

"But it's hungry." Sorka broke off more bits and lobbed them at the three hatchlings.

The other two scurried to secure a share of the bounty. To Sean's dismay, Sorka had crawled out of their hiding place and was offering the foremost hatchling a piece directly from her fingers. Sean made a grab for her but missed, bruising his chin on the rock.

Sorka's creature took the offered piece and then climbed into her hand, snuffling piteously.

"Oh, Sean, it's a perfect darling. And it can't be a lizard. It's warm and feels soft. Oh, do take a sandwich and feed the others. They're starving of the hunger."

Sean spared a glance at the dam and realized with intense relief that she was far more concerned with getting the others fed than with coming after the three renegades. His fascination with the creatures overcame caution. He grabbed a sandwich and, kneeling beside Sorka, coaxed the nearer brown dragonet to him. The second brown, hearing the change in its sibling's cries, spread its wet wings and, with a screech, joined it in a frantic dive. Sean found that Sorka was right: the critters had pliant skins and were warm to the touch. They did not feel at all lizardlike.

In short order, the sandwiches had been reduced to bulges in lizard bellies, and Sorka and Sean had unwittingly made lifelong friends. They had been so preoccupied with their three that they had failed to note the disappearance of the others. Only the empty shards of discarded eggs in a hollow of the rock bore witness to the recent event.

"We can't just leave them here. Their mother's gone," Sorka said, surprised by the abandonment of dragonet kin.

"I wasn't going to leave mine any road," Sean said, slightly derisive of her quandary. "I'm keeping 'em. I'll keep yours, too, if you don't want to bring it back to Landing. Your mother won't let you have a wild thing."

"This one's not wild," Sorka replied, taking offense. With her forefinger, she stroked the back of the tiny bronze lizard curled in the crook of her arm. It stirred and snuggled closer, exhaling on something remarkably like a purr. "My mother's great with babies. She used to save lambs that even my father thought might die."

Sean was pacified. He had put the browns in his shirt, one on either side, and tightened the leather belt he had dared requisition. The ease with which he had accomplished that at the Stores building had encouraged him to trust Sorka. It had also proved to his father that the "others" were fairly distributing the wealth of matériel carried to Pern in the spaceships. Two days after getting his belt, Sean began to see proper new pots replacing discarded tins over the campfire, and his mother and three sisters were wearing new shirts and shoes.

The brown dragonets felt warm against his skin and a bit prickly where their tiny spikes pressed, but he was more than pleased with his success. They only had three toes, the front one folded against the back two. Everyone in his father's camp had been hunting for lizard—well, dragonet—nests and snake holes along the coast. They looked for signs of the legendary lizards for fun, and hunted the snakes for safety. The scavenging reptiles were dangerous to people who camped in rough shelters of woven branches and broad-leaf fronds. Reptiles had eaten their way into the shelters and had bitten sleeping children in their blankets. Nothing was safe from their predatory habits. And they were not good eating.

Sean's father had caught, skinned, and grilled several snakes. He had sampled a tiny bite of each variety and instantly had to wash his mouth out, as the snake flesh stung and caused his mouth to swell. So the order had gone to everyone in the camp: snare and kill the vermin. Of course, as soon as they had terriers or ferrets to go down the holes, they could make short work of the menace. Porrig Connell had been upset because the other members of the expedition seemed not to understand how urgent it was for his people to have dogs. The animals were not pets—they were necessary adjuncts of his folk's life-style. It was proving the same on Pern as on Earth: the Connells were the last to get anything useful and the first to be given the back of the hand. But he had had each of his five families put in for a dog.

"Your dad'll be pleased," Sorka said, expansive in her own pleasure. "Won't he, Sean? Bet they'll be better even than dogs at going after snakes. Look at the way they attacked the mottleds."

Sean snorted. "Only because the hatchlings were being attacked."

"I doubt it was just that. I could almost feel the way they hated the snakes." She wanted to believe that the flying lizards were unusual, just as she had always believed that their marmalade tom, Duke, was the best hunter in the valley, and old Chip the best cattle dog in Tipperary. Doubt suddenly assailed her. "But maybe we should leave them here for their dam."

Sean frowned. "She was shooing the others off to the sea fast enough."

Of one mind, they rose and, walking carefully so as not to disturb their sleeping burdens, headed for the summit of the headland.

"Oh, look!" Sorka cried, pointing wildly just as something pulled the tattered body of a hatchling under the water. "Oh, oh, oh." Sean watched impassively. Sorka turned away, clenching her fists. "She's not a very good mother after all."

"Only the best survive," Sean said. "Our three are safe. They were smart enough to come to us!" Then he turned, cocking his head and peering at her through narrowed eyes. "Will yours be *safe* at Landing? They've been after us to bring 'em specimens, you know. 'Cause my dad's special at trapping and snaring."

Sorka hugged her sleeping charge closer to her body. "My father wouldn't let anything happen to this lad. I know he wouldn't."

Sean was cynical. "Yeah, but he's not head of his group, is he? He has to obey orders, doesn't he?"

"They just want to *look* at life-forms. They don't want to cut 'em up or anything."

Sean was unconvinced, but he followed Sorka as she moved away from the sea and made her way through the undergrowth to the edge of the plateau.

"See ya tomorra?" Sean asked, suddenly loath to give up their meetings now that their mutual vigil had now come to an end.

"Well, tomorrow's a workday, but I'll see you in the evening?" Sorka didn't even pause a moment to think about her reply. She was no longer hampered by the stern tenets of Earth restrictions on her comings and goings. She was beginning to accept her safety on Pern as easily as she accepted her responsibility to work for her future there. Sean was also part of that sense of personal safety, despite his innate distrust of all but his own people. Even if Sean was unaware of it, a special link had been forged between Sean and her after their momentous experience on the rock head.

"Are you sure these creatures will hunt the snake?" Porrig Connell asked as he examined one of Sean's sleeping acquisitions. It remained motionless when he extended one of the limp wings.

"If they're hungry," Sean replied, holding his breath lest his father inadvertently hurt his little lizard.

Porrig snorted. "We'll see. At least it's a creature of this place. Anything's better than being eaten alive. One of the blue mottled ones took a huge chunk out of Sinead's babee last night."

"Sorka says the snakes can't get in *their* house. Plastic keeps 'em out."

Porrig gave another of his skeptical grunts, then nodded toward the sleeping hatchling. "Watch 'em now. They're your problem."

At Residence Fourteen in Asian Square, there was considerably more enthusiasm about Sorka's creature. Mairi dispatched Brian to bring his father from the veterinary shed. Then she made a little nest in one of the baskets she had been weaving from the tough Pernese reeds, lining it with dried plant fiber. Tenderly she transferred the creature from Sorka's arm to its new bed, where it immediately curled itself into a ball and, with a tremendous sigh that inflated its torso to the size of its engorged belly, fell deeper into sleep.

"It's not really a lizard, is it?" she said, softly striking the warm skin. "It feels like good suede. Lizards are dry and hard to the touch. And it's smiling. See?"

Obediently Sorka peered down and smiled in response. "You should have seen it wolf down the sandwiches."

"You mean, you've had no lunch?" Aghast, Mairi immediately bustled about to remedy that situation.

Though the communal kitchens catered for most of the six thousand regular inhabitants of Landing, more and more of the family units were beginning to cook for themselves for all but the evening meal. The Hanrahan's home was a typical accommodation for a family: one medium-sized bedroom, two small, a larger room for general purposes, and a sanitary unit; all the furnishings but the treasured rosewood dower chest were salvaged from the colony ships or made by Red in his infrequent spare time. At one end of the largest room was a food-preparation unit, compact but adequate. Mairi prided herself on her culinary skills and was enjoying a chance to experiment with new foods.

Sorka was halfway through her third sandwich when Red Hanrahan arrived with zoologist Pol Nietro and microbiologist Bay Harkenon.

"Don't wake the little thing," Mairi instantly cautioned them.

Almost reverently the three peered at the sleeping lizard. Red Hanrahan let the specialists monopolize it while he gave his daughter a hug and a kiss, ruffling her hair with affectionate pride. "Who's the clever girl!" he exclaimed.

He sat down at the table, stretching his long legs underneath, and slid his hands into his pockets as he watched the two tut-tutting over a genuine Pernese native.

"A most amazing specimen," Pol remarked to Bay as they straightened.

"So like a lizard," she replied, smiling with wonder at Sorka. "Will you please tell us exactly how you enticed the creature to you?"

Sorka hesitated only briefly, then, at her father's reassuring nod, she told them all she knew about the lizards, from her first sight of the little gold beast guarding her eggs, to the point where she had coaxed the bronze one to eat from her hand. She did not, however, mention Sean Connell, though she knew from the glances her parents exchanged that they mised that he had been with her.

"Were you the only lucky one?" her father asked her in a low voice while the two biologists were engrossed in photographing the sleeping creature.

"Sean took two brown ones home. They have an awful time with snakes in their camp."

"There're homes waiting for them on Canadian Square," her father reminded her. "And they'd have the place to themselves."

All the ethnic nomads in the colony's complement had been duly allotted living quarters, thoughtfully set to the edge of Landing, where they might not feel so enclosed. But after a few nights, they had all gone, melting into the unexplored lands beyond the settlement. Sorka shrugged.

Then Pol and Bay began a second round of questions, to clarify her account.

"Now, Sorka, we'd like to borrow your new acquisition for a few hours." Bay emphasized the word "borrow." "I assure you we won't harm a—well, a patch of its hide. There's a lot we can determine about it simply from observation and a judicious bit of hands-on examination."

Sorka looked anxiously at her parents.

"Why don't we let it get used to Sorka first?" Red said easily, one hand resting lightly on his daughter's clenched fists. "Sorka's very good with animals; they seem to trust her. And I think it's far more important right now to reassure this bitty fellow than find out what makes it tick." Sorka remembered to breathe and let her body relax. She knew she could count on her father. "We wouldn't want to scare it away. It only hatched this morning."

"Zeal motivates me," Bay Harkenon said with a rueful smile. "But I know you're right, Red. We'll just have to leave it in Sorka's capable care." The woman gathered herself to rise when her associate cleared his throat.

"But if Sorka would keep track of how much it eats, how often, what it prefers—" Pol began.

"Besides bread and sandwich spread," Mairi said with a laugh.

"That would improve our understanding." Pol had a charming grin that made him appear less gray and frowzy. "And you say that all you had to do was entice it with food?"

Sorka had a sudden mental image of the rather stooped and unathletic Pol Nietro lurking in bushes with a basket of goodies, luring lizards to him.

"I think it had something to do with its being so dreadfully hungry after it hatched," she replied thoughtfully. "I mean, I've had sandwiches in my pockets every morning this week on the beach, and the dam never came near me for food."

"Hmmm. A good point. The newly hatched are voracious." Pol continued to mumble to himself, mentally correlating the information.

"And the adults actually held food for the hatchlings?" Bay murmured. "Fish and insects? Hmm. Sort of an imprinting ritual, perhaps? The juveniles could fly as soon as the wings dried? Hmmm. Yes. Fascinating. The sea would be the nearest source of food." She gathered up her notes and thanked Sorka and her parents. Then the two specialists left the house.

"I'd best go back myself, loves," Red said. "Good work, Sorka. Just shows what old Irish know-how can achieve."

"Peter Oliver Plunkett Hanrahan," his wife immediately chided him. "Start thinking Pernese. Pernese. Pernese." With each repetition she raised her voice in mock emphasis.

"Pernese, not Irish. We're Pernese," Red obediently chanted. Grinning unrepentantly, he did a dance step out of the house to the tempo of "Pernese, Pernese."

That night, to Sorka's intense and embarrassed surprise, and to the total disgust of her envious brother, she was called upon to light the evening bonfire. When Pol Nietro announced why, there were cheers and vigorous applause. Sorka was astonished to see that Admiral Benden and Governor Boll, who had made a point of attending that little evening ceremony, were shouting and clapping like everyone else.

"It wasn't just me," Sorka said in a loud clear voice as she was formally presented with the torch by the acting mayor of Landing. "Sean Connell got two brown lizards, only he isn't here tonight. But you should know that he found the nest first, and both of us watched it."

She knew that Sean Connell would not care if he was given due credit or not, but she did. With that thought, she plunged the burning brand into the heart of the bonfire. She jumped back quickly as the dry material caught and flared brightly.

"Well done, Sorka," her father said, lightly resting his hands on her shoulders. "Well done."

Sorka and Sean remained the only proud owners of the pretty lizards for nearly a full week, even though there was an evening rush to the beaches and headlands. But bit by bit, nests were staked and vigilantly guarded. Guided by the routine that Sorka had accurately reported, several more of the little creatures were finally acquired. And her name for the creatures—"dragonets"—was adopted popularly.

The acquisition, as Sorka soon discovered, had two sides. Her little dragonet, whom she nostalgically named Duke after her old marmalade tomcat, was voracious. It ate anything at three-hour intervals, the first night disturbing the entire square with its hungry keening. Between feedings, it slept. When Sorka noticed that its skin was cracking, her father prescribed a salve, prudently concocted of local fish oils, with the help of a pediatrician and a biologist. The pediatrician was so pleased with the result that she had the pharmacist make up more as an ointment for dry skin in general.

"Duke is growing, and his skin is stretching," was Red's diagnosis.

The male designation was arbitrary, since no one had been able to examine the creature closely enough to discover its sex, or even if it had any. The golden dragonets had demonstrated a generally more feminine role in egg-laying, though one of the biologists qualified that by reminding people that the males of some species on Earth were the egg-tenders. The dead skin flakes were assiduously collected for analysis. The eager zoologists had not been able to X-ray Duke, for he seemed to know the moment someone had designs on him. On the second day of his advent, the zoologists had attempted to place him under the scope, while Sorka waited nervously in the next room.

"My word!"

"What?"

Sorka heard the startled exclamations from Pol and Bay at the same moment that Duke reappeared above her head, considerably agitated. Dropping to her shoulder with cries of relief and anger, he wrapped his tail firmly about her neck and hooked his talons into her hair, scolding furiously, his many-faceted eyes rippling with angry reds and oranges.

The door behind Sorka opened suddenly, and Pol and Bay burst into the room, their eyes wide with amazement.

"He just appeared," the girl told the two scientists.

Recovering their composure, the two exchanged glances. Pol's broad face became wreathed in a smile, and Bay looked remarkably pleased.

"So the Amigs do *not* have a monopoly on telekinetic abilities," Bay said with a smug smile. "I always maintained, Pol, that they could not be unique in the galaxy."

"How did he do that?" Sorka asked, not quite certain as she remembered other instances of perplexingly rapid departures.

"Duke must have been frightened by the scope. He is rather small, and it does look menacing," Bay said. "So he teleported himself away. Fortunately back to you, whom he considers his protector. The Amigs use teleportation when threatened. A very useful capability."

"I wonder if we can discover how the little creatures *do* it?" Pol mused.

"We could try the Eridani equations," Bay suggested.

Pol looked at Duke. The lizard's eyes were still red with anger, and he continued to cling tenaciously to Sorka, but he had folded his wings to his back.

"To try them, we need to know more about this chap and his species. Perhaps if you held him, Sorka?" Pol suggested.

Even with Sorka's gentle reassurance, Duke would not permit himself to be placed under the scope. After a half hour, Pol and Bay reluctantly allowed their unwilling subject to be taken away. Reassuring him every step, Sorka carried her still-outraged lizard to his birthplace. Sean was there, stretched out in the shade cast by the bushes, his two browns curled up against his neck. They heard Sorka coming and peered up at her, their eyes whirling a mild blue-green. Duke chirped a greeting to which they replied in kind.

"I was just getting some sleep," Sean muttered petulantly, not bothering to open his eyes to see who had arrived. "M'da made me bunk in with the babees to see if these fellers would scare off the snakes."

"Well, did they?" Sorka asked when he seemed to be falling asleep again.

"Yup." Sean yawned hugely and swatted idly at an insect. One of the browns immediately snapped it out of the air and swallowed it.

"They do eat anything." Sorka's tone was admiring. "Omnivorous, Dr. Marceau called them." She sat down on the rock beside Sean. "And they can go between places when they're scared. Dr. Nietro tried to scope Duke and made me leave the room. The next thing I knew Duke was clinging to me like he'd never let go. They said he can teleport. He uses telekinesis." She was proud that she had gotten the words out without stumbling over them.

Sean opened one eye and cocked his head to stare up at her. "What does that mean?"

"He can project himself out of danger instantly."

Sean gave a huge yawn. "Yeah? We've both seen them do their disappearing act. And they don't do it always because of danger." He yawned again. "You were smart to take only one. If one isn't eating, the other is. What with that and guarding the babees, I'm fair knackered." He closed his eye again, settled his hands across his chest, and went back to sleep.

"I shall play gold then and guard you, lest a big nasty mottled blunt-nose comes and takes a bite out of you!"

She did not rouse him even when she saw a flight of the lizards in the sky, looping and diving in an aerial display that left her breathless. Duke watched with her, crooning softly to himself, but despite her initial consternation that he might choose to join them, he did not even ease his tailhold about her neck. Before she returned home, Sorka left Sean a jar of the ointment that had been made for Duke's skin.

Sorka was not the only person on Pern watching aerial acrobatics that day. Half a continent to the south and west, Sallah Telgar's heart was in her mouth as she watched Drake Bonneau pull the little air sled out of a thermal elevator above the vast inland lake that he was campaigning to call Drake's Lake. No member of their small mining expedition would deny him that privilege, but Drake had a tendency to beat a subject to death. Similarly, he would not stop showing off; he seemed bent on stunning everyone with his professional skill. His antics were a foolish waste of power, Sallah thought, and certainly not the way to her heart and esteem. He had taken to hanging around her quarters, but so far he had met with no great success.

Ozzie Munson and Cobber Alhinwa emerged from the shelter where they had just stored their gear and paused to see what Sallah was staring at.

"Oh, my word, he's at it again," Ozzie said, grinning maliciously at Sallah.

"He'll crash hisself," Cobber added, shaking his head, "and that bleeding lake's so deep we'd never find 'im. Or the sled. And we need that."

Seeing Svenda Olubushtu coming to join them, Sallah hastily turned and headed for the main shelter of the small prospecting camp. She did not care to listen to Svenda's snide, jealous remarks. It was not as if Sallah encouraged Drake Bonneau. On the contrary, she had emphatically, publicly, and frequently made her disinterest plain enough.

Maybe I'm going about discouraging him the wrong way, she thought. Maybe if I'd run after him, hang on his every word, and ambush him every chance I get, the way Svenda's doing, he'd leave me alone, too.

In the main shelter, she found Tarvi Andiyar already marking the day's findings on the big screen, muttering to himself as he did so, his spidery fingers flicking at the terminal keys so fast that even the word processor had trouble keeping up with him. No one understood him when he talked to himself like that; he was speaking in his first language, an obscure Indic dialect. When asked about his eccentricity, he would respond with one of his heart-melting smiles.

"For other ears to hear this beautiful liquid language, so it will be spoken even here on Pern, so that there will be one person alive who still speaks it fluently, even after all these centuries," he always told those who asked. "Is it not a lovely language, lilting, melodic, a joy to the ear?"

An intuitive, highly trained mining engineer, Tarvi had a reputation of being able to trace elusive veins through many subterranean shifts and faults. He had joined the Pern expedition because all the glorious hidden "blood and tears of Mother Earth," as he chose to describe the products of mining, had been pried from her bosom. He had prospected on First, too, but the alien metals had eluded his perceptions and so he had traveled across a galaxy to ply his trade in what he called his "declining years."

As Tarvi Andiyar had only reached his sixth decade, that remark generally brought the reassurances he required from the kindly, or hoots of derision from those who knew his ploys. Sallah liked him for his wry and subtle wit, which he generally turned on his own shortcomings, and would never think to use to offend anyone else.

Since Sallah had first encountered him after coldsleep, he had not put even so much as an ounce more on his long, almost emaciated frame. "My family has had generations of gurus and mahatmas, all intent on fasting for the purification of their souls and bowels, until it has become a genetic imperative for all Andiyars to be of the thinness of a lathe. But I am strong. I do not need bulk and thews and bulging muscles. I am every bit as strong as the strongest sumo wrestler." Everyone who had seen him work all day without respite beside Ozzie and Cobber knew that his claim was no idle boast.

Sallah found herself more attracted to the lanky engineer than to any of the other men in the colony. But if she could not impress on Drake Bonneau how little she cared for him, she was equally unable to get closer to Tarvi.

"What's the tally, Tarvi?" she asked, nodding to Valli Lieb, who was already relaxing with a quikal drink.

One of the first things human settlers seemed to do on any new world was to make an immediate and intensive search for fermentables, and to devise an alcoholic beverage in the quickest possible time. Every lab at Landing, no matter what its basic function, had experimented with distilling or fermenting local fruits into potable beverages. The quikal still had been the first piece of equipment assembled when the mining expedition had set up its base camp, and no one had objected when Cobber and Ozzie had spent the first day producing imbibables from the fermented juices they had brought along. Svenda had berated them fiercely, while Tarvi and Sallah had merely carried on with the surveying. That first evening in the camp the drink had been more than a tradition: it was an achievement.

As Svenda entered the shelter, Sallah poured herself a glass of quikal. Valli moved over on the bench to make room for her. Valli looked freshly washed and in far better shape than when she had emerged from the brush that afternoon, covered with slime but bearing some very interesting samples for assay.

At that moment they heard the sound of the sled landing outside the shelter. Svenda craned her neck to watch Drake's progress up from the pad; she barely moved as Ozzie and Cobber brushed past her to enter the room.

"What was the assay, Valli?" Sallah asked.

"Promising, promising," the geologist said, her face glowing with achievement. "Bauxite has so many uses! This strike alone makes this expedition profitable."

"However, your find—" Cobber bowed formally to Valli. "—will be far easier to work in an open pit."

"Ha! We have enough to mine both," Ozzie said. "High-grade ore's always needed."

"And," Tarvi put in, joining them at the table though he refused the drink Svenda always offered him, "there is copper and tin enough within reasonable distance so that a mining town could profitably be established by this beautiful lake, with hydroelectric from the falls to power refineries, and a good waterway to transport the finished products to the coast, and thence to Landing."

"So," Svenda asked, "this site is viable?" She looked about her with an air of possession that struck Sallah as slightly premature. Charterers had first choice, before contract specialists.

"I shall certainly recommend it," Tarvi said, smiling in the avuncular way he had that always annoyed Sallah. He was not old. He was very attractive, but if he kept thinking of himself as everyone's uncle, how could she get him to really look at her? "I *have* recommended it," he went on. "Especially as that slime into which you fell today, Valli, is high-yield mineral oil." When the cheers had subsided, he shook his head. "Metals, yes. Petroleum, no. You all know that. To establish this as an effective colony, we must learn how to function efficiently at a lower technological level. That's where the skill comes in, and how skills are remembered."

"Not everyone agrees with our leaders on that score," Svenda said, scowling.

"We signed the charter and we all agreed to honor it," Valli said, quickly glancing at the others to see if anyone else concurred with Svenda.

"Fools," was the blond girl's derisive rejoinder. Slopping more quikal into her beaker, Svenda left the shelter.

Tarvi looked after her, his mobile face anxious.

"She's all wind and piss," Sallah said softly to him.

He raised his eyebrows, his dark eyes regarding her expressionlessly for a moment. Then his usual smile reappeared, and he patted her shoulder—unfortunately just as one would pat an obedient child. "Ah, and here is Drake with our supplies and news of our comrades."

"Hey, where is everyone?" Drake demanded the moment he entered, well laden with bundles. "There's more in the sled, too."

Sallah dropped her head to hide her expression. "We're celebrating, Drake," Valli said, taking him a glass of quikal. "Two new finds, both of them rich and easily worked. We're in business."

"So, the Drake's Lake Mining and Refinery is in business?"

Everyone laughed and, when he raised his glass in a toast, no one refuted the title.

"And I've news for you," he said after he drank. "We're all to go back to Landing three days from now."

His announcement was met with great consternation. Grinning with anticipated pleasure, Drake raised his free hand for silence. "For a Thanksgiving."

"For this? How'd they know?" Valli asked.

"That should be in the fall, after harvest," Sallah said.

"Why?" was Tarvi's simple response.

"For this auspicious start to our new life. The last load from the starships has reached Landing. We are officially landed."

"Why make a fuss over that?" Sallah asked.

"Not everyone is a workaholic like you, my lovely Sallah," Drake said, pinching her chin affectionately. Seeing that he meant to kiss her, Sallah ducked away, grinning to take away the sting of her rejection. He pouted. "Our gracious leaders have so decided, and it is to be the occasion of many marvelous announcements. All the exploratory teams are being called back, and a grand time will be had by all."

Sallah was almost resentful. "We only got here last week!"

As an escape from several unpalatable but unprovable conclusions, she had taken on the assignment of flying the geologists and miners to the immense inland lake where the EEC survey had reported ore concentrations. She had hoped that distance might provide some objective answers to the events she had witnessed.

A week before, returning one evening to the *Mariposa* to look for a tape she had left on board during one of her early stints as Admiral Benden's pilot, she had seen Kenjo emerging from the small rear service hatch, a brace of sacks in each hand. Curious, she had followed him as he hurried off into the shadows. Then he had seemed to disappear. She hid behind a bush and waited until he had reemerged empty-handed. Then she retraced his steps, and tried to find out where he had put his burden.

After some scrambling about, a couple of bruised shins, and a scraped hand, she had stumbled into a cave—and she was appalled to see the amount of fuel he had purloined. Tons of it, she judged, checking a tag for the quantity, all stashed in easily handled plasacks. The rock fissure was well hidden at the extreme end of the landing grid behind a clump of the tough thorny bushes that the farmers were clearing from the arable acres.

Two nights later, she had overheard a disturbing conversation between Avril and Stev Kimmer, the mining engineer whom Sallah had seen her with the day the landing site had been announced.

"Look, this island is stuffed with gemstones," Avril was saying, and Sallah, dropping into the shadow of the delta wing of the shuttle, could hear the sound of plasfilm being unrolled. "Here's the copy of the original survey report, and I don't need to be a mining specialist to figure out what these cryptic symbols mean." The plasfilm rippled as Avril jabbed her finger at various points. "A fortune for the taking!" There was a ring of triumph in her wheedling voice. "And I intend to take it."

"Well, I grant you that copper, gold, and platinum are useful on any civilized world," Stev began.

"I'm not talking industrial, Kimmer," Avril said sharply. "And I don't mean little stones. That ruby was a small sample. Here, read Shavva's notes."

Kimmer snorted in dismissal. "Exaggerations to improve her bonus!"

"Well, I have forty-five carats of exaggeration, man, and you saw it. If you're not in this with me, I'll find someone who can take a challenge."

Avril certainly knew how to play her hook, Sallah thought grimly.

"That island's not on the schedule for years," Stev pointed out.

Avril gave a low laugh. "I can navigate more than spaceships, Stev. I'm checked out on a sled and I'm as free as everyone else on this mudball to look for the measly amount of stake acres I'm entitled to as a contractor. But you're charter, and if we pool our allotments, we could own the entire island."

Sallah heard Kimmer's intake of breath. "I thought the fishers wanted the island for that harbor."

"They only want a harbor, not an island. They're fishermen, dolphineers. The land's no use to them."

He muttered, shifting his feet uneasily.

"Who'd know anyhow?" Avril demanded silkily. "We could go in, on the weekends, begin on the most accessible stuff, stash it in a cave. There're so many that you could search for years and never find the right one. And we wouldn't have to draw attention to our activities by staking it officially, unless we're forced to."

"But you said there was stuff in the Great Western Range."

"And so there is," Avril agreed with a little chuckle. "I also know where. A short hop from the island."

"You've got it all worked out, haven't you?" Kimmer's voice had an edge of sarcasm.

"Of course," Avril agreed easily. "I'm not going to live out the rest of my life in this backwater, not when I've discovered the means to live the style of life I very much prefer." Again there was that rippling laugh and then a long silence, broken by the sound of moist lips parting. "But while I'm here, and you're here, Kimmer, let's make the most of it. Here and now, under the stars."

Sallah had slipped away, both embarrassed and disgusted by Avril's blatant sexuality. Small wonder Paul Benden had not kept the woman in his bed. He was a sensual man, Sallah thought, but unlikely to appreciate Avril's crude abandon for long. Ju Adjai, elegant and serene, was far more suitable, even if neither appeared to be rushing a noticeable alliance.

But Avril's voice had dripped with an insatiable greed. Had Stev Kimmer heard what Sallah had? Or had her enticement clouded his thinking? Sallah had always been aware of Pern's gemstone wealth. The Shavva Ruby had been as much part of the legend of Pern as the Liu Nugget. Pern's distance from the Federated Sentient Planets outweighed any major temptation its gem deposits might have held for the greedy. But if a person did manage to return to Earth with a shipload of gems, he or she would undoubtedly be able to retire to a sybaritic life-style.

Avril's plot would hardly deplete Pern's resources. What worried Sallah was *how* Avril would contrive the fuel for such a journey. Sallah knew that there was fuel left in the Admiral's gig, the *Mariposa*. That was not common knowledge, but as a pilot, Avril would have access to that information. Judging by the computations Avril had made during her time on the *Yokohama*, Sallah knew that the woman could actually make it to an uninhabited system. But then what?

Sallah had liked surveying with Ozzie, Cobber, and the others, and she had been kept too tired to think of her dilemma. But with return to Landing imminent, her questions came flooding back. While she had no compunction about reporting Avril, she realized that she would also have to mention Kenjo's activities. She wished she knew why Kenjo had held back fuel. Did he have some crazy notion about exploring the two moons? Or the wayward planet which was expected to cross Pern's orbit in roughly eight years?

It was impossible to imagine Kenjo being involved with someone like Avril Bitra. Sallah was certain that the obvious animosity between the two was not feigned. She suspected that to Kenjo flying was both a religion and an incurable disease. But he did have all of Pern to fly over, and the packs that powered the colony's air sleds would, if used circumspectly, allow for several decades of such flight.

What worried Sallah most was the possibility, however remote, of Avril's discovering Kenjo's cache. She had thought of confiding in one of the other pilots, but Barr Hamil could not handle such a problem, Drake would not take it seriously, and Jiro, Kenjo's copilot, would never betray his superior. She did not know the others well enough to judge their reactions to such a disclosure. Go to the top, she told herself. This sort of thing is safest there. She was sure that Ongola would listen to her. And he would know whether or not to burden Paul and Emily with her suspicions.

Damn! Sallah's fists clenched at her sides. Pern was supposed to be above petty schemes and intrigues. We're all working to a common goal, she thought. A secure, bountiful future, without prejudice. Why must someone like Avril touch that beautiful vision with her sour egocentricity?

Then Ozzie touched her arm, bringing her out of her depressing thoughts.

"You'll gimme a dance, Sallah?" he asked in his slightly nasal twang, his eyes twinkling with a challenge.

Sallah grinned and accepted. As soon as she returned to Landing, she would find Ongola and tell him. Then she would be able to trip the light fantastic with an easy conscience.

"And then," Ozzie went on irrepressibly, "Tarvi can dance with you and give me time to rest my sore toes."

Tarvi gave her a look of rueful assent, not having much choice, Sallah realized, with so many witnesses and without a chance to prepare an excuse. But she was grateful to sly old Ozzie.

By the time the mining party returned to Landing, the fire was well started in Bonfire Square and the party was gathering momentum. From her high vantage point as she swung the sled to the perimeter and down to the strip, Sallah almost did not recognize the utilitarian settlement. Lights were on in almost every window, and every lamp standard glowed. A dais had been erected across one side of Bonfire Square, and colored spotlights strung on a frame above it. Drake had said that there was a call out for anyone who could play an instrument to take a turn that evening. The white cubes of old plastic packers dotted the dais to serve as stools for the musicians.

Tables and chairs had been brought from residences and set up in a freshly mowed space beyond the square. Firepits had been dug to roast huge wherries; on smaller spits the last of the frozen meats brought from Earth browned along with several other carcasses. The aroma of roasting meat and grilling fish was mouth-watering. The colonists were all dressed in their best clothes. Everyone was bustling around, helping, toting, arranging, and fixing the last of the delicacies brought from the old worlds and saved for one last gorge on the new.

Sallah parked her sled crosswise on the landing grid, thinking that if more were set down at random along the straightaway, the *Mariposa* parked at the other end of the field would not have sufficient space for takeoff. But how long would there be that many sleds at Landing?

"Hey, hurry up, Sallah," Ozzie called as he and Cobber jumped out of the sled.

"Gotta check in at the tower," she said, waving cheerfully at them to go on.

"Oh, leave it the once," Cobber suggested, but she waved them on again.

Ongola was just leaving the meteorology tower as she reached it. He gave her a resigned nod and opened the door again, noticing as he did so the position of her sled. "Wise to leave it like that, Sallah?"

"Yes. A precautionary measure, Commander," she said in a tone intended to warn him that she had come on a serious errand.

He did not seat himself until she was halfway through her suspicions, and then he lowered himself into the chair with such weariness that she hated herself for speaking out.

"Forewarned is forearmed, sir," she said in conclusion.

"It is, indeed, Mister Telgar." His deep sigh stressed the return of doubt. He motioned her to be seated. "How much fuel?"

When she reluctantly gave him the precise figures, he was surprised and concerned.

"Could Avril know of Kenjo's hoard?" Ongola sat up so quickly that she realized he found her suspicions of the astrogator far more worrying than Kenjo's theft. "No, no," he corrected himself with a quick wave of his hand. "their dislike of each other is genuine. I will inform the admiral and the governor."

"Not tonight, sir," Sallah said, inadvertently raising her hand to protest. "It's only because this was the first chance I've had to approach you . . ."

"Forewarned is forearmed, Sallah. Have you mentioned these suspicions to anyone else?"

She shook her head vigorously. "No, sir! It's bad enough suspecting there are maggots in the meat without offering anyone else a bite."

"True! Eden is once again corrupted by human greed."

"Only one human," Sallah felt obliged to remind him.

He held up two fingers significantly. "Two, Kimmer. And who else was she speaking to on board?"

"Kimmer, Bart Lemos, and Nabhi Nabol, and two other men I've never met."

Ongola did not seem surprised. He took a deep breath and sighed before he put both hands on his thighs and rose to his full height. "I am grateful, and I know that the admiral and the governor will also be grateful."

"Grateful?" Sallah stood, feeling none of the relief she had hoped to gain from telling her superior.

"We had actually anticipated some problems as people began to realize that they are *here,*" Ongola said, stabbing one long finger downward, "and cannot go anywhere else. The euphoria of the crossing is over; tonight's celebration is planned to defuse a rebound as that realization sinks in. Well-fed, well-oiled people who have tired themselves with dancing are unlikely to plot sedition."

Ongola opened the door, gesturing courteously for her to precede him. No one locked doors on Pern, even doors to official administrative offices. Sallah had been proud of that fact, but now she was worried.

"We're not that stupid, Sallah," Ongola said, as if he had read her mind. He tapped his forehead. "This is still the best memory bank ever invented."

She gave a sigh of relief and managed a more cheerful expression.

"We still have a great deal to be thankful for on Pern, you know," he reminded her.

"Indeed I do!" she replied, thinking of her dance with Tarvi.

By the time she had washed, changed into her own finery, and reached Bonfire Square, the party was in full swing and the impromptu orchestra was playing a polka. Halting in the darkness beyond all that light and sound, Sallah was astonished at the number of unexpected musicians who were stomping time as they waited their turns.

The music changed constantly as new musicians replaced those who had already played. To Sallah's utter amazement, even Tarvi Andiyar produced pan pipes and played an eerie little melody, quite haunting and a quiet change after the more raucous sets.

The informal group went from dance tunes to solos, calling on the audience to sing old favorites. Emily Boll took a turn on the keyboard, and Ezra Keroon enthusiastically fiddled a medley of hornpipes that had everyone foot-tapping while several couples did hilarious imitations of the traditional seamen's dance.

Sallah had enjoyed not one dance with Tarvi, but two. In the middle of the second, as they swayed to an ancient tune in three-quarter time, there came a heart-stopping moment when it seemed as if Pern, too, had decided to dance to the new tunes it heard. Every dish on the trestle tables rattled, dancers were thrown off balance, and those seated felt their chairs rock.

The quake lasted less than the time between two heartbeats and was followed by complete and utter silence.

"So Pern wants to dance, does it?" Paul Benden's amused voice rang out. He jumped to the musicians' platform, arms outspread as if he considered the quake an oblique sign of welcome. His comment caused whispers and murmurs, but it eased the tension. Even as Paul signaled the musicians to resume their music, he was scanning the audience, looking for certain faces.

Beside Sallah, Tarvi gave an almost imperceptible nod of his head and dropped his arms away from her. "Come, we must go check the rhythm of this dance."

Sallah tried to hide her intense disappointment at having her dance with Tarvi cut short. The quake had to be given precedence. She had never felt an earth tremor before, but that had not prevented her from instantly understanding what had just occurred. Even as she and Tarvi made their way from the dancing square, she moved warily, as if to forestall the surprise of another shock.

Jim Tillek gathered his mariners to see that the boats were moored well within the newly reinforced breakwater, and hoped that if there were a tsunami, it would dissipate its force against the intervening islands.The dolphineers, with the exception of Gus, who was coerced into remaining behind to play his accordion, went to the harbor to speak to the marine mammals. They could signal the arrival of the tsunami and estimate its destructiveness.

Patrice de Broglie took a group to go set seismic cores, but in his professional opinion the shock had been a very gentle one, originating from a far-distant epicenter.

Sallah got to finish her dance with Tarvi, but only because he was told that the absence of too many specialists might cause alarm.

By morning, the epicenter had been located, east by northeast, far out in the ocean, where volcanism had been mentioned by the EEC team. As there were no further shocks penetrating to the mainland, the geologists were able to dispel the ripple of uncertainty that had marred the Thanksgiving festivities.

When Tarvi wanted to join Patrice to investigate the epicenter, Sallah volunteered to pilot the big sled. She did not even mind that the sled was crowded with curious geologists and packed with equipment. She saw to it that Tarvi occupied the right hand driving seat.

After the Thanksgiving celebration, the colonists settled down to more routine work. The dolphins had a high old time tracking the tsunami wave; it had, as Tarvi had predicted, raced across the Northern Sea, spending the worst of its violence on the eastern extrusion and the western tip of the northern continent and the big island. Jim Tillek's harbor was safe, although combers brought a ridge of bright red seawrack well up the beaches. The deep-sea plant was unlike anything so far discovered, and samples were rushed to the lab for analysis. An edible seaweed would be valuable.

The dolphins were excited by the earthquake, for they had sensed its imminence from the reactions of the larger marine forms that scurried for safety, and they were pleased to learn of such awareness in the life of their new oceans. As Teresa had told Efram in indignant clicks and hisses, they had rung and rung the seabell installed at the end of the jetty, but no one had come. The marine rangers had had their work cut out to soothe and placate the blues and bottlenoses.

"What was the sense," Teresa, the biggest blue, had demanded, "of going through all that mentasynth infection if you humans don't come to hear what we have to tell you?"

Meanwhile, high-quality copper, tin, and vanadium ores were assayed in the north at the foot of a great range, fortuitously near a navigable river by which ore could be carried down to the great estuary. Tarvi, who was now head of mine engineering on Pern, had inspected the site with that mining team's leader, and they had proposed to the council that a secondary settlement there would be feasible. Ore could be processed in situ and shipped downriver, saving a lot of time, effort, and trouble. The power resources committee agreed that the nearby cataracts would provide ample hydroelectric power. The council proposed to bring the matter up at the next monthly congregation. In the meantime, the geology teams were to continue their explorations of both continents.

Other progress was being made on land and sea. Wheat and barley were thriving; most of the tubers were doing well; and though several species of squash were having trouble, those crops were being sprayed with nutrients. Unfortunately, the roots of cucumbers and all but two of the gourds seemed to be susceptible to a Pernian fungus-worm, and unless the agronomists could combat it with a little cross-parasitism, they might lose the entire family Cucurbitacae. Technology was looking into the problem.

The orchard stock, bar a few samples of each variety, had bloomed and was leafing well. Transplants of two varieties of Pern fruit plants appeared to thrive near Earth types, and technology was hoping for some symbiosis. Two Pernian food plants showed evidence of being attacked by a human-brought virus, but it was too early to tell if it would prove symbiotic or harmful. Land suitable for rice cultivation still had not been found, but the colony cartographer, busy translating probe pictures to survey maps, thought that the southern marshlands might work out.

Joel Lilienkamp, the stores managers, reported no problems and thanked everyone, especially the children, for doing such a grand job of bringing in edible stuffs. The mariners, too, got special thanks for their catches. Some of the indigenous fishlike creatures were very tasty despite their appearance. He once again warned people to be careful of the fins on what they had dubbed "packtails," for they would infect any cuts or scratches. He would gladly supply gloves now that plastics was able to produce a tough, thin film for handwear.

On the zoological front, Pol Nietro and Chuck Havers delivered a cautious report on the success of gestations. Some of each big species were progressing well, but the initial turkey eggs had not survived. Three bitches were expecting imminently, and there were seventeen kittens from four tabbies, though one mother cat had given birth to only one. Six more bitches and the other two female cats would be in heat soon and would shortly be inseminated or receive embryos. It had regretfully been decided not to use the Eridani techniques, especially mentasynth on the dogs, due to the considerable trouble with such adaptations on Earth. Some of the stock, and indeed many of the human beings, had ancestors who had been so "enhanced," and their descendants still showed signs of extreme empathy, something that dogs apparently could not adapt to.

Geese, ducks, and chickens had no problems, and were laying regularly. They were kept in outdoor runs, too valuable yet to be allowed to range free, and the runs were much visited by both adults and children. It took nearly six weeks for the omnivorous wherries, as the EEC team had named the awkward fliers, to discover that new source of food and for hunger to overcome their cautious, though some termed it cowardly, nature. But when they finally attacked, they attacked with a vengeance.

Fortunately, by that time there were thirty of the little dragonets in Landing. Although smaller than their adversaries, the dragonets were more agile aerial fighters and seemed able somehow to communicate with one another so that as soon as one wherry had been driven off, one dragonet, usually a big bronze, would keep pace with it to be sure it left the area, while the other dragonets would go to assist their fellows in fending off the next attacker.

Watching from the crowd of onlookers, Sorka noticed something very odd in the dragonets' staunch defense: her Duke had appeared to attack one very aggressive wherry with what looked suspiciously like a little flame. Certainly there was smoke puffing up above the combatants, and the wherry broke off its attack and fled. It happened so fast that she was not sure what she had seen, so she did not mention the phenomenon to anyone.

There was always a cloud of smell accompanying wherries, like the sulfurous odor of the river estuary and the mud flats. If the fliers were anywhere upwind their presence was obvious. The dragonets smelled cleanly of sea and salt and sometimes, Sorka noticed when Duke lay curled on her pillow, a little like cinnamon and nutmeg, spices that would soon be memories unless there was more success in the greenhouses.

There was no question in the colonists' minds that the dragonets had preserved the poultry from danger.

"By all that's holy! What warriors they make," Admiral Benden declared respectfully. He and Emily Boll had seen the attack from their vantage point in the met tower and hurried to help conduct the defense.

Though startled and unprepared, the settlers had rushed to the poultry run, grabbing up brooms, rakes, sticks—whatever was near to hand. The firemen, who were well drilled and had already had to control small fires, arrived with firehoses, which held off the few wherries that evaded the little defenders. Adults and kids herded the squawking, frightened poultry back into their hutches. One of the funnier sights, Sorka told Sean afterward, was watching the very dignified scientists trying to catch chicks. Although some people bore scratches from the raking talons of the wherries, there would have been more—and probably serious—casualties if the dragonets had not intervened.

"Too bad they're not bigger," the admiral remarked, "they'd make good watch animals. Maybe our biogeneticists can create a few flying dogs for us." He inclined his head respectfully toward Kitti and Wind Blossom Ping. Kitti Ping gave him a frosty nod. "Not only did those dragonets use their own initiative, but, by all that's holy, I swear they were communicating with each other. Did you see how they set up a perimeter watch?

And how they combined their attacks? Superb tactics. Couldn't have improved on it myself."

Pol Nietro, himself impressed by the incident, was momentarily between phases of his scheduled projects and not the sort of personality to put leisure time to leisure use. So, when order had been restored and reliable young colonists set as sentinels against a repeat of the incursion, he and Boy paid a visit to Asian Square.

Mairi Hanrahan smiled at his request. "You're in luck, Pol, for she happens to be home. Duke's getting an extra-special meal for his defense of the poultry yard."

"Ah, he was there, then."

"Sorka would have it that he led the fair of dragonets," Mairi said in a low voice, her eyes twinkling with maternal pride and tolerance. She ushered him into their living room, which had been transformed from utilitarian to homey, with bright curtains at the windows, and pots of flowering plants, some native and some obviously from Terran seed. Several etchings made the walls seem less bare, and brightly colored pillows improved the comfort of the plastic chairs.

"Fair of dragonets? Like a pride of lions? Or a gaggle of geese? Yes, a very 'fair' description," Pol Nietro said, his eyes twinkling at mother and daughter. "Not that you're apt to have that kind of cooperation in the ordinary 'fair.'"

"Pol Nietro, if you're casting aspersions on Donnybrook Fairs . . ." Mairi began with a grin.

"Cast aspersions, Mairi? Not my way at all." Pol winked at her. "But that *fair* of dragonets proved very useful. They did, indeed, seem to work well together to a common goal. Paul Benden noticed this particularly and wants Kitti and myself to—"

Mairi caught his arm, her expression altered. "You wouldn't—"

"Of course not, my dear." He patted her hand reassuringly. "But I think Sorka can help us, and Duke, if they're willing. We have already amassed quite a good deal of information about our small friends. Their potential has just taken a quantum leap. And our understanding of them! We brought no creatures with us to ward off such vicious aerial scavengers as the wherries."

Sorka was feeding a nearly sated Duke, who sat upright, tail extended on the top of the table, the tip twitching with a more decisive movement each time he daintily secured the morsel Sorka offered him. There was about him an odd, not completely pleasant odor which, out of deference to his heroism, she was trying to ignore.

"Ah, the servant is worthy of his hire," Pol said.

Sorka gave him a long look. "I don't mean to be cheeky, sir, but I don't think of Duke as a servant of any kind. And he certainly proved he was a friend to us!" She waved her hand to indicate the entire settlement.

"He and his . . . cohorts," Pol said tactfully, "most certainly proved their friendship today." He said down beside Sorka, watching the little creature pinch the next piece of food in its claws. Duke regarded the morsel from all sides, sniffed, licked, and finally took a small bite. Pol watched admiringly.

Sorka giggled. "He's stuffed, but he never turns down food." Then she added, "Actually, he's not eating as much as he used to. He's down to one meal a day, so he may be reaching maturity. I've kept notes on his growth, and really, sir, he does seem to be as big as the wild ones."

"Interesting. Do please give me your records, and I shall add them to the file." Pol shifted his body a bit. "Really, you know, this is a fascinating evolution. Especially if those plankton eaters the dolphins report could represent a common ancestor for the tunnel snakes and dragonets."

Mairi was surprised. "Tunnel snakes *and* dragonets?"

"Hmm, yes, for life evolved from the seas here on Pern just as it did on Earth. With variations, of course." Pol settled happily into his lecturing mode with an attentive if incredulous audience. "Yes, an aquatic eellike ancestor, in fact. With six limbs. The first pair—" He pointed at the dragonet still clutching his morsel in his front pincers. "—originally were nets for catching. See the action of the front claw against the stationary back pair. The dragonets dropped the net in favor of three digits. They opted for wings instead of stabilizing middle fins, while the hind pair are for propulsion. The dry-land adaptation, our tunnel snake, was to make the front pair diggers, the middle set remained balancers, especially when they have food in the front pair, and the rear limbs are for steering or holding on. Yes, I'm sure we'll find that the plankton eaters are like the common ancestors of our good friends here." Pol beamed warmly down at Duke, who was deliberating taking a fresh morsel from Sorka. "However . . ." He paused.

Sorka waited politely, knowing that the zoologist had some purpose in his visit.

"Would you happen to know of any undisturbed nests?" he asked finally.

"Yes, sir, but it's not a big clutch, and the eggs are rather smaller than others I've seen."

"Ah, yes, perhaps the eggs of the smaller green female," Pol said, placatingly. "Well, since the green is not as protective of her nest as the gold, she will suffer no great pangs if we borrow a few. But I did want to ask you one other, greater favor. I particularly remember your mentioning seeing the body of a hatchling in the water. Is this a frequent hazard?"

Sorka considered that and replied in the same objective tone of voice. "I think so. Some of the hatchlings just don't make it. Either they can't feed themselves enough to make up for the hatching trauma," she began to explain. She didn't see the slight grin tugging at Pol Nietro's mouth. "Or they are struck down by wherries. You see, just before hatching, the older dragonets bring seaweed to form a ring about the clutch, and offer fish and crawlies and anything else they can find to the hatchlings."

"Hmm, definitely imprinting, then," Pol murmured.

"By the time they've filled their stomachs, their wings have dried, and they can fly off with the rest of the fair. The older dragonets do a first-rate job of keeping off snakes and wherries, to give the babies a chance. One day, though, Sean spotted some eellike thing attacking from the sea during a high tide. The hatchling didn't have a chance."

"Sean is your elusive but oft-mentioned ally?"

"Yes, sir. He and I discovered the first nest together and kept watch on it."

"Would he assist us in finding nests, and . . . the hatchlings?"

Sorka regarded the zoologist for a long moment. He had always kept his word to her, and he had been very good about Duke that first day. She decided that she could trust him, but she was also aware of his high rank in Landing, and what he might be able to do for Sean.

"If you promise, *promise*—and I'd vouch for you, too—that his family gets one of the first horses, he'll do just about anything for you."

"Sorka!" Mairi was embarrassed by her daughter's proposal. The girl spent entirely too much time with that boy and was learning some bad habits from him. But to her amazement, Pol smiled cheerfully and patted Sorka's arm.

"Now, now, Mairi, your daughter has good instincts. Barter is already practiced as an exchange system on Pern, you know." He regarded Sorka with proper solemnity. "He's one of the Connells, is he not?" When she nodded solemnly, he went on briskly. "In point of fact, that is the first name on the list to receive equines. Or oxen, if they prefer."

"Horses. Horses are what they've always had," Sorka eagerly affirmed.

"And when can I have a few words with this young man?"

"Anytime you want, sir. Would this evening do? I know where Sean is likely to be." Out of lifelong habit, she glanced at her mother for consent. Mairi nodded.

On consultation, Sean agreed that there were only green eggs nearby, but suggested that they would do well to look on the beaches a good distance from Landing's well-trampled strands. Sorka had found him on the Head, his two dragonets fishing in the shallows for the finger fish often trapped between tides.

"May we request your services in this venture, Sean Connell?" Pol Nietro asked formally.

Casually, Sean cocked his head and gave the zoologist a long and appraising look. "What's in it for me to go off hunting lizards?"

"Dragonets," Sorka said firmly.

Sean ignored her. "There aint no money here, and me da needs me in the camp."

Sorka moved restlessly beside Pol, unsure if the scientist would rise to the occasion. But Pol had not been head of a prestigious zoology department in the huge university on First without learning how to deal with touchy, opinionated fellows. The young rascal who eyed him with ancient, inherited skepticism merely presented a slightly different aspect of a well-known problem. To any other young person, the zoologist might have offered the chance to light the evening bonfire, which had become a much-sought-after privilege, but he knew that Sean would not care about that.

"Did you have your own pony on Earth?" Pol asked, settling himself against a rock and folding his short arms across his chest.

Sean nodded, his attention caught by such an unexpected question.

"Tell me about him."

"What's to tell? He's long gone to meat, and even them what ate him is probably worms, too."

"Was he special in some way? Apart from being special to you?"

Sean gave him a long sideways look, then glanced briefly at Sorka, who kept her face expressionless. She was not going to get involved further; she was feeling the slightest twinge of guilt for having given Pol a hint about Sean's deepest desire.

"He was part Welsh mountain, part Connemara. Not many like him left."

"How big?"

"Fourteen hands high," Sean said almost sullenly.

"Color?"

"Steel gray." Sean frowned, growing more suspicious. "Why d'ya wanna know?"

"D'you know what I do on this planet?"

"Cut things up."

"That, too, of course, but I also combine things, among them, traits, color, gender. That is what I and my colleagues generally do. By a judicious manipulation of gene patterns, we can produce what the client—" Pol waved one hand toward Sean. "—wants."

Sean stared at him, not quite understanding the terms used and not daring to hope what Pol Nietro seemed to be suggesting.

"You could have Cricket again, here on Pern," Sorka said softly, her eyes shining. "He can do it, too. Give you a pony just like Cricket."

Sean caught his breath, darting glances from her to the old zoologist who regarded him with great equanimity. Then he jerked his thumb at Sorka. "Is she right?"

"In that I could produce a gray horse—if I may venture to suggest that you're too tall now for a pony—with all the physical characteristics of your Cricket, yes, she's correct. We brought with us sperm as well as fertilized eggs from a wide variety of the Terran equine types. I know we have both Connemara and Welsh genotypes. They're both hardy, versatile breeds. It's a simple matter."

"Just to find lizard eggs?" Sean's suspicious nature overcame his awe.

"Dragonet eggs." Sorka doggedly corrected him. He scowled at her.

"We're trading eggs for eggs, young man. A fair exchange, with a riding horse from your egg in the bargain, altered to your specifications as a gratuity for your time and effort in the search."

Sean glanced once more at Sorka, who nodded reassurance. Then, spitting into the palm of his right hand, he extended it to Pol Nietro. Without hesitation, the zoologist sealed the bargain.

The speed with which Pol Nietro organized an expedition left many of his colleagues as well as the administration staff gasping for breath. By morning, Jim Tillek had agreed that they could use the *Southern Cross* if he captained the crew. He was asked to provision it for a coastal trip of up to a week's length; the Hanrahans and Porrig Connell had given their permission for Sorka and Sean to go; and Pol had persuaded Bay Harkenon to bring along her portable microscope and a quantity of specimen cases, slides, and similar paraphernalia. To Sorka's surprise and Sean's amusement, Admiral Benden was at the jetty to wish them good luck with the venture, and helped the crew cast off the stern lines. With that official blessing, the *Southern Cross* glided out of the bay on a fine brisk breeze.

Landbred Sean was not all that happy about his first sea voyage, but he managed to suppress both fear and nausea, determined to earn his horse and not to show weakness in front of Sorka, who showed every evidence of enjoying the adventure. He spent most of the voyage sitting with his back against the mast, facing forward and stroking his brown dragonets, who liked to sleep stretched out on the sunny deck. Sorka's Duke remained perched on her shoulder, one pincer holding delicately to her ear to balance himself while his tail was lightly but firmly wrapped about her neck. From time to time, she would nuzzle him reassuringly or he would croon some comment in her ear just as if he was certain of her understanding.

The forty-foot sloop, *Southern Cross,* could be sailed with a crew of three, slept eight, and had been designed to serve as an exploratory ship as well as a fast courier. Jim Tillek had already sailed as far west as the river they had christened the "Jordan," and, along with a crew to measure volcanism, as far east as the island volcano whose eruption had interrupted the Thanksgiving feast. He was hoping to get permission to make the longer crossing to the large island off the northern continent, and to explore the delta of the river proposed to carry the ore or finished metals from the projected mining site. He had, he told the enthralled Sorka, sailed all the seas and oceans of Earth during his leaves from captaining a merchantman on the Belt runs, and up as many rivers as were navigable: Nile, Thames, Amazon, Mississippi, St. Lawrence, Columbia, Rhine, Volga, Yangtze, and less well known streams.

"Course, I wasn't doing that as a professional man, and there wasn't much call on a sailor on First yet, so this expedition was my chance to ply my hobby as trade, as 'twere," he confided. "Damned glad I came!" He inhaled deeply. "The air here's fabulous. What we used to have back on Earth. Used to think it was the ozone! Take a deep breath!"

Sorka inhaled happily. Just then Bay Harkenon emerged from the cabin, looking much better than she had when she had hastily descended to be nauseated in private.

"Ah, the pill worked?" Jim Tillek inquired solicitously.

"I cannot thank you enough," the microbiologist said with a tremulous but grateful smile. "I'd no idea I was susceptible to motion sickness."

"Had you ever sailed?"

Bay shook her head, the clusters of gray curls bobbing on her shoulders.

"Then how would you know?" he asked affably. He squinted into the distance, where the peninsula and the mouth of the Jordan River were already visible. Portside, the towering Mount Garben—named after the senator who had done so much to smooth the expedition's way through the intricacies of the Federated Sentient Planets' bureaucracy—dominated the landscape, its cone suitably framed against the bright morning sky. There had been some lobbying to name its three small companions after Shavva, Liu, and Turnien, the original EEC landing party, but no decision had yet been made at the monthly naming sessions held around the evening campfire after the more formal official sittings of the council.

Captain Tillek dropped his gaze to the charts and, using his dividers, measured the distance from the jetty to the river mouth, and again to the land beyond.

"Why do the colors stop here?" Sorka asked, noticing that the bulk of the chart was uncolored.

Grinning in approval, he tapped the chart. "Fremlich did this for me from the probe pics, and they've been accurate to the last centimeter so far, but as we ourselves walk across the land and sail the coast, I color it in appropriately. A good way of knowing where we've been and where we've yet to go. I've also added notations that a sailor might need, about prevalent winds and current speeds."

It was only then that Sorka noticed those additional marks. "It's one thing to see, and another to know, isn't it?"

He tweaked one of her titian braids. "Indeed, it is being there that matters."

"And we'll really be the first people—here?" She laid the tip of her forefinger on the peninsula.

"Indeed we shall," Tillek said with heartfelt satisfaction.

Jim Tillek had never been so contented and happy before in a life that had already spanned six decades. A misfit in a high-tech society because of his love of seas and ships, bored by the monotonous Belt runs to which his lack of tact or incorruptible honesty restricted him, Tillek found Pern perfect, and now he had the added fillip of being one of the first to sail its seas and discover their eccentricities. A strongly built man of medium height, with pale blue, far-seeing eyes, he looked his part, complete with visored cap pulled down about his ears and an old guernsey wool sweater against the slight coolness of the fresh morning breeze. Though the *Southern Cross* could have been sailed electronically from the cockpit with the touch of buttons, he preferred to steer by the rudder and use his instinct for the wind to trim the sheets. His crew were forward, making all lines fair on the plasiplex decks and going about the routine of the little ship.

"We'll put in at dusk, probably about here, where the chart tells me there's a deep harbor in a cove. More color to be added. We might even find what we're looking for there, too." He winked at Sorka and Bay Harkenon.

When the *Southern Cross* was anchored in six fathoms, Jim took the shore party to the beach in the little motorboat. Sean, who had had quite enough company for a while, told Sorka to search for dragonet nests to the east while he went west along the beach. His two browns circled above his head, calling happily as they flew. Galled at the way Sean ordered the girl about, Jim Tillek was about to take the lad to task, but Pol Nietro sent him a warning look and the captain subsided. Sean was already ducking into the thick vegetation bordering the strand.

"We'll have a hot meal for you when you return," Pol called after the two youngsters. Sorka paused to wave acknowledgment.

When they returned at dusk for the promised food, both children reported success.

"I think the first three I found are only greens," Sorka said with quiet authority. "They're much too close to the water for a gold. Duke thinks so, too. He doesn't seem to like greens. But the one we found farthest away is well above high-tide marks, and the eggs are bigger. I think they're hard enough to hatch soon."

"Two green clutches and two I'm positive are gold," Sean said briskly, and began to eat, pausing only to offer his two browns their share of his meal. "There's a lot of 'em about, too. Are you going to take back all you can find?"

"Heavens, no!" Pol exclaimed, throwing both hands up in dismay. His white hair, wiry and thick, stood out about his head like a nimbus, giving him a benign appearance that matched his personality. "We won't make *that* mistake on Pern."

"Oh, no, never," Bay Harkenon said, leaning toward Sean as if to touch him in reassurance. "Our investigative techniques no longer require endless specimens to confirm conclusions, you know."

"Specimens?" Sean frowned, and Sorka looked apprehensive.

"Representative would perhaps be the better word."

"And we'd use the eggs . . . of the green, of course," Pol added quickly, "since the female greens do not appear to be as maternally inclined as the gold."

Sean was confused. "You don't want a gold's eggs at all?"

"Not all of them," Bay repeated earnestly. "And only a dead hatchling of the other colors if one can be obtained. We've had more than enough green casualties."

"Dead is the only way you'd get one," Sean muttered.

"You're likely correct," Bay said with a little sigh. She was a portly woman in her late fifth decade but fit and agile enough not to hinder the expedition. "I've never been able to establish a rapport with animals." She looked wistfully at Sorka's bronze lying in the total relaxation of sleep around the girl's neck, legs dangling down her chest, the limp tail extending almost to her waist.

"A dragonet's so hungry when it's born, it'll take food anywhere it can," Sean said with marked tactlessness.

"Oh, I don't think I could deprive someone of—"

"We're all supposed to be equal here, aren't we?" Sean demanded. "You got the same rights as anyone else, y'know."

"Well said, young nipper," Jim Tillek said. "Well said!"

"If the dragonets were only a little bigger," Pol murmured, as much to himself as to the others, and then he sighed.

"If dragonets were only a little bigger what?" Tillek asked.

"Then they'd be an equal match for the wherries."

"They already are!" Sean said loyally, stroking one of his browns. If he had named them, he kept their names to himself. He had trained them to answer his various whistled commands. Sorka felt too shy to ask him how he had done it. Not that Duke ever disobeyed her—once he figured out what she wanted.

"Perhaps you're right," Pol said, giving his head a little shake.

"Tinkering isn't something lightly undertaken. You know how many efforts abort or distort." Bay smiled to ease her gentle chiding.

"Tinker?" Sean came alert.

"They didn't mean you, silly," Sorka assured him in a low voice.

"Why would you want to . . . ahem . . . manipulate," Jim Tillek asked, "critters that have been doing quite well in protecting themselves for centuries. And us."

"Out of the stew of creation so few survive, and often not the obvious, more perfectly designed or environmentally suited species," Pol said with a long patient sigh. "It is always amazing to me what does win the evolutionary race to become the common ancestors of a great new group. I'd never have expected anything as close to our vertebrates as wherries and dragonets on another planet. The really strange coincidence is that our storytellers so often invested a four-legged, two-winged creature in fantasy, although none ever existed on Earth. Here they are, hundreds of light-years away from the people who only imagined them." He indicated the sleeping Duke. "Remarkable. And not as badly designed as the ancient Chinese dragons."

"Badly designed?" the seaman asked, amused.

"Well, look at him. It's redundant to have both forelimbs and wings. Earth avian species opted for wings instead of forelimbs, though some have vestigial claws of what had once been the forefinger before the limb became a wing. I'll grant you that a curved rear limb is useful for springing off the ground—and the dragonet's are powerful, with muscles into the back to provide assistance—but that long back is vulnerable. I wonder how they arrange their mechanics so that they can sit up for so long without moving." Pol peered at the sleeping Duke and touched the limp tail. "There is one slight improvement: the excretory hole in the fork of the tail instead of under it. And there are dorsal nostrils and lungs, which are a distinct improvement. Humans are very poorly designed, you know," he went on, happy to be able to exercise his favorite complaint to a rapt audience.

"I mean, surely you can see how ridiculous it is to have an air pipe—" He touched his nose. "—that crosses the food pipe." He touched his rather prominent Adam's apple. "People are always choking themselves to death. And a vulnerable cranium: one good crack, and the concussion can cause impairment if not fatality. Those Vegans have their brains well protected in tough internal sacs. You'd never concuss a Vegan."

"I'd rather have bellyaches in my middle than headaches," Tillek said in a droll tone. "Though, from what I saw once, some of the other Vegan operating mechanisms are exceedingly unhandy, particularly the sexual and reproductive arrangements."

Pol snorted. "So you think having the playground between the sewers makes more sense?"

"Didn't say that, Pol," Jim Tillek answered hurriedly with a glance at the two children, though neither were paying the adults much heed. "It's a bit handier for us, though."

"And more vulnerable. Oh my, oh my, there I go again, falling into the lecture attitude. But there are endless ways in which we humans could be profitably improved . . ."

"We are doing that, though, aren't we, Pol, dear?" Bay said kindly.

"Oh, yes, cybernetically we do, and *in vitro* we can correct certain gross genetic mistakes. It's true that we are allowed to use the Eridani mentasynth, though personally I don't know whether our response to it is a boon or not. It makes people too empathic with their experimental animals. But we can't do much yet, of course, with the laws that the Pure Humans forced through to prohibit drastic changes."

"Who'd want to?" Tillek asked with a frown.

"Not us," Bay assured him hastily. "We don't have that kind of need on this world. But I sometimes feel that the Pure Human Life Group was wrong to oppose alterations that would permit humans to use those water worlds in Ceti IV. Lungs exchanged for gills and webbing on hands and feet is not that great or blasphemous an adaptation. The fetus still goes through a similar stage *in utero,* and there's good evidence for a more aquatic past for adults. Think how many planets would be open to humans if we weren't so limited to land areas that met our gravitational and atmospheric requirements! Even if we could provide special enzymes for some of the dangerous gases. Cyanides have kept us out of so many places. Why . . ." She threw up her hands as words failed her.

Sean was peering at the two specialists with some suspicion.

"Campfire talk," Sorka told him sagely. "They don't mean it."

Sean snorted and, carefully positioning his two brown dragonets, rose to his feet. "I plan to be up tomorrow before dawn. Best time to catch the dragonets feeding and know who's minding the nests."

"Me, too," Sorka said, standing.

Tillek had rigged shelters well above the high-tide marks, protection against the sudden squalls that seemed characteristic of the early summer season. Thermal blankets had been stitched into sleeping bags, and Sorka gratefully crawled into one. Duke, without apparently waking, accommodated himself to her new position. She had a little trouble falling asleep because, for a while, the beach seemed to heave beneath her, mimicking the motions of the waves.

A little warning chirp from Duke roused her. Snores drifted over from the adults, but as her eyes grew accustomed to the predawn darkness, she saw Sean rising. She could just see him turn his head toward her and then westward. With an economy of movement he crept to the ashes of the previous night's fire and rummaged quietly in the supply sacks, taking several items which he stuffed into his shirt.

Sorka waited until he was out of sight and then she rose. Then, after taking a pack of rations and one of the red fruits they had gathered before dinner, she left a note telling the adults that she and Sean had gone to check nests and would be back soon after dawn to report.

As she trotted along the beach, she ate the red fruit, discarding the blemished side where a mold had gotten at it, just as she had once eaten windfall apples and thrown away the brown bits back on Earth. At a little distance from each of the nests, she had piled small cairns of white, ocean-smoothed stones so that she could find each clutch without stepping into it. She found the first two with no problem and hurried toward the third, the one she thought might be a gold's nest. There was a faint trace of brightness in the eastern sky, and she wanted to be hidden in the bushes before day actually broke.

It was wonderful to be alone, and safe, in a part of a world that had never felt the tread of feet. Sorka had studied the EEC survey reports and maps often enough to know that those intrepid people had not been on that particular beach. She exulted in the special magic of being first and sighed at being so privileged. Her earlier desire to be able to tag a special place with *her* name had altered to a dream of finding the most beautiful spot on the new world, a really unique place for which she, too, could be remembered. Better still would be for the colonists to wish to name a mountain or a river or a valley after Sorka Hanrahan because of something special that she had done.

She was so lost in that dream that she nearly stumbled over the cairn and into the half-buried clutch. Duke saved her from the error with a warning cheep.

She stroked his little head in gratitude. If she could alter one thing about Duke, it would be to give him speech. She had learned to interpret his various noises accurately and was able to understand what other dragonets said to their owners, but she wished she could communicate with Duke in a common language. But someone had said that forked tongues could not manage speech, and she certainly did not want any drastic changes in Duke—especially not in his size. Any bigger and he would not fit on her shoulder so comfortably.

Maybe she should have a chat with the marine rangers who worked with the dolphins. They communicated with one another about complex matters. It was just as likely that the dragonets did, too, judging by the way they had routed the wherries. Even Admiral Benden had commented on it.

Thinking of the hero of Cygnus, she decided that she, too, must use careful strategy and hide her tracks. The gold dragonets were a lot smarter than the stupid green ones. She found a thickly fronded branch from the underbrush and covered her footprints in the dry sand, retreating into the brush before making her way back to a good vantage point close to but obscured from the beach and the nest.

Dawn coincided with a cheerful morning chorus as a fair of dragonets swooped down to the foreshore. Only the gold approached the nest; the others, brown and bronze and blue, remained a discreet distance from it. Watching their bodies outlined against the white sands, Sorka could appreciate the difference in their sizes. The golden female was the largest, taller in the shoulder by the span of two fingers than the bronzes, who seemed to be the next in size, though one or two of the browns were nearly as big. The blues were definitely smaller, moving with quick nervous steps, examining seaweeds, discarding some and hauling others toward the nest with many smug chirps. The bronzes and browns seemed to be discussing something, murmuring and cheeping to themselves while the blues were clearly interested only in what might be edible. Or were they? The nest was being surrounded by a circle of weed. When it was completed, the browns and bronzes got busy, depositing the scuttling sea things she had seen at Duke's hatching.

With an almost peremptory screech, the gold female rose from the nest, swooping down over the heads of the bronzes and browns and dipping wings at the blues as she raced toward the sea. The others followed, not as gracefully, Sorka thought, but swiftly. She saw them climb over the gently lapping surf and then suddenly dive at the waves, chirping triumphantly as they fished. Then, abruptly, they all disappeared. One moment they were there, suspended above the ocean; the next moment the sky was completely clear of flashing dragonet bodies. Sorka blinked in astonishment.

Then she had an idea: If the eggs were that close to hatching, and if she could get one back to Bay Harkenon in time for her to feed it, Bay would finally have a creature of her own. The scientist was a nice, kind lady, not the least bit stuffy like some of the section heads were, and a dragonet would be a companion to her.

Sorka didn't think about it any further; she acted. Darting out of her hiding place, she streaked to the nest, made a grab for the nearest egg on the top of the pile, and scurried as fast as she could back to the underbrush.

She was only just in time, the branches still swaying from her swift passage, when the dragonets were back again, in what seemed to be greater numbers than before. The little golden one landed right by the eggs while bronzes, browns, and blues were depositing helplessly flapping fish within the seaweed circle. Suddenly the welcoming chorus began, and Sorka was torn between the desire to watch the magical moment of hatching and the need to get her purloined egg to Bay in time. Then she felt the egg, which she had tucked under her pullover for warmth and protection, move against her skin.

"Don't you dare make a sound, Duke!" she whispered harshly when she heard Duke's chest begin to rumble. She caught his little jaw between her fingers and glared straight into his faceted eyes, which had begun to whirl with happy colors. "She'll kill me!"

He clearly understood her warning and hunched closer to

her, clinging with sharp nails to her hair and hiding his face against her braid. Then she crawled backward from the beach edge until she was screened sufficiently to risk standing up. Dead fronds and branches tangled her feet as she ran, and she encountered a disheartening variety of thorny bushes and needly plants. But she plunged on.

When she could no longer hear the cries of the dragonets, she turned west and crashed back out to the beach. She pelted down the sands as fast as she could, ignoring the stitch in her side in deference to the antics of the egg beating at her ribs. Duke circled about her head, keening with obediently muted anxiety.

Surely she must be almost back at the camp. Was that the first cairn she had passed, or the second? She stumbled, and Duke cried out in terrible alarm, a shrill strident shriek like the cries of the peacocks that had inhabited her father's farm, a ghastly sound like someone in extreme agony. He swooped, tugging valiantly at her shoulder, as if he himself could support her.

His shriek had been sufficient to rouse the sleepers. Jim Tillek was the first one to struggle to his feet, which got tangled in the bag for the first few steps. Pol and Bay were more laggard until they recognized Sorka.

Sorka, ignoring both Tillek's urgent queries and helping hands, staggered to the plump microbiologist, dropping heavily to her knees and fumbling to get the egg into Bay's hands for she could feel a crack beginning to run along the shell.

"Here! Here, this is yours, Bay!" she gasped, grabbing the astonished woman's hands and closing them about the egg.

Bay's reaction was to thrust it back to Sorka, but the girl had thrown herself toward the supply packs, rummaging for something edible, fumbling to open a packet of protein bars and break one into tiny pieces.

"It's cracking, Sorka. Pol! What do I do with it? It's cracking all over!" Bay exclaimed uncertainly.

"It's yours, Bay, an animal that will love only you," Sorka

said in gasps, floundering back with full hands. "It's hatching. It'll be yours. Here, feed it these. Pol, Captain, see what you can find under the seaweed for it to eat. You be bronzes. See, watch what Duke's going after."

Duke, chirping with exultation, was dragging a huge branch of seaweed up from the high-tide line.

"Just bundle the seaweed up, Pol," Tillek said moments later as he demonstrated.

"It's cracked!" Bay cried, half-afraid, half-delighted. "There's a head! Sorka! What do I do now?"

Twenty minutes later the risen sun shone on a weary but excited quartet as Bay, with the most beatific and incredulous expression on her face, cradled a lovely golden dragonet on her forearm. Its head was an ornament on the back of her hand, its forearms loosely encircled her wrist. Its distended belly had support from Bay's well-fleshed limb, its hind legs dangled by her elbow, and its tail was lightly twined around her upper arm. A slight noise, similar to a snore, could be discerned. Bay stroked the sleeping creature from time to time, amazed by the texture of its skin, by the strong but delicate claws, the translucent wings, and the strength of the newborn's tail about her arm. She constantly extolled its perfections.

Jim Tillek regenerated the fire and served a hot drink to counteract the chilly breeze from the sea.

"I think we should go back to the nest, Pol," Sorka said, "to see if . . . if . . ."

"Some didn't make it?" Jim finished for her. "You need to eat."

"But then it'll be too late."

"It's probably too late already, young lady," Tillek said firmly. "And you've acquitted yourself superbly anyhow, delivering the gold. That's the highest status of the species, isn't it?"

Pol nodded, peering detachedly at Bay's sleeping charge. "I don't think any other biologist actually has one yet. Ironic that."

"Always the last to know, huh?" Jim asked, screwing his

eyebrows sardonically but grinning. "Ah, what have we here?" He pointed his long cooking fork at the figure plodding from the west. "He's got something. Can you make it out better, Sorka, with your young eyes?"

"Maybe he's got more eggs and you'll have one, too, Pol and Jim."

"I tend to doubt Sean's altruism, Sorka," Pol remarked dryly. She flushed. "Now, now, child. I'm not being critical. It's a difference of temperament and attitude."

"He's carrying something, and it's larger than an egg, and his two dragonets are very excited. No," Sorka amended. "They're upset!"

On her shoulder, Duke raised up on to his hind legs, uttering one shrill query. She could feel him sag as he received an answer, and he gave a little moan, almost a sob, she thought. She reached up to stroke him. He nuzzled her hand as if he appreciated her sympathy. She could feel the tension in his small frame, and in the way his feet gripped her pullover. Once again she was glad that her mother had reinforced the fabric to prevent his claws from puncturing through to her skin. She turned her head, rubbing his side with her cheek.

Everyone watched as Sean made his way toward the camp. Soon his bundle could be distinguished as layers of wide leaves, closely wrapped and bound with green climber vine. He was aware of their scrutiny and he looked tired. Sorka thought he also looked unhappy. He came right up to the two scientists and carefully deposited his bundle by Pol.

"There you are. Two of 'em. One barely touched. And some of the green eggs. Had to search both nests to find some that snakes hadn't sucked dry."

Pol laid one hand on Sean's offering. "Thank you, Sean. Thank you very much. Are the two . . . from a gold's clutch or a green's?"

"Gold's, of course," Sean said with a disgusted snort. "Greens rarely hatch. They're snake-eaten. I got there just in time." He looked almost challengingly at Sorka.

She did not know what to say.

"So did Sorka," Jim Tillek replied proudly, nodding to Bay.

Only then did Sean see the sleeping dragonet. A fleeting look of surprise, admiration, and annoyance crossed his face, and he sat down with a thump.

Sorka did not quite meet his eyes. "I didn't do as well," she heard herself saying. "I didn't get what we were sent after. You did."

Sean grunted, his face expressionless. Above his head, his browns exchanged news with her bronze in a rapid fire of cheeps, chirps, and murmurs. Then each gave a flip to its wings to close them back and settled in the sun to catch the warming rays.

"Chow's up," Jim Tillek said. He began filling plates with fried fish and rings of one of the fruit nuts that was improved by cooking.

"So, Ongola, what have you to report?" Paul Benden asked.

Emily Boll poured a measure of Benden's precious brandy into three glasses and passed them around before taking her own seat. Ongola used the interval to organize his thoughts. The three had gathered, as they often did, in the meteorology tower beside the landing grid now used by the sleds and the one shuttle that had been altered for sparing use as a cargo carrier.

Both admiral and governor, naturally pale of skin, had become almost as brown as the swarthy Ongola. All three had worked hard in the fields, in the mountains, and on the sea, actively participating in every aspect of the colony's endeavors.

Once the colonists took up their stake acres and Landing's purpose had been accomplished, the ostensible leaders would turn consultants, with no more authority than other stakeholders. The council would convene regularly to discuss broad topics and redress problems that affected the entire colony. A yearly democratic meeting would vote on any issues that required the consent of all. Magistrate Cherry Duff administered justice at Landing and would have a circuit for grievances and any litigation. By the terms of the Pern Charter, charterers and contractors alike would be autonomous on their stake acres. The plan was idealistic, perhaps, but as Benden repeatedly insisted, there was more than enough land and resources to allow everyone plenty of latitude.

There had been no more than a few grumbles so far about Joel Lilienkamp's disposition of supplies and matériel from their stores. Everyone knew that once the imported supplies were exhausted, all would have to learn to make do with what they had, to replace with their own industry, or to barter with the appropriate crafters. Many people prided themselves on being able to improvise, and everyone took good care of irreplaceable tools and equipment.

Between the weekly informal gatherings and the monthly mass meeting where most administrative matters were put to a democratic vote, the colony was running smoothly. An arbitration board had been voted on at one of the first mass meetings, comprising three ex-judges, two former governors, and four nonlegal people who would hold their offices for two years. The board would look into grievances and settle such disputes as might occur about staking acres or contractual misunderstandings. The colony had four trained legists and two attorneys, but it was hoped that the need for such representations would be minimal.

"There is no dispute so bitter that it cannot be arbitrated by an impartial board or by a jury of peers," Emily Boll had stated fervently and persuasively at one of the earliest mass meetings attended by everyone, including sleeping babies in their cradles. "Most of you know war firsthand." She had paused dramatically. "Wars of attrition over land and water, wars of terrible annihilation in space itself. Pern is now far, far from those former battlefields. You are here because you wished to avoid the contagion of territorial imperatives that has plagued humans since time began. Where there is a whole planet, with diverse and magnificent lands and wealth and prospects, there is no longer a need to covet a neighbor's possessions. Stake your own acres, build your homes, live in peace with the rest of us, and help us all build a world truly a paradise."

The power of her ringing voice and the sincerity of her fervent phrases had, on that glorious evening, motivated everyone to fulfill that dream. Also a realist, Emily Boll knew very well that there were dissident factors among those who had listened so politely before giving her a cheering ovation. Avril,

Lemos, Nabol, Kimmer, and a handful of others had already been tagged as possible troublemakers. But Emily devoutly hoped that the dissidents would become so involved in their new lives on Pern that they would have little time, energy, or occasion to indulge in intrigue.

The charter and the contracts had incorporated the right to discipline the signatories for "acts against the common good." Such acts had as yet to be defined.

Emily and Paul had argued about the necessity for any sort of penal code. Paul Benden favored the "punishment fitting the crime" as an object lesson for miscreants and frequent breakers of the "peace and tranquility of the settlement." He also preferred to mete out community discipline on the spot, shaming offenders in public and requiring them to do some of the more disagreeable tasks necessary to the running of the colony. So far that rough justice had been sufficient.

Meanwhile, the discreet surveillance continued on a number of folk, and Paul and Emily met with Ongola from time to time to discuss the general morale of the community and those problems that were best kept discreet. Paul and Emily also made sure to be constantly accessible to all the colonists, hoping to solve small discontents before they could grow into serious problems. They kept official "office hours" six days of the established seven-day week.

"We may not be religious in the archaic meaning of the word, but it makes good sense to give worker and beast one day's rest," Emily stated in the second of the mass meetings. "The old Judean Bible used by some of the old religious sects on Earth contained a great many commonsensible suggestions for an agricultural society, and some moral and ethical traditions which are worthy of retention"—she held up a hand, smiling benignly—"but without any hint of fanatic adherence! We left *that* back on Earth along with war!"

While the two leaders knew that even that loose form of democratic government might be untenable once the settlers had spread out from Landing to their own acres, they did hope that the habits acquired would suffice. Early American pioneers on that western push had exhibited a keen sense of independence and mutual assistance. The later Australian and New Zealand communities had risen above tyrannical governors and isolation to build people of character, resource, and incredible adaptability. The first international Moonbase had refined the art of independence, cooperation, and resourcefulness. The original settlers on First had been largely the progeny of ingenious Moon and asteroid-belt miner parents, and the Pern colony included many descendants of those original pioneering groups.

Paul and Emily proposed to institute yearly congregations of as many people from the isolated settlements as possible to reaffirm the basic tenets of the colony, acknowledge progress, and apply the minds of many to address any general problems. Such a gathering would also be the occasion for trading and social festivities. Cabot Francis Carter, one of the legists, had proposed setting aside a certain area, midway on the continent, that would be the center for these annual assemblies.

"That would be the best of all possible worlds," Cabot had said in a mellifluous bass voice that had often stirred Supreme Courts on Earth and First. Emily had once told Paul that Cabot was the most unlikely of their charter members, but it was his legal guild that had produced the actual charter and rammed it through the bureaucracy to be ratified by the FSP council. "We may not achieve it on Pern. But we can damn sure try!"

Alone with Emily and Ongola, Paul recalled that stirring challenge as he ticked off names on his long callused fingers. "Which is why I think we should continue to keep tabs on people like Bitra, Tashkovich, Nabol, Lemos, Olubushtu, Kung, Usuai, and Kimmer. The list is, mercifully, short, considering our numbers. I'm not adding Kenjo, because he's shown absolutely no connection with any of the others."

"I still don't like it. Secret surveillance smacks too much of the subterfuges used by other governments in more parlous times," Emily said grimly. "It feels demeaning to myself and to my office to use such tactics."

"There's nothing demeaning in knowing who's agin you," Paul argued. "An intelligence section has always proved invaluable."

"In revolutions, wars, power struggles, yes, but not here on Pern."

"Here as well as everywhere else in the galaxy, Em," Paul replied forcefully. "Mankind, not to mention Nathi, and even the Eridanites to some degree, prove in many ways that greed is universal. I don't see the bounty of Pern changing that trait."

"Forgo that futile old argument, my friends," Ongola said with one of his wise, sad smiles. "The necessary steps have already been taken to defunction the gig. I have, as you recommended—" He inclined his head to Paul. "—stripped the gig of several minor but essential parts in the ignition system, the effect of which would be obvious early on, and substituted two dud chips in the guidance module, something that would not be so obvious." He gestured out the window. "Sleds are allowed to park any which way, effectively but surreptitiously blocking the gig from taking off. But I don't really know why she would."

Paul Benden winced, and the other two looked away from him, knowing that he had allowed himself to be too intimate with her for an injudicious length of that outward voyage.

"Well, I'd be more worried if Avril knew about that cache of Kenjo's," Paul said. "Telgar's figures indicate that there's half a tank's worth for the *Mariposa*." He grimaced. He had found it hard enough to believe that Kenjo Fusaiyuko had scrounged so much fuel. Paul had a grudging admiration for the sheer scope of the theft, even if he could not understand the motive, and especially for the risks that Kenjo had gotten away with during all those fuel-saving shuttle trips.

"Avril favors us so seldom with her company that I don't

worry that she'd discover the hoard," Emily said with a wry smile. "I've also managed to have Lemos, Kimmer, and Nabol assigned to different sections, with few occasions to return here. 'Divide and conquer,' the man said."

"Inappropriate, Emily," Paul replied, grinning.

"If, and I do stress that improbability, Avril should discover and use Kenjo's purloined fuel," Ongola began, holding up a finger for each point, "manage to find the missing pieces, and fly the gig out of here undetected, she would have a half-full tank. She would not then drain the ships' reserves to a danger point. Frankly, we would be well rid of her and whoever she deigns to take with her. I think we dwell too much on the matter. Those seismic reports from the eastern archipelago are far more worrying. Young Mountain is smoking again and twitching its feet."

"I agree," Paul said, quite willing to turn to the more immediate problem.

"Yes, but for what purpose did Kenjo take so much fuel?" Emily asked. "You haven't answered that question. Why would he risk the safety of passengers and cargo? And he is a genuinely eager colonist! He's already chosen his stake acreage."

"A pilot of Kenjo's ability risked nothing," Paul replied smoothly. "His shuttle flights were without incident. I do know that flying is his life."

Ongola regarded the admiral in mild surprise. "Hasn't he done enough flying for one lifetime?"

Paul smiled with understanding. "Not Kenjo. What I do completely appreciate is that flying a mere power sled is a come-down, a loss of prestige, face, considering the kind of craft he's flown and where he's been. You say that he's chosen his acres, Emily? Where?"

"Down beyond what people are beginning to call the Sea of Azov, as far away from Landing as he can get but on rather a pleasant plateau, to judge by the probe report," Emily replied.

She hoped that the meeting would conclude soon. Pierre had promised her a special meal, and she found that she was enjoying those quiet dinners far more than she had thought she would.

"Howinell is Kenjo going to get those tons of fuel there?" Benden asked.

"I suspect we'll have to wait and see," Ongola replied with the trace of a smile on his lips. "He's got the same right as everyone else to use power sleds to transport his goods, and he's done some close trading with work units at the commissary. Shall I have a word with Joel about Kenjo's requisitions?"

Emily glanced quickly at Paul, who was adamant in his defense of Kenjo. "Well, I don't like unsolved riddles. I'd prefer some sort of explanation, and I think you would, too, Paul." When Benden nodded reluctantly, Emily said that she would speak to Joel Lilienkamp.

"Which brings us back to that third tremor," Paul Benden said. "How's work progressing on buttressing the stores warehouses and the one with all the medical supplies? We can't afford to lose such irreplaceable items."

Ongola consulted his notes. He wrote with a bold angular script that looked, from Emily's angle, like ancient manuscript ornamentations. All three of them, as well as most section heads, had made a point of reverting to less sophisticated methods of note-taking than speech processors. The power packs, whose rechargeability was good but not infinite, were to be reserved for essential uses, so everyone was rediscovering the art of calligraphy.

"The work will be completed by next week. The seismic net has been extended as far as the active volcano in the eastern archipelago and to Drake's Lake."

Paul grimaced. "Are we going to let him get away with that?"

"Why not?" Emily asked, grinning. "No one's contesting it. Drake was the first to see it. A community settling there would have ample space to grow, and plenty of industry to support it."

"Is it scheduled for a vote?" Paul asked after an appreciative sip of his brandy.

"No," Ongola said with another hint of a grin. "Drake is still campaigning. He doesn't want any opposition, and whatever there might have been is now worn down."

Paul snorted, and Emily cast her eyes upward in amused exasperation with the flamboyant pilot. Then Paul pensively regarded the remainder of the brandy in his glass. As Emily went on to the next point on their informal agenda, he took another sip, rolling the liquor around in his mouth, savouring the soon-to-be-exhausted beverage. He could and did drink the quikal but found it harsh to a palate trained to subtleties.

"We are proceeding well in general terms," Emily was saying briskly. "You heard that one of the dolphins died, but Olga's death was accepted by her community with considerable equanimity. According to Ann Gabri and Efram, they had expected more fatalities. Olga was, apparently," she added with a grin, "older than she said she was and hadn't wished to let her last calf go into the unknown without her."

All three chuckled and followed Paul's lead as he raised a toast to maternal love.

"Even our . . . nomads . . . have settled in," Emily went on, after checking her notepad. "Or, rather, spread out." She tapped it with her pencil, still unused to handwriting notes but struggling to get accustomed to archaic memory assists. The only voice-activated device still operable was the surface interface with the main computer banks on the *Yokohama,* but it was rarely used anymore. "The nomads've made rather a lot of inroads on clothing fabrics, but when those are depleted, that's the end of it and they'll have to make their own or trade, the same as the rest of us. We have located all the campsites. Even on foot, the Tuareg contingent can travel astonishing distances, but they camp for a while, in two separate sections."

"Well, they've a whole planet to lose themselves in," Paul said expansively. "Have they posed any other problems, Ongola?"

The dark man shook his heavy head, lowering the lids of his deep-set eyes. He was agreeably surprised by the nomads' smooth transition to life on Pern. Every week each tribe sent a representative to the veterinary sheds. The forty-two mares brought in coldsleep by the colony were all in foal, and the nomads' leaders had accepted the fact that a mare's gestation period was eleven months on Pern as it had been on Earth.

"As long as the vets keep their sense of humor. But Red Hanrahan seems to understand their ways and deals with them."

"Hanrahan? Didn't his daughter find the dragonets?"

"She and a boy, one of the travelers," Ongola replied. "They also provided the corpses which the bios have been clucking over."

"Could be useful creatures," Benden said.

"They already are," Emily added stoutly.

Ongola smiled. One day, Ongola thought, he would find a nest at the critical hatching point and he would have one of those charming, friendly, nearly intelligent creatures as a pet. He had once learned Dolphin, but he had never been able to overcome his fear of being constricted underwater to share their world properly. He needed space about him. Once, when Paul was sharing one of the long watches with him on the journey to Pern, the admiral had argued most eloquently that the dangers of outer space were even more inimical to human life than those of inner sea.

"Water is airless," Paul had said, "although it contains oxygen, but when and if the Pure Lives' hold on human adaptations is broken, humans will be able to swim without artificial help. Space has no oxygen at all."

"But you are weightless in space. Water presses down on you. You feel it."

"You'd better not feel space," Paul had replied with a laugh, but he had not argued the point further.

"Now, to more pleasant matters," Paul said. "How many contract marriages are to be registered tomorrow, Emily?"

Emily smiled, riffling pages of her notepad to come to the next seventh-day sheet, since that had become the usual time for such celebrations. In order to widen the gene pool in the next generation, the charter permitted unions of varying lengths, first insuring the support of a gravid woman and the early years of the resultant child. Prospective partners could choose which conditions suited their requirements, but there were severe penalties, up to the loss of all stake acres, for failing to fulfill whatever contract had been agreed and signed before the requisite number of witnesses.

"Three!"

"The numbers are falling off," Paul remarked.

"I've done my bit," Ongola said, slyly glancing at the two staunchly single leaders.

Ongola had courted Sabra Stein so adroitly that neither of his close friends had realized he had become attached until the couple's names had appeared on the marital schedule six weeks earlier. In fact, Sabra was already pregnant, which had led Paul to remark that the big gun was not firing blanks. He had let his bawdy humor disguise his relief, for he knew that Ongola still grieved for the wife and family of his youth. Ongola's hatred of the Nathi and his implacable desire for revenge had sustained the man throughout the war. For a long while, Paul had worried that his favorite aide and valued commander might be unable to alter that overpowering hatred even in a more peaceful clime.

"Emily, has Pierre consented yet?" Ongola asked, a knowing grin lighting a somber face that even his present felicitous state did not completely brighten.

Emily was astonished. She had thought that she and Pierre had been discreet. But she had recently noticed in herself a tendency to smile more easily and to lose the thread of conversations for no apparent reason.

She and Pierre were an unlikely combination of personalities, but that was half the pleasure of it. Their relationship had begun quite unexpectedly about the fifth week after Landing, when Pierre had asked her opinion of a casserole composed entirely of indigenous ingredients. He administered the mass catering of Landing, and very well, she thought, considering the wide range of tastes and dietary requirements. He had started to serve her special dishes when she ate at the big mess hall. Then, when she would often have to work through the lunch hour, Pierre de Courci would bring over the tray she ordered.

"If I were the possessive type, I would keep his cooking to myself," she replied. "Kindly remember that I am past childbearing, an advantage you men have over me. How about it, Paul? Will you do your bit?" Emily knew that her tone had a snap to it, born of envy. None of her children, all adults, had wished to accompany her on a one-way journey.

Unperturbed, Paul Benden merely smiled enigmatically and sipped at his brandy.

"Caves!" Sallah cried, nudging Tarvi's arm and pointing to the rock barrier in front of them. Sunlight outlined openings in its sheer face.

He reacted instantly and enthusiastically, with the kind of almost innocent joy of discovery that Sallah found so appealing in him. The continually unfolding beauties of Pern had not palled on Tarvi Andiyar. Each new wonder was greeted with as much interest as the last one he had extolled for its magnificence, its wealth, or its potential. She had wangled ruthlessly to get herself assigned as his expedition pilot. They were making their third trip together—and their first solo excursion.

Sallah was playing it cautiously, concentrating on making herself so professionally indispensible to Tarvi that an opportunity to project her femininity would not force him to retreat into his usual utterly courteous, utterly impersonal shell. She had seen other women who made a determined play for the handsome, charming geologist rebuffed by his demeanor; they were surprised, puzzled, and sometimes hurt by the way he eluded their ploys. For a while, Sallah wondered if Tarvi liked women at all, but he had shown no preference for the acknowledged male lovers in Landing. He treated everyone, man, woman, and child, with the same charming affability and understanding. And whatever his sexual preference, he was nonetheless expected to add to the next generation. Sallah was already determined to be the medium and would find the moment.

Perhaps she had found it. Tarvi had a special fondness for caves; he had at various times called them orifices of the Mother Earth, entrances to the mysteries of her creation and construction, and windows into her magic and bounty. Even though this was Pern, he worshipped the same mystery that had dominated his life so far.

Their current trip was to make an aerial reconnaissance of the location of several mineral deposits noted by the metallurgy probes. Iron, vanadium, manganese, and even germanium were to be found in the mountainous spine that Sallah was aiming at as they followed the course of a river to its source. She was also operating under the general directive that unusual sites should be recorded and photographed to offer the widest possible choice. Only a third of those with stake acreage had made their selection. There was a subtle pressure to keep everyone in the southern continent—at least in the first few generations—but there was no such directive in the charter. The broad, long river valley that lay to their right as they approached the precipice was, to Sallah's mind, the most beautiful they had seen so far.

Rene Mallibeau, the colony's most determined vintner, was still looking for the proper type of slope and soil for his vineyards, though to get his project started he had actually released some of his hoard of special soils from their sealed tanks for his experiments in viniculture. Quikal was not a universally accepted substitute for the traditional spirits. Despite being poured through a variety of filters with or without additives, nothing could completely reduce the raw aftertaste. Rene had been promised the use of ceramic-lined metal fuel tanks which, once thoroughly cleansed, would provide him with wine vats of superior quality. Of course, once the proper oak forests had reached adequate size for use as staves, his descendants could move back to the traditional wooden barrel.

"Rather spectacular, that precipice, isn't it, Tarvi?" Sallah said, grinning rather foolishly, as if the view were a surprise that she herself had prepared for him.

"Indeed it is. 'In Xanadu did Kublai Khan,'" he murmured in his rich deep voice.

"'Caverns measureless to man'?" Sallah capped it, careful not to sound smug that she recognized his source. Tarvi often quoted obscure Sanskrit and Pushtu texts, leaving her groping for a suitable retort.

"Precisely, O moon of my delight."

Sallah suppressed a grimace. Sometimes Tarvi's phrases were ambiguous, and she knew that he did not mean what his phrase suggested. He would not be so obvious. Or would he? Had she penetrated that bland exterior after all? She forced herself to contemplate the immense stone bulwark. Its natural fluted columns appeared carved by an inexperienced or inattentive sculptor, yet the imperfection contributed to the overall beauty of the precipice.

"This valley is six or seven klicks long," she said quietly, awed by the truly impressive natural site.

From the steep, right-angled fall of a spectacular *diedre,* the palisade led in a somewhat straight line for about three klicks before falling back into a less perfectly defined face that sloped down in the distance to meet the floor of the valley. She angled the sled to starboard, facing upriver, and they were nearly blinded by the brilliant sunlight reflecting from the surface of the lake that had been charted by the probe.

"No, land here," Tarvi said quickly, actually catching her arm to stress his urgency. He was not much given to personal contact, and Sallah tried not to misinterpret excitement for anything else. "I must see the caves."

He released the safety harness and swiveled his seat around. Then he walked to the back of the sled, rummaging among the supplies.

"Lights, we'll need lights, ropes, food, water, recording devices, specimen kit," he muttered as his deft movements filled two backpacks. "Boots? Have you on proper boots . . . ah, those will do, indeed they will. Sallah, you are always well prepared." He compounded his inadvertent injury to her feelings by one of his more ingratiating smiles.

Once again, Sallah shook her head over her whimsical fancy, which had managed to settle on one of the most elusive males of her acquaintance. Of course, she consoled herself, anything easily had is rarely worth having. She landed the sled at the base of the towering precipice, as near to the long narrow mouth of the cave as she could.

"Pitons, grappling hook—that first slab looks about five meters above the scree. Here you are, Sallah!"

He handed her pack over, waiting only long enough to see her grab a strap before he released the canopy, jumped down, and was striding toward the towering buttress. With a resigned shrug, Sallah flipped on beacon, comm unit, and recorder for incoming messages, fastened her jacket, settled the rather hefty pack on her back, and followed him, closing the canopy behind her.

He scrambled up the scree and stood with one palm flat against the slab, looking up its imposing and awesome spread, his face rapt with wonder. Gently, as in a caress, he stroked the stone before he began to look right and left, assessing how best to climb to the cave. He flashed her an ingenuous smile, acknowledging her presence and assuming her willingness.

"Straight up. Not much of a climb with pitons."

The climb proved strenuous. Sallah could have used a breather as she crawled onto the ledge, but there was the cave opening, and nothing was going to deter Tarvi from immediate entrance and a leisurely inspection. Ah, well, it was just 1300 hours. They had time in hand. She rolled to her feet, unlatching the handlight from her belt just a few seconds after he had done the same, and was at his side as he peered into the opening.

"Lords, gods, and minor deities!"

His invocation was a mere whisper, solemn and awed, a susurrous echo. The vast initial cavern was larger than the cargo hold of the *Yokohama*. Sallah made that instant comparison, remembering how eerie that immense barren space had seemed on her last trip, and in the next second, she wondered what the cavern would look like occupied. It would make a spectacular great hall, in the tradition of medieval times on Earth—only even more magnificent.

Tarvi held his breath, hesitantly extending his still-dark handlight, as if reluctant to illuminate the majesty of the cavern. She heard his intake of breath, in the manner of one steeling himself to commit sacrilege, and then the light came on.

Wings whirred as shadows made silent sinuous departures to the darker recesses. They both ducked as the winged denizens departed in flight lines just clearing their heads, though the cave entrance was at least four meters high. Ignoring the exodus, Tarvi moved reverently into the vast space.

"Amazing," he murmured as he shined the light up and judged that the shell of the outer wall above them was barely two meters thick. "A very thin face."

"Some bubble," Sallah said, feeling impious and wanting to regain her equilibrium after her initial awe. "Look, you could carve a staircase in that," she said, her light picking out a slanting foot of rock that rose to a ledge where a large darkness indicated yet another cave.

She spoke to inattentive ears, for Tarvi was already prowling about, determining the width of the entrance and the dimensions of the cave. She hurried after him.

The first chamber of the cave complex measured an awesome fifty-seven meters deep at its widest, tapering at either end to forty-six meters on the left and forty-two meters on the right. Along the back wall, there were innumerable irregular openings at random levels; some were on the ground level leading into apparent tunnel complexes, most of which were high enough to admit Tarvi's tall frame with considerable head space; others, like great dead eyes, peered down from higher up the inside wall. Entranced as Tarvi was by their discovery, he was a trained scientific observer. With Sallah's aid, he began to draft an accurate plan of the main chamber, the openings of secondary ones, and the tunnel complexes leading inward. He penetrated each to a depth of a hundred meters, roped to a nervous Sallah who kept glancing back at the cave's opening for the reassuring sight of the waning day.

His rough notes were refined by the light of the gas fire on which Sallah cooked their evening meal. Tarvi had elected to camp far enough into the cave to be protected from the stiff breeze that blew down the valley, and far enough to the left so as not to interfere with the habits of the cave's natural residents. Later, a low flame from the protected gas fire would discourage most of Pern's wildlife from investigating the intruders.

Somehow, in the cave Sallah did feel like an intruder, though she had not previously been bothered by that notion. The place was truly awe-inspiring.

Tarvi had gone down to the sled to bring up more drafting tools and the folding table over which he had hunched almost immediately. With no comment, he had eaten the stew she had carefully prepared, absently handing back his plate for a second helping.

Sallah was of two minds about Tarvi's concentration. On the one hand, she was a good cook and liked to have her skill acknowledged. On the other hand, she was as glad that Tarvi was distracted. One of the pharmacists had given her a pinch of what she swore was a potent indigenous aphrodisiac; Sallah had used it to season Tarvi's share. She did not need it herself, not with her mind and body vibrating to his presence and their solitude. But she was beginning to wonder if the aphrodisiac was strong enough to overcome Tarvi's enchantment with the cave. Just her luck to get him to herself for a night or two and then have him be totally enthralled by Dear Old Mother Earth in Pernese costume. But she had not bided her time to waste a sterling opportunity. She could wait. All night. And tomorrow. She had enough of the joy dust to use the next night, too. Maybe it just took a while to act.

"It is truly magnificent in its proportions, Sallah. Here, look!" He straightened his torso, arching his back against his cramped muscles, and Sallah came up behind him, knelt, and considerately began to knead his taut shoulder muscles as she peered over his shoulder.

The two-dimensional sketch had been deftly drawn with bold lines: he had added back, front, and side elevations, truthfully ending them where his measurements ended. But that only made the cavern more imposing and mysterious.

"What a fort it would have been in the olden days!" He looked toward the black interior, his wide liquid eyes shining, his face alight as imagination altered the chamber before him. "Why, it would have housed whole tribes. Kept them secure for years from invasion. There's fresh water, you understand, down the third left-hand tunnel. Of course, the valley itself would be defensible and this the protected inner hold, with that daunting slab to defeat climbers. There are no less than eighteen different exits from the main chamber."

She had worked her hands up the column of his neck, then across the trapezius muscles, and down to the deltoids, massaging firmly but letting her fingers linger in a movement that she had found immensely effective on other occasions when she had wished to relax a man.

"Ah, how kind you are, Sallah, to know where the muscles bind." He twisted slightly, not to evade her seeking, kneading fingers but to guide them to the sorest points. He pushed the low table to one side so that his arms could fall naturally to his lap as he rotated his head. "There's a point, eleventh vertebrae . . ." he suggested, and she dutifully found the knot of muscle and smoothed it expertly. He sighed like a lithe dark feline being stroked.

She said nothing, but moved ever so slightly forward so that her body touched his. As she walked her fingers back to his neck, she dared to press against him so that her breasts lightly touched his shoulder blades. She could feel her nipples harden at the contact, and her respiration quickened. Her fingers ceased to knead and began to caress, moving down over his chest in long slow motions. He caught her hands then, and she could feel the stillness of him, a stillness of mind and breath, as his body began to tremble slightly.

"Perhaps this is the time," he mused as if alone. "There will never be a better. And it must be done."

With the suppleness that was as much a trademark of Tarvi Andiyar as his ineffable charm, he gathered her in his arms, pulling her across his lap. His expression, oddly detached as if examining her for the first time, was not yet quite the tender, loving expression she had so wished to evoke. His expressive and large brown eyes were almost sad, though his perfectly shaped lips curved in an infinintely gentle smile—as if, the thought intruded on Sallah's delight in her progress, he did not wish to frighten her.

"So, Sallah," he said in his rich low and sensual voice, "it is you."

She knew she should interpret that cryptic remark, but then he began to kiss her, his hands suddenly displaying an exceedingly erotic mind of their own, and she no longer wished to interpret anything.

Four mares, three dolphins, and twelve cows produced their young at precisely the same moment, or so the records for that dawn hour stood. Sean had even agreed to allow Sorka to observe the birth of the foal designated for him by Pol and Bay. He had maintained a pose of skepticism over the color and sex of the creature although, three days previously, he had already witnessed that the first of the draft animals produced for his father's group was exactly as requested, a sturdy bay mare with white socks and a face blaze who had weighed over seventy kilos at birth and would be the image of the long-dead Shire stallion whose sperm had begot her.

Some wit had quipped that Landing's records were turning into the biblical begottens of Pern's chronicle. In two years, the new generation was well begun and increasing daily. Human births were less minutely reported than the successes of animalkind, but at least as well celebrated.

Sheep and the Nubian strain of goats that had somehow adapted where other tough breeds had failed grazed Landing's meadows and would soon go to farm-stake acres in the temperate belts of the southern continent. The growing herds and flocks were patrolled by such a proliferation of dragonets that the ecologists were becoming concerned that the animals would lose their natural abilities to fend for themselves. The tame dragonets were proving to be extraordinarily faithful to the humans who had impressed them at hatching, even after their voracious appetites abated with maturity and they were well able to forage on their own.

The biology department was learning more about the little creatures every day. Bay Harkenon and Pol Nietro had discovered of a particularly surprising phenomenon. When Bay's little queen mated with a bronze that Pol had impressed, the sensuality of their pets surprised them with its intensity. They found themselves responding to the exciting stimulus in a human fashion. After the initial shock, they came to a mutual conclusion and took a larger residence together. Awed by the empathic potential of the dragonets, Bay and Pol asked for, and got, Kitti Ping's permission to try mentasynth enhancement on the fourteen eggs that Bay's Mariah had conceived in her mating flight. They fussed considerably more over the little golden Mariah than was necessary, but neither the dragonet nor her clutch suffered. When Mariah produced her enhanced eggs in a specially constructed facsimile of a beach, Bay and Pol were smugly pleased.

Incorporation of mentasyth, which had originally been developed by the Beltrae, a reclusive Eridani hive culture, sparked latent empathic abilities. Dragonets had already demonstrated such an ability, amounting to an almost telepathic communication with a few people. The dragonets were clearly a remarkable evolutionary attempt which, like dolphins, had produced an animal that understood its environment—and controlled it. So, inspired by the success of the dolphins' mentasynth enhancement, Bay and Pol hoped that the dragonets would come to an even closer empathy with people.

Initially, humans from Beltrae who had been "touched" were regarded with great suspicion, of course, but as soon as their remarkable empathic powers with animals and other people were realized, the technique became widespread. Many groups eventually had valued healers whose abilities had been amplified that way. Luckily, that all happened well before the Pure Human group became powerful.

From their studies of the tunnel snakes and wherries, Bay and Pol had come to an appreciation of the potential of the charming and useful dragonets. It had taken many experiments with dragonet tissues, and with several generations of the little tunnel snakes, to incorporate the mentasynth system successfully, but longtime experience with such species as dolphins—and, of course, man—paid off.

Everyone in Landing had come to have a working knowledge of the habits of the dragonets, biological as well as psychological, for there was good cause to be grateful to the creatures and to tolerate their few natural excesses. Theoretically, Bay had known that some of the owners seemed to feel the "primitive urges" of the creatures: hunger, fear, anger, and an intense mating imperative. She had simply never thought that she would be as vulnerable as her younger colleagues. It had been an exceedingly delightful surprise.

Red and Mairi Hanrahan were thankful that Sorka and Sean had impressed—the word, meaning the act of imprinting a dragonet, had somehow crept into the language—dragonets that would not want to mate with each other. They still did not approve of Sorka's close attachment to the boy and felt that she was too young to be subject to irresistible sensual urges.

On that morning, nearly twelve months after Landing, the mare Sean had chosen to produce his promised foal was laboring to give birth, there was no doubt that Sorka, who had turned thirteen, and Sean, two years older, were in rapport with their eagerly anticipating dragonets. The two browns and the bronze had perched on the top rail of the stable partition, their eyes whirling with growing excitement as they crooned their birth song. The little chestnut mare dropped to the straw to deliver the forelegs and head of her foal. Above, the rafters of the barn seemed to ripple with its temporary adornment of the dragonet population of Landing, crooning and chirping continual encouragement.

Dragonets were sentimental about births and missed none in Landing, bugling in high-pitched tenor voices at each new arrival. Fortunately, they discreetly remained outside human habitations. The colony's obstetricians had lately been working nonstop and had drafted the nurses and taken on apprentices.

An array of dragonets on a roof became an irrefutable sign of impending birth: the dragonets were never wrong. The obstetricians could gauge the labor's progress by the growing intensity of the dragonets' welcoming song. The chorus might deprive neighbors of sleep, but most of the community took it in good humor. Even the most jaundiced had seen the dragonets protecting the flocks and herds, and had to appreciate their value.

The chestnut mare heaved again, extruding the foal farther. Since its legs, head, and forequarters were wet with birth fluids, Sean could not distinguish the animal's color. Then the rest of the body emerged, followed, with a final push, by the hindquarters. There was no doubt that he was not only darkly dappled but male. With a crow of incredulous joy, Sean dropped to the little fellow's head to mop it dry, even before the mare could form her bond. Tears streaming down her dusty face, Sorka hugged herself in joy. Dimly she heard the excited comments of the other animal midwives sharing the large barn.

"He's the only colt," her father said, returning to Sean and Sorka. "As ordered." Though the colony actually needed as many female animals as it could breed, Sean's preference for a colt had been duly considered. And one local stallion would be a safeguard, though there were more than enough varied sperms in reserve. "Grand fellow, though," Red remarked, nodding his head approvingly. "Make a good sixteen hands, if I'm any judge. A sturdy nine stone, I'd say. Fine good fellow, and she bore him like a trooper." He stroked the neck of the little mare, who was licking the colt as he suckled her with vigor. "Come now, Sorka," he went on, seeing her tear-streaked face. "I'll keep my promise that you'll have a horse, too." He gave her a reassuring hug.

"I know you will, Da," she said, burrowing into his chest. "I'm crying because I'm so happy for Sean. He didn't believe Bay, you know. Not for one moment."

Red Hanrahan laughed softly, for it wouldn't do for Sean to hear. Not that the boy was aware of anything but the colt, twisting its stump of a tail as if that would speed its suckling. For once, Sean's customary wary, often cynical expression had softened with amazed tenderness as he devoured the colt with his eyes.

After Sorka gave her father a hug for his assurances, she stepped away from him, and her bronze glided down to her shoulder, chattering in a happy social tone as he wrapped his tail possessively about her neck. Then Duke leaned down Sorka's chest, his eyes sparkling blue and green as he, too, examined the new arrival closely. Encouraged, Sean's brown pair dropped to the lower rail of the foaling box, exchanging cheeps and chirps with Duke.

"You approve?" Sean asked them, grinning despite the challenge in his tone.

Bobbing their heads up and down vigorously, they extended wings, each complaining that the other's wing was in the way, then they flicked their wings to their backs and assured Sean volubly that they approved. He grinned back at them.

"He's a real beauty, Sean. Just what you wanted," Sorka said.

Unaccountably Sean shook his head, looking dubious. "Too young to tell if he'll match Cricket."

"Oh, you are the utter limit!" Sorka snapped angrily. She left the box, nearly jamming the door rail as she closed it with considerable vehemence.

"What'd I say?" Sean demanded of Red Hanrahan.

"I think you'll have to figure that one out yourself, boyo!" Red clapped him on the shoulder, torn between amusement and a certain concern for his daughter. "Give the mare her feed before you leave, will you, Sean?"

As Red Hanrahan walked down the aisle, checking on the other new arrivals, he considered Sorka's behavior. She was thirteen but a well-developed girl who had been menstruating for nearly a year. That she doted on Sean was patent to everyone but Sean. He tolerated her. As did Sean's family. Mairi and

Red had talked it over, wary of the boy's background though both Hanrahans acknowledged that it was time to discard old attitudes and opinions.

Sean, too, had made several notable concessions. Whether spurred by competition with Sorka or mere male arrogance, he had improved his reading and writing skills and frequently used a viewer to scan veterinary texts in Red's office. Red had carefully cultivated the boy's interest and encouraged him to help with the breeding stock. The boy unquestionably had a way with animals, not just horses, though he ignored sheep altogether.

"Sean says sheep are for stealing, trading, and eating," Sorka told her father when he had remarked on that exception.

Mairi did worry occasionally that Sorka was inevitably partnered with Sean when they were assigned together to the zoological expeditions. But, as Sorka blithely explained, she got along with Sean, and they were both more used to handling animals and wildlife than urban-bred young people. As long as they did their obligatory share of work for the colony, and enjoyed it, they were ahead of the game. Sean was also making more of a contribution to Landing's efforts than most of his people. It was just that Sean and Sorka were becoming linked together in the collective Landing mind, Mairi wistfully remarked one evening to Red. To his surprise, Red found himself in the position of devil's advocate. But then, like Sorka, he had grown accustomed to Sean's ways and knew what to ignore.

Sorka's exhibition of female exasperation that morning was the first of its kind, to Red's knowledge, and he wondered ruefully if her patience with Sean's obtuseness was exhausted, or if their relationship was merely entering a new phase. Sorka had been given an appropriate theoretical education in sexual relationships but until today had shown only a patient acceptance of Sean's behavior and eccentricities. He would have to talk with Mairi. When he got the chance.

"Red! Reeeeddd!" another veterinarian called in alarm.

Red ran to consult. It was not until much later that night

that he remembered the problem of Sorka and Sean, but Mairi was already long asleep and, as well as being in the second trimester of a pregnancy, she was working hard enough in the creche to deserve her rest.

The westward-jutting finger of the northern continent pointed directly at the big island, which loomed lavender above the gray of the morning sea. Avril had lifted off from the desert camp well before dawn, leaving a message that she was taking a day off. The others would not mind, and she was as tired of Ozzie Munson and Cobber Alhinwa as they were of her.

Yesterday, the two miners had found some really good turquoise and refused to tell her where, tantalizing her with brief glimpses of the very fine sky-blue–banded rock. She had known when they came into camp the previous evening that they were excited about the hunk that they were tossing back and forth. She had merely asked to see it, and had allowed herself to become irritated when the two miners had responded with secrecy. She would have to be very cautious with those two, she thought. They thought themselves so clever. Anyhow, turquoise, though valued for its rarity on Earth, was not really worth the trouble of ingratiating herself to those two jerks.

Then, at supper, when they were still whispering between themselves and glancing at her with sly smiles, she began to wonder if they had heard something in particular to make them react as they had to her polite and diffident query.

She tried to remember if they had ever teamed up with Bart Lemos. But he was at Andiyar's ore mountain. He must, for once, have kept quiet about the gold nuggets that he had been panning out of a mountain stream above the camp. Obedient to the pact they had made on the *Yoko,* he had given them to her to hide in her cache at Landing. She had not confided much of her scheme to him, for, given a few mugs of quikal, Bart Lemos would give anyone his life history.

Maybe Stev Kimmer was not as good a choice of ally as she had initially thought, hearing his sly and witty complaints during the last year of that interminable journey to this godforsaken planet. He was more attractive than the others; in fact, he was extremely attractive and, more importantly, lusty, with a willingness to experiment that the much vaunted Admiral Benden had never displayed. A bit of a bore in bed, our dear admiral. Damn Paul Benden. Why had he turned so cool toward her? After all those protestations of admiration and devotion. She had been so certain that she had felt the marriage contract in her hand. Then, a scant year away from their destination, when Rukbat had grown from a spark to a gleam in the blackness of space, Benden had altered. He suddenly had had no time for her at all. Well, he would find out what Avril Bitra was made of. And then it would be too late.

Colonizing had seemed like a good idea back on Earth when the excitement of the Nathi War had died down. Any alternative, save First Centauri, which everyone knew was controlled by the First Families and founding companies, was no better than Earth or moldering at grade on a lumbering merchantman. She had even toyed with the challenge of navigating mining ships within the Belts until the Roosevelt Dome had exploded for no apparent reason, killing all but a handful of the ten thousand inhabitants. The chance to rule a new world had drawn her. Over the years, she had had enough experience with psycho profiles to know how to control her pulse and what answers to give to the asinine questions that were supposed to separate truth from fiction. And so she had been accepted as astrogator for the Pern expedition.

But since she had failed to capture Paul Benden, who would be Pern's first leader—in her estimation, the less colorful Emily Boll would be overshadowed by the more flamboyant admiral once they landed on Pern—she had decided that living the rest of her life in obscurity at the end of the Milky Way was insupportable. She was, after all, a competent astrogator and, given a ship, charts, and a deep-sleep tank, she could make her way to some other civilized and sophisticated planet that catered to the life-style she wished to enjoy.

She had begun with Stev Kimmer, partly just to ease the pain of losing Paul Benden. When she had noticed that Bart Lemos managed to attach himself to her whenever Stev was on duty, she encouraged him, too. Nabhi Nabol joined the group one evening, along with several others. Bart and Nabhi were pilots, each with a useful secondary skill: Bart in mining, and Nabhi in computers. Stev was a mechanical engineer with an uncanny ability to diagnose computer failures and rearrange chips to do twice the work they had been designed to handle.

For the plan taking shape in her mind, she assembled useful cronies. Most were contractors like herself, or small-stake charterers beginning to feel that they had been shortchanged on their deals. In the back of Avril's mind was the notion that it would be fun to see if she could foment sufficient discord to overthrow their benevolent leaders and rule Pern on her own, instead of as Paul Benden's consort. But that would have to wait for a propitious moment once the colony had been settled in and troubles began.

So far, except for minor hitches, there had been no trouble of the type that she could use for her purposes. Everyone was too busy scurrying around, settling in, raising livestock, and zipping here and there looking at real estate. She despised the colonists for being so enthusiastic about the ghastly empty wasteland of a world, with its noisy wildlife and the thousands of things that crawled, wriggled, or flew. There was not a decent useful animal native to the entire planet, and she was getting very tired of eating fish or wherry, which sometimes tasted more like fish than what came out of the sea. Even tank-beef would have been an acceptable substitute.

More and more her determination to leave this wretched backwater world was reinforced. But she would leave it in style, and the hell with the rest of them.

Stev Kimmer was essential to that escape. He was constructing an emergency beacon for her from parts he had "found" on the *Yokohama;* without that essential piece of equipment, her scheme would have to be aborted. Kimmer had to be kept on the mark, too, for when she wanted to appropriate the captain's gig.

More important was his willingness to participate in her plan to stake the right sections of the island to prospect for the gemstones that she knew were there. Grandmama Shavva had left her single remaining descendant a legacy that had to be grasped.

Kimmer was to requisition a sled for seven days in a quite legitimate search for a stake. He was supposed to imply that he was looking about the southern continent. As a veteran of the Nathi War, he had twice Avril's allotment. That the charterers had more than any contractor, including herself, the astrogator, who had delivered them safely to the wretched place, was a fact that had never set well with her.

Damn Munson and Alhinwa. They could have told her where they had unearthed the turquoise. Pern was a virgin world, with metal and mineral aplenty, untouched as yet by careless prospectors and greedy merchants. There was plenty for everyone. Back on sophisticated worlds, any large, well-colored hunks of that sky-blue stone would be snatched up by ardent collectors—the higher the asking price the more collectible!

And why had she not heard from Nabhi? She suspected that he might be trying to run a program of his own, instead of the one she had set. She would have to watch that one: he was a devious sort. Much as she was. In the long run, she had the upper hand, since she was the astrogator, and Nabhi did not have the skills required to get home by himself. He had to have her, but she did not have to have him—unless it suited her. Nabol was not as good overall for her purposes as Kimmer was, but he would do in a pinch.

She had almost bridged the distance between continent and island and could see waves lashing the granite rock. She veered to port, looking for the mouth of the natural harbor where the long-dead survey team had made camp. She had told Kimmer to meet her there. She felt better about being someplace that had already been occupied. She could not stand listening to the idiot colonists going on and on about being "first" to see that or "first" to step there, or the naming arguments that continually dominated conversation night after night around the bonfire. Shit in Drake's Lake! Fatuous ass! Lousy gravity-ball player!

She corrected her course as she spotted the two natural spurs of rock that formed a breakwater to the roughly oval natural harbor. Kimmer would have hid the sled anyhow just in case . . . She caught herself and snorted in sour amusement. As if anyone on this goody-good world is checking up on anyone else! "We are all equal here." Our brave and noble leaders have so ordained it. With equal rights to share in Pern's wealth. You just bet. Only I'll get my equal share before anyone else and shake this planet's dirt off my boots!

Just as she passed over the breakwater, she saw the glint of metal under the lush foliage to starboard on a ledge above the sandy shoreline. Nearby was the smoke of Kimmer's small fire. She landed her sled neatly beside his.

"You were right about this place, baby," he greeted her, a closed fist upraised and shaken in victory. "I got here yesterday afternoon, good tail wind all the way, so I did a decco. And see what I found first thing!"

"Let me see," she said, displaying a bright breathless eagerness, though she did not at all like his presumptive solo explorations.

He smiled broadly as he slowly opened his fingers and let his hand drop so that she could see the large gray rock he held. Her eagerness drained with discouragement until he turned the stone just slightly and she caught the unmistakable glint of green, half buried in one end.

"Fardles!" She snatched the stone from his hand and whirled to the sun, which had risen over the ocean by then. She wet her finger and rubbed at the green glint.

"I also found this," Kimmer said.

Looking up, she saw him holding a squarish green stone the size of a spoon bowl, rough-edged where it had been prized from a limestone cavity.

She almost threw away the rock with its still-hidden treasure in her eagerness to take the rough emerald from him. She held it to the sun, saw the flaw, but had no complaint about the clear deep green. She weighed it in her hand. Why, it had to be thirty or forty carats. With a clever lapidary to cut beyond the flaw, there would be fifteen carats of gemstone. And if that stone was just a sample . . . The idea of apprenticing as a gemstone cutter and using that magnificent jewel to learn on amused her.

"Where?" she demanded, her breath constricted with urgency.

"Over there." He half turned, pointing up into the thick vegetation. "There's a whole cave of them embedded in the rock."

"You just walked in and it winked at you?" She forced herself to speak lightly, amusedly, smiling up approvingly at his beaming face. He looked so bloody pleased with himself. She continued to smile but ground her teeth.

"I've *klah* for you," he said, gesturing to the fire where he had rigged a spit and a protecting rock for his kettle.

"That abominable stuff," she exclaimed. She had a fleet-incurred preference for strong coffee, and the last had been served at that pathetic Thanksgiving shindig—and spilled when the tremor had shaken the urns from their stands. The last coffee from Earth had seeped, undrunk, into the dirt of Pern.

"Oh, if you use enough sweetening, it's not all that bad." He poured her a cup even though she had not said that she wanted one. "They say it's got as much caffeine in it as coffee or tea. The secret's in drying the bark thoroughly before grinding and steeping it."

He had lashed sweetener into the cup and handed it to her,

expecting her to be grateful for his thoughtfulness. She could not afford to alienate Kimmer even if he sounded revoltingly like a good little colonist, approving of good colonial substitutes.

"Sorry, Stev," she said, smiling apologetically at him as she took the cup. "Early morning nerves. I really do miss coffee."

He gave a shrug. "We won't for long, now, will we?"

She kept her smile in place, wondering if he knew how inane he sounded. Then, she cautioned herself severely, if she had only been more careful with Paul, she might have been first lady on Pern. What *had* she done wrong? She could have sworn she would be able to maintain his interest in her. All had gone perfectly right up until they entered the Rukbat system. Then it had been as if she no longer existed. And I got them here!

"Avril?"

She came back to the present at the impatience in Stev Kimmer's voice. "Sorry!" she said.

"I *said* that I've already got food for the day, so as soon as you finish that we can go."

She tipped her cup, watching the dark liquid momentarily stain the white sand. She jiggled the cup to scatter the last drops, put it upside down by the fire like a good little colonist, and rose to her feet, smiling brightly at Kimmer. "Well, let's go!"

PART TWO
Thread

4.5.08 Pern

Perhaps it was because people were so accustomed to dragonets after nearly eight years of close association that they no longer paid much attention to the creatures' behavior. Those who noticed their unusual antics thought that the dragonets were merely playing some sort of a new game, for they were inventively amusing. Later people would remember that the dragonets attempted to herd the flocks and herds back to the barns. Later marine rangers would remember that the bottlenoses Bessie, Lottie, and Maximilian had urgently tried to explain to their human friends why the indigenous marine life was rushing eastward to a food source.

At her home in Europe Square, Sabra Ongola-Stein actually thought that Fancy, the family dragonet, was attacking her three-year-old son at play in the yard. The little gold was grabbing at Shuvin's shirt, attempting to haul him from his sandpile and his favorite toy truck. As soon as Sabra had rescued the boy, batting at Fancy, the dragonet had hovered over her, cheeping with relief. It was puzzling behavior to be sure, but, though the fabric of the shirt was torn, Sabra could see no marks on Shuvin's flesh from the dragonet talons. Nor was Shuvin crying. He merely wanted to go back to his truck while Sabra wanted to change his shirt.

To her utter surprise, Fancy tried to duck into the house with them, but Sabra got the door closed in time. As she leaned against it, catching her breath, she noticed through the rear window that other dragonets were acting in the most peculiar fashion. She was somewhat reassured by the fact that there had never been reports of dragonets *hurting* people, even in the ardor of mating, but that did not seem to be what was agitating them, because greens were wheeling as frantically as the other colors. Greens always got out of the way when a gold was mating. And it was certainly the wrong time for Fancy to be in season.

As Sabra changed Shuvin's shirt, deftly handling the little boy's squirms, she realized that the cries that penetrated the thick plastic walls of the house sounded frightened. Sabra knew the usual dragonets sounds as well as anyone in Landing. What could they be frightened of?

The large flying creature—perhaps a very big wherry—that had been occasionally spotted soaring near the Western Barrier Range would be unlikely to range so far east. What other danger could there be on a fine early spring morning? That smudge of gray cloud far off on the horizon suggested rain later on in the day, but that would be good for the crops already sprouting in the grain fields. Maybe she should get the clothes in off the line. Sometimes she missed the push-button conveniences that back on old Earth had eliminated the drudgery of monotonous household tasks. Too bad that the council never considered requiring miscreants to do domestic duties as punishment for disorderly conduct. She pulled Shuvin's shirt down over his trousers, and he gave her a moist, loving kiss.

"Truck, Mommie, truck? Now?"

His wistful question made her aware, suddenly, of the silence, of the absence of the usual cheerful cacophony of dragonet choruses which was the background to daily life in Landing and in nearly every settlement across the southern continent. Such a complete silence was frightening. Startled, restraining Shuvin who wanted urgently to get back out and play in the sand, Sabra peered out the back window, then through the plasglas behind her. She saw not a dragonet in sight. Not even on Betty Musgrave-Blake's house where there had been the usual natal congregation. Betty was expecting her second child; and Sabra had seen Basil, the obstetrician, arriving with Greta, his very capable apprentice midwife.

Where were the dragonets? They never missed a birth.

As well established as Landing was, one was still supposed to report anything unusual on Pern. She tried Ongola's number on the comm unit, but it was engaged. While she was using the handset, Shuvin reached his grubby hand up to the door pull and slid it open, with a mischievous grin over his shoulder at his mother as he performed that new skill. She smiled her acquiescence as she tapped out Bay's number. The zoologist might know what was amiss with her favorite critters.

Well east and slightly south of Landing, Sean and Sorka were hunting wherry for Restday meals. As the human settlements spread, foragers were having to go farther afield for game.

"They're not even trying to hunt, Sorka," Sean said, scowling. "They've spent half the morning arguing. Fardling fools." He lifted one muscular brown arm in an angry gesture to his eight dragonets. "Shape up, you winged wimps. We're here to hunt!"

He was ignored as his veteran browns seemed to be arguing with the mentasynths, most aggressively with Sean's queen, Blazer. That was extraordinary behavior: Blazer, who had been genetically improved by Bay Harkenon's tinkering, was usually accorded the obedience that any of the lesser colors granted the fertile gold females.

"Mine, too," Sorka said, nodding as her own five joined Sean's. "Oh, jays, they're coming for *us!*" Slackening her reins, she began to tighten her legs around her bay mare but stopped when she saw Sean, wheeling Cricket to face the oncoming dragonets, hold up an imperious hand. She was even more startled to see the dragonets assume an attack formation, their cries clamors of unspeakable fright and danger.

"Danger? Where?" Sean spun Cricket around on his

haunches, a trick that Sorka had never been able to teach Doove despite Sean's assistance and her own endless patience. He searched the skies and stayed Cricket as the dragonets solidly turned their heads to the east.

Blazer landed on his shoulder, swirling her tail about his neck and left bicep, and shrieked to the others. Sean was amazed at the interaction he sensed. A queen taking orders from browns? But he was distracted as her thoughts became vividly apprehensive.

"Landing in danger?" he asked. "Shelter?"

Once Sean had spoken, Sorka understood what her bronzes were trying to convey to her. Sean was always quicker to read the mental images of his enhanced dragonets, especially those of Blazer, who was the most coherent. Sorka had often wished for a golden female, but she loved her bronzes and brown too much to voice a complaint.

"That's what they all give me, too," Sorka said, as her five began to tug various parts of her clothing. Though Sean could hunt bare to the waist, she bobbled too much to ride topless comfortably; her sleeveless leather vest provided support, as well as protection from the claw holds of the dragonets. Bronze Emmett settled on Doove's poll long enough to secure a grip on one ear and the forelock, trying to pull the mare's head around.

"Something big, something dangerous, and shelter!" Sean said, shaking his head. "It's only a thunderstorm, fellas. Look, just a cloud!"

Sorka frowned as she looked eastward. They were high enough on the plateau to have just a glimpse of the sea.

"That's a funny-looking cloud formation, Sean. I've never seen anything like it. More like the snowclouds we'd have now and again in Ireland."

Sean scowled and tightened his legs. Cricket, picking up on the dragonets' urgent fears, pranced tensely in place in the piaffe he had been taught, but it was clear that he would break into a mad gallop the minute Sean gave him his head. The stallion's eyes were rolling white in distress as he snorted. Doove, too, was fretting, spurred by Emmett's peculiar urgency.

"Doesn't snow here, Sorka, but you're right about the color and shape. By jays, whatever it's raining, it's damned near visible. Rain here doesn't fall like that."

Duke and Sean's original two browns saw it and shrieked in utter frustration and terror. Blazer trumpeted a fierce command. The next thing Sean and Sorka knew, both horses had been spurred by well-placed dragonet stabs across their rumps into a headlong stampede which the massed fair of dragonets aimed north and west. Rein, leg, seat, or voice had no effect on the two pain-crazed horses, for whenever they tried to obey their riders, they got another slash from the vigilant dragonets.

"Whatinell's got into them?" Sean cried, hauling on the hackamore that he used in place of a bit in Cricket's soft mouth. "I'll break his bloody nose for him, I will."

"No, Sean," Sorka cried, leaning into her mare's forward plunge. "Duke's terrified of that cloud. All of mine are. They'd never hurt the horses! We'd be fools to ignore them."

"As if we could!"

The horses were diving headlong down a ravine. Sean needed all his skill to stay on Cricket, but his mind sensed Blazer's relief that she had succeeded in moving them toward safety.

"Safety from what?" he muttered in a savage growl, hating the feeling of impotence on an animal that had never disobeyed him in its seven years, an animal that he had thought he understood better than any human on the whole planet.

The headlong pace did not falter, even when Sean felt the gray stallion, fit as he was, begin to tire. The dragonets drove both horses onward, straight toward one of the small lakes that dotted that part of the continent.

"Why water, Sean?" Sorka cried, sitting back and hauling on Doove's mouth. When the mare willingly slowed, Duke and the other two bronzes screamed a protest and once again gouged her bleeding rump.

Neighing and white-eyed with fear, the mare leapt into the water, nearly unseating her rider. The stallion plunged beside her, galled by the spurred talons of Sean's dragonets.

The lake, a deep basin collecting the runoff from the nearby hills, had little beach and the horses were soon swimming, determinedly herded by the dragonets toward the rocky overhang on the far side. Sean and Sorka had often sunbathed on that ledge; they enjoyed diving from their high perch into the deep water below.

"The ledge? They want us *under* the ledge? The water's fardling deep there."

"Why?" Sorka still asked. "It's only rain coming." She was swimming beside Doove, one hand on the pommel of her saddle, the other holding the reins, letting the mare's efforts drag her forward. "Where'd they all go?"

Sean, swimming alongside Cricket, turned on his side to look back the way they had come. His eyes widened. "That's not *rain*. Swim for it, Sorka! Swim for the ledge!"

She cast a glance over her shoulder and saw what had startled the usually imperturbable young man. Terror lent strength to her arm; tugging on the reins, she urged Doove to greater efforts. They were nearly to the ledge, nearly to what little safety that offered from the hissing silver fall that splatted so ominously across the woods they had only just left.

"Where are the dragonets?" Sorka wailed as she crossed into the shadow of the ledge. She tugged at Doove, trying to drag the mare in behind her.

"Safer where they are, no doubt!" Sean sounded bitterly angry as he forced Cricket under the ledge. There was just room enough for the horses' heads to remain above the level of the water, but there was no purchase for their flailing legs.

Suddenly both horses ceased resisting their riders and began to press Sean and Sorka against the inner wall, whinnying in abject terror.

"Jack your legs up, Sorka! Balance against the inside wall!" Sean shouted, demonstrating.

Then they heard the hiss on the water. Peering around the frightened horses' heads, they could actually see the long, thin threads plunging into the water. The lake was suddenly roiling and cut every which way with the fins of the minnows that had been seeded in the streams.

"Jays! Look at that!" Sean pointed excitedly to a small jet of flame just above the lake's surface that charred a large tangle of the stuff before it landed in the water.

"Over there, too!" Sorka said, and then they heard the agitated but exultant chatter of dragonets. Crowded back under the ledge, they caught only fleeting glimpses of dragonets and the unexpected flames.

All at once Sorka remembered that long-ago day when she had first witnessed the dragonets defending the poultry flocks. She had been certain then that Duke had flamed at a wherry. "That happened before, Sean," Sorka said, her fingers slipping on his wet shoulder as she grabbed at it to get his attention. "Somehow they breathe fire. Maybe that's what the second stomach is for."

"Well, I'm glad they weren't cowards," Sean muttered, cautiously propelling himself to the opening. "No," he said in a relieved voice, expelling a big sigh. "They're by no means cowards. C'mere, Sorka."

Glancing anxiously at Doove, Sorka joined Sean and cried out with surprised elation. Their fair of dragonets had been augmented by a mass of others. The little warriors seemed to take turns diving at the evil rainfall, their spouts of flame reducing the terror to char, which fell as ashes to the surface of the lake, where quick fish mouths gobbled it up.

"See, Sorka, the dragonets are protecting this ledge."

Sorka could see the menacing rain falling unimpeded to the lake on either side of the dragonet fire zone.

"Jays, Sean, look what it does to the bushes!" She pointed to the shoreline. The thick clumps of tough bushes they had ridden through only moments before were no longer visible, covered by a writhing mass of "things" that seemed to enlarge as they watched. Sorka felt sick to her stomach, and only intense concentration prevented her from heaving her breakfast up. Sean had gone white about the mouth. His hands, moving rhythmically to keep him in position in the water, clenched into fists.

"No bleeding wonder the dragonets were scared." He smashed impotent fists into the water, sending ripples out. Sorka's Duke appeared instantly, hovering just outside and peering in. He waited just long enough to squeak a reassurance, and then literally disappeared. "Well, now," Sean said. "If I were Pol Nietro, I'd call that instantaneous flit of theirs the best defense mechanism a species could develop." A long thread slithered from the ledge and hung a moment in front of their horrified eyes before a flame charred it.

Revolted, Sean splashed water on the remains, whisking the floating motes away from Sorka and himself. Behind them the horses' breathing showed signs of real distress.

"How long?" Sean said, gliding over to Cricket's head and soothing the horse with his hands. "How long?"

"It is *not* mating activity," Bay told Sabra when she called, "and it is a totally irrational pattern of behavior." Her mind riffling through all she knew and had observed about the dragonets, Bay continued to peer out her window. As she watched, a sled lifted from a parking spot near the met tower, and it headed at full speed toward the storm. "Let me check my behavioral files and have a word with Pol. I'll call you back. It really is most unusual."

Pol was working on the vegetable patch behind their home. He saw her coming and waved cheerfully, tipping back his visored cap and mopping his brow. The garden soil had been carefully enriched and enhanced by a variety of Terran beetles and worms that were as happy to aerate the soil of Pern as of Earth and augmented the local, lazier kinds. Bay saw Pol stop, his hand in midwipe, and stare about him; she guessed he had only then noticed the absence of the dragonets.

"Where've they all gone?" He glanced toward other residential squares and Betty's empty roof. "That was sudden, wasn't it?"

"Sabra's just been on to me. She said their Fancy appeared to attack little Shuvin. For no reason, although her claws did not pierce the skin. Fancy then attempted to enter the house with them. Sabra said she sounded frightened."

Pol raised his eyebrows in surprise and continued to wipe his brow and then the hat band before recovering his head. Leaning on his hoe, he glanced all around. It was then that he saw the gray clouds.

"Don't like the look of that, m'luv," he said. "I'll take a bit of a break until it blows over." He smiled at her. "While we access your notes on the menta-breed. Fancy's a menta, not a native."

Suddenly the air was full of shrieking, screaming, bugling, and very frightened dragonets.

"Where have they been, the little pests?" Pol demanded, snatching off his cap to wave it furiously in front of his face. "Faugh! They stink!"

Bay pinched her nostrils, hurrying toward the refuge of the house. "They do, indeed. Positively sulfurous."

Six dragonets detached themselves from the swirling hundreds and dove for Bay and Pol, battering at their backs and screeching to hurry them forward.

"I do believe they're driving us into the house, Pol," Bay said. When she stopped to study the eccentric behavior, her queen grabbed a lock of her hair, and the two bronzes secured holds on the front of her tunic, pulling her forward. Their cries grew more frantic.

"I believe you're correct. And they're doing it to others, too."

"I've never seen so many dragonets. We don't normally

have such a concentration here," Bay went on, cooperating to the point of a lumbering jog trot. "Most of them are wilds! Look how much smaller some queens are. A preponderance of greens as well. Fascinating."

"Extremely," Pol remarked, mildly amused that the dragonets who were their particular friends had entered the house and were cooperating in a joint effort to close the door behind the humans. "Most remarkable."

Bay was already sitting down at the terminal. "Patently, it's something harmful to them as well as to us."

"I'd prefer them to settle," Pol said. Their dragonets were flitting about the lounge and into the bedroom, the bathroom, and even the addition to the house that had been made into a small but well-equipped home laboratory for the two scientists. "This is a bit much. Bay, tell your queen to settle, and the others will follow suit."

"Tell her yourself, Pol, while I access the behavioral program. She'll obey you as well as me."

Pol attempted to coax Mariah to land on his arm. But the moment she touched down she was off again, and the others after her. A tidbit of her favorite fish was ignored. Pol was no longer amused. He looked out the window to see if others were experiencing the same mass hysteria and noticed that the squares had been cleared of people. He could see clouds of dust over by the veterinary barns, and the dark dashes of dragonets attempting to herd the animals. He could also hear the distant discord of frightened beasts.

"There had better be an explanation for this," he murmured, pausing behind Bay to read the screen. "My word, look at Betty's house!" He pointed over the screen and out the window toward a structure fully clothed in dragonets. "My God, should I call them to see if they need help?"

When he put his hand out to reach for the door pull, Mariah, screaming with anger, dove at his hand and pushed it away, scratching him.

"Don't go, Pol. Don't go out, Pol! Look!"

Bay had half risen from her chair and remained frozen in the semicrouch, a look of utter horror on her face. As Pol threw a protective arm about her shoulders, they both heard the hiss of the terrible rain that fell on Landing. They could see the individual elongated "raindrops" strike the surface, sometimes meeting only dust, other times writhing about the shrubs and grasses, which disappeared, leaving behind engorged sluglike forms that rapidly attacked anything green in their way. Pol's nicely sprouting garden became a waste of squirming grayish "things," bloating larger within seconds on each new feast.

Mariah let out a raucous call and disappeared from the house. The other five dragonets followed instantly.

"I don't believe what I saw," Pol said in an amazed whisper. "They're teleporting in droves, almost formations. So the telekinesis was developed as a survival technique first. Hmm."

The hideous rain had advanced, spreading its mindless burden behind and inexorably falling across Pol's neatly patterned stonework patio toward the house.

"They can't devour stone," Pol remarked with clinical detachment. "I trust our silicon plastic roof provides a similar deterrent."

"The dragonets have more than one unexplored skill, Pol, my dear," Bay said proudly and pointed.

Outside, their dragonets were swooping and soaring, breathing flame to incinerate the attacking life-form before it could reach the house.

"I would be happier if I knew the things could not penetrate plastic," Pol repeated with a slight tremor in his voice, looking up at the opaque roof. He winced and hunched in self-protection as he heard a slithering impact, then another, then saw the flame spurt briefly in gouts across the dark roof material.

"Well, that's a relief," he said, straightening his shoulders.

"They did strike the roof, however, until the dragonets,

bless their little hearts, set them ablaze." Bay peered out the window facing Betty Musgrave-Blake's house. "My word! Look at that!"

The house seemed to be ringed by fiery whirls and gouts as an umbrella of dragonets frantically made certain that not a single piece of the grotesque rain reached the home of a woman in labor.

Pol had the presence of mind to collect his binoculars from the clutter on a shelf. He turned them on the fields and the veterinary sheds. "I wonder if they'll protect our livestock. There're too many animals to get all safely under shelter. But dragonets do seem to be massing in that area."

Keenly interested in the safety of the herds and flocks they had helped to create, Pol and Bay took turns watching. Bay suddenly dropped the glasses, shuddering as she passed them wordlessly to Pol. She had been shocked by the sight of a full-grown cow reduced in a few moments to a seared corpse covered by masses of writhing strings. Pol altered the focus and then groaned in helpless dismay, dropping the binoculars.

"Deadly, they are. Voracious, insatiable. It would appear they consume anything organic," he murmured. Taking a deep, resolute breath, he raised the binoculars again. "And, unfortunately, to judge by the marks on the roofs of some of those shelters we put up first, carbon-based plastics, too."

"Oh, dear. That could be terrible. Could this be a regional phenomenon?" Bay asked, her voice still trembling. "There were those odd circles on the vegetated areas, the ones in the original survey fax . . ." Turning away from the disaster, she sat down at the keyboard and, clearing the screen, began to call up files.

"I hope no one is foolish enough to go out after those last few cows and sheep," Pol said, an edge to his voice. "I hope they got all the horses in safely. The new equine strain is too promising to lose, even to a ravening disaster."

Almost as an afterthought the alarm klaxon on the meteorology tower began to bleat.

"Now that's a bit after the fact, old fellow," Pol said, turning to focus the binoculars on the tower. He could see Ongola in the tower, holding a rag against his cheek. The sled that had gone out to investigate the storm was parked so close to the tower entrance that Pol guessed that Ongola had probably dived directly from sled to the tower door.

"No, the sound carries and sets off the relays," Bay said absently as her fingers flew over the keys.

"Ah, yes, I'd forgot that. Quite a few people went out on hunting parties this morning, you know."

Bay's quick fingers stilled, and she turned slowly in the swivel chair to stare at Pol, her face ashen.

"There now, old dear, so many people have dragonets now, and at least one of the smarter mentas you developed." He crossed to her and gave her a reassuring pat on the head. "They've done a first-class job of warning and protecting us. Ah! Listen!"

There was no mistaking the exultant warble of the dragonets that always heralded a birth. Despite the bizarre disaster occurring on Pern at that moment, a new life had entered it. The welcome did not, however, interfere with the protective net of flame about the house.

"The poor baby! To be born now!" Bay mourned. Her plump cheeks were drawn, her eyes sunken in her face.

Heedless of the stinging pain on the left side of his face, Ongola kept one finger on the klaxon even as he began calling out to the other stations on the network.

"Mayday! Mayday! Mayday at Landing! Take shelter! Get livestock under cover! Extreme danger. Shelter all living things." He shuddered, recalling the horrific sight of two wayward sheep consumed in an eye-blink by the descending vileness. "Shelter under rock, metal, in water! An unnatural rain heading westward in uneven fall. Deadly! Deadly! Shelter. Mayday from Landing. Mayday from Landing. Mayday from

Landing!" Drops of blood from his head and neck dripped in punctuation to his terse phrases. "Cloud unnatural. Rainfall deadly. Mayday from Landing! Take shelter! Mayday. Mayday."

His own home was barely visible through the sheeting fall, but he did see the gouts of flame above those houses in Landing still occupied. He accepted the amazing reality of the thousands of dragonets massing to assist their human friends, of the living, flaming shield over Betty Musgrave-Blake's home, of the multitude swirling above the veterinary sheds and the pastures, and he remembered that Fancy had tried to fly into the window where he had been sitting out his watch. When he had suddenly realized that none of the meteorological devices were registering the cloud mass approaching steadily from the east, he had phoned Emily at her home.

"Go have a look, Ongola. Looks like just a good stiff equinoctial squall, but if the water-vapor instruments are not registering, you'd better check the wind speed and see if there's hail or sleet in the clouds. There're hunters and fishers out today, as well as farmers."

Ongola had gotten close enough to the cloud to register its unusual composition—and to see the damage it did. He tried to raise Emily on the sled's comm unit. When that did not work, he tried to reach Jim Tillek at Harbor Control. But he had taken the nearest sled, a small, fast one that did not have the sophisticated equipment the bigger ones did. He tried every number he could think of and only reached Kitti, who generally stayed in her home, frail in her tenth decade despite prostheses that gave her some mobility.

"Thank you for the warning, Ongola. A prudent person is well advised. I will contact the veterinary sheds for them to get the livestock under cover. A hungry rain?"

Ongola had thrown the little sled to its maximum speed, hoping that there was enough power in the packs to withstand such a drain. The sled responded, but he only just made it back to the tower, the engine dying just as he touched ground.

The stuff pelted down on the sled canopy. He had not managed to outrun the leading edge. He grabbed the flight-plan board, an inadequate shield from the deadly rain but better than nothing. Taking a deep breath, he punched auto-close, then ducked out. He took three long strides, more jump than run, and made it to the tower door just as a tangle descended. The tilted edge of the board deflected the stuff right onto the unprotected left side of his head. Screaming with pain, Ongola batted the stuff from his ear just as a dragonet came flaming up to his assistance. Ongola shouted a "Thanks" for the dragonet's aid as he threw himself inside and slammed the door. Automatically, he threw the bolt, snorting at useless instinct, and took the steps to the tower in twos and threes.

The stinging pain continued, and he felt something oozing down his neck. Blood! He blotted at the injury with his handkerchief, noticing that the blood was mixed with black fragments, and he became aware of the stench of burned wool. The dragonet's breath had scorched his sweater.

The warning delivered, he was flipping on the recording when a second stinging pain on his left shoulder made him glance down. He saw the front end of a waving strand that did not look at all like wool. The pain seemed to accompany the strand. He had never undressed as fast as he did then. And he was just fast enough: the strand had become thicker and was moving with more rapidity and purpose. Even as he watched in horror at his close escape, the wool was ingested, and the grotesque, quivering segment left in its place filled him with revulsion.

Water! He reached for both the water pitcher and the klah thermos and emptied them over the . . . the thing. Writhing and bubbling, it slowly subsided into a soggy inert mass. He stamped on it with as much satisfaction as he had felt destroying Nathi surface positions.

Then he looked at his shoulder and saw the thin bloodied line scored in his flesh by his close encounter with that deadly piece of thread. A convulsive shudder took hold of his body, and he had to grab a chair to keep from falling to his knees.

The comm unit began to bleat at him. Taking several deep breaths, he got to his feet and back on duty.

"Thanks for the klaxon, Ongola. We had just time enough to batten down the hatches. Knew the critters were telling us something but howinell could we guess *that?*" Jim Tillek reported from the bridge of the *Southern Star.* "Thank the powers that be, our ships are all siliplex."

Monaco Bay harbor office reported overturned small craft and was instigating rescues.

The infirmary reported that human casualties in and about Landing had been minimal: mainly dragonet scratches. They had the dragonets to thank for saving lives.

Red Hanrahan at Vet said that they had lost fifty to sixty assorted livestock of the breeding herds pastured about Landing, thanking the good fortune of having just shipped out three hundred calves, lambs, kids, and piglets to new homes the previous month. There were, however, large numbers at nearby stakes that did not have stabling facilities and were in the path of the abominable rain. Red added that all of the animals left loose to graze could be considered lost.

Two of the larger fishing vessels reported severe burn injuries for those who had not made it under cover in time. One of the Hegelman boys had jumped overboard and drowned when the things landed in a clump on his face. Maximilian, escorting the *Perseus,* had been unable to save him. The dolphin had added that native marine life was swarming to the surface, fighting over the drowning wrigglers. He himself did not much like the things: no substance.

Messages were rapidly stacking up on Ongola's board; he rang Emily to send him some assistance.

The captain of *Maid of the Sea,* fishing to the north, wanted to know what was happening. The skies about him were clear to the southern horizon. Patrice de Broglie, stationed out at Young Mountain with the seismic team, asked if he should send his crew back. There had been only a few rumbles in the past weeks, though there were some interesting changes in the gravity meter graphs. Ongola told him to send back as many as he could, not wanting to think what might have happened to homesteads in the path of that malevolent Threadfall.

Bonneau phoned in from Drake's Lake, where it was still night and very clear. He offered to send a contingent.

Sallah Telgar-Andiyar got through from Karachi Camp and said that assistance was already on its way. How widespread was the rain? she wanted to know.

Ongola shunted all those calls when the first of the nearby settlements reported.

"If it hadn't been for those dragonets," said Aisling Hempenstahl of Bordeaux, "we'd all be—have been eaten alive." Her swallow was audible. "Not a green thing to be seen, and all the livestock gone. Except the cow the dragonets drove into the river, and she's a mess."

"Any casualties?"

"None I can't take care of myself, but we've little fresh food. Oh, and Kwan wants to know do you need him at Landing?"

"I'd say yes, indeed we do," Ongola replied fervently. Then he tried again to raise the Du Vieux, the Radelins, the Grant van Toorns, the Ciottis, and the Holstroms. "Keep trying these, Jacob." He passed the list over to Jacob Chernoff, who had brought three young apprentices to help. "Kurt, Heinrich, try the River numbers, Calusa, Cambridge, and Vienna." Ongola called Lilienkamp at Stores. "Joel, how many checked out for hunting today?"

"Too many, Ongola, too many." The tough Joel was weeping.

"Including your boys?"

Joel's response was the barest whisper. "Yes."

"I am sorry to hear that, Joel. We've organized searches. And the boys have dragonets."

"Sure, but look how many it took the protect Landing!" His voice rose shrilly.

"Sir." Kurt tugged urgently at Ongola's bare elbow. "One of the sleds—"

"I'll get back to you, Joel." Ongola took the call from the sled. "Yes?"

"Whaddya do to kill this stuff, Ongola?" Ziv Marchane's anquished cry sent a stab of pure terror and fury to Ongola's guts.

"Cautery, Ziv. Who is it?"

"What's left of young Joel Lilienkamp."

"Bad?"

"Very."

Ongola paused and closed his eyes tightly for a moment, remembering the two sheep. "Then give him mercy!"

Ziv broke the connection, and Ongola stared at the console, paralyzed. He had given mercy several times, too many times, during the Nathi War when his men had been blown apart after Nathi hits on his destroyer. The practice was standard procedure in surface engagements. One never left one's wounded to Nathi mercy. Mercy, yes, it was mercy to do so. Ongola had never thought that necessity would ever arise again.

Paul Benden's vibrant voice broke through his pained trance. "What in hell's happening, Ongola?"

"Wish the hell I knew, Admiral." Ongola shook his head and then gave him a precise report and a list of casualties, known or suspected.

"I'm coming in." Paul had staked his claim on the heights above the delta on the Boca River. It would soon be dawn there. "I'll check other stakes on the way in."

"Pol and Kitti want samples if they can be safely got—of the stuff in the air. It scores holes through thin materials, so be sure to use heavy-gauge metal or siliplex. We've got enough of what ate our fields bare. I've sent all our big sleds out to track the frigging Fall. Kenjo's flying in from Honshu in that augmented speeder of his. The stuff just came out of nowhere, Paul, nowhere!"

"Didn't register on anything? No? Well, we'll check it all out."

The absolute confidence in Paul Benden's voice was a tonic for Ongola. He had heard that same note all through the Cygnus Battle and he took heart.

He needed it. Before Paul Benden arrived late that afternoon, the casualties had mounted to a frightening total. Only three of the twenty who had gone hunting that morning had returned: Sorka Hanrahan, Sean Connell, and David Catarel, who had watched, helpless, from the water as his companion, Lucy Tubberman, dissolved under the rain on the riverbank despite the frantic efforts of their dragonets. He had deep scores on his scalp, left cheek, arms, and shoulders, and he was suffering from shock and grief.

Two babies, obviously thrust at the last moment into a small metal cabinet, were the only survivors of the main Tuareg camp on the plains west of the big bend in the Paradise River. Sean and Sorka had gone to find the Connells, who had last been reported on the eastern spur of Kahrain Province. No one answered from the northern stakes on the Jordan River. It looked bad.

Porrig Connell had, for once, listened to the warnings of the dragonets and had taken shelter in a cave. It had not been large enough to accommodate all his horses, and four of the mares had died. When they screamed outside, the stallion had gone berserk in the confines of the cave, and Porrig had had to cut his throat. There was no fodder for the remaining mares, so Sean and Sorka returned with hay and food rations. Then they went off to search for other survivors.

The Du Vieux and Holstroms at Amsterdam Stake, the Radelins and Duquesnes at Bavaria, and the Ciottis at Milan Stake were dead; no trace remained of them or their livestock. The metals and heavy-gauge, silicon-based plastic roofing, though it was heavily pocked, remained as the only evidence of their once thriving settlement. They had used the newly pressed vegetable-fiber slabs for their homes. No one on Pern ever would use such building material again.

From the air, the swath of destruction cut by the falling threadlike rain was obvious, the fringes seething with bloated wormlike excrescences which squadrons of dragonets attacked with flaming breath. The path ended seventy-five klicks beyond the narrow Paradise River, where it had annihilated the Tuareg camps.

By evening, the exhausted settlers fed their dragonets first, and left out mounds of cooked grain for the wild ones that would not approach near enough to be hand-fed.

"Nothing was said about this sort of thing in the EEC report," Mar Dook muttered in a bitter tone.

"Those wretched polka dots no one ever explained," Aisling Hempenstahl said, her voice just loud enough to be heard.

"We've been investigating that possibility," Pol Nietro said, nodding to a weary Bay, who was resting her head against his shoulder.

"Nevertheless, I think we should arrive at some preliminary conclusions before tomorrow," Kitti said. "People will need facts to be reassured."

"Bill and I looked up the reports we did on the polka dots—" Carol Duff-Vassaloe smiled grimly. "—during Landing Year. We didn't investigate every site, but the ones we examined where tree development could be measured suggests a time lapse of at least a hundred and sixty or seventy years. I think it's rather obvious that it was this terrible life-form which caused the patterning, turning all organic material it meets into more of itself. Thank heavens most of our building plastics are silicon-based. If they were carbon-based, we'd all have been killed, without a doubt. This infestation—"

"Infestation?" Chuck Havers's voice broke in incredulous anger.

"What else to call it?" Phas Radamanth remarked in his dogmatic fashion. "What we need to know is how often it occurs? Every hundred and fifty years? That patterning was planet-wide, wasn't it, Carol?" She nodded. "And how long does it last once it occurs?"

"Last?" Chuck demanded, appalled.

"We'll get the answers," Paul Benden said firmly.

The colony's two psychologists flew in late that evening when the infirmary was still crowded with the injured and shocked, and set to work immediately to help reduce traumas. Cherry Duff had suffered a stroke at the news, but was recovering splendidly. Joel and his wife were both prostrated by the loss of their sons. Bernard Hegelman had submerged his own grief to comfort his shattered wife and the other families bereft by loss.

Sean and Sorka had tirelessly sledded in the wounded they located. Even those uninjured were dazed, some weeping uncontrollably until sedated, others pathetically quiet. Porrig Connell had sent his eldest daughter and his wife to help cope with the survivors, while he stayed with his extended family in the cave.

"The first time Porrig Connell ever did anything for anyone else," his son remarked under his breath to Sorka, who berated him for such cynicism. "He wants to use Cricket to service the rest of his mares when they foal. He expects me to give up *my* stallion because he hadn't trained his!"

Sorka wisely said nothing.

With one exception, the distant holdings had contacted Landing, offering either assistance or sympathy. The one exception was the Big Island mining camp, comprised of Avril Bitra, Stev Kimmer, Nabhi Nabol, and a few others. Ongola, running over the log, noticed the absence.

Kenjo, appearing like magic from his distant Honshu plateau, headed the aerial survey. By nightfall, he and his team produced accurate maps and pics of the extent of the terrible "Threadfall," as it soon came to be called. The original complement of biologists reconvened at Landing to ascertain the nature of the beast. Kitti Ping and Wind Blossom lent their special skills to analyze the life-forms as soon as samples were brought in.

Unfortunately too many, acquired at considerable danger to the volunteers, were found apparently moribund in the metal or heavy plastic containers in which they had been contained. Seemingly, after about twenty minutes, all the frenetic activity, the replications of the original strand several thousand times into big wriggling "sausages," ceased. The form unraveled, blackened, and turned into an utterly lifeless, sticky, tarry mess, within a tougher shell.

The captain of the *Mayflower,* which had been trawling at the ragged northern edge of the Fall, inadvertently discovered a segment of Thread in a pail of fish bait, slapped on a tight lid, and reported the find to Landing. He was told to keep it alive, if possible, by judicious feeding until it could be flown to Landing.

By then, the Thread had to be housed in the biggest heavy-gauge plastic barrel on board the *Mayflower.* Ongola transported the tightly sealed barrel, using a long steel cable attached to the big engineering sled. Only when the crew saw the sled disappearing in the distance would they come on deck. The captain was later astonished to learn that his act was considered one of extreme bravery.

By the time the pulsing life-form reached Landing, it coiled, a gross meter long and perhaps ten centimeters in circumference, resembling a heavy hawser. Double-thick slabs of transparent silicon-based building plastic, tightly banded with metal strips, were rigged into a cage, its base quikplased to the floor. Several thin slits with locking flaps were created. A hole the size of the barrel opening was incised in the top, the barrel lid readied, and with the help of grimly anxious volunteers the terrible creature was transferred from barrel to cage. The top opening was sealed as soon as the life-form was dropped into the plastic cube.

One of the men scrambled for a corner to be sick in. Others averted their faces. Only Tarvi and Mar Dook seemed unmoved by the creature's writhing as it engulfed the food that had been placed in the cube.

In its urgency to ingest, the thing rippled in waves of gray, greasy colors: sickly greens, dull pink tones, and an occasional streak of yellow flowed across its surface, the image sickeningly distorted by the thick clear plastic. The outer covering of the beast seemed to thicken. The thick shell probably formed at its demise, the observers guessed, for such remains had been found in rockly places where the organism had starved. The interior of the beast evidently deteriorated as rapidly as it had initially expanded. Was it really alive? Or was it some malevolent chemical entity feeding on life? Certainly its appetite was voracious, although the very act of eating seemed to interfere with whatever physical organization the beast had, as if what it consumed hastened its destruction.

"Its rate of growth is remarkable," Bay said in a very calm voice, for which Pol later praised her, saying that it had provided an example to the others, all stunned by the sight of that gross menace. "One expects such expansion under the microscope but not in the macrocosm. Where can it have come from? Outer space?"

Blank silence met her astonishing query, and those in the room exchanged glances, partly of surprise, partly of embarrassment at Bay's suggestion.

"Do we have any data on the periodicity of comets in this system?" Mar Dook asked hopefully. "That eccentric body? Something brought in from our Oort cloud? Then there's the Hoyle-Wickramansingh theory, which has never been totally discredited, citing the possibilty of viruses."

"That's one helluva virus, Mar," Bill Duff said skeptically. "And didn't someone on Ceti III confound that old theory?"

"Considering it drops from the skies," Jim Tillek said, "why couldn't it have a space origin? I'm not the only one who's noticed that red morning star in the east getting brighter these past weeks. A bit of coincidence, isn't it, that the planet with the crazy orbit is coming right into the inner planets, right at the same time this stuff hits us? Could that be the source? Is there any data in the library on that planet? On this sort of thing?"

"I'll ask Cherry. No," Bill Duff corrected himself before anyone could remind him that the redoubtable magistrate was indisposed. "I'll access the information myself and bring back hardcopy to study." He hurried from the room as if glad to have a valid excuse to leave.

"I'll get a sample from that section pressing against the lower slot," Kwan Marceau said, gathering up the necessary implements in the rush of someone who dared not consider overlong what he was about to do.

"A record's being kept of the . . . intake?" Bay asked. She could not quite say "food," remembering what the creatures had already consumed since they had fallen on Pern.

"Now, to judge the frequency of . . . intake"—Pol seized gratefully on that euphemism—"sufficient to keep the . . . organism alive."

"And to see how it dies," Kitti added in a voice so bland that it rang with satisfaction.

"And why all its ilk died in this first infestation," Phas Radamanth added, pulling the EEC pics out of the welter of hardcopy in front of him.

"*Did* all die?" Kitti asked.

By morning, with no report from scientists who had worked through the night, the muttering began: a still-shocked whisper over morning klah; a rumor that began to seep into every office and the hastily reopened living quarters on the abandoned residential squares. A huge blaze had been started the previous evening and continued to burn at Bonfire Square. Torches, pitched and ready to be lit, had been piled at each corner, and more were added to the piles throughout the day.

Many of the lighter sleds that had been on the ground at Landing needed new canopies. Sweeping out the detritus of putrid Thread shells was undertaken with masks and heavy work gloves.

There was a new and respectful title for the winged friends: fire-dragons. Even those who had previously scorned the creatures carried tidbits for them in their pockets. Landing was dotted with fat-bellied dragonets sleeping in the sun.

By lunchtime, a meal was served from the old communal kitchens, and rumor was rife. By midafternoon, Ted Tubberman and a fellow malcontent, their faces streaked and drawn by grief, led bereaved relatives to the door of the containment unit.

Paul and Emily came out with Phas Radamanth and Mar Dook.

"Well? Have you discovered what that thing is?" Ted demanded.

"It is a complex but understandable network of filaments, analogous to a Terran mycorrhiza," Mar Dook began, resenting Tubberman's manner but respecting his grief.

"That explains very little, Mar," Ted replied, belligerently sticking out his chin. "In all my years as a botanist, I never saw a plant symbiont dangerous to humans. What do we get next? A death moss?"

Emily reached out to touch Tubberman's arm in sympathy, but he jerked away.

"We have little to go on," Phas said in a sharp tone. He was tired, and working all night near the monstrosity had been a terrible strain. "Nothing like this has ever been recorded on any of the planets humans have explored. The nearest that has been even imagined were some of the fictional inventions during the Age of Religions. We're still refining our understanding of it."

"It's still alive? You're *keeping* it alive!" Ted was livid with irrational outrage. Beside him, his companions nodded agreement as fresh tears streamed down their faces. Murmuring angrily among themselves, the delegation crowded closer to the entrance, every one of them seeking an outlet for frustration and impotent grief.

"Of course, we have to study it, man," Mar Dook said, keeping his voice steady. "And find out exactly what it is. To do that, it must be fed to . . . continue. We've got to ascertain if this is only the beginning of its life cycle."

"Only the beginning!" Tubberman cried. Paul and Phas leapt forward to restrain the grief-mad botanist. Lucy had been his apprentice as well as his daughter, and the two had shared a deep and affectionate bond. "By all that's holy, I'll end it now!"

"Ted, be rational. You're a scientist!"

"I'm a father first, and my daughter was . . . devoured by one of those creatures! So was Joe Milan, and Patsy Swann, Eric Hegelman, Bob Jorgensen, and . . ." Tubberman's face was livid. His fists clenched at his sides, his whole body strained with rage and frustration. He glared accusingly at Emily and Paul. "We trusted you two. How could you bring us to a place that devours our children and all we've achieved the past eight years!" The murmurs of the delegation supported his accusation. "We"—his wide gesture took in the packed numbers behind him—"want that thing dead. You've had long enough to study it. C'mon, people. We know what we have to do!" With a final bitter, searing look at the biologists, he turned, roughly pushing aside those in his path. "Fire kills it!"

He stomped off, raging. His followers left with him.

"It won't matter what they do, Paul," Mar Dook said, restraining Paul Benden from going after Ted. "The beast is moribund now. Give them the corpse to vent their feelings on. We've about finished what examinations we can make anyhow." He shrugged wearily. "For all the good it does us."

"And that is?" Paul inquired encouragingly. Mar Dook and Phas gestured to him and Emily to reenter the containment unit where Pol, Bay, and the two geneticists were still writing up their notes.

Wearily, Mar Dook scrubbed at his face, his sallow skin

nearly gray as he slumped onto a table that was littered with tapes and slide containers. "We now know that it is carbon based, has complex, very large proteins which flick from state to state and produce movement, and others which attack and digest an incredible range of organic substances. It is almost as if the creature was designed specifically to be inimical to our kind of life."

"I'm glad you kept that to yourself," Emily said wryly, looking over her shoulder at the door swinging shut on a view of the angry group heading away.

"Mar Dook, you can't mean what you just said," Paul began, resting both hands on the shoulders of the weary biologist. "It may be dangerous, yes—but designed to kill *us?*"

"That *is* just a thought," Mar Dook replied, looking a bit sheepish. "Phas here has a more bizarre suggestion."

Phas cleared his throat nervously. "Well, it's come out of the blue so unexpectedly, I wondered if it could possibly be a weapon, preparing the ground for an invasion?" Dumbfounded, Paul and Emily stared at him, aware of Bay's sniff of disagreement and the amused expression on Kitti Ping's face. "That is not an illogical interpretation, you know. I like it better than Bay's suggestion, that this might be only the beginning of a life cycle. I dread what could follow."

Paul and Emily glanced around them, stunned by such a dreadful possibility. But Pol Nietro rose from his chair and cleared his throat, a tolerant expression on his round face.

"That is also a suggestion from the fiction of the Age of Religions, Mar," Pol said with a wry smile. He glanced apologetically at his wife and then noticed Kitti Ping's reassuring smile. He felt heartened. "And, in my opinion, highly improbable. If the life cycle produced inimical forms, where are the descendants of subsequent metamorphoses? The EEC team may have erred in considering the polka dots nondangerous, but they also discovered no other incongruous life-forms.

"As for an invasion from outer space, every other planet in this sector of space was found to be inimical to carbon-based life-forms." Pol began to warm to his own theory and saw Emily recovering from the shock of the other revelations. "And we have determined that *that*—" He jerked his thumb at the discolored cube. "—is carbon based. So that would seem to more or less limit it to this system. And we will find out how." Pol's burst of explanation seemed to have drained the last of his energy, and he leaned wearily against the high laboratory stand. "I believe I'm right, though. Airing the worst possible interpretations of the data we have gleaned has cleared the air, so to speak." He gave a little, almost apologetic shrug and smiled hopefully at Phas and Bay.

"I still feel we have missed something in our investigations," Phas said, shaking his head. "Something obvious, and important."

"No one thinks straight after forty hours on the trot," Paul said, clasping Phas by the shoulder to give him a reassuring shake. "Let's look at your notes again when you've had some rest and something to eat, away from the stench in here. Jim, Emily, and I will wait and deal with Ted's delegation. They're overreacting." He sighed. "Not that I blame them. Sudden grief is always a shock. However, I personally would rather plan for the worst that can happen. As you've suggested several dire options, we won't be surprised by anything that happens. And we should plan to reduce its effects on the settlements."

Paul had a quiet word with one of the psychologists, whose opinion was that the thwarted tensions of the bereaved might be eased by what he termed "a ritual incineration." So they stepped aside when Ted Tubberman and his adherents demanded the cube and destroyed it in a blazing fire. The resultant stench gagged many, which helped to speed the dispersal of the onlookers. Only Ted and a few others remained to watch the embers cool.

The psychologist shook his head slowly. "I think I'll keep an eye on Ted Tubberman for a while," he told Paul and Emily. "That was apparently not enough to assuage his grief."

Telescopes were trained on the eccentric planet early the

next morning. Its reddish appearance was due, Ezra Keroon suggested, to the aggregated dust swirls it had brought in from the edge of the system. Despite the lack of any proof, the feeling among the observers was that the planet was somehow responsible for the disaster.

During the day, Kenjo's group discovered traces of an earlier fall on Ierne Island, which a witness remembered as more of a rainstorm littered with black motes than a fall of Thread. A scout sent to the northern continent reported traces of recent destruction across the eastern peninsula there. That discovery dispersed the vain hope that the Fall was unique or confined to a specific area. A review of the probe pics from the EEC did nothing to alleviate tension, for the fax incontrovertibly showed the Fall two hundred years before to have been widespread. They figured that the event must have happened just prior to the team's arrival. The demand to know the extent and frequency of the falls increased ominously.

To assuage mounting fears and tension, Betty Musgrave-Blake and Bill Duff undertook to review the survey's original botanical data. Ted Tubberman was the only trained botanist who had survived, but he spent his days tracking down every Thread shell and his evenings burning the piles. The psychologists continued to monitor his aberrant behavior.

Based on the original data, Betty and Bill deduced a two-hundred-year gap between incursions, allowing a span of ten to fifteen years for the vegetation to regenerate on the damaged circles after taking into account the age of some of the largest trees in and near the previous occurrence. Betty delivered their conclusion as a positive statement, meant to engender optimism, but she could provide no answer to the vital question of how long the deadly rain would continue to fall.

In an attempt to disprove Mar's theory of purposeful design or Phas's equally disturbing suggestion of invasion, Ezra Keroon spent that day on the link with the *Yokohama*'s mainframe. His calculations confirmed beyond question that the eccentric planet had an orbit of 250 years. But it only stayed in the inner system for a little while, the way Halley's comet periodically visited Sol. It was too much to suppose there was no connection, and, after consulting Paul and Emily, Ezra programmed one of the *Yokohama*'s few remaining probes to circumnavigate the planet and discover its composition and, especially, the components of its apparently gaseous envelope.

Though all reports were honestly and fully presented to the community as soon they came in, by evening speculation had produced alarming interpretations. Grimly the more responsible members tried to calm those who gave way to panic.

Then a perplexed Kenjo sought Betty out with a disturbing observation. She immediately informed Paul and Emily, and a quiet meeting was arranged with those who were able to discuss the situation with some detachment.

"You all know that I've overflown to map the damage," Kenjo began. "I didn't know what I'd seen until I'd seen it often enough to realize what was *not* there." He paused, as if steeling himself for rebuke or disbelief. "I don't think all thread starved to death. And crazy Tubberman hasn't gotten as far as I have. In most places, there are shells! But in nine circles that I have seen—and I landed to be sure I make no mistake—there were no shells." He made a cutting gesture with both hands. "None. And these circles were by themselves, not in a group, and the area—demolished—was not as big as usual." He glanced at each of the serious faces about him. "I see. I observe. I have pics, too."

"Well," Pol said, heaving a weary sigh and absently patting the folded hands of his wife beside him at the table. "It is biologically consistent that to perpetuate a species many are sent and few are chosen. Perhaps the journey through space vitiates most of the organisms. I'm almost relieved that a few can survive and flourish. It makes more sense. I prefer your theory to some of the others that have been bruited about."

"Yes, but what do they become in the next metamorphosis?" Bay wondered, her face reflecting depression. Sometimes being right was another sort of failure.

"We'd better find out," Paul said, glancing around for support. "Is there one nearby, Kenjo?" When the pilot pointed to its position on the map, Paul nodded. "Good, then. Phas, Pol, Bill, Ezra, Bay and Emily, just slip out of Landing in small sleds. Let's see if we can prevent a new batch of wild notions. Report back here as soon as you can."

Paul sent Betty back to her home and her new baby, telling her to rest. Boris Pahlevi and Dieter Clissman were summoned and set to work designing a comprehensive computer program to analyze the data as it continued to come in. Then Paul and Ongola settled back to wait tensely for the other specialists to return.

Pol, Bay, and Phas were the first back, and they brought little good news.

"All the insects, slug-forms, and grubs we found on those sites," Phas reported, "appear harmless enough. Some of them have already been catalogued, but," he added with a shrug, "we've barely begun to identify creatures and their roles in the ecology of this planet. Kenjo was right to alert us. Clearly some of the Thread survives to propagate itself, so Bay's theory is the most viable to date." Phas seemed relieved. "But I won't rest easy until we have discovered the entire cycle."

Late in the afternoon of the third day after that first Fall, an almost hysterical call came in from Wade Lorenzo of Sadrid in Macedonia Province. Jacob Chernoff, who took the call, immediately contacted Ongola and Paul at the administration building. "He says it's coming straight across the sea, right at him, sir. His stake is due west on the twenty-degree line. I'm holding him on channel thirty-seven."

Even as Paul picked up the handset and punched for the channel, he located the coastal stake of Sadrid on the big map of the continent.

"Get everyone in under silicon plastic," he ordered. "Use fire to ignite the stuff where it hits the suface. Use torches if necessary. D'you have any dragonets?"

The stakeholder's deep breath was audible as he fought for

self-control. "We have some dragonets, sir, and we've two flamethrowers—used 'em to cut down bush. We thought it was just a very bad rain squall until we saw the fish eating. Can't you come?"

"We'll get there as soon as possible!"

Paul told Jacob to tell no one of the new Fall.

"I don't want to cause more panic than there already is, sir," Jacob agreed.

Paul smiled briefly at the boy's fervor, then dialed Jim Tillek at the Monaco Bay harbormaster's office. He inquired if there were any trawlers southwest near Sadrid.

"Not today. Any trouble?"

So much for trying to sound casual, Paul thought. "Can you get here to admin without appearing to rush?"

Ongola was looking grimly at the map, his eyes flicking from Macedonia to Delta. "Your Boca River Stake is not that far from Sadrid," he told the admiral.

"I noticed." Paul dialed the channel link to his stake and in terse sentences told his wife the grim news and instructed her on what precautions to take. "Ju, it may not reach us but . . ."

"It's best to be on the safe side with something like this, isn't it?"

Paul was proud of her calm response. "I'll give you an update as soon as we've got one. With any luck, you've got at least an hour's leeway if it's just now at Sadrid. I'll be there as soon as I can. Quite possibly, Boca's far enough north. This stuff seems to fall in a southwesterly drift."

"Ask her if her dragonets are acting normally," Ongola suggested.

"Sunning themselves, as always at this time of day," Ju replied. "I'll watch them. They really do anticipate this stuff?"

"Ongola thinks so. I'll check with you later, Ju."

"I've just got through to the Logorides at Thessaly," Ongola said. "They might be in the path. Had we better warn Caesar at Roma Stake? He's got all that livestock."

"He was also smart enough to put up stone buildings, but

call him and then find out if Boris and Dieter have run their new program. I wish the hell we knew when it started, how far it'll travel," Paul muttered anxiously. "I'll organize transport." He dialed the main engineering shed and asked for Kenjo.

"There's more Thread? How far away?" Kenjo asked. "Sadrid? On the twentieth? I've got something that could make it in just over an hour." There was a ripple of excitement in Kenjo's usually even tone. "Fulmar worked out jet-assist units on one of the medium sleds. Fulmer thinks we could get seven hundred kph out of it, at least, even fully loaded. More if we run light."

"We're going to have to pack as many of the flamethrowers as possible plus emergency supplies. We'll use HNO_3 cylinders—they'll be like using fire *and* water at once on the Thread. Pol and Bay don't weigh much, and they'll be invaluable as observers. We need at least one medic, a couple of joats, Tarvi, Jim, and me. Eight. All right, then, we'll be with you directly." Paul turned to Ongola. "Any luck?"

"Since we can't tell them when it started, they want to know when it ends," Ongola said. "The more data we can give them, the more accurate they will be . . . next time. Am I among the eight?"

Paul shook his head with regret. "I need you here to deal with any panic. Blast it, but we've got to get organized for this."

Ongola snorted to himself. Paul Benden was already a legend in organizing and operating at high efficiency in emergency situations. Observers, crew, and supplies boarded the augmented sled within twenty minutes of the initial call, and it was airborne and out of sight before Ongola heard the muted roar of its improved drive.

Kenjo drove the sled at its maximum speed, passengers and supplies securely strapped in safety harnesses. They sped across the verdant tip of the untouched peninsula past the Jordan River, and then out to sea where the turbulence of sporadic but heavy squalls added more discomfort to an already rough ride in a vehicle not designed for such velocities.

"No sign of the leading edge of Fall. Half of that cloud to the south of us is more squalls," Paul said, looking up from the scope and rubbing his eyes. "Maybe, just maybe," he added softly, "those squalls also saved Sadrid."

Despite the excessive speed, the journey, mainly over water, seemed to continue endlessly. Suddenly, Kenjo reduced speed. The sea became less of a blur to starboard, and on the port side, the vast, approaching land was just visible through the mist of squall. Sunlight broke through cloud to shine impartially on tossing vegetation and denuded alleys.

"It's an ill wind," Jim Tillek remarked, pointing to the sea, which was disturbed more by underwater activity than by wind. "By the way, before I left Monaco Bay, I sent our finny friends to see what they could find out."

"Good heavens!" Bay exclaimed, pressing her face against the thick plastic canopy. "They can't have made it here so fast."

"Not likely," Jim replied, chuckling, "but the locals are feeding very well indeed."

"Stay seated!" Kenjo cried, fighting the yoke of the sled.

"If the dolphins can find out where it started . . . Data, that's what Dieter and Boris need." Paul resumed manning the forward scope. "Sadrid wasn't entirely lucky," he added, frowning. "Just as if someone had shaved the vegetation off the ground with a hot knife," he muttered under his breath, and turned away. "Get us down as fast as possible, Kenjo!"

"It was the wind," Wade Lorenzo told the rescue team. "The wind saved us, and the squall. Came down in sheets, but it was water, not Thread. No, we're mostly okay," he assured them, pointing to the dragonets, grooming themselves on the rooftrees. "They saved us, just like I heard they did at Landing." The younger children were just being shepherded out of one of the larger buildings, wide-eyed with apprehension as they looked about them. "But we don't know if Jiva and Bahka are all right. They were trawling." He gestured hopelessly to the west.

"If they went west and north, they'd've had a good chance," Jim told him.

"But we are ruined," Athpathis added. The agronomist's face was a picture of defeat as he indicated the ravaged fields and orchards.

"There're still plenty of seedlings at Landing," Pol Nietro assured him, patting his back with clumsy sympathy. "And one can grow several crops a year in this climate."

"We'll be back to you later," Paul said, helping to unload flamethrowers. "Jim, will you organize the mop-up here? You know what to do. We've got to track the main Fall to its end. There you are, Wade. Go char the bastards!"

"But Admiral—" Athpathis began, the whites of his large fearful eyes accentuated in his sun-darkened face.

"There's two other stakes in the way of this menace," Paul said, climbing back into the sled and fastening the hatch.

"Straight to your place, Paul?" Kenjo asked, lifting the sled.

"No, I want you to go north first. See if we can find Jiva and Bahka. And until we find the edge of the Fall."

As soon as Kenjo had hoisted the sled, he slapped on the jet assist, slamming his passengers back into their seats. But almost immediately he eased back on the power, "Sir, I think it's missed your place."

Instantly Paul pressed his eyes to the scope and, with incredible relief, saw the vegetation along the beach tossing in the wake of squall winds. Reassured, he could concentrate on the job at hand without divided priorities.

"Why, it just cuts off," Bay said, surprised.

"Rain, I think," Pol remarked as he, too, craned his neck to see out the siliplex canopy. "And look, isn't that an orange sail?"

Paul looked up from the scope with a weary smile. "Indeed it is, and intact. Mark your position, Mister Fusaiyuki, and let's get to Caesar's with all available speed." He took a more comfortable position in his seat and gripped the arm rests.

"Aye, aye, sir."

The six passengers once again endured the effects of speed and, once again, Kenjo's abrupt braking. That time he added such a turn to port that the sled seemed to spin on its tail.

"I've marked my position, Admiral. Your orders, sir?"

Paul Benden's spine gave an involuntary shudder, which he hoped was due more to the unexpected maneuver than to Kenjo's naval address.

"Let's follow the path and see how wide a corridor it punches. I'll contact the other stakes to stand down from the alert."

He permitted himself to contact his wife first and gave her a brief report, as much to lock the details in his own mind as to relieve hers.

"Shall I send a crew to help?" she asked. "Landing's report says the stuff often has to be burnt to be killed."

"Send Johnny Greene and Greg Keating in the faster sled. We've spare flamethrowers with us."

Others volunteered to send their sons, and Paul accepted those offers. Caesar Galliani, making the same offer, added that he wanted his sons back in time to milk the big Roma herd.

"I was right, wasn't I," the vet said with a chuckle, "to spend so much energy on stone buildings?"

"You were indeed, Caesar."

"There's nothing like stone walls to make you feel secure. The boys'll be on their way as soon as you give me a position. You'll keep us posted, won't you, Admiral?"

Paul winced at that second unconscious use of his former rank. After seven happy years as a civilian agronomist, he had no wish to resume the responsibilities of command. Then his eyes were caught by the circles of destruction, so hideously apparent from the air, interspersed with untouched swaths where squally rain had drowned Thread before it could reach the surface. Rain and dragonets! Fragile allies against such devastation. If he had his way . . . Paul halted that train of thought. He was not in command; he did not wish to be obliged to take command. There were younger men to assume such burdens.

"I make the corridor fifty klicks wide, Admiral," Kenjo announced. Paul realized that the others had been quietly conferring on details.

"You can watch vegetation disintegrating by the yard," Bay said anxiously. She caught Paul's eyes. "Rain isn't enough."

"It helped," Tarvi answered her, but he, too, looked at Paul.

"We've got reinforcements coming from Thessaly and Roma. We'll scorch where we have to on our way back to Sadrid. Set down where you can, Kenjo. Landing will need to know the details we've gotten today. Data they want, data they'll have."

By the time all the available HNO_3 cylinders were exhausted, so were the crews. Pol and Bay had followed diligently after the flamethrower teams, taking notes on the pattern of the stuff, grateful that squall activity had somewhat limited the destruction. When Paul had thanked the men from Thessaly and Roma, he told Kenjo to make reasonable speed to Sadrid to collect Jim Tillek.

"And so we must arm ourselves with tongues of flame against this menace to our kind and generous planet," Tarvi said softly to Paul as they finally headed eastward toward a fast-approaching night. "Will Sadrid be safe now?"

"On the premise that lightning doesn't strike twice in the same place?" Paul's tone was droll. "No promises can be made on that score, Tarvi. I am hoping, however, that Boris and Dieter will soon come up with a few answers." Then, his expression anxious, he turned to Pol. "This couldn't fall at random, could it?"

"You prefer the theory that it's planned? No, Paul, we've established that we're dealing with an unreasoning, voraciously hungry organism. There isn't a discernible intelligence," Pol replied, clenching and releasing his fist, surprised at his own vehemence, "much less a trace of sentience. I continue to favor Bay's theory of a two- or three-stage life cycle. Even so, it is only remotely possible that intelligence develops at a later stage."

"The wherries?" Tarvi asked facetiously.

"No, no, don't be ridiculous. We've traced them back to a sea eel, a common ancestor for both them and the dragonets."

"The dragonets were more of a help than I expected," Tarvi admitted. "Sallah insists they've a high level of intelligence."

"Pol, have you or Bay attempted to measure that intelligence when you used mentasynth enhancement?" Paul Benden asked.

"No, not really," Pol replied. "There's been no need to, once we demonstrated that an enhanced empathy made them more biddable. There have been other priorities."

"The main priority as of now is establishing the parameters of this menace," Paul muttered. "We'd all better get some rest."

Once the rescue team had returned to Landing, it was impossible to deny the fact of the new incursion. Despite a comm silence on their trip, rumors were inevitable.

"The only good thing about it," Paul told Emily as he consumed a hastily prepared meal, "was that it was sufficiently far away from here."

"We still don't have enough data to establish either frequency or probable corridors of the stuff," Dieter Clissmann announced. "The dolphins apparently could not find out where or when it started. Marine life doesn't keep time. Boris is adding in random factors of temperature variations, high- and low-pressure areas, frequency of rain, and wind velocity to the data." He gave a long sigh, combing thick hair back from his forehead. "Drowns in the rain, huh? Fire and water kill it! That's some consolation."

Few were as easily consoled. There were even some at Landing who were relieved that other sections of the continent had suffered the same disaster. The positive benefit of fear and horror was that emergency measures were no longer resisted. Some had felt that precautions emanating from Landing violated their charter autonomy. The more outspoken revised their objections when pictures of the devastation on the Sadrid corridor—as Pol termed it—were distributed. After that, Ongola and his communications team were kept busy briefing distant stakeholders.

Tarvi drafted a crew to work round the clock, adapting empty cylinders into flamethrowers and filling them with HNO_3. The easily made oxidant had not only proved to be very effective at destroying Thread but could be synthesized cheaply from air and water, using only hydroelectricity, and was not a pollutant. Most importantly, dragonet hide and human skin were usually not severely damaged from spillage. A wet cloth, applied within about twenty seconds, prevented a bad burn. Kenjo led a group in rigging holders for flamethrowers on the heavier sleds. He was adamant that the best defense was not only offense but aerial. He had many willing supporters among those at Landing who had lived through the First Fall.

Fire was the top choice for weapon. As one wit said, since no one had ever figured out how to make rain on demand, fire was the only reliable defense. Even the most ardent supporters of the dragonets did not wish to rely totally on their continued assistance.

There were not hands enough to do all the jobs required. Twice Paul and Emily were called in to arbitrate labor-pirating. The agronomists and veterinarians hastily reinforced livestock shelters. Caves were explored as possible alternate accommodations. Empty warehouses at Landing were made into shelters for any stakeholders who wished to house stock for safety's sake. Joel Lilienkamp insisted that due to the worker shortage the holders themselves would have to reinforce any buildings they preempted. Many stakeholders felt that that was Landing's job; some were unwilling to leave their stakes unless, and until, assured of safe quarters. In eight years, the population of the settlers had increased far beyond the point where the original site could house even half the current numbers.

Porrig Connell remained in his cave, having discovered that there were sufficient interlinking chambers to accommodate his entire extended family and their livestock. In addition to stabling for his mares and foals, he had also constructed a stallion box in which Cricket had been made very comfortable. Magnanimously, he allowed the survivors of some other families to remain in his cavesite until they found their own.

Because they had been the colony's leaders, Paul Benden and Emily Boll—as well as Jim Tillek, Ezra Keroon, and Ongola—found that many decisions were being referred to them, despite the fact that they had stepped down from their previous administrative duties.

"I'd far rather they came to me than to Ted Tubberman." Paul remarked wearily to Ongola when the former communications officer brought him the latest urgent queries from outlying stakes. He turned to the psychologist Tom Patrick, who had come to report on the latest round of gripes and rumors. "Tom?"

"I don't think you can stall a showdown much longer," he said, "or you and Emily will lose all credibility. That would be a big error. You two may not want to take command, but someone will have to. Tubberman's constantly undermining community effort and spirit. He's so totally negative that you ought to be thankful that most of the time he's out trying singlehandedly to clear the continent of rotting Threadshell. Grief has totally distorted his perceptions and judgment."

"Surely no one believes his ranting?" Emily asked.

"There're just enough long-buried gripes and resentments, and good honest gut-fear, right now that some people do listen to him. Especially in the absence of authorized versions," Tom replied. "Tubberman's complaints have a certain factual basis. Warped, to be sure." The psychologist shrugged, raising both hands, palms up. "In time, he'll work against himself—I hope. Meanwhile he's roused a substantial undercurrent of resentment which had better be countered soon. Preferably by you gentlemen and Emily and the other captains. They still trust you, you know, in spite of Tubberman's accusations."

"So the Rubicon must be crossed again," Paul said whimsically, and exhaled. He caught himself rubbing his left thumb against the insensitive skin of his replacement fingers and stopped. Leaning wearily back in his chair, he put both hands behind his head as if supporting an extra weight.

"I can lead a meeting, Paul," Cabot said when Paul contacted him on a secured comm channel, "but they subconsciously consider you and Emily their leaders. Force of habit."

"Any decision to reinstate us must be spontaneous," Paul replied after a long and thoughtful pause. Slowly Emily nodded. The last days had aged both admiral and governor. "The matter must be handled strictly on the charter protocol, though by all that's holy, I never anticipated having to invoke those contingency clauses."

"Thank all the powers that be that they're there," Cabot said fervently. "It'll take an hour or two to organize things here. Oh, by the way, we also had a few messages across the river early yesterday morning. Didn't notice until about noon today. Hit the southern edge of Bordeaux. We gave Pat and his crew a hand. All's safe here." With that, he rang off, leaving Paul dumbfounded.

"After our little brush with the stuff," Cabot said when he arrived in person, "I'm beginning to appreciate the gravity of the colony's situation." A hopeful smile, not echoed by the expression in his keen gray eyes, curved his strong mouth. "Is it as bad as rumor has it?"

"Probably. Depends on the source of the rumor," Paul answered with an honest grimace.

"Depends on whether you're an optimist or pessimist," Jim

Tillek added. "I've been in worse fixes on the asteroid runs and come out with life and lung. I prefer to have a planet to maneuver in, on, over. And the seas."

Cabot's smile faded as he regarded the five people gathered discreetly in the met tower.

"Most of what we *know,*" Paul said, "is negative. But—" He began to refute the prevalent rumors by ticking them off on his strong, work-stained fingers. "The Threads are unlikely to be the forerunner of an alien invasion. It was not unique to this area. It did strike the planet in much the same way, to judge by the EEC records, almost exactly two hundred years ago. It may or may not emanate from the eccentric planet, which has a two-hundred-and-fifty-year orbit. And although we do not know what its life cycle is, or even if it does have one—that is the most viable theory—Thread is not the initial stage of tunnel snakes, for example, who have a much more respectable lineage, nor of any of the other kinds of life we've had a look at so far."

"I see." Cabot slowly nodded his handsome leonine head as he fingered his lips in thought. "No reassuring forecast available?"

"Not yet. As Tom here recommends, we need a forum in which to air grievances and correct misconceptions," Paul went on. "It didn't miss Boca Stake because Paul Benden owns it, or drop on Sadrid because they're the newest, or stop short of Thessaly because Gyorgy was one of the first charterers to claim his stake. We can, and will, survive this hazard, but we cannot have the indiscriminate conscriptions of technicians and able-bodied workers. It is apparent to anyone pausing to think that we also cannot survive if everyone hares off in opposite directions. Or if some of the wilder notions, including Tubberman's, are not dismissed and morale restored."

"In short, what you want is a suspension of autonomy?"

"Not what I want," Paul replied clearly and with emphasis, "but a centralized administration"—Cabot grinned at the admiral's choice of words—"will be able to efficiently organize available workers, distribute matériel and supplies, and make sure that the majority survive. Joel Lilienkamp locked up Stores today, claiming inventory, to prevent panic requisitions. People must realize that this *is* a survival situation."

"Together we stand, divided we fall?" Cabot used the old saying with respect.

"That's it."

"The trick will be in getting all our independent spirits to see the wisdom," Tom Patrick said, and Cabot nodded agreement.

"I must emphasize," Paul went on, looking quickly at Emily, who nodded approval, "that it doesn't matter who administers during the emergency so long as some authority is recognized, and obeyed, that will ensure survival."

After a pause, Cabot added thoughtfully, "We're years from help. Did we burn all our bridges?"

Considerable surprise and relief permeated Landing the next morning when Cabot Francis Carter, the colony's senior legist, broadcast the announcement that a mass meeting was scheduled for the following evening. Representatives of every major stake, charter, or contract, would be expected to attend.

By the night of the meeting, the electricians had managed to restore power to one end of Bonfire Square by means of underground conduits. Where lamps were still dark, torches had been secured to the standards. The lighted area was filled with benches and chairs. The platform, originally constructed for musicians for the nightly bonfires, contained a long table, set with six chairs along one side. There was light enough to see those who took places there.

When neither Paul Benden nor Emily Boll appeared, a murmur of surprise rippled around those assembled. Cabot Francis Carter led Mar Dook, Pol and Bay Harkenon-Nietro, Ezra Keroon, and Jim Tillek onto the stage.

"We have had time to mourn our losses," Cabot began, his

sonorous voice easily reaching to the very last bench. Even the children listened in silence. "And they have been heavy. They could have been worse, and there can't be one among us who doesn't give thanks to our small fire-breathing, dragonlike allies.

"I don't have all bad news for you tonight. I wish I had better. We can give a name to the stuff that killed some of our loved ones and wiped out five stakes: it's a very primitive mycorrhizoid life-form. Mar Dook here tells me that on other planets, incuding our own Earth, very simple fungi can be generally found in a symbiotic association with trees, the mycelium of the fungus with the roots of a seed plant. We've all seen it attack vegetation—"

"And just about anything else," Ted Tubberman shouted from the left-hand side of the audience.

"Yes, that is tragically true." Cabot did not look at the man or attempt to lighten the tone of the meeting, but he intended to control it. He raised his voice slightly. "What we are only just beginning to realize is that the phenomenon is planetwide and the last occurrence was approximately two hundred years ago." He paused to allow the listeners to absorb that fact, then stolidly held up his hands to silence the murmurs. "Soon we will be able to predict exactly when and where this Threadfall is likely to strike again, because, unfortunately, it will. But this is *our* planet," he stated with an expression of fierce determination, "and no damned mindless Thread is going to make us leave."

"You stupid bastard, we *can't* leave!" Ted Tubberman jumped to his feet, wildly waving clenched fists in the air. "You fixed it so we'll rot here, sucked up by those effing things. We can't leave! We'll all die here."

His outburst started a sullen, murmurous roll in the audience. Sean, sitting with Sorka to the edge of the crowd, was indignant.

"Damnfool loud mouth charterer," Sean murmured to Sorka. "He knew this was a one-way trip, only now everything's not running smooth enough for him, it has to be *someone's* fault." Sean snorted his contempt.

Sorka shushed him to hear Cabot's rebuttal.

"I don't look at our situation as hopeless, Tubberman," Cabot began, his trained voice drowning the murmurs in a firm, confident, and determined tone. "Far from it! I prefer to think positively. I see this as a challenge to our ingenuity, to our adaptability. Mankind has survived more dangerous environments than Pern. We've got a problem and we must cope with it. We must solve it to survive. And survive we will!" When Cabot saw the big botanist gathering breath, he raised his voice. "When we signed the charter, we all knew there'd be no turning back. Even if we could, I, for one, wouldn't consider running home." His voice became rich with contempt for the faint of heart, the coward, and the quitter. "For there's more on this planet for me than First or Earth ever held! I'm not going to let this phenomenon do me out of the home I've built, the stock I plan to raise, the quality of life I enjoy!" With a contemptuous sweep of his hand, he dismissed the menace as a minor inconvenience. "I'll fight it every time it strikes my stake or my neighbors', with every ounce of strength and every resource I possess.

"Now," he went on in a less fervent tone, "this meeting has been called, in the democratic manner outlined by our charter, to make plans on how best to sustain our colony during this emergency. We are, in effect, under siege by this mycorrhizoid. So we must initiate measures and develop the necessary strategy by which to minimize its effect on our lives and property."

"Are you suggesting martial law, Cabot?" Rudi Shwartz demanded, rising to his feet, his expression carefully guarded.

Cabot gave a wry chuckle. "As there is no army on Pern, Rudi, martial law is impossible. However, circumstances force us to consider suspending our present autonomy in order to reduce the damage which this Thread apparently can—and will—do to both the ecology of the planet and the economy of this colony. I'm suggesting that a reversion to the centralized government of our first year on Pern be considered at this point in time." His next words rose to a near bellow to drown out the protests. "*And* whatever measures are required to ensure the survival of the colony, unpalatable though they may be to us as individuals who have enjoyed our autonomy."

"And these measures have already been decided?" someone asked.

"By no means," Cabot assured the woman. "We don't even yet know that much about our—adversary—but plans must be made now, for every possible contingency. We know that Thread falls on a worldwide scale, so sooner or later it will affect every stake. We have to minimize that danger. That will mean centralization of existing food supplies and matériel, and a return to hydroponics. It definitely means that some of you technicians will be asked to return to Landing, since your particular skills can be best exercised here. It means we're all going to have to work together again instead of going our separate ways."

"What option do we have?" another woman asked in the slight pause that followed. She sounded resigned.

"Some of you have fairly large common stakes," Cabot answered in the most reasonable of tones. "You could probably do quite well on your own. Any central organization here at Landing would have to consider the needs of its population first, but it wouldn't be the case of 'Never Darken Our Doorstep Again.'" He gave a brief reassuring smile in her general direction. "That's why we meet here tonight. To discuss all the options as thoroughly as the charter's conditions and the colony's prospects were initially discussed."

"Wait just a minute!" Ted Tubberman cried, jumping to his feet again, spreading out his arms and looking around, his chin jutting forward aggressively. "We've got a surefire option, a realistic one. We can send a homing capsule to Earth and ask for assistance. This is a state of emergency. We need help!"

"I told ya," Sean murmured to Sorka, "squealing like a stuck pig. Earth lands here, girl, and we make for the Barrier Range and stay lost!"

"I wouldn't bet on Earth sending any," Joel Lilienkamp said from the front of the audience, his words drowned by the cries of colonists agreeing with Ted.

"We don't need Earth mucking about Pern," Sean cried, jumping to his feet and flourishing his arm. "This is *our* planet!"

Cabot called for order, but very little of the commotion subsided. Ezra Keroon got to his feet, trying to help. Finally, making a megaphone of his hands, he bellowed his message. "Hold it down, now, friends. I have to remind you all—*listen to me!*—it'd be over ten years before we got a reply. Of any kind."

"Well, I for one don't want old Terra," Jim Tillek said over the loud reaction to that, "or even First, poking their noses in *our* business. That is, if they'd bother to respond. For sure, if they condescended to help, they'd mortgage all of us to the hilt for aid. And end up owning all the mineral rights and most of the arable land. Or have you all forgotten Ceti III? I also don't see why a central administration during this emergency is such a big deal. Makes sense to me. Share and share alike!"

A low murmur of agreement could be clearly heard, although many faces wore discouraged or sullen expressions.

"He's right, Sorka," Sean said in a voice loud enough for others around him to hear.

"Dad and Mother think so, too," Sorka added, pointing to her parents, who were sitting several rows ahead.

"We've got to send a message," Ted Tubberman shouted, shaking off the attempts of his immediate neighbors to make him sit down. "We've got to tell them we're in trouble. We've a right to help! What's wrong in sending a message?"

"What's wrong?" Wade Lorenzo shouted from the back of the audience. "We need help right now, Tubberman, not ten to thirty years from now. Why, by then, we'd probably have the thing licked. A Fall's not all that bad," he added with the confidence of experience. He sat down amid hoots and shouts of dissent, mainly from those who had been at Landing during the tragedy.

"And don't forget that it took half a century before Earth went to Ceti III's assistance," Betty Musgrave-Blake said, jumping to her feet.

Other comments were voiced.

"Yeah, Captain Tillek's right. We've got to solve our own problems. We can't wait for Earth."

"Forget it, Tubberman."

"Sit down and shut up, Tubberman."

"Cabot, call him to order. Let's get on with this meeting."

Similar sentiments rose from all sides.

His neighbors forced the botanist down and, dismayed by the lack of support, Ted shook off the compelling hands and crossed his arms defiantly on his chest. Tarvi Andiyar and Fulmar Stone moved to stand nearby. Sallah watched apprehensively, although she knew full well the strength belied by Tarvi's lean frame.

Sean nudged Sorka. "They'll shut him up, and then we can get to the meat of all this talking," he said. "I hate meetings like this—people sounding off just to make a noise and act big when they don't know what they're talking about."

Raising a hand to be recognized, Rudi Shwartz again got to his feet. "If, as you've suggested, Cabot, the larger stakes could remain self-governing, how would a central government be organized? Would the large stakes be at all responsible to it?"

"It's more a matter of the fair allocation of food, materials, and shelter, Rudi," Joel Lilienkamp said, rising, "rather than—"

"You mean, we don't have enough food?" an anxious voice broke in.

"For now, we do, but if this Threadstuff is planetwide . . . we all see what it did to Landing's fields," Joel went on, motioning to the dark, ravaged area, "and if it keeps coming back, well—" A woman made a protest of dismay that was clearly audible. "Well," he went on, hitching up his trousers, "everyone deserves a fair share of what we've got. I see nothing wrong with going back to hydroponics for a while. We did just fine for fifteen years on shipboard, didn't we? I'll take any odds we can do it again."

His jovial challenge met with mixed reactions, some cheering, others clearly apprehensive.

"Remember, too, folks, that Thread doesn't affect the sea," Jim Tillek said, his cheerfulness unforced. "We can live, and live well, from the sea alone."

"Most early civilizations lived almost entirely from the sea," Mairi Hanrahan cried in a ringing, challenging tone. "Joel's right—we can use alternate methods of growing. And, as long as we can harvest the sea for fresh protein, we'll be just fine. I think we all ought to buck up, instead of collapsing under the first little snag." She stared significantly at Ted Tubberman.

"Little snag?" he roared. He would have shoved through the crowd to get to Mairi if he had not been restrained. Tarvi and Fulmar moved in closer to him.

"Hardly a *little* snag," Mar Dook said quickly, raising his voice over the ripple of mixed remonstrance and support. "And certainly tragic for many of us. But let's not fight among ourselves. It's equally useless for us to bitch that the EEC team did not do a thorough inspection of this planet and grossly misled us. But this world has already proved that it can survive such an incursion and regenerate. Are we humans any less resilient with the resources we have at hand?" He tapped his forehead significantly.

"I don't want just to survive, hand to mouth," Ted Tubberman shouted, his chin jerking out belligerently, "cooped up in a building, wondering if those things are going to eat their way through to me!"

"Ted, that's the biggest bunch of bilgewash I've ever heard

from a grown man," Jim Tillek said. "We got a bit of a problem with our new world that I sure as hell am going to help solve. So quit your bitching, and let's figure out just how to cope. We're here, man, and we're going to survive!"

"I want us to send home for help," someone else said, calm but firm. "I feel that we're going to need the defenses a sophisticated society can supply, especially as we brought so little technology with us. And most especially if this stuff returns so often."

"Once we've sent for help, we have to take what is sent," Cabot said quickly.

"Lili, what odds are you taking that Earth would send us help?" Jim Tillek asked.

Ted Tubberman jumped to his feet again. "Don't bet on it. Vote on it! If this meeting's really democratic, that is, let's vote to send a mayday to Federated Sentient Planets."

"I second the motion," one of the medics said, along with several others.

"Rudi," Cabot said, "appoint two other stewards and let's take a hand vote."

"Not everyone's here tonight," Wade Lorenzo pointed out.

"If they don't wish to attend a scheduled meeting, they will have to abide by the decision of those who did," Cabot replied sternly. He was met with shouts of agreement. "Let the vote be taken on the motion before us. Those in favor of sending a homing capsule to the Federated Sentient Planets for assistance, raise their hands."

Hands were duly raised and counted by the stewards, Rudi Shwartz taking note of the count. When Cabot called for those opposed to sending for help, the majority was marked. As soon as Cabot announced the results, Ted Tubberman was vituperative.

"You're damned fools. We can't lick this stuff by ourselves. There's no place safe from it on this planet. Don't you remember the EEC reports? The entire planet was eaten up. It took more than two hundred years to recover. What chance have we?"

"That is enough, Tubberman," Cabot roared at him. "You asked for a vote. It was taken in sight of all, and the *majority* has decided against sending for help. Even if the decision had been in favor, our situation is serious enough so that certain measures must be initiated immediately.

"One priority is the manufacture of metal sheeting to protect existing buildings, no matter where they are. The second is to manufacture HNO_3 cylinders and flamethrower components. A third is to conserve all materials and supplies. Another problem is keeping a good eastern watch at every stake until a pattern can be established for Threadfall.

"I'm asking that we temporarily reinstate Emily Boll and Paul Benden as leaders. Governor Boll kept her planet fed and free despite a five-year-long Nathi space embargo, and Admiral Benden is by far the best man to organize an effective defense strategy.

"I'm calling for a show of hands now, and we'll make it a proper referendum when we know exactly how long the state of emergency will last." A ripple of assent greeted his crisp, decisive statements. "Rudi, prepare for another count." He waited a moment as the crowd shifted restlessly. "Let's have a show of hands on implementing those priorities tonight, with Admiral Benden and Governor Boll in charge."

Many hands were immediately thrust in the air, while others came up more slowly as the undecided took heart from their neighbors' resolution. Even before Rudi gave him the count, Cabot could see that the vote was heavily in favor of the emergency measures.

"Governor Boll, Admiral Benden, will you accept this mandate?" he asked formally.

"It was rigged!" Ted Tubberman shouted. "I tell you, rigged. They just want to get back into power again." His accusations broke off suddenly as Tarvi and Fulmar pushed him firmly back down on the bench.

"Governor? Admiral?" Cabot ignored the interruption. "You two still have the best qualifications for the jobs to be done, but if you decline, I will accept nominations from the floor." He waited expectantly, giving no hint of his personal preference in the matter and paying no attention to the restless audience and the rising murmur of anxious whispers.

Slowly Emily Boll rose to her feet. "I accept."

"As I do," Paul Benden said, standing beside the governor. "But only for the duration of this emergency."

"You believe that?" Tubberman roared, breaking loose from his restrainers.

"That is quite enough, Tubberman," Cabot shouted, appearing to lose his professional detachment. "The majority supports this temporary measure even if you won't." Slowly the audience quieted. Cabot waited until there was complete silence. "Now, I've saved the worst news until I was certain we were all resolved to work together. Thanks to Kenjo and his survey teams, Boris and Dieter believe that there is a pattern emerging. If they're right, we have to expect this Thread to fall again tomorrow afternoon at Malay River and proceed across Cathay Province to Mexico on Maori Lake."

"On Malay?" Chuck Kimmage jumped to his feet, his wife clutching his arm, both of them horrified. Phas had managed to find and warn all the other stakers at Malay and Mexico, but Chuck and Chaila had arrived just before the meeting, too late to be privately informed.

"And all of us will help preserve your stakes," Emily Boll said in a loud firm voice.

Paul jumped up on the platform, raising his hands and glancing at Cabot for permission to speak. "I'm asking for volunteers to man sleds and flamethrowers. Kenjo and Fulmar have worked out a way of mounting them. Some are already in place on what sleds they could commandeer. Those of you with medium and large sleds just volunteered them. The best way to get the Thread is while it's still airborne, before it has a chance to land. We will also need people on the ground, mopping up what does slip through."

"What about the fire-lizards, or whatever you call 'em? Won't they help?" someone asked.

"They helped us that day at Landing," a woman added, a note of fearful apprehension making her voice break.

"They helped at Sadrid Stake two days ago," Wade said.

"The rain helped a lot, too," Kenjo added, not at all convinced of assistance from a nonmechanical quarter.

"Any of you with dragonets would be very welcome in ground crews," Paul went on, willing to entertain any possible reinforcements. But he, too, was skeptical; he had been too busy to attach a dragonet, though his wife and older son had two each. "I particularly need those of you who've had any combat or flight experience. Our enemy isn't the Nathi this time, but it's our world that is being invaded. Let's stop it, tomorrow and whenever it's necessary!"

A spontaneous cheer went up in response to his rousing words and was repeated, growing in volume as people got to their feet, waving clenched fists. Those on the platform watched the demonstration, relieved and reassured. Perhaps only Ongola took note of those who remained seated or silent.

If Dieter and Boris were correct, the oncoming Fall would give the Kahrain peninsula a near miss, beginning at approximately 1630 hours, roughly 120 klicks northwest of the mouth of the Paradise River, 25 degrees south. Dieter and Boris were not sure if the fall would extend as far southwestward as Mexico on Lake Maori, but precautions were being taken there as well.

Acting Commander Kenjo Fusaiyuki assembled his squadrons at the required point. Though Thread drowned in the sea, his teams would at least have some practice throwing flame at the "real thing."

"Practice" was not the appropriate term for the chaos that resulted. Kenjo was reduced to snarling peremptory orders over the comm unit as the inept but eager sled pilots plummeted through the skies after Thread, frequently favoring one another with a glancing touch of thrown HNO_3.

Fighting Thread required entirely different techniques from hunting wherry or scoring a hit on a large flying machine driven by a reasonably intelligent enemy. Thread was mindless. It just fell—in a slanting southwesterly direction, occasionally buffeted into tangles by gusting winds. It was the inexorability of that insensate fall that infuriated, defeated, depressed, and frustrated. No matter how much was seared to ash in the sky, more followed relentlessly. Nervous pilots swooped, veered, and dove. Unskilled gunners fired at anything that moved into range, which more often than not was another sled chasing down a tangle of Thread. Nine domesticated dragonets fell victim to such inexpertise, and there was suddenly a marked decrease in the number of wild ones who had joined the fray.

In the first half hour of the fall, seven sleds were involved in midair collisions, three badly damaged and two with cracked siliplex canopies which made them unairworthy. Even Kenjo's sled bore scorch marks. Four broken arms, six broken or sprained hands, three cracked collarbones, and a broken leg put fourteen gunners out of action; many others struggled on with lacerations and bruises. No one had thought about rigging any safety harnesses for the flame-gunners.

A hasty conference between the squadron leaders was called on a secured channel at the beginning of the second hour while the Fall was still over water. The squadron leaders—Kenjo, Sabra Stein-Ongola, Theo Force, and Drake Bonneau—and Paul Benden, as leader of the ground-support crews—decided to assign each squadron their own altitude level at hundred-meter intervals. The squadron would fly in a stacked wedge formation back and forth across the fifty-klick width of the Thread corridor. The important factor was for each wedge of seven sleds to stick to its designated altitude.

Once the sleds began to maintain their distances, midair collisions and scorchings were immediately reduced. Kenjo led the most capable fliers at ground level to catch as much missed Thread as possible and to inform the surface crews where tangles got through. Paul Benden coordinated the movements of the fast ground-skimmers, which carried teams with small portable flamers. Channels were kept open to air, ground, and Landing. Joel Lilienkamp organized replacement of empty HNO_3 cylinders and power packs. A medical team remained on standby.

By mid-Fall, Paul knew that his ground-support teams were too thinly spread to be truly effective, even though there were, fortunately, substantial stretches where Thread landed on stony or poor soil and shriveled and died quickly. Toward the end, when weary pilots were running low on energy and the sled power packs were nearly depleted, more Thread got through. It seemed to be part of the growing bad luck that it fell over thick vegetation and the home farm of the Mexico Stake.

The abrupt end of the Fall, on the verge of Maori Lake and the main buidings of Mexico, came as a distinct shock to those who had been concentrating so hard on destroying Thread. Squadron leaders ordered their fighters to land on the lakeside while they had a chance to confer with the ground-crew marshals. Those at Mexico who had not been in ground defense provided hot soup and klah, fresh bread, and fruit, and had prepared an infirmary in one of the houses. Tarvi and the Karachi team had managed to complete metal roofing just before the Fall reached the area. Then Joel Lilienkamp's supply barge arrived with fresh power packs and HNO_3 cylinders.

The day was not over yet. Pilots cruised slowly back over the Fall corridor, checking for any "live" Thread. Paul drove himself and his sweat-smeared, soot-covered, weary teams back toward Malay Stake and the coast to try to spot signs of a secondary infestation where no shell or dissolving matter was visible. Only two such points were discovered and, on Paul's order, the ground was saturated with sustained blasts of HNO_3.

One of the ground crew on that detail told the admiral that he thought that was a waste of fuel. "The dragonets weren't at all concerned, Admiral. They are when there's Thread."

"We take no chances at this stage," Paul replied, a slight smile removing any hint of rebuke. He did not look upon the fiery bath as an overkill. The dragonets were palpably alerted by Thread, but were obviously unaware of the presence of the second, and possibly more fearful, stage of its life cycle.

However, Paul Benden's respect for the dragonets was increased by their diligent searching out of newly fallen Thread. Several times during the Fall, he spotted the fair of dragonets fighting alongside Sean Connell and the redheaded Hanrahan girl. The creatures seemed to be obeying orders. Their movements had a discipline, while other groups flitted about in a kind of chaotic frenzy.

On almost too many occasions, Paul saw the little creatures suddenly disappearing just when one seemed certain to be seared by the fiery breath of another. He found himself wishing that sleds had that sort of ability, or even more agility. Sleds were not the most efficient fighter craft. He recalled his admiration of the dragonets during the wherry attack. From accounts of their now legendary "umbrella" defense of Landing from the First Fall, he knew that hundreds of wild ones had assisted their domesticated kin. They could be splendid reinforcements. Paul wondered what the chances were to mobilize *all* the dragonets to be trained by Connell and Hanrahan.

The present Fall had left denuded patches on the surface, but despite all initial bungling and the inexperience of sled and ground crews, the devastation was not as widespread as in the first horrific Fall.

Most of the exhausted fighters chose to remain the night at Malay Stake. Pierre de Courci took it upon himself to act as chef, and his team had prepared baked fish and tubers in great pits on the beach. Weary men, women, and youngsters sat around the reassuring bonfires, too spent to talk, glad enough just to have survived the rigors of the day.

Sean and Sorka opened an emergency clinic on the Malay beach to tend the wounded fire-dragonets, slathering numbweed on Threadscored wings and seared hide.

"D'you think that once Sira stops crying, my bronze and brown will come back?" Tarrie Chernoff asked. She was dirty with black grease and vegetation-green stains, her wher-hide jerkin showing numerous char spots, new and old, but like all devoted fire-dragonet owners, she was caring for her creature before seeing to her own relief.

Sean shrugged noncommittally, but Sorka laid a reassuring hand on Tarrie's arm. "They usually do. They get pretty upset when one of their own fair's hurt, especially a queen. You get a good night's sleep and see what the morning brings."

"Why'd you give her false comfort like that, Sorka?" Sean asked in a low voice when Tarrie had trudged back to the bonfires, her comforted queen cradled in the crook of her arm. "You know bloody well by now that if it's hurt badly enough, a fire-lizard doesn't come back." Sean was grim. He and Sorka had been lucky with their fair so far, but then, he had seen to it that their dragonets had the discipline to survive.

"She needs a good night's sleep without worrying herself sick. And a lot do come back."

Sorka gave a weary sigh as she closed the medicine case. She arched her back against tired back muscles. "Give me a rub, would you, Sean? My right shoulder." She turned her back to him and sighed in relief as his strong fingers kneaded the strain away.

Sean's hands felt marvelous on her back; he knew just how to ease away the tension. Then his hands moved caressingly up the nape of her neck and lovingly into her hair. Tired as she was, she responded to the silent question. She stepped away from him, smiling as she looked quickly about to see where their fair had taken themselves.

"They've all found quiet nests to curl up in." Sean's low voice was suggestive.

"Then let's find us one of our own." She caught his hand and led him off the beach and into a thick grove of arrow-leaf plants that they had helped save from Threadscore.

Revived by the hot meal and a generous beaker of a very smooth quikal fermented by Chaila Xavior-Kimmage from local fruits, Paul and Emily quietly organized a discreet council, which they held in one of the unscathed Malay outbuildings. Besides the admiral and the governor, Ongola, Drake, Kenjo, Jim Tillek, Ezra Keroon, and Joel Lilienkamp attended.

"We'll do better next time, Admiral," Drake Bonneau assured Paul with a cocky salute. Kenjo, entering behind him, regarded the tall war ace with amused condescension. "Today taught us that this Thread requires entirely different flight and strike techniques. We'll refine that wedge maneuver so nothing gets through. Sled pilots must drill to maintain altitude patterns. Gunners must learn to control their blasts. It's more than just holding the button down. We had some mighty close encounters. We lost some of the little dragonets, too. We can't risk so many lives, much less the sleds."

"We can repair the sleds, Drake," Joel Lilienkamp remarked dryly before Paul spoke, "but power packs won't last forever. We can't afford to expend them uselessly on drills. Despite our resupply system, which I bet I can improve, nine pilots had to glide-land at Maori. That's clumsy management. That wedge formation, by the way, Drake, is economical on the packs. But it still takes days to recharge exhausted ones. How long will this stuff keep falling, Paul?" Joel looked up from his calculating pad.

"We haven't established that yet," Paul said, his left thumb rubbing his knuckles. "Boris and Dieter are collating information from the pilot debriefing."

"Hellfire, that's not going to tell us what we need to know, Paul," Drake said, his weary tone a complaint. "Where does this stuff come *from?*"

"Probe's gone off," Ezra Keroon said. "It'll be a couple a more days before any reports come back."

Drake continued almost as if he had not heard. "I want to find out if the stuff mightn't be more vulnerable in the stratosphere. Even if we only have ten pressurized sleds, would a high-altitude strike be more effective? Does this junk hit the atmosphere in clumps and then disperse? Can we develop a defense less clumsy than flamethrowers? We need to know more about this enemy."

"It doesn't fight back," Ongola remarked, rubbing his temples to ease the pounding sort of headache that battle had always given him.

"True," Paul replied with a grim smile as he turned to Kenjo. "I wonder if we would gain any useful data from an orbital reconnaissance flight? How much fuel in the *Mariposa*'s tanks?"

"If I pilot it, enough for three, maybe four flights," Kenjo replied, deliberately avoiding Drake's eyes, "depending on how much maneuvering is required and how many orbits."

"You're the man for it, Kenjo," Drake said with a flourish of his hand and a rueful expression. "You can land on a breath of fuel." Kenjo, smiling slightly, gave a short, quick bow from the waist. "Do we know when, or where, the stuff hits us again?"

"We do," Paul assured them in a flat tone. "If the data is correct, and it was today, stakeholders are lucky. It strikes in two places: 1930 hours across Araby to the Sea of Azov, "—his expression reflected his continued regret at the loss of Araby's original stakeowners—"and 0330 from the sea across the tip of Delta. Both those areas are unoccupied."

"We can't let that stuff go unchecked anywhere, Paul," Ezra said in alarm.

"I know, but if we're going to have to mount crews every three days, we'll all soon be exhausted."

"Not everything needs to be protected," Drake said, unfolding his flight map. "Lots of marsh, scrub land."

"The Fall will still be attended," Paul said in an inarguable tone of voice. "Look on it as a chance to refine maneuvers and train teams, Drake. It is undeniably best to get the stuff while it's airborne. Thread didn't eat through as much land today, but we can't to afford to lose wide corridors every time it hits us."

"Draft some more of those dragonets," Joel suggested facetiously. "They're as good on the ground as in the air."

Emily regarded him sadly as the others grinned. "Unfortunately they just aren't big enough."

Paul turned around in his chair to give the governor a searching look. "That's the best idea today, Emily."

Drake and Kenjo looked at each other, puzzled, but Ongola, Joel, and Ezra Keroon sat up, their expressions expectant. Jim Tillek grinned.

There were five main islands off the southern coast of Big Island and several small prominences, the remains of volcanoes poking above the brilliant green-blue sea. The one Avril and Stev were eagerly approaching was no more than the crater of a sunken volcano. Its sides sloped into the sea, providing a narrow shore, except to the south where the lip of the crater was lowest. Avril was bouncing with impatience as Stev nosed the prow of the little boat up onto the north shore.

"That Nielsen twit couldn't possibly be right," she muttered, hopping on to the pebbly beach before he had shut off the power. "How could we have missed a whole beach full of diamonds?"

"We had more promising sites. Remember, Avril?"

Steve watched her scoop up a handful of the black stones and sift them through her fingers. She kept only the largest, which she thrust at him.

"Here! Scan it!" As he inserted the palm-sized stone into the portable scanner, she looked about in angry agitation. "It makes no sense. They can't all be black diamonds. Can they?"

"This one is!"

She took back the stone and held it up to the sun for a moment. "And this one?" She grabbed up a fist-sized rock and pushed it at him, but he was quick enough to see her slip the first stone into her pouch. "It's lucky that Nielsen kid's only our apprentice. All this is—ours—too!"

"We'll,"—Stev had not missed Avril's quick alteration—"have to be careful not to glut the market." He put the big stone into the scanner with eager and not quite steady fingers. "It is indeed black diamond. Around four hundred carats and relatively unflawed. Congratulations, my dear, you've struck it rich."

She grimaced at his mocking tone and snatched the diamond from him, clasping it against her almost protectively. "It can't all be black diamond," she muttered. "Can it?"

"Why not? There's nothing to keep diamonds from being hatched from a volcano, if you have the right ingredients and sufficient pressure at some point in time. I grant you, this might be the only beach composed of black diamond, or any diamond, in the universe, but that's what"—Stev's grin was pure malice—"*you* have here."

She glanced at him, her eyes weary, and managed an easy smile. "What *we* have, Stev." She leaned into him, her skin warm against his. "This is the most exciting moment of my life." She wound her free hand about his neck and kissed him passionately, her body pressing against him until he felt the diamond gouging his ribs.

"Not even diamonds must come between us, my love," he murmured, taking it from her resisting fingers and dropping it behind him into the open sled.

Stev was not unduly surprised the next morning when he found that both Avril and the fastest sled were gone from their Big Island mining camp. He made a second check in the rock hollow where he knew Avril secreted the more spectacular gemstones that had been found. It was empty.

Stev grinned maliciously. She might have ignored the mayday from Landing, but he had not. He had followed what was happening on the southern continent, and kept an eye to the east whenever a cloud appeared. He had made contingency plans. He doubted that Avril had. He would have liked to see her expression when she found out that Landing was swarming with industrious people, the takeoff grid crammed with sleds and technicians. So he roared with amusement when one of their apprentices anxiously reported that she could not find Avril anywhere.

Nabhi Nabol was not at all pleased.

Kenjo achieved orbit with a minimum of fuel expenditure. He kept his mind on the task at hand, feeling the upward thrust of the versatile craft, and the glorious elation of release from gravity. He could wish that all his cares would fall away as easily. But he had not lost his touch with spacecraft. He slid appreciative fingers down the edge of the console.

The last three days had been frantic, servicing the *Mariposa*'s dormant systems, checking any possible fatigue or perishing of essential parts. He had even allowed Theo Force to command his squadron when Thread fell over the mountains southeast of Karachi and brushed Longwood, on Ierne Island. It was more important for him to recommission the *Mariposa*. Ongola had spared some time to tune the comm unit circuits and help with the terminal checks. The little ship had been designed for inactivity in the vacuum of space, and although the more important circuits had been stored in vacuum containers, there was always the fear that some minor but critical connection had *not* been properly scrutinized. But finally all systems had proved go-green, and a trial blast of her engines had been reassuringly loud and steady—and Kenjo had objected when forced to rest the last twelve hours before takeoff.

"You may be a bloody good jockey, Kenjo, but there are better mechanics on Pern than you," Paul Benden had told him in no uncertain terms. "You need rest *now,* to keep you alert in space where we can't help you."

A flight plan had been calculated to allow Kenjo to be in the position where Boris and Dieter had predicted the next batch of Thread would enter Pern's atmosphere. Their program indicated that Thread fell in approximately seventy-two-hour bursts, give or take an hour or two. Kenjo's mission was to measure the accuracy of their program, to determine the composition of Thread prior to entry, and, if possible, to trace its trajectory backward. Also, last but scarcely least, he was to destroy it before it entered the atmosphere. The next Fall was due to hit Kahrain Province, just above the deserted Oslo Landing, continue on to fall over Paradise River Stake, and end in the Araby Plains.

Kenjo was a hundred miles below the empty spaceships, but that was too far away for them to register on his scope. Nevertheless he strained to see them, magnifying the viewscope to its limit. Then he shrugged. The ships were past history. He was going to make a new contribution, an unparalleled one. Kenjo Fusaiyuko would discover the source of Thread, eradicate it once and for all, and be a planetary hero. Then no one would condemn him for "conserving" so much fuel for his private use. He could relieve his sense of honor and his scouring bouts of conscience.

Building his extra-light aircraft had been most rewarding. He had found the design on tape in the *Yokohama*'s library, in the history-of-airflight section. It was not the most fuel efficient, even when he had redesigned the engine, but what he had saved from each shuttle drop had made that saucy plane possible. Flying it over his isolated Honshu Stake in the Western Barrier Range had given him satisfaction far beyond his imagining, even if it had given rise to rumors of a large, and hitherto unknown, flying creature. His wife, patient and calm, had ventured no opinion on his avocation, aiding him in its construction. A mechanical engineer, she managed the small hydroelectric plant that served their plateau home and three small stakes in the next valley. She had given him four children, three of them sons, was a good mother, and even managed to help him cultivate the fruit trees that he raised as a credit crop.

She was safe from Thread, for they had cut their home right into the mountain, using wood only on the interior. She had been quite willing to help him carve a hangar for his aircraft with the stone-cutters he had borrowed from Drake Bonneau. But she did not know that he had a second, well-concealed cave in which to store his hoard of liquid fuel. He had not yet managed to transfer all of it to Honshu from the cave at Landing.

Yes, no one would object to what Kenjo had done when he brought them the information they sought. And he would see to it that it took three or four missions to do so. He had missed the tranquility and the challenge of deep space. How pitiful his little atmospheric craft was in comparison to the beautiful, powerful *Mariposa*. How clumsy the sled he had flown as a squadron leader. He had finally returned to his true medium—space!

The ship's alarms went off, and moments later the pinging began. He was in the midst of a shower of small ovoids. With a cry once uttered by long-dead Japanese warriors, Kenjo fired his starboard repulsors and grinned when the screen blossomed with tiny stars of destruction.

Avril Bitra was livid. She could not believe the change in Landing, especially as she had counted on it being nearly deserted. When Stev had talked her into taking apprentices so that no one would question exactly what it was they were doing on Big Island, Landing's population had been down to a mere two hundred.

But the Landing she found was crawling with people. There were lights everywhere, and people bustling about despite the late hour. Worst of all, the landing strip was crowded with sleds, large, small, and medium, and technicians swarmed about—and the *Mariposa* was not there! What under the suns had happened?

She had settled her sled to one edge of the strip, near where she had last seen the little space gig. She fumed impotently again over that disappointment. She had a fortune with which to depart this wretched mudball. She had even managed to shake off any companions. She had no qualms about leaving Stev Kimmer. He had been useful, as well as amusing—until just lately, until he had assessed those black diamonds. Yes, she had been right to leave immediately, before he thought to dismantle the sleds or do something drastic so that she would be forced to take him with her. Where in all the hells of seventeen worlds was the *Mariposa*? Who was using up the fuel she needed to get her to the colony ships? She struggled to control her rage. She had to think!

Belatedly she remembered the mayday. She wished now that she had listened in. Well, it could not have been that serious, not with Landing a hive of industry. Still, that could work in her favor. With so many people around, no one would notice another worker poking about.

She shivered, suddenly aware of the chill in the night air of the plateau. She was accustomed to the tropical climate of Big Island. Cursing inventively under her breath, she rooted through the sled's storage compartments and found a reasonably clean coverall. She also girded on the mechanic's belt she found beneath the coverall. It was probably Stev's—he was always well equipped. She smirked. Not always prepared, however.

Before she left to hunt for the *Mariposa,* she would have to hide the sled. In the darkness, she tried to locate at least one of the dense shrubs that grew at the edge of the strip, but she could not find any. Instead she stumbled into a small hole that proved large enough to conceal her sacks of treasure. She retrieved them from the sled, dropped them into the hole, piled loose stone and dirt over them, and then shone her handbeam over the spot to see if they were well hidden. After a few minor adjustments, she was satisfied.

With brazen strides she walked down the grid to the lights and activity.

Glancing out of the ground-floor window of the met tower where Drake Bonneau was conducting a training session, Sallah Telgar-Andiyar thought she had to be mistaken: the woman only *looked* like Avril Bitra. She was wearing a tool belt and strode purposefully toward a stripped-down sled. Yet no one else Sallah knew had that same arrogant walk, that provocative swing of the hip. Then the woman stopped and began to work on the sled. Sallah shook her head. Avril was at Big Island; she had not even responded to the mayday, or to the more recent recall to Landing for pilot duty. No one had seen her, or really cared to, but Stev Kimmer's genius with circuits would have been invaluable. Ongola was trying to get Paul Benden to *order* the return of Big Island miners.

"Don't keep your fingers on the release button." Drake's voice penetrated her moment of inattention.

Poor fellow, Sallah thought. He was trying to teach all the eager youngsters how to fight Thread. If half of what Tarvi had told her about the deadly menace was true, it was devilish to combat.

"Always sweep from bow to stern. Thread falls in a sou'westerly direction, so if you come in under the leading edge, you char a larger portion." Drake was running out of space on the operational board, which he had covered with his diagrams and flight patterns. Sallah had yet to fight the stuff, so she had paid attention—until the moment when she had thought she recognized Avril.

The day had had the quality of a reunion for the shuttle pilots. All the old crowd, with the exception of Nabhi Nabol and Kenjo, had answered the summons. Sallah knew where Kenjo was; she was a trifle envious of him, and was glad of Nabol's absence. He would certainly have sneered to be in the company of all the young ones who had earned their flying tickets since Landing. Why, she had known some of them as adolescents.

Settling in at Karachi had eaten more time than she realized. And it had brought so many changes, such as the dragonets perched on young shoulders or curled up on hide-trousered legs. Her own three—a gold and two bronzes—had, just like her older children, picked up some basic manners. They were perched on the top shelves of the big ready room. Two were mentas, and she wondered if they understood what was going on before their watchful rainbow eyes.

Drake's imperative warning interrupted her musing. "*Don't* deviate from your assigned altitude. We're trying to rig cruising devices that will warn you hair-trigger pilots when you're out of line. We've got to maintain flight levels to avoid collisions. We've got more people to fly than sleds to fly in. *You,"* he said, jabbing his finger at his audience, "can be replaced. The sled cannot, and we're going to need every one we can keep in the air.

"Now, a sweep from bow to stern in a one-second blast chars as much Thread for the range of these throwers. Catch the end of the stuff and fire runs back up most of it. Don't waste the HNO_3." His rapid-fire use of the chemical designation made it sound more like "agenothree," Sallah thought, losing concentration once again. Damn, she must pay attention, but she was so used to listening for sounds, not words. And silences. The silence all children made when they were being naughty or trying out forbidden things. And hers were inventive. She felt her lips widen in a proudly maternal smile, then disciplined her expression as Drake's eyes fastened on her face.

She already missed her three older children dreadfully. Ram Da, Sallah's sturdy, reliable seven-year-old son, had promised to look out for Dena and Ben. Sallah had brought three-month-old Cara with her—the baby was safely installed with Mairi Hanrahan's lot—so she was not totally deprived. But Tarvi was back at Karachi, extruding metal sheets on a round-the-clock basis, slaving as hard as the people he drove to their limits.

". . . and make each cylinder last as long as possible," Drake was saying. "Conserve agenothree and power, and you'll last longer in the flight line. Which is where you're needed. Now, most of you have had experience with turbulence. *Don't* shuck your safety harness until you're on the ground. The lighter sleds can be flipped on landing if the wind suddenly gusts, because they're nose-heavy with the flame-thrower mounts."

With Tarvi on such a schedule, it was just as well that she had work of her own to do, Sallah thought. He had little enough time for her, and she would not even have the comfort of sleeping beside him—or be able to rouse him to a dawn lusting when he was too drowsy to resist her caresses.

What was wrong with her? she wondered for the millionth time. She had not trapped Tarvi. The mutual need and passion that day in the cave could not have been faked. When the chance union had resulted in pregnancy, he had immediately offered to make a formal arrangement. She had not insisted, but she had been much relieved that the initiative had been his. He had been considerate, tender, and solicitous throughout the gestation, and sincerely overjoyed when his firstborn was a strong, healthy boy. He adored all his children, rejoicing at their birth and in their development. It was his wife he avoided, dismissed, ignored.

Sallah sighed, and her old friend Barr shot her a quizzical glance. Sallah smiled and gave a shrug, intimating that Drake had caused her reaction. What would her life have been like with Drake Bonneau, happily ensconced on his lake? Svenda looked complacent, boasting about limiting her childbearing to two. Drake might act the confident flyboy in public, but the previous night he had been noticeably dancing attendance on his imperious wife. Sallah had always thought that Drake was more "show" than "do." Yet for all Tarvi's eccentricities, Sallah preferred the geologist and treasured those ever more rare occasions when she could rouse him to passion. Perhaps that was the problem: Tarvi should be allowed the initiative. No, she had tried that tack, and had gone through a miserable year before she thought of her "dawn attacks."

She had learned some Pushtu phrases from Jivan and artlessly she had inquired about feminine names. Whomever Tarvi called for at the height of passion, it was not another woman. Or another man, from all she could discover.

"So," Drake said, "here is the roster for the next Fall. Remember, it's a double hit, at Jordan and at Dorado. We're going to send you Dorado squadrons on ahead so you can be well rested by the time you have to fight." Again Drake's eagle gaze swept his adoring students. "Now, back to your sleds to lend the technicians what assistance you can. House lights'll go out at midnight. We all need our rest," he concluded cheerfully as he waved their dismissal.

Svenda quickly moved to his side, her scowl a deterrent to those who approached Drake with private questions.

"When did you get in, Sallah?" Barr asked, turning with her usual friendly grin. "I only arrived in from our stake around noon. No one of the old group knew when you'd make it. I didn't realize this thing was so serious until I saw what it had done on my way up."

Sallah laughed. Barr's bubbling personality had not changed a micro, though her figure had rounded. "How many kids do you have now, Barr?" Sallah asked. "We've sort of lost track of each other with you on the other side of the continent."

"Five!" Barr managed a girlish giggle, glancing slyly at Sallah. "The last was a set of twins, which I'd never have expected. Then Jess told me that he was a twin, and twin births were common in his family. I could have strangled him."

"You didn't, though."

"Naw! He's a good man, a loving father, and a hard worker." Barr gave a sharp nod of her head at each virtue, grinning at Sallah again. Then her mobile face changed to one of concern. "Are you all right, Sallah?"

"Me, certainly. I've four kids. Brought Cara with me. She's only three months old."

"Is she at Mairi's or Chris MacArdle-Cooney's?"

"At Mairi's. We'd better check that roster and see when we're on duty. Where's Sorka these days?" Sallah had also lost track of the redheaded Hanrahan girl. "I saw all the others."

"Oh, she's living with another vet. Over on Irish Square."

"How appropriate!" Suddenly Sallah felt a surge of resentment, something to do with the freedom young people had and her frustration with Tarvi's diffidence, along with the sudden realization that she had relatively few responsibilities at that moment and that her professional skills were once again in demand. "C'mon, let's go find a drink and catch up on our lives!"

Sorka and Sean arrived at their quarters from different directions, Sean from an unexpected meeting with Admiral Benden, Sorka from the barn. She knew by his jarring stride that Sean was barely containing a fine fit of rage. He held it back until they were inside the house.

"Damn fool, hell'n'damned fool," he said, slamming the door behind him. "That pompous, pig-headed, butt-stupid git."

"Admiral Benden?" she inquired, surprised. Sean had never had reason to criticize the admiral, and he had been proud to be called to a special interview.

"That stupid admiral wants a cavalry unit!"

"Cavalry?" Sorka paused as she picked their evening meal out of the freezer compartment.

"To charge about the countryside with flamethrowers, no less!"

"Doesn't he realize horses hate fire?"

"He does now." Sean went past her to the small cabinet, hauled out a bottle of quickal, and held it up suggestively.

"Yes, please. If I don't unwind, too, my food won't do me any good at all." She curtailed her anxiety. The need for a drink indicated how tense he was, for Sean was not a drinking man.

"We don't have to eat up above, do we?" he asked, jerking his head over his shoulder in the direction of the reestablished community kitchen.

"No, I raided Mother's freezer." She set the container in the warming unit and dialed the appropriate time.

Sean handed over her glass and raised his in a toast. "To idiot admirals who are very good in space and real dumb wash-out stupid about animals. As if we had enough horses to waste in such an asinine caper. He also envisions me training squadrons of fire-lizards"—Sean had persisted in using his own name for them—"swooping down on Thread at command. He even feels that he should have one, too. He doesn't effing know they won't be hatching till summer! That is, if those flyboys don't flame 'em all down."

Sorka had never seen Sean so infuriated. He paced about, his face flushed, throwing his left arm out in extravagant gestures, sipping at his drink between phrases as he vented his anger. He flicked his head to flip the sun-lightened hair out of his eyes. A grimace made him appear inscrutable, almost frightening in his anger. On one level she listened to his words, agreeing with his anxieties and opinions; on another, she reveled in the fact that beneath the contained, almost coldly detached impression he gave most people, there was such a passionate, intelligent, critical, rational, and dedicated personality.

Sorka did not quite know when she had realized that she loved him—it seemed that she always had—but she remembered the day she realized that he loved her: the first time he had exploded in her presence over a minor incident. Sean would never have permitted himself that luxury if he had not felt totally secure in her presence, if he had not unconsciously needed her soothing affection and reassurance. Watching him work off his aggravation, Sorka permitted herself a small smile which she tactfully hid behind her glass.

"Now, Sean, the admiral paid you a compliment, too," she remarked. She caught his surprised glance and smiled. "By consulting *you*. I noticed, even if you didn't, that he watched us out there on the Malay corridor, saw how well our fair behaved. And I'm sure that he knows that you're more likely than anyone else to discover where the queens are hiding their eggs."

"Humph. Yes, I guess that's true enough." Somewhat mollified, Sean continued to pace, but with less agitation.

Sorka loved Sean in every mood, but his infrequent explosions fascinated her. His anger had never been directed at her;

he rarely criticized, and then only in a crisp impersonal tone. Some of her girlfriends had wondered how she could stand his taciturn, almost sullen moodiness, but Sorka had never found him sullen in her company. Generally he was thoughtful, unwilling to offend even in a complete disagreement, and certainly a man who kept his own counsel—unless horses were at risk. His lithe figure was graceful even as he thudded back and forth, his heels pounding and leaving dents in the thick wool carpet she had woven for their home. She let his tirade continue, amused by the language in which he described the probable antecedents of the admiral, whom he usually respected, and the idiocy of the entire biological team who tampered with creatures whose natures they had not the wit to understand.

"Well, did you offer to find the admiral a dragonet egg when the time's right?" she asked when he paused for breath after another elaboration of the stupidity of brass asses.

"Ha! I will if I can." He spun on his heel and sprawled beside her on the couch, his face suddenly still, rage and frustration dissipated, his eyes on the amber liquid in his glass. From his expression, she knew that something else was worrying him deeply. She waited for him to continue. "You know as well as I do that we haven't caught a glimmer of any of the wild ones around here. They've made themselves scarce since the Sadrid Fall. Jays, if there were anywhere safe on this planet, they'd find it!"

"There were a lot helping us at the Malay corridor."

"Up until some ijiits started flaming them, too!" Sean finished the last of his drink to drown his disgust. "We won't get the wild ones to help at all if that gets about." He poured himself another drink. "Say, where're yours?" he asked suddenly noticing that the usual perches were vacant.

"Same place yours are, out and about," she answered in a mild tone.

Then Sean began to laugh, as much at himself as at the fact that he had only just realized that his fire-lizards had made themselves scarce the moment he left the admin building.

"Not surprising, is it?" she teased, grinning back at him. He shoved one arm behind her shoulders and pulled her, unresisting, closer to him. "When Emmett told me Blazer was in a tizzy over your righteous wrath, I told mine they'd have to find their own food tonight. They don't like cheesy things anyway."

"It's not often we get a night alone," Sean said softly, his voice a seductive whisper in her ear. "Finish your drink, red-headed gal." He ruffled her fringe, then his hand traveled in a caress down her cheek to her chin. "And turn off the cooker," he added just before he kissed her.

Sorka did as she was told, well pleased. It was awkward having to invent excuses to send the dragonets off on specious errands. But even when they were not in season, the creatures delighted in strong emotions, and with thirteen in a chorus of encouragement, the entire neighborhood would know what was happening in the Hanrahan-Connell quarters.

Later that night, when the sounds of Landing's industry were muted, Sorka wondered if she had conceived. Sean slept neatly and quietly beside her, his fingers lightly encircling her upper arm. She had never mentioned a formal arrangement to Sean, or ever pointed out the common assumption of Landing's population that they were a tempered team. She and Sean were of one mind in nearly everything they did, utilizing their veterinary apprenticeship to breed strong horses, finding the very best among the genetic stock available from either the banks or the live stallions. They were soon to sit their final exams in veterinary medicine and they had located the perfect spot for a home—a valley halfway down the Eastern Barrier Range. Sean had taken Red to see the proposed Killarney Stake, and her father had approved emphatically of their choice. Sorka took that as a tacit approval of their still informal union.

Although Sorka's parents had acquiesced, Porrig Connell

still treated her formally as a guest he wished to see less often. His wife had never ceased in her efforts to bring her son back to his proper hearth. She had chosen another daughter-in-law for Sean and sometimes embarrassed all concerned by pushing the girl at Sean on every opportunity.

"I won't breed so close, Mam," Sean had informed her when she had nagged him once too often. "It's bad for the blood. Lally Moorhouse's father was your first cousin. We need to spread the gene pool, not enclose it."

Sorka had overheard, but she knew Sean well enough by then not to be hurt that he had said no more about choosing. Perhaps he had not known then that he loved fifteen-year-old Sorka Hanrahan, who was already certain where her heart had been given.

She had been seventeen before he had touched her with any kind of passion, and that had been a night to remember. Their roles had become reversed: she, the wanton; he, the hesitant, tender lover. Her ardent response to his gentle overtures had surprised and pleased them both, but they had not moved to separate quarters until she had passed her eighteenth birthday. It had become a custom in their generation to have a trial period prior to a formal declaration before the magistrate.

Sorka wanted Sean's child badly. Ever since that hideous half hour, treading water under a stone ledge, she had been aware of their mortality. She wanted something of Sean—just in case. Not that he was wild or incautious, but the Lilienkamp boys had not been reckless, and certainly poor Lucy Tubberman had not. So many people had been wiped out in that First Fall.

Sorka did not want to be left with nothing of Sean. She had not tried before to conceive, because pregnancy would have interfered with their plans for Killarney Stake: they needed the work credits for every acre they could purchase. She worried that there was something wrong with her that she had not gotten pregnant before, with all the incautious fooling around that she and Sean had enjoyed. But she was no longer fooling. That night she had meant business.

Wind Blossom opened the door to Paul Benden, Emily Boll, Ongola, and Pol and Bay Harkenon-Nietro. Gracefully inclining her head in welcome, she held the door wide for them to enter.

Kitti Ping was seated on a padded chair that, Paul decided, must be raised off the ground under its cover, giving it the semblance of an archaic throne. She looked imposing, a feat for someone half his height. A beautiful soft woven rug had been tucked about a frail body, and a long-sleeved tunic with elaborate embroideries also increased her general look of substance and authority. She raised one delicate hand, no larger than his oldest daughter's, and indicated that they were to be seated on the stools set in an irregular circle in front of her.

As Paul doubled his long legs to sit, he realized that she had achieved a subtle advantage over her visitors. Amused by the tactic, he smiled up at her and thought he could detect the merest hint of an acknowledgment.

Only a few strong ethnic traditions had survived the Age of Religions, but the Chinese, Japanese, Maori, and Amazon-Kapayan were four that had retained some of their ancient ways. In Kitti's Pernese house, which was exquisitely furnished with heirlooms from her family, Paul knew better than to disrupt a hospitality ritual. Wind Blossom served the visitors fragrant tea in delicate porcelain cups. The little plantation of tea bushes, grown to sustain the lovely ceremony, had been a casualty in the First Fall. Paul was poignantly aware that the cup of tea he sipped might be the last he would ever taste.

"Has Mar Dook had a chance to inform you, Kitti Ping, that he had several tea bushes in reserve in the conservatory?" Paul asked when everyone had had time to savor the beverage.

Kitti Ping inclined her head in a deep bow of gratitude and

smiled. "It is a great reassurance."

Such a bland reply gave him no opening wedge. Paul moved restlessly, trying to find a comfortable position on the stool, and he knew that Pol and Bay were bursting to discuss the reason for the interview.

"All of us would be more reassured, Kit Ping Yung"—Abruptly he modulated his voice which sounded so much louder after her delicate response. —"If we had . . . some form of reliable assistance in combating this menace."

"Ah?" Her pencil-thin eyebrows rose, and then her tiny hands made a vague gesture about the armrests.

"Yes." Paul cleared his throat, annoyed at himself for being so gauche, and more annoyed that he could be so disconcerted by a trivial seating arrangement. She must know why he had arranged the private conference. "The truth is we are very badly positioned to defend ourselves against Thread. Bluntly, we will run out of resources in five years. We do not have the equipment to manufacture either sleds or power packs when what we brought are worn out. Kenjo's attempt to destroy Thread in space was only partially successful, and there isn't much fuel left for the *Mariposa*.

"As you know, none of the colony ships carried any defensive or destructive weaponry. Even if we could construct laser sweep beams, there isn't fuel enough to move even one ship into an effective position to annihilate the pods. Nevertheless the best way to protect the surface is to destroy this menace in the air.

"Boris and Dieter have confirmed our worst fears: Thread will sweep across Pern in a pattern that will denude the planet unless we can stop it. We cannot entertain much hope that Ezra Keroon's probe will bring us any useful information." Paul spread his hands with the hopelessness that threatened to overwhelm him.

Kitti raised her delicate eyebrows in unfeigned surprise. "The morning star is the source?"

Paul sighed heavily. "That is the current theory. We'll know more when the probe returns its survey."

Kitti Ping nodded thoughtfully, her willow-slender fingers tightening on the armrests.

"We are, Kit Ping Yung," Emily said, sitting even more erect on her stool, "in a desperate situation."

Paul Benden was heartened in an obscure way to see the governor as much like a nervous schoolchild as himself. Pol and Bay nodded encouragement. Kitti Ping and Wind Blossom, who stood slightly behind her grandmother's left side, waited patiently.

"If the dragonets were only larger, Kitti," Bay broke in, her manner unusually brusque, "intelligent enough to obey commands, they'd be an immense help to us. I was able to use mentasynth to enhance their own latent empathies, but that's a relatively simple matter. To breed large enough dragonets—dragons—we need them *big*—" Bay stretched her arms full length and flicked her fingers to indicate room size. "—intelligent, obedient, strong enough to do the job needed: flame Thread out of the sky." She ran out of words then, knowing very well how Kitti Ping Yung felt about bioengineering beyond simple adjustments to adapt creatures to new ecological parameters.

Kitti Ping nodded again while her granddaughter regarded her with surprise. "Yes, size, strength, and considerable intelligence would be required," she said in her softly audible voice. Hiding her hands in the cuffs of her long sleeves and folding them across her stomach, she bent her head and was silent for so long that her audience wondered if she had nodded off in the easy sleep of the aged. Then she spoke again. "And dedication, which is easy to instill in some creatures, impossible in others. The dragonets already possess the traits you wish to enhance and magnify." She smiled, a gentle, faintly apologetic smile of great sadness and compassion. "I was the merest student, though a very willing and eager one, in the Great Beltrae

Halls of Eridani. I was taught what would happen if I did this or that, enlarged or reduced, severed that synapse or modified this gene pattern. Most of the time what I was taught to do worked, but, alas," she added, raising one hand warningly, "I never knew why sometimes the modification failed and the organism died. Or should have. The Beltrae would teach us the how but never the why."

Paul sighed deeply, despair threatening to overwhelm him.

"But I can try," she said. "And I will. For though my years are nearly accomplished, there are others to be considered." She turned to smile gently upon Wind Blossom, who ducked her head with humility.

Paul shook his head, not quite believing what she had just said.

"You will?" Bay exclaimed, jumping to her feet. She stopped just short of rushing to Kitti's raised chair.

"Of course I will *try*!" Kitti raised one tiny hand in warning. "But I must caution you that success cannot be assumed. What we undertake is dangerous to the species, could be dangerous for us, and cannot be guaranteed. It is good fortune of the highest degree that the little dragonets already possess so many of the qualities required in the genetically altered animal that suits the urgent need. Even so, we may not be able to achieve the exact creature, or even be sure of a genetic progression. We have no sophisticated laboratory equipment, or methods of analysis which could lighten our burden. We must let repetition, the work of many hands and eyes, replace precision and delicacy. The task is appropriate, but the means are barbaric."

"But we have to try!" Paul Benden said, rising to his feet with clenched fists.

All medical staff not on duty in the infirmary or on ground crew duty, the veterinarians, and the apprentices, Sean and Sorka included, worked shifts as Kitti Ping's project was given top priority. Anyone with training in biology, chemistry, or laboratory procedures of any kind—sometimes even those with nimble fingers who could be put to work preparing slides, or those convalescing from Threadfall injuries who could watch monitors—were drafted into service. Kitti, Wind Blossom, Bay, and Pol extracted a genetic code from the chromosomes of the fire-dragonets. Although the creatures were not of Earth, their biology proved not too dissimilar to work with.

"We succeeded with the chiropteroids on Centauri," Pol said, "and they had chains of silicons as their genetic material."

A great deal of schedule-juggling was required in order to muster enough people to fight Fall over populated areas. The detailed sequence of Threadfall, established by the exhausted team of Boris Pahlevi and Dieter Clissmann, gave a structure to which even Kitti's project had to bow. The resultant four-shift roster attempted to provide everyone with some time for themselves—both to relax and to care for their own stakes—though some of the specialists ignored such considerations and had to be ordered to sleep.

Everyone over the age of twelve was brought in when Thread fell. The hope that Kenjo, in the *Mariposa,* could deflect Thread pods in the upper reaches of the atmosphere turned out to be ineffective. The predicted double Fall—over Cardiff in mid-Jordan and Bordeaux in Kahrain, and over Seminole and Ierne Island—was patchy, but the gaps perversely did not include occupied sites.

More double Falls could be anticipated: on the thirty-first day after First Fall, Thread would sweep across Karachi camp and the tip of the Kahrain peninsula; three days later a single land corridor would range from Kahrain across Paradise River Stake, while a second Fall would pass harmlessly at sea well above the tip of Cibola Province. After another three days, a dangerous double would hit Boca Stake and the thick forests of lower Kahrain and Araby, stocks of the one real wood vitally needed to shore up mine pits at busy Karachi Camp and Drake's Lake.

Ezra spent hours in the booth that housed the link with the *Yokohama*'s mainframe, scanning the naval and military histories to find some means of combating the menace. He also sought, with much less optimism, obscure equations or devices that might be able to alter the orbit of the planet. Then the next Fall could, perhaps, be avoided. Meanwhile, however, the present pass had seeded Pern's orbit with spirals of the encapsulated Thread, a danger that the colonists would have to face no matter what. He also did comparisons with data from Kitti's program, delving into science files, using his security ID to access secret or "need to know" information. He was waiting, too, for the probe's findings to be relayed back to him. And because everyone knew where to find Ezra, he often intercepted complaints and minor problems that would have added unnecessary burdens to the admiral and the governor.

Kenjo was sent on three more missions, each time trying to find a more efficient way of destroying enough Thread in space to justify the expenditure of precious fuel. The gauges on the *Mariposa* dropped only slightly with each trip, and Kenjo was commended on his economy. Drake was openly envious of the space pilot's skill.

"Jays, man," Drake would say. "You're driving it on the fumes!"

Kenjo would nod modestly and say nothing. He was, however, rather relieved that he had not managed to transfer all the fuel sacks to their hiding place at Honshu. All too soon, he would have to broach that supply to ensure continued trips into space. Only there did he feel totally aware and alive in every sense and nerve of his body.

But each time he brought back useful information. Thread, it turned out, traveled in a pod that burned away when it hit the atmosphere of Pern, leaving an inner capsule. About 15,000 feet above the surface, the inner capsule opened into ribbons, some of which were not thick enough to survive in the upper reaches. But, as everyone at Landing well knew, plenty fell to the surface.

Most of the sleds were unpressurized, so they had an effective ceiling of 10,000 feet. There was still only one way to clear the Thread from the skies: by flamethrowers.

With Thread due to fall on the Big Island Stake on Day 40, Paul Benden ordered Avril Bitra and Stev Kimmer to return to Landing. When Stev asked what Landing needed in the way of the ores mined at Big Island, Joel Lilienkamp was more than happy to supply a list. So when they arrived at Landing with four sleds crammed canopy-high with metal ingots, no one mentioned their long delinquency.

"I don't see Avril," Ongola commented as the sleds were being unloaded at the metals supply sheds.

Stev looked at him, slightly surprised. "She flew back weeks ago." He peered back at the landing grid and saw the sun glint off the *Mariposa*'s hull. "Hasn't she reported in?" Ongola shook his head slowly. "Well, now, fancy that!" Stev's gaze lingered thoughtfully on the *Mariposa* just long enough for Ongola to notice. "Maybe Thread got her!"

"Maybe her, but not the sled," Ongola replied, knowing that Avril Bitra was too adept at preserving her skin to be scored. "We'll keep an eye out for her."

Threadfall charts were displayed everywhere and constantly updated; previous Falls were deleted and future ones limited to the next three, so that people could plan a week ahead. Avril could not have stopped ten minutes in Landing without learning of the dangers of Thread. Ongola reminded himself that he must remove that guidance chip from the *Mariposa* as soon as Kenjo landed. He knew exactly how the space pilot had extended the fuel; he did not want anyone else, especially Avril Bitra, to discover how. Admiral Benden had been right about Kenjo. Ongola did not want to be right about Bitra!

"Where do you want me to work now I'm back, Ongola?" Stev asked with a wry grin.

"Find out where Fulmar Stone needs you most, Kimmer. Glad to see you in one piece."

Avril had stayed around Landing that night just long enough to know that she did not wish to be conscripted into any of the several teams who could use her special skills. The only skill she preferred to employ—space navigation—was thwarted. So, before dawn broke on Landing and before anyone noticed the existence of a spare sled, she lifted it again, loaded with useful supplies, both food and matériel.

She touched down on the rocky height above the ravaged Milan Stake, where she had a clear view of Landing and, more importantly, a good view of the busy, illuminated grid where the *Mariposa* would touch down. She spent the early morning hours using the metal sheets she had filched to arrange an umbrella over the sled's siliplex canopy. She preferred to take every precaution against the deadly airborne stuff. By midmorning she had camouflaged her eyrie and tuned the sled's scope on her objective. She was rewarded by a provocative view of Kenjo's return.

By listening carefully to all the channels available on the sled's comm unit, she managed to discover the facts of his mission and its limited success.

Over the next several days, she began to feel secure in her hideout. Because of the old volcanoes, most air traffic took corridors well to either side of her. During the morning the shadow of the biggest peak lurked over the retreat, like a broad digit pointing directly at her. It was enough to make her flesh creep. She had no real appreciation of views, although the fact that she could look up the Jordan to the bay, or down toward Bordeaux meant that she was unlikely to be surprised. She began to relax and wait. Considering the reward, she had trouble practicing patience.

"Have you *any* progress to report, Kitti?" Paul Benden asked the tiny geneticist.

He had never found that close surveillance improved performance, but he needed some morsel of encouragement to lighten the depression of his people. The psychologists reported a lowering of morale as the second month of Threadfall ground on. The initial enthusiasm and resolution was being eroded by fierce work schedules and few distractions. Landing's facilities, once generous, were crowded with technicians drafted into the laboratories and stakeholders' families returned to the dubious safety of the first settlement.

No one was idle. Mairi Hanrahan had made a game for the five- and six-year-olds with good motor control to assemble control panels by the colors of the chips. Even the most awkward ones could help gather fruits and vegetables from the undamaged lands, or compete with one another in collecting the unusual-colored seaweeds from the beaches after high tides or storms. The seven- and eight-year-olds were permitted to help fish with handlines under the watchful eyes of experienced fishermen. But even the youngest toddlers were beginning to react to mounting tensions.

There was considerable talk about allowing more holders to return to their stakes and fly out from their homes to meet Thread. But that would mean splitting up the supply depots and disarranging the work schedules of the more valuable technicians. Paul and Emily finally had to remain adamant on the centralization.

That night Kitti regarded Paul and Emily with a wise and compassionate smile. As she sat erect on the stool by the massive microbiological unit, its minute laser units pushed back from the manipulation chamber, she did not appear fatigued; only her bloodshot eyes showed the strain of her labors. A program was running with whispering clicks, flashing incomprehensible displays on its several monitors. Kitti paused briefly to regard a graph on one screen and a set of equations on another before she returned her gaze to the anxious men.

"There is no way, Admiral, to accelerate gestation, not if you wish a healthy, viable specimen. Not even the Beltrae managed to hasten that process. As I mentioned in my last reports, we pinpointed the cause of our original failures and made the necessary corrections. Time-consuming, I realize, but well worth the effort. The twenty-two bioengineered prototypes we now have are proceeding well into the first semester. We all"—her delicate hand made a graceful sweeping gesture that included all the technicians working in the huge laboratory block—"are immensely cheered by such a high rate of success." She turned her head slightly to watch the flicker of a reading. "We constantly monitor the specimens. They show the same responses as the little tunnel snakes whose development we understand well. Let us earnestly hope that all proceeds without incident. We have been infinitely fortunate so far. Patience is required of you now."

"Patience," Paul echoed ruefully. "Patience is in very short supply."

Kitti raised her hands in a gesture of impotence. "Day by day, the embryos grow. Wind Blossom and Bay continue to refine the program. In two days we shall start a second group. We shall continue to refine the manipulations. Always seeking to improve. We do not stand still. We move forward.

"Our task is great and full of responsibility. One does not irresponsibly change the nature and purpose of any creature. As it was said, the person of intellect is careful in the differentiation of things, so that each finds its place. Before completion, deliberation and caution are the prerequisites of success."

Kitti then smiled a courtly dismissal of the two leaders and turned her complete attention to the rapidly shifting monitors. Paul and Emily executed equally courteous bows to her slender back and left the room.

"Well," Paul began, shrugging off his frustration, "that's that."

"What city wasn't built in a day, Paul?" Emily asked whimsically.

"Rome." Paul grinned at Emily's astonishment at his prompt reply. "Old Earth, first century, I think. Good land fighters and road builders."

"Militarists."

"Yes," Paul said. "Hmm . . . They also had a way of keeping people content. They called it circus. I wonder . . ."

On the forty-second day after First Fall, with Thread crossing uninhabited parts of Araby and Cathay and falling harmlessly in the Northern Sea above Delta, missing Dorado's western prong, Admiral Benden and Governor Boll decreed a day of rest and leisure for all. Governor Boll asked department heads to schedule work loads to allow everyone to participate in the afternoon feast and evening dancing. Even the most distant stakeholders were invited to come for whatever time they could spare. Admiral Boll asked for two squadrons of volunteers to fly Thread at 0930 over the eastern corridor, and another two to be ready in the early evening to check the western one.

The platform on Bonfire Square was gay with multicolored bunting, and a new planetary flag was hoisted on the pole to flap in the breeze. Tables, benches, and chairs were placed around the square, leaving its center clear for dancers. Vats of quickal were to be broached, and Hegelman would produce ale—no one wished to think that it might be the last made for a long while. Joel Lilienkamp released generous supplies without grudge. "Thank the kids that gathered them! Child labor can be efficient," he said with a grin. The Monaco Bay fishermen brought in shining loads of fish and the more succulent seaweeds to be baked in the big, long-unused pits; twenty farm stakes donated as many steers to turn on spits; Pierre de Courci had worked all the previous night, baking cakes and making extravagant sweets. "Better to fatten humans than Thread!" He was always happiest when overseeing a large effort.

"It's good to hear music and singing and laughter," Paul murmured to Ongola as they wandered from one group to another.

"I think it would be a good custom to establish," Ongola replied. "Something to look forward to. Reunites old friends, improves bonds, gives everyone a chance to air and compare." He nodded to the group that included his wife, Sabra, Sallah Telgar-Andiyar, and Barr Hamil-Jessup, chatting and laughing together, each with a sleepy child on her lap. "We need to gather more often."

Paul nodded, then glanced at his wrist chrono and, swearing softly under his breath, went off to lead the volunteers against the western Fall.

Ongola was not feeling exactly top of the mark the next morning when he arrived for his watch at the met tower. In fact, he had called in first at the infirmary, where the pharmacist had given him a hangover tablet and assured him that he was one of many. But her comment about disturbing casualties during that Threadfall had only made his headache worse.

The report that awaited him at the met tower was a shock and a surprise. One sled had been totaled and its crew of three killed; a second sled had been badly crumpled, the starboard gunner killed, and pilot and port gunner badly injured in the midair head-on collision. Someone had not been obeying the altitude restrictions. Ongola groaned involuntarily as he read the casualty list: Becky Nielson, mining apprentice just back from Big Island—she had been safer after all with Avril; Bart Nilwan, a very promising young mechanic; and Ben Jepson. Ongola rubbed his eyes to clear the blur. Bob Jepson was the other dead pilot. Two in the same family. Those twins! Farting around in break-ass fashion instead of following orders! Stinkin' air! What could he say to their parents? A minor Fall with a party to come back to, and they died!

Ongola put his hand on the comm unit, about to dial administration. Then he heard someone tapping hesitantly at the door.

"Come!" he called.

Catherine Radelin-Doyle stood there, her eyes round, her face pale.

"Yes, Cathy?"

"Sir, Mr. Ongola . . ."

"Either will do." He mustered an encouraging smile. Considering the amount of trouble Cathy could get into, from stumbling into caves at an early age, to marrying the most feckless joat on the planet, he wondered at her shy demeanor. She was, poor child, just one of those people to whom events tended to occur with no connivance from themselves at all.

"Sir, I've found a cave."

"Yes?" he encouraged when she hesitated. She was constantly finding caves.

"It wasn't empty."

Ongola sat up straight. "It had a lot of fuel sacks in it?" he asked. If Catherine had found it, would Avril? No, Avril did not have the same sort of luck Catherine had.

"However did you know, Mr. Ongola?" She looked faint with relief.

"Possibly because I know they're there."

"You do? They are? I mean, they weren't put there by 'them'?"

"No, by us." He wanted to make as little fuss about Kenjo's

hoard as possible. He had been counting the dwindling numbers and wondering why Kenjo seemed so complacent after each trip. Ongola flicked a glance at the corner of the shadowed shelving where the guidance chips were hidden in their dark-foam case.

Catherine suddenly sank to the nearest chair. "Oh, sir, you don't know what a fright it gave me. Thinking that someone else was here, because everyone *knows* there's so little fuel left. And then to see . . ."

"But you saw nothing, Catherine," Ongola told her crisply. "Nothing whatever. There's no cave worth noticing down that particular crevasse and you won't say a thing about it to anyone else. I will personally tell the admiral. But you will tell no one."

"Oh no, sir."

"This information cannot—I repeat, can*not*—be divulged to any other person."

"That's right, Mr. Ongola." She nodded solemnly several times. Then she smiled winsomely. "Shall I keep on looking?"

"Yes, I think you'd better. And find something!"

"Oh, but I have, Mr. Ongola, and Joel Lilienkamp says they're going to be excellent storage space." Her face clouded briefly. "But he didn't say for what."

"Go, Cathy, and find something . . . else."

She left, and Ongola had barely returned to brooding over the first serious losses to their defense when Tarvi came storming up the stairs.

"It's been staring us in the face, Zi," he said, swinging his arms in one of his expansive gestures. His face was alight with enthusiasm, although his skin looked a bit gray from the excesses of the night before.

"What?" Ongola was in no mood for puzzles.

"Them! There!" Tarvi gestured extravagantly out the northern windows. "All the time."

It was probably the headache, Ongola thought, but he had no idea what Tarvi was talking about.

"What do you mean?"

"All this time we have been slavering away at mining ore, refining, molding it, adding weeks to our labors, when all the time we've had what we need in front of us."

"No puzzles, Tarvi."

Tarvi's expressive eyes widened in surprise and consternation. "I give you no puzzles, Zi, my friend, but the source of much valuable metals and materials. The shuttles, Zi, the shuttles can be dismantled and their components used for our specific purposes here and now. Theirs is done. Why let them slowly decay on the meadow?" Tarvi emphasized each new sentence with a flick of long fingers out the window and then, exasperated with Ongola's incomprehension, he hauled the man to his feet and pointed a very long, slightly dirty forefinger directly at the tail fins of the old shuttles. "There. We'll use them. Hundreds of relays, miles of the proper flex and tubing, six small mountains of recyclable material. Have you any idea of how much is in them?" In an instant, all the exuberance drained from the volatile geologist. He put both hands on Ongola's shoulders. "We can replace the sled we lost today even if we cannot replace those marvelous young lives or comfort their stricken families. The parts make a new whole."

Work dulled the edge of the sorrow that hung over Landing at the loss of four young people. The two survivors reluctantly admitted that the Jepson twins, toward the end of that Fall, had indulged in some fatal foolery. Ben's sled had been scheduled for servicing after the Fall because its previous pilot had reported a sluggish reaction on port side turns. The sled had been considered safe enough for what should have been a monitoring flight.

Rather than prevent other such collisions, the next few Falls saw a rash of them even as Tarvi's crew began to strip the first shuttle and Fulmar's teams began to service and replace from the bonanza of salvage.

The longest hours were still put in at Kitti Ping's laboratory, monitoring the development of the specimens for any signs of aberration from the program.

"Patience," was Kitti's response to all queries. "All proceeds vigorously."

Three days after the midair collision, Wind Blossom discovered her grandmother still at the electronic microscope, apparently peering at yet another slide. But when Wind Blossom touched Kitti's arm, the movement produced an unexpected result. The dainty fingers slipped from their relaxed position on the keyboard, and the body slumped forward, only kept upright by the brace that held her to the stool for her long sessions at the microscope. Wind Blossom let out a moan and dropped to her knees, holding one tiny cold hand to her forehead.

Bay heard her disconsolate weeping and came to see what had happened. Instantly she called to Pol and Kwan, then phoned for a doctor. Once Wind Blossom had followed the gurney carrying her grandmother's body out of the room, Bay straightened her plump shoulders and stood at the console. She asked the computer if it had finished its program.

PROGRAM COMPLETED flashed on the screen—almost indignantly, Bay thought in the portion of her mind that was not sorrowing. She tapped out an information query. The screen displayed a dazzling series of computations and ended with REMOVE UNIT! DANGER IF UNIT IS NOT IMMEDIATELY REMOVED!

Astonished, Bay recognized the paraphernalia on the workspace beside the electronic microscope. Kitti Ping had been manipulating gene patterns again, a complicated process that Bay found as daunting as Wind Blossom did, despite Kitti Ping's encouragements. So Kitti had made those infinitesimal alterations in the chromosomes. Bay felt the chill of a terrible apprehension sweep through her plump body. She pressed her lips together. That moment was not the time to panic. They must not lose what Kitti Ping had been making of the raw material of Pern.

With hands that were not quite steady, she unlocked the

microcylinder, removed the tiny gel-encapsulated unit, and placed it in the culture dish that Kitti had readied. An agony as severe as a knife stab almost doubled Bay up, but she fought the grief and the knowledge that Kit Ping Yung had died to produce that altered egg cell. The label was even prepared: *Trial 2684/16/M: nucleus #22A, mentasynth Generation B2, boron/silicon system 4, size 2H; 16.204.8.*

Walking as fast as her shaky legs would permit and gradually recovering her composure, Bay took the final legacy of the brilliant technician to the gestation chamber and put it carefully beside the forty-one similar units that held the hopes of Pern.

"*That* was the second probe to malfunction," Ezra told Paul and Emily, his quiet voice ragged with disappointment. "When the first one blew up, or whatever, I thought it a mischance. Even vacuum isn't perfect insulation against decay. Probe motors could misfire, their recording device clog somehow or other. So I refined the program for the second one. It got exactly as far as the first one, and then every light went red. Either that atmosphere is so corrosive even our probe enamels melt, or the garage on the *Yokohama* has somehow been damaged, and the probes, too. I dunno, guys."

Ezra was not much given to agitated gestures but he paced up and down Paul's office, strutting and waving his arms about him like a scarecrow in a high wind. The last few days had wearied and aged him. Paul and Emily exchanged concerned glances. Kitti Ping's death had been such a shock, following so closely on the sled collision disaster. The geneticist had seemed so indestructible, despite the fact that everyone knew of her physical frailty. She had exuded a quality of immortality, however false that had proved.

"Whose theory was it that we were being bombarded from outer space to reduce us to submission?" Ezra asked, stopping suddenly in his tracks and staring at the two leaders.

"Ah, c'mon now, Ezra!" Paul was bluntly derisive. "Think a

minute, man. We're all under a strain, but not one that makes us lose our wits. We all know that there are atmospheres that can and have melted probes. Furthermore—" He halted, not certain what would suffice to reassure Ezra, and himself.

"Furthermore, the organism attacking us," Emily went on with superb composure, "is hydrocarbon based, and if it comes from that planet, its atmosphere is not corrosive. I favor malfunction."

"My opinion, too," Paul said, nodding his head vigorously. "Fardles, Ezra, let's not talk ourselves into more problems than we've got."

"We've *got*"—Ezra brought both fists down on the desk—"to probe that planet, or we won't know enough to combat the stuff. Half the settlers want to know the source and destroy it so we can get back to our lives. Rake up the debris and forget all this."

"What aren't you telling us, Ezra?" Emily asked, cocking her head slightly and regarding the captain with an unflinching gaze.

Ezra stared back at her for a very long moment, then straightened from his half crouch over the desk and began to smile wryly.

"You've been sitting in the interface booth long hours, Ezra, and you weren't playing tiddlywinks while the programs were running," Emily went on.

"My calculations are frightening," he said in a low voice, glancing over each shoulder. "If the program is in any way accurate, and I've run it five times now from start to finish, we have to put up with Thread for long after that red planet crosses out of the inner system."

"How long will that be?" Paul felt his fingers gripping the arm rests and made a conscious effort to relax them while he tried to recall some reassuring facet of planetary orbits.

"I get between forty and fifty years!"

Emily grimaced, her mouth forming an O of surprise before she slowly exhaled. "Forty or fifty years, you say."

"If," Ezra added grimly, "the menace originated from that planet."

Paul caught his eyes and saw the ineffably weary and discouraged look in them. "If? There is another alternative?"

"I have discerned a haze about the planet, irrespective of its atmospheric envelope. A haze that spreads backward in this system and swirls along the eccentric's path. I cannot refine that telescope enough to tell more. It could be space debris, a nebulosity, the remnants of a cometary tail, a whole bunch of things that are harmless."

"But if it should be harmful?" Emily asked.

"That tail would take nearly fifty years to diffuse out of Pern's orbit, some into Rukbat—the rest, who knows?"

There was a long moment of silence.

"Any suggestions?" Paul asked finally.

"Yes," Ezra said, straightening his shoulders with a wrench. He held up two fingers. "Take a trip to the *Yokohama*, find out what's bugging the probes, and send two of 'em down to the planet to gather as much information as we can. Send the other two along the line of that cometary dust and use the *Yoko*'s more powerful space scope with no planetary interference to see if we can identify its source and components." Ezra then locked his fingers together and cracked his knuckles, a habit that always made Emily shudder. "Sorry, Em."

"At least you can recommend some positive action," Paul went on.

"The big question is, Paul, is there enough fuel to get someone to the *Yoko* and back? Kenjo's already made more trips than I thought possible."

"Good pilot," Paul said discreetly. "There's enough for what we need now. Kenjo will pilot, and did you wish to go with him?"

Ezra shook his head slowly. "Avril Bitra has the training for the job."

"Avril?" Paul gave a harsh bark and then shook his head,

grinning sourly. "Avril's the last person I'd put on the *Mariposa* for any reason. Even if we knew where she is."

"Really?" Ezra looked at Emily for an explanation, but she shrugged. "Well, then, Kenjo can double. No," he corrected himself. "If something's wrong with the probes, we'd need a good technician. Stev Kimmer. He's back, isn't he?"

"Who else?" Paul jotted down names rather than worry Ezra with more suspicions.

"Kenjo is a very capable technician," Emily insisted.

"There should be two on the mission, for safety's sake," Ezra said, furrowing his brow. "This mission has got to give us the results we need."

"Zi Ongola," Paul suggested.

"Yes, the very one," Ezra agreed. "If he runs into any trouble, I can have Stev at the interface for expert advice."

"Forty years, huh?" Emily said, watching Paul underline the two final choices on the pad. "Rather longer than we'd bargained for, my friend. Let's start training replacements."

Inevitably their thoughts went to Wind Blossom, so obviously a frail vessel to continue the work her grandmother had begun.

Avril's suspicious nature was aroused not by anything she heard, although what she did not hear was as significant, but by what she saw in the weary hours she manned the sled's scope. It was usually trained on the *Mariposa,* sitting at the far end of the landing grid. The night before every one of Kenjo's jaunts he had done exterior and internal checks of the craft. Fussy Fusi! Her use of the nickname was not quite derisive, because she simply could not figure out how he had managed to stretch the small reserve of fuel on the *Mariposa* as far as he already had. She had seen some activity about it last night but no sign of Kenjo. In fact, with neither moon out, she had just barely seen the shifting of shadow that indicated activity about the craft. She had been quite agitated. The only thing that reassured her was that several figures were involved. But no one entered the gig. That perplexed her.

At first light, so early that no one was yet working the donks at the skeleton of the shuttle that had been the center of considerable activity all week, she was surprised to see Fulmar Stone and Zi Ongola approaching the vessel. Her apprehension, honed by weeks of waiting, spurred her to remove the protective cover from her sled in preparation for a quick departure. At full speed, she could reach the landing grid in less than fifteen minutes. Early morning traffic into Landing would be sufficient to give her cover.

She had a moment's anxiety thinking that perhaps the *Mariposa* had developed a problem and they were scavenging replacement parts from the shuttle. Kenjo had flown a mission three days before with his usual economical takeoff and landing. She had to hand it to him—he was gliding in smoothly with no power at all. Only where was he getting the fuel to lift?

The three men, moving with almost stealthy speed, slipped inside the little spaceship and closed the airlock. Well, the access to the engines was through exterior panels, so she began to relax. They remained inside the ship for three hours, long enough for a full interior systems check. But that did not presage a usual flight. Maybe the *Mariposa* was bollixed. Scorch Kenjo for ineptitude. The *Mariposa* had to be spaceworthy. Avril swore.

Or had something happened to Kenjo so that Ongola was taking the ship up? But how? There could not be much fuel left. So why were they checking internal systems? Why were they making yet another jaunt? Displeased, Avril finished her preparations to fly.

Sallah Telgar-Andiyar was feeding her daughter her breakfast in the shady covered porch of Mairi Hanrahan's Asian Square house when she caught sight of a familiar figure striding down the path. It was covered by loose overalls, and a peaked cap was pulled well down over the face, but the walk was undeniably Avril's, especially from the rear. Never mind the greasy hands, the exhaust pipe carried so ostentatiously in one hand, the clipboard in the other. That was Avril, who only sullied her hands for a good cause. No one had seen her since she had left Big Island. Sallah continued to watch until Avril mingled in with the crowd at the main depot, where technicians jostled one another for parts and matériel.

Ever since Sallah had overheard Avril's conversation with Kimmer, she had known the woman would attempt to leave Pern. Did Avril know of Kenjo's fuel dump? Irritably Sallah shook her head. Cara blinked her huge brown eyes and stared apprehensively at her mother.

"Sorry, love, your mother's mind is klicks away." Sallah gathered more puree on the spoon and deposited it into Cara's obediently open mouth. No, Sallah told herself fiercely, because she wanted to believe it so badly, Avril could not have discovered that fuel: she had been too busy mining gemstones on Big Island. At least, up until three weeks before. And where has Avril been since then? Sallah asked herself. Watching while Kenjo flew the *Mariposa*? That would certainly set Avril Bitra to thinking hard.

Well, Sallah was due on her shift soon anyway, and as luck would have it, the sled she was servicing was on the grid. She would have a clear view of the *Mariposa* and those who approached it. If Avril came anywhere near, Sallah would set up an alarm.

There had been no talk of Kenjo making another attempt to clear Thread in the atmosphere. Then, too, Kenjo's flights were usually plotted for the dawn window, and Sallah's shift began well past that time.

It all happened rather quickly. Sallah was walking toward the sled she was servicing as Ongola and Kenjo, suited for space travel, left the tower with Ezra Keroon, Dieter Clissmann, and two other overalled figures whom Sallah was astonished to recognize by their postures as Paul and Emily. Ongola and Kenjo had the appearance of men listening to last-minute instructions. Then they continued on, almost at a stroll, toward the *Mariposa,* while the others turned back into the met tower. Suddenly another suited figure began to walk across the grid on a path that would intercept Ongola and Kenjo. Even in the baggy space gear the figure walked as only Avril did!

Sallah grabbed the nearest big spanner and started at a jog-trot across the grid. Ongola and Kenjo disappeared behind the pile of discarded sled parts at the edge of the field. Avril had begun to run, and Sallah increased her own pace. She lost sight of Ongola and Kenjo. Then she saw Arvil pick up a short strut from the pile and disappear out of sight.

Rounding the pile, Sallah saw both Kenjo and Ongola flat on the ground. Blood covered the back of Kenjo's head and Ongola's shoulder and neck. Sallah ran flat out, ducking down to keep scrap heaps between her and the *Mariposa.* As it was, she just made it as the airlock was closing. She threw herself inside and felt something scrape her left foot; there was an immense hissing, and then she blacked out.

Mairi Hanrahan thought it odd that Sallah had not rung at lunchtime to tell her she was delayed. With so many small ones to feed, every mother tried to be there at mealtimes. Mairi got one of her older children to feed Cara instead, thinking that something very important must have demanded Sallah's attention.

None of the people at the met tower or admin building expected any contact from Ongola or Kenjo while the shuttle was moving through the ionized atmosphere. Ezra, seated at the desk of the voice-activated interface, could follow its course via the activated monitor screens on board the *Yokohama*. The *Mariposa* was closing fast and soon reached the docking port. "Safely there," Ezra announced when he rang through to both tower and administration.

Half an hour later, children playing at the edge of the grid came screaming back to their teacher about the dead men. Actually, Ongola was still barely alive. Paul met the medic team at the infirmary.

"He'll live, but he's lost more blood than I like," the doctor told the admiral. "What 'n hell happened to him and Kenjo?"

"How was Kenjo killed?" Paul asked.

"The old blunt instrument. The paras found a bloodied strut nearby. Probably that. Kenjo never knew what hit him."

Paul was not sure he did either, for his legs suddenly would not support him. The doctor beckoned fiercely for one of the paras to help the admiral to a seat and poured a glass of quikal.

Paul tried to dismiss the eager hands. The implications of

the two deaths greatly disturbed him. There was no antidote for Kenjo's loss, though the wretched quikal eased the intense shock that had rocked him. In the back of his mind, as he knocked back the drink, he wondered where Kenjo had cached the rest of the fuel. Why, Paul seethed at himself, had he not asked the man before? He could have done so any time before or after the last few flights Kenjo had taken in the *Mariposa.* As admiral, he knew exactly how much fuel had been left in the gig on its last drop. Now it was too late! Unless Ongola knew. He had mentioned to Paul that there was not much left at the original site, but that Kenjo had been supplying the *Mariposa.* The figures Sallah had initially reported to Ongola indicated a lot more fuel than Paul had seen in that cave the other night. Well, the misappropriation—yes, that was the right term—had had a final appropriate usage. Maybe Kenjo's wife knew where he had stored the remainder.

Paul consoled himself with that thought. Kenjo's wife would certaintly know if there were more fuel sacks at the Honshu stake. He forced himself to deal with present issues: a man had been murdered and another lay close to death on a planet that had, until that moment, witnessed no capital crime.

"Ongola will survive," the doctor was saying, pouring Paul a second shot. "He's got a splendid constitution, and we'll work any miracle required. We could probably have saved Kenjo if we'd got there earlier. Brain-dead. Drink this—your color's lousy."

Paul finished the quikal and put the glass down with a decisive movement. He took a deep breath and rose to his feet. "I'm fine, thanks. Get on with saving Ongola. We'll need to know what happened when he recovers consciousness. Keep the rumors down, people!" he added, addressing the others in the room.

He strode out of the emergency facility and turned immediately for the building that housed the interface chamber and Ezra. As he walked, he reviewed the puzzle that rattled his orderly mind. He had seen the *Mariposa* take off. Who had flown her? He stopped off to collect Emily from her office, briefing her on the calamity. Ezra was surprised by the arrival of both admiral and governor; the *Mariposa*'s current flight was being treated as routine.

"Kenjo's dead and Ongola seriously injured, Ezra," Paul said as soon as he had closed and locked the door behind them. "So, who's flying the *Mariposa*?"

"Gods in the heavens!" Ezra leapt to his feet and pointed to the monitor, which clearly showed the safely docked *Mariposa*. "The flight was precalculated to hit the right window, but the docking process was left to the pilot. It was very smoothly done. Not everyone can do that."

"I'll run a check on the whereabouts of pilots, Paul," Emily said, picking up a handset.

Paul glared at the monitor. "I don't think we need to do that. Call—" Paul had started to say "Ongola" and rubbed his hand across his face. "Who's at the met tower?"

"Jake Chernoff and Dieter Clissmann," Emily reported.

"Then ask Jake if there's any unmodified sleds on the grid. Find out exactly where Stev Kimmer, Nabol Nahbi, and Bart Lemos are. And—" Paul held up a warning hand. "—if anyone's seen Avril Bitra anywhere."

"Avril?" Ezra echoed, and then clamped his mouth firmly shut.

Suddenly Paul swore in a torrent of abusive language that made even Ezra regard him with amazement, and slammed out of the room. Emily concentrated on finding the pilots and had completed her check before Paul returned. He leaned back against the closed door, catching his breath.

"Stev, Nabhi, and Lemos are accounted for. Where did you go?" Emily asked.

"To check Ongola's space suit. Doc says he'll recover from his injuries. The strut just missed severing the shoulder muscle and leaving him a cripple. But—" Paul held up a crystal packet between forefinger and thumb. "No one is going to get very far in the *Mariposa*." He nodded grimly as Ezra realized what the admiral was holding. "One of the more essential parts of the guidance system! Ongola had not yet put it in place."

"Then how did—Avril?" Emily asked, pausing for confirmation. Paul nodded slowly. "Yes, it has to be Avril, doesn't it? But why would she want to get to the *Yoko*?"

"First step to leaving the system, Emily. We've been stupidly lax. Yes, I know we have this," he acknowledged when Emily pointed to the chip panel. "But we shouldn't have allowed her to get that far in the first place. And we all knew what she was like. Sallah warned us, and the years . . ."

"And recent unusual events," Ezra put in, mildly hinting that Paul need not excoriate himself.

"We should have guarded the *Mariposa* as long as she'd an ounce of fuel in her."

"We also ought to have had the sense to ask Kenjo where he was getting all the fuel," Ezra added.

"We knew that," Emily said with a wry grin.

"You did?" Ezra was amazed.

"At least Ongola took no chances," Paul went on, wincing as he remembered the sight of the man's battered shoulder and neck. "This—" He put the guidance chip very carefully down on the shelf above the worktop. "—was Ongola's special precaution, done with Kenjo's complete concurrence."

Emily sat down heavily in the nearest chair. "So where does that leave us now?"

"The next move would appear to be Avril's." Ezra shook his head sadly. "She's got more than enough fuel to get back down."

"That is not her intention," Paul said.

"Unfortunately," Emily said, "she has a hostage, whether she knows it or not. Sallah Telgar-Andiyar is also missing."

Sallah returned to consciousness aware of severe discomfort and a throbbing pain in her left foot. She was bound tightly and efficiently in an uncomfortable position, her hands behind her back and secured to her tied feet. She was floating with her side just brushing the floor of the spacecraft; the lack of gravity told her that she was no longer on Pern. There was a rhythmic but unpleasant background noise, along with the sounds of things clattering and slipping about.

Then she recognized the monotonous and vicious sounds to be the curses of Avril Bitra.

"What in hell did you *do* to the guidance systems, Telgar?" she asked, kicking at the bound woman's ribs.

The kick lifted Sallah off the floor, and she found herself floating within inches of the face of an enraged Avril Bitra. Probably the only reason Sallah was still breathing was because the cabin of the *Mariposa* had its own oxygen supply. Kenjo would have charged the tanks up to full, wouldn't he? Sallah asked herself in a moment of panic as she continued to float beyond Avril. The other woman was suited; the helmet sat on the rack above the pilot's seat, ready for use.

Avril reached up and grabbed Sallah's arm. "What do you know about this? Tell me and be quick about it, or I'll evacuate you and save the air for me to breathe!"

Sallah had no doubt that the woman was capable of doing just that. "I know nothing about anything, Avril. I saw you stalking Ongola and Kenjo and knew you were up to something. So I followed you and got in the airlock just as you took off."

"You followed me?" Avril lashed out with a fist. The impact caused both women to bounce apart. Avril steadied herself on a handhold. "How dare you?"

"Well, as I hadn't seen you in months and longed to know how you were faring, it seemed a good idea at the time." Hang for the fleece, hang for the sheep, Sallah thought. She could not shrug her shoulders. What had she done to her foot? It was an aching mess.

"Bloody hell. You've flown this frigging crate. How do I override the preflight instructions? You must know that."

"I might if you'd let me see the console." She saw hope, and then manic doubt, in Avril's eyes. Sallah was not lying. "How could I possibly tell from over here? I don't know where we are. I've been just another Thread sledder." Even to a woman slightly paranoid, the truth would be obvious. Sallah warned herself to be very careful. "Just let me look."

She did not ask to be untied although that was what she desperately wanted—needed. Her right shoulder must have been bruised by her fall into the cabin, and all the muscles were spasming.

"Don't think I'll untie you," Avril warned, and contemptuously she pushed Sallah across the cabin. Grabbing a handhold, she corrected Sallah's spin to a painful halt against the command console. "Look!"

Sallah did, though hanging slightly upside down was not the best position for the job. She had to think carefully, for Avril had piloted shuttles and knew something of their systems. But the *Mariposa,* though small, was designed to traverse interplanetary distances, dock with a variety of stations or other craft, and had the sophisticated controls to perform a considerable variety of maneuvers in space and on a planetary surface. Sallah dared to hope that much of its instrumentation would be unfamiliar to Avril.

"To find out what this ship just did," she instructed, "hit the return button on the bottom tier of the greens. No, the port side."

Avril jerked at Sallah, tweaking strained arm and back muscles and jamming Sallah's head against the viewscope. Sallah's long hair was freed completely from its pins and flowed over her face.

"Don't get cute!" Avril snapped, her finger hovering on the appropriate button. "This one?"

Sallah nodded, floating away again. Avril punched the button with one hand and hauled her back into position with the other. Then she caught the handhold to keep herself in place.

Every action has a reaction, Sallah thought, trying to clear her head of pain and confusion.

The monitor came up with a preflight instruction plan.

"The *Mariposa* was programmed to dock here on the *Yoko*." It was nice to know where she was, Sallah reflected. "Once you hit the power, you couldn't alter its course."

"Well," Avril said, her tone altering considerably. "I wanted to come here first anyhow. I just wanted to come on my own." Sallah, hair falling over her face, felt a lessening of the tension that emanated from the woman. Some of the beauty returned to a face no longer contorted with frustration. "I don't need you hanging about, then." Avril reached up and gave Sallah's body a calculated shove that sent her to the opposite end of the cabin, to bump harmlessly against the other wall and then hover there. "Well, I'll just get to work."

How long Sallah was suspended in that fashion she did not know. She managed to tilt her head and get her hair to float away from her eyes, but she did not dare to move much—action produced reaction, and she did not wish to draw attention to herself. She ached all over, but the pain in her foot was almost unbearable.

A tirade of malevolent and resentful oaths spun from Avril's lips. "None of the programs run, of all the frigging luck. Nothing runs!"

Sallah had just enough time to duck her head to avoid Avril's projectile arrival against her. As it was, she went head over heels in a spin that Avril, laughing gleefully, assisted until the rotation made Sallah retch.

"You bitch woman!" Avril stopped Sallah before she could expel more vomit into the air. "Okay! If that's the way of it, you know what I need to know. And you're going to tell me, or I'll kill you by inches." A spaceman's knife, with its many handle-packed implements, sliced across the top of Sallah's nose.

Then she felt the blade none too gently cutting the bindings on her hands and feet. Blood rushed through starved arteries, and her strained muscles reacted painfully. If she had not been in free-fall, she would have collapsed. As it was, the agony of release made her sob and shake.

"Clean up your spew first," Avril said, shoving a slop jar at her.

Sallah did as she was told, grateful for the lack of gravity, grateful for the release, and wondering what she could do to gain an upper hand. But she had little opportunity to enjoy her freedom, for Avril had other ways of securing her prisoner's cooperation.

Before Sallah realized what was happening, Avril had secured a tether to the injured foot and tweaked the line. Pain, piercing like a shard of glass, shot through Sallah's leg and up to her groin. There was too little left in her stomach to throw up. Avril jerked Sallah over to the console, pushed her into the pilot's chair, and tied her down, twiching her improvised lead line to remind Sallah of her helplessness.

"Now, check the fuel on board, check the quantity in the *Yoko*'s tanks—I've done that, I know the answers, so don't try anything clever." A jerk against Sallah's injured foot reinforced the threat. "Then enter a program that gets me out of this wretched asshole of a midden system."

Sallah did as she was told, though her head ached and her eyes blurred repeatedly. She could not suppress her surprise at the amount of fuel in the *Mariposa*'s tanks.

"Yes, someone was holding back on it. You?" There was a jerk on the line.

"Kenjo, I suspect," Sallah replied coolly, managing to suppress a cry. She was determined not to give Avril any satisfaction.

"Fussy Fusi? Yes, that computes. I thought he'd given up all too tamely! Where did he hide it?" The line tightened. Sallah had to bite hard on her lip against a sob.

"Probably at his stake. It's back of beyond. No one goes there. He could hide anything there."

Avril snorted and remained silent. Sallah made herself breathe deeply, forcing more adrenaline into her system to combat pain, fatigue, and fear.

"All right, compute me a course to . . ." Avril consulted a notebook. "Here."

Only because Sallah already knew the coordinates did she recognize the numbers. Avril wished to go to the system nearest them, a system that, though uninhabited, was closer to the populated sectors of space. The course would stretch the *Mariposa* to the end of available fuel, even if Avril also drained the *Yoko*'s tanks. It gave Sallah no consolation to think that the little ship might drift for centuries with Avril safe and composed in deep sleep. Unless, just maybe, Ongola had tampered with the sleep tanks, too. She liked that idea. But she knew Ongola too well to presume that kind of foresight.

Unfortunately, the Avrils of the galaxy could make themselves at home in any time and culture. So if Avril went into deep sleep, eventually someone, or something, would rescue her and the *Mariposa*. Sallah did not need to see them to know that Avril had several fortunes' worth of gemstones and precious metals aboard the *Mariposa*. There had never been any doubt in anyone's mind why Avril had chosen Big Island as her stake, but no one had cared. But then, no one would have imagined that she would be mad enough to attempt to leave Pern, even with Threadfall threatening the planet.

Wondering why Avril, who was an astrogator, after all, had not been able to complete laying in such a simple course, Sallah did as she was ordered. She had more experience than Avril did with the *Mariposa*'s drive board. But the program was not accepted. ERROR 259 AT LINE 57465534511 was the message.

Avril jerked hard on the line, and Sallah hissed against the burning, crippling pain in her foot.

"Try again. There's more than one way of entering a course."

Sallah obeyed. "I'll have to go around the existing parameters."

"Reset the entire effing thing but plot that course," Avril told her.

As Sallah began the more laborious deviation into the command center of the gig's course computer, she was aware that Avril had picked up a long narrow cylinder from the rack by her helmet. She fiddled with it, humming tunelessly under her breath, seemingly thoroughly delighted with herself.

When Sallah finally tapped the "return" tab, she became aware of Avril's intense interest in the flickering console. She chanced a look at what the woman had been fondling. It was a homemade capsule. Not a homer—they were thicker and longer—but something more like the standard beacon. Suddenly she clearly saw Avril's plan.

Avril would take the *Mariposa* as far away from the Rukbat system as possible and then direct the distress beacon toward shipping lanes. Every planetary system involved with the Federated Sentient Planets, and some life-forms who were not, traced distress beacons to origin. The devices, automatically released when a ship was destroyed, were often traced by those who wished to turn whatever profit they could on the flotsam.

Avril's plan was not as insane as it seemed. Sallah felt certain that Stev Kimmer had intended to take the trip with her, to be rescued by the distress beacon he had made for her.

Words flashed on the screen. NO ACCESS WITHOUT STANDARD FCP/120/GM.

"Fuck it! That's all I could get out of it. Try again, Telgar." Avril pressed Sallah's foot against the base of the console module, increasing the pain to the point where Sallah felt herself losing consciousness. Avril viciously pinched her left breast. "You don't pass out on me, Telgar!"

"Look," Sallah said, her voice rather more shaken than she liked, "I've tried twice, you've tried. I've tried the fail-safe I was taught. Someone anticipated you, Bitra. Open up this panel and I'll tell you if we've been wasting effort." She was trembling not only with pain but with the effort not to relieve her bladder. But she did not dare to ask even that favor.

Swearing, her face livid with frustration and rage, Avril deftly removed the panel, kicking the console in her frenzy. Sallah leaned as far away as her bonds permitted, hoping to escape any stray blows.

"How did they do it? What did they take, Telgar, or I'll start carving you up." Avril flattened Sallah's left hand over the exposed chips, and her knife blade cut through the little finger to the bone. Pain and shock lanced through Sallah's body. "You don't need this one at all!"

"Blood hangs in the air just like vomit and urine, Bitra. And if you don't stop, you'll have both in free-fall!"

They locked eyes in a contest of wills.

"What . . . did . . . they . . . remove?" With each word Avril sawed against the little finger. Sallah screamed. It felt good to scream, and she knew that it would complete the picture of her in Avril's mind: soft. Sallah had never felt harder in her life.

"Guidance. They removed the guidance chip. You can't go anywhere."

The blade left her finger, and Sallah stared in fascination at the drops of blood that formed and floated. The contemplation took her mind off Avril's ranting until the woman snagged her shoulder.

"Are all the spare parts on the planet? Did they strip everything from the *Yoko*?"

Sallah forced her attention away from the blood and the pain, clamping down on all but the important consideration: how to thwart Avril without seeming to. "I'd say that there would be guidance chips left in the main board that could be substituted."

"There'd better be." Avril slipped the knife through the cord that bound Sallah to the pilot's seat. "Okay. We suit up and head for the bridge."

"Not before I go to the head, Avril," Sallah replied. She nodded at her hand. "And attend to this. You don't want blood on the chips, you know." She let herself scream with the pain of the jerk to her foot. She felt she had handled her submission well. Avril would have suspected a more immediate capitulation. "And another boot."

Finally Sallah could spare a dispassionate look at her foot. Half her heel was missing, and a puddle of blood rocked slowly back and forth, moved by the agitation of Avril's kicks.

"Wait!" Avril had also noticed the blood. She spun away to the lockers by the hatch and came back with a space suit and a dirty cloth. "There! Strip!"

Sallah tied up her finger with the least soiled strip of cloth and used the rest to bind her foot. It hurt badly, and she could feel that fragments of her work boot had been jammed into the flesh. She was allowed the use of the head, while Avril watched and made snide cracks about maternal changes in a woman's body. Sallah pretended to be more humiliated than she actually felt. It made Avril feel so superior. The higher the summit, the harder the fall, Sallah thought grimly. She struggled into the space suit.

"She's left the gig, Admiral," Ezra said suddenly into the tense silence in the crowded interface chamber. Tarvi had been called in. Silent tears streamed down his face. "She's passed the sensors at the docking area. No," he corrected himself, "two bodies have passed the sensors." Tarvi let out a ragged sob but said nothing.

Bit by bit, the pieces had been put together to solve the puzzle of Sallah's disappearance and Avril Bitra's reappearance.

A technician, working on a remount job on the sled nearest Sallah's, remembered seeing her leave her task and wander toward the scrap pile at the edge of the grid. He had also noticed Kenjo and Ongola walking to the *Mariposa*. He had not seen anyone else in that vicinity. Shortly afterward he had seen the *Mariposa* lift off.

Once someone thought to look for it, the sled Avril had used was easily spotted. It carried none of the modifications that all other Pernese sleds bore; it had been left at the edge of the grid, among others that had been called in for servicing. Stev Kimmer was called in to identify it. She had removed every trace of her occupancy, although Stev pointed to scrape marks that were new to him. He also kept his personal comments about his erstwhile partner to himself, though his expression had been sufficiently grim for Paul and Emily to suspect that he had been double-crossed. For one moment he had hesitated. Then, with a shrug, he had answered every question they asked him.

"She won't get anywhere," Emily said, firmly, striving for optimism.

"No, she won't." Paul looked at the guidance cartridge, not daring to glance in Tarvi's direction.

"Couldn't she replace it from similar chips on the bridge?" Tarvi asked, his face an odd shade, his lips dry, and his liquid eyes tormented.

"Not the right size," Ezra said, his expression infinitely sad. "The *Mariposa* was more modern, used smaller, more sophisticated crystals."

"Besides," Paul added heavily, "the chip she really needs is the one Ongola replaced with a blank. Oh, she can probably set a course and it will appear to be accepted. The ship will reverse out of the dock, but the moment she touches the firing pin, it'll just go straight ahead."

"But Sallah!" Tarvi demanded in an anguished voice. "What will happen to my wife?"

Sallah waited until Avril had reversed the *Mariposa* from the dock, let it drift away from the *Yokohama*'s bulk, and ignited the *Mariposa*'s tailflame before she operated the comm unit. Avril had done as much damage to the circuitry in the bridge console as she could, but she had forgotten the override at the admiral's position. As soon as she left the bridge, Sallah accessed it.

"*Yokohama* to Landing. Come in, Ezra. You must be there!"

"Keroon here, Telgar! What's your position?"

"Sitting," Sallah said.

"Goddamn it, Telgar, don't be facetious at a time like this," Ezra cried.

"Sorry, sir," Sallah said. "I don't have visuals." That was a lie, but she did not wish anyone to see her condition. "I'm accessing the probe garage. There is no damage report for that area. You've three probes left. How shall I program them?"

"Hellfire, girl, don't talk about probes now! How're we going to get you down?"

"I don't think you are, sir," she said cheerfully. "Tarvi?"

"Sal-lah!" The two syllables were said in a tone that brought her heart to her mouth and tears to her eyes. Why had he never spoken her name that way before? Did it mean the long-awaited avowal of his love? The anguish in his voice evoked a spirit tortured and distressed.

"Tarvi, my love." She kept her voice level though her throat kept closing. "Tarvi, who's with you there?"

"Paul, Emily, Ezra," he replied in broken tones. "Sallah! You must return!"

"On the wings of a prayer? No. Go to Cara! Get out of the room. I've got some business to do, Pern business. Paul, make him leave. I can't think if I know he's listening."

"Sallah!" Her name echoed and reechoed in her ears.

"Okay, Ezra, tell me where you want them."

There was a choking, throat-clearing noise. "I want one to go to the body of the cometary, the second to circumnavigate." Ezra cleared his throat again. "I want the other to follow the spiral curve of that nebulosity. If the big scope is operable, I'd like bridge readings all along that damned thing. We can't track it with the telescope we have here—not powerful enough for the definition we need. Never thought we'd need the big one, so we didn't dismantle it." He was maundering, Sallah thought affectionately, to get himself under control. Did she hear someone crying through that conversation? Surely Governor Boll or the admiral would have been kind enough to get Tarvi out of the room.

Then she needed to concentrate on the information Ezra was giving her to encode the duties and destinations of the individual probes.

"Probes away, sir," she said, remembering the last time she had given that response. She saw Pern on the big screen; she had never thought that she would again see from space the world she had come to know as her home. "Now I'm sending some data for Dieter to decipher. Avril said she'd killed both Ongola and Kenjo. Has she?"

"Kenjo, yes. Ongola will pull through."

"Old soldiers don't die easy. Look, Ezra, what I'm sending for Dieter are some notations I made on available fuel. Ongola will know what I mean. And I've sent down Avril's course. She went off in the right direction, but I saw a very odd-looking crystal in that guidance system, one I never saw on the *Mariposa* when I was driving her. Am I right? She won't go anywhere?"

"Once Bitra hits the engine button, she goes in a straight line."

"Very good," Sallah said with a feeling of immense satisfaction. "The straight and narrow for our dear departed friend. Now, I'm activating the big scope. I'll program it to report through the interface to you. All right?"

"Give me the readings yourself, Mister Telgar," Ezra ordered gruffly.

"I don't think so, Captain," she said, glad to rely on the impersonal address. She visualized Ezra Keroon's thin frame hunched over the interface. "I don't have that much time. Only the oxygen in my tanks. They were full when Avril let me put them on, but she told me she was switching off the bridge's independent system. I have no reason to doubt her. That's another reason why I'm switching the scope's readings to you. Space gloves are good, but they don't allow for fine tunings. I just about managed some repairs to the mess Avril made of the console. Jury rig at least, so . . . when someone gets a chance to get up here, most everything will work."

"How much time do you have, Sallah?"

"I don't know." She could feel the blood reaching to her calf in the big boot, and her left glove was full. How much blood did a person have? She felt weak, too, and she was aware that it was getting harder to breathe. It was all of a piece. She would miss knowing Cara better.

"Sallah?" Ezra's voice was very kind. "Sallah, talk to Tarvi. We can't keep him out of here. He's like a madman. He just wants to talk to you."

"Oh, sure, fine. I want to talk to him," she said, her voice sounding funny even to herself.

"Sallah!" Tarvi had managed to get his voice under control. "Get out of here, all of you! She's mine now. Sallah, jewel in my night, my golden girl, my emerald-eyed ranee, why did I never tell you before how much you mean to me? I was too proud. I was too vain. But you taught me to love, taught me by your sacrifice when I was too engrossed in my other love—my worklove—to see the inestimable gift of your affection and kindness. How could I have been so stupid? How could I have failed to see that you were more than just a body to receive my seed, more than an ear to hear my ambitions, more than hands to— Sallah? Sallah! Answer me, Sallah!"

"You—loved—me?"

"I do love you, Sallah. I do! Sallah? Sallah! *Salllllaaaaah!*"

"What do you think, Dieter?" Paul asked the programmer as he consulted the figures Ezra had given them.

"Well, this first lot of figures gives us over two thousand liters of fuel. The second is a guesstimate of how much Kenjo used on the four missions he flew and what was used by the *Mariposa* today. There's a substantial quantity unused somewhere down here on the surface. The third set is evidently what was left in the *Yoko*'s tanks and is now in the *Mariposa*'s. But, I do point out, as Sallah does, that there's enough in the *Yoko*'s sumptank for centuries of minor orbital corrections."

Paul nodded brusquely. "Go on."

"Now this section is the course Bitra tried to set. The first course correction should have been initiated about now." Dieter frowned at the equations on his monitor. "In fact, she should be plunging straight toward our eccentric planet. Maybe we'll find out sooner than we knew what the surface is like."

"Not that Avril is likely to stand by and give us any useful information as—as Sallah did." Dieter looked up at the savage tone of the admiral's voice. "Sorry. C'mon. You've the right. And if something goes wrong . . ." Paul left the sentence dangling as he led Dieter down the corridor to the interface room.

Emily had gone with Tarvi to give him what comfort she could, so Ezra was manning the room alone. He looked as old as Paul felt after the wringing emotions of the day.

"Any word?"

"None of it for polite company," Ezra said with a snort. "She's just discovered that the first course correction hasn't occurred." He turned the dial so that the low snarl of vindictive curses was plainly audible.

Paul grinned maliciously at Dieter. "So you said." He turned on the speakers.

"Avril, can you hear me?"

"Benden! What the hell did that bitch of yours do? How did she do it? The override is locked. I can't even maneuver. I knew I should have sawn her *foot* off."

Ezra blanched and Dieter looked ill, but Paul's smile was vindictive. So Avril had underestimated Sallah. He took a deep breath of pride in the valiant woman.

"You're going to explore the plutonic planet, Avril darling. Why don't you be a decent thing and give us a running account?"

"Shove it, Benden. You know where! You'll get nothing out of me. Oh, shit! Oh, shit! it's not the—oh, shiiiitt."

The sound of her final expletive was drowned by a sizzling roar that made Ezra grab for the volume dial.

"Shit!" Paul echoed very softly. "'It's not the . . . '—the what? Damn you, Avril, to eternity! It's not the *what*?"

Emily and Pierre, along with Chio-Chio Yoritomo, who had been Kenjo's wife's cabinmate on the *Buenos Aires* and her housemate on Irish Square, took the fast sled to Kenjo's Honshu Stake. While most of Landing knew about Kenjo's death and Ongola's serious illness, there had been no public announcement. Rumor had been busy discussing the "unknown" assailant.

When Emily returned that night, she brought a sealed message to the admiral.

"She told us," Emily said dryly, "that she would prefer to stay on at Honshu to work the stake herself for her four children. She has few needs and would not trouble us."

"She is very traditional," Chio-Chio told the admiral breathlessly. "She would not show grief, for that belittles the dead." She shrugged, eyes down, her hands clenching and unclenching. Then she looked up, almost defiant in her anger. "She was like that. Kenjo married her because she would not question what he did. He asked me first, but I had more sense, even if he *was* a war ace. Oh!" She brought her arm up to hide her face. "But to die like that! Struck from behind. An ignominious death for one who had cheated it so often!" Then she turned and fled from the room, her sobbing audible as she ran out into the night.

Emily gestured for Paul to open the small note, which was well sealed by wax and stamped with some kind of marking. He broke it open and unfolded the thick, beautiful, handmade paper. Then, mystified, he handed it to Emily and Pierre.

"'There were two caves cut, to judge by the amount of fuel used and rubble spilled. One cave housed the plane. I do not know where the other was,'" Emily read. "So he did manage to remove some of the fuel? How much?"

"We'll see if Ezra can figure it out—or Ongola, when he recovers. Pierre?" Paul asked the chef for a pledge of silence.

"Of course. Discretion was bred in my family for generations, Admiral."

"Paul," the admiral corrected him.

"For something like this, old friend, you are the admiral!" Pierre clicked his heels together and inclined his body slightly from the waist, smiling with a brief reassurance. "Emily, you are tired. You should rest now. Paul, tell her!"

Paul laid one hand on Pierre de Courci's shoulder and took Emily's arm with the other. "There is one more duty for the day, Pierre, and you'd best be with us."

"The bonfire!" Emily pulled back against Paul's arm. "I'm not sure I—"

"Who can?" Paul broke in when she faltered. "Tarvi has asked it."

All three walked with reluctant steps, joining the trickle of others going in the same direction, down to the dark Bonfire Square. Each house had left one light burning. The thinly scattered stars were brilliant, and the first moon, Timor, was barely a crescent on the eastern skyline.

By the pyramid of thicket and fern, Tarvi stood, his head down, a man as gaunt as some of the branches that had been cast into the pile. Suddenly, as if he knew that all were there who would come, he lit the brand. It flared up to light a face haggard with grief, with hair that straggled across tear-wet cheeks.

Tarvi raised the brand high, turning slowly as if to place firmly in his memory the faces of all those in attendence.

"From now on," he shouted harsely, "I am not Tarvi, nor Andiyar. I am Telgar, so that her name is spoken every day, so that her name is remembered by everyone for giving *us* her life today. Our children will now bear that name, too. Ram Telgar, Ben Telgar, Dena Telgar, and Cara Telgar, who will never know her mother." He took a deep breath, filling his chest. *"What is my name?"*

"Telgar!" Paul replied as loud as he could.

"Telgar!" cried Emily beside him, Pierre's baritone repeating it a breath behind her. *"Telgar!"*

"Telgar! Telgar! Telgar! *Telgar! Telgar!*" Nearly three thousand voices took up the shout in a chant, pumping their arms until Telgar thrust the burning torch into the bonfire. As the flame roared up through the dry wood and fern, the name crescendoed. *"Telgar! Telgar! Telgar!"*

The shock of Sallah Telgar's death reverberated across the continent. She had been well known, both as shuttle pilot during debarkation and as an able manager of the Karachi camp. Her courage, however, gave an unexpected boost to morale, almost as if, because Sallah had been willing to devote the last moments of her life to benefit the colony, everyone had to strive harder to vindicate her sacrifice. Or so it seemed for the next eight days until some disturbing rumors began to circulate.

"Look, Paul," Joel Lilienkamp began even before he had closed the door behind him. "Everyone's got a right to access Stores. But that Ted Tubberman's been taking out some unusual stuff for a botanist."

"Not Tubberman again," Paul said, leaning back in his chair with a deep sigh of disgust. Tarv—Telgar, Paul corrected himself, had phoned the previous day, asking if Tubberman had been authorized to scrounge in the shuttle they were dismantling.

"Yes," Joel said. "If you ask me, he's only accessing half his chips. You've got enough on your plate, Paul, but you gotta know what that fool's doing. I'll bet my last bottle of brandy he's up to something."

"At Wind Blossom's request, Pol has denied him further access to the biology labs," Paul said wearily. "Seems he was acting as if *he* was in charge of bioengineering. Bay doesn't like him much, either."

"She's not alone," Joel replied, lowering himself to a chair and scrubbing at his face. "I want your permission to shut the shop door in his face, too. I caught him in Building G, which houses the technically sensitive stuff. I don't want anyone in there without my authorization. And there he was, bald-faced and swaggering like he had every right, he and Bart Lemos."

"Bart Lemos!" Paul sat up again.

"Yeah. He, Bart, and Stev Kimmer're doing a good-old-buddy bit these days. And I don't like the rumors my sources tell me they're spreading."

"Stev Kimmer's in on it?" Paul was surprised.

Joel shrugged. "He's mighty thick with 'em."

Paul rubbed his knuckles thoughtfully. Bart Lemos was a gullible nonentity, but Stev Kimmer was a highly skilled technician. Paul had put a discreet monitor on the man's activities after Avril's departure. Stev had gone on a three-day bender and been found asleep in the dismantled shuttle. Once he had recovered from the effects of quikal, he had gone back to work. Fulmar said that other mechanics did not like pairing with him because he was taciturn, if not downright surly. The thought of Tubberman having access to Kimmer's expertise made Paul uneasy. "What exactly have you heard, Lili?" he asked.

"A load of crap," the little storesman said, folding his fingers across his chest. "I don't think anyone with any sense buys the notion that Avril and Kenjo were in league. Or that Ongola killed Kenjo to keep them from taking the *Mariposa* to go for help. But I'll warn you, Paul, if Kitti's bioengineering program doesn't show positive results, we could be down the tubes. I'll lay odds you and Emily are going to be asked to reconsider sending off that homing capsule."

The previous evening, Paul had discussed that expedient with Emily, Ezra, and Jim. Keroon had been the fiercest opponent of a homing-capsule Mayday, which he termed an exercise in futility. As Paul remarked, such technological help was, at the earliest, ten years away. And the chance that the FSP would move with any speed to assist them was depressingly slim. To send for help seemed not only a rejection of Sallah's sacrifice but a cowardly admission of failure when they had not exhausted the ingenuity and resourcefulness of their community.

"What sort of material has Ted been requisitioning, Lili?" Paul asked.

Joel extracted a wad of paper from his thigh pocket and made a show of unfolding and reading from it. "Grab bag from hydroponics to insulation materials, steel mesh and posts, and some computer chips that Dieter says he couldn't possibly need, use, or understand."

"Did you happen to ask Tubberman what he needed them for?"

"I happened to just do that very thing. A bit arrogant he was, too. Said they were needed for his experiments"—Joel was clearly dubious about their value—"to develop a more effective defense against the Thread until help comes."

Paul grimaced. He had heard the botanist's wild claims that *he*, not the biologists and their jumped-up mutated lizards, would protect Pern. "I don't like that 'till help comes' bit," Paul murmured, gritting his teeth.

"So, tell me to lock him out, Paul. He may be a charterer, but he's overspent his credit and then some." He waved the sheet. "I got records to prove that."

Paul nodded. "Yes, but next time he presents a list, get him to tell you what he wants, then shut the door. I want to know what he's up to."

"Restrict him to his stake," Joel said, rising to his feet, an expression of genuine concern on his round face, "and you'll save all of us a lot of aggro. He's a wild card, and you can't be sure where he'll bounce up next."

Paul grinned at the storesman. "I'd be glad to, Lili, but the mandate doesn't permit that kind of action."

Joel snorted derisively, hesitated a moment longer, and then, shrugging in his inimitable fashion, left the office.

Paul did not forget the conversation, but the morning brought more pressing concerns. Despite the best efforts of

Fulmar and his engineering crews, three more sleds had failed airworthiness tests. That meant using more ground crews, the last line of defense and the most enervating for people already worked to the point of exhaustion. Neither Paul nor Emily recognized the significance of three separate reports: one from the veterinary lab, saying that their supply rooms had been rifled overnight; another from Pol Nietro, reporting that Ted Tubberman had been seen in bioengineering; and the third from Fulmar, saying that someone had made off with one of the exhaust cylinders from the dismantled shuttle.

When Joel Lilienkamp's angry call came through, Paul had little trouble arriving at a conclusion.

"May his orifices congeal and his extremities fall off," Joel cried at the top of his voice. "He's got the homing capsule!"

Shock jolted Paul out of his chair, while Emily and Ezra regarded him in astonishment. "Are you sure?"

"Of course I'm sure, Paul. I hid the carton in among stove pipes and heating units. It hasn't been misplaced, but who the hell could *know* that carton #45/879 was a homing capsule?"

"Tubberman took it?"

"I'll bet my last bottle of brandy he did." Joel spoke so fast that his words slurred. "The fucker! The crap-eater, the slime-producing maggot!"

"When did you discover it gone?"

"Now! I'm calling from Building G. I check it out at least once a day."

"Could Tubberman have followed you?"

"What sort of a twat do you think I am?" Joel was as apoplectic at such a suggestion as he was about the theft. "I check every building every day and I can tell you exactly what was requisitioned yesterday and the day before, so I fucking well know when something's missing!"

"I don't doubt you for a moment, Joel." Paul rubbed his hand hard over his mouth, thinking rapidly. Then he saw the anxious expressions of Emily and Ezra. "Hold on," he said into the handset, and reported what Joel had said.

"Well," Ezra replied, a look of intense relief passing over his gaunt features. "Tubberman couldn't launch a kite. He can barely maneuver a sled. I wouldn't worry about him."

"Not him. But I worry a lot about Stev Kimmer and Bart Lemos being seen in Tubberman's company lately," Paul said quietly. Ezra seemed to deflate, burying his head in his hands.

"Ted Tubberman has had it," Emily said, placing the folder she had been studying onto the table in a precise manner and rising to her feet. "I don't give a spent chip for his position as a charterer or the privacy of his stake. We're searching Calusa." She gave Ezra a poke in the shoulder. "C'mon, you'll know what components he'd need."

They all heard the sound of running feet, then the door burst in and Jake Chernoff erupted into the office.

"Sir, sorry, sir," the young man cried, his face flushed, his chest heaving from exertion. "Your phone—" He pointed excitedly at the receiver in the admiral's hand. "Too important. Scanners at met—something blasted off from Oslo Landing, three minutes ago—and it wasn't a sled. Too small."

As one, Paul, Emily, and Ezra made for the door and ran to the interface chamber. Ezra fumbled at the terminal in his haste to implement the program. An exhaust trail was plainly visible, on a northwestern heading. Cursing under his breath, Ezra switched to the *Yoko*'s monitor, which was tracking the blip. For a long moment they watched, rigid with fury and frustration. Then Ezra straightened his long frame, his hands hanging limply.

"Well, what's done's done."

"Not completely," Emily said, her voice harsh as she separated each syllable in a curious lilt. She turned to Paul, her eyes very bright, her lips pursed, and her expression implacable. "Oslo Landing, hmmm? That capsule was just launched. Let's go get the buggers."

Leaving Ezra to monitor the capsule's ascent, Paul and Emily left at a run. The first three big men they encountered on their way to the grid were commandeered to assist. Paul spotted Fulmar and told him to pilot Kenjo's augmented sled.

"Don't ask questions, Fulmar," Paul said, peremptorily seconding two more burly technicians. "Just head us toward Jordan, and everyone keep their eyes open for sled traffic." He reached for the comm unit as he shrugged into his harness. "Who's in the tower? Tarrie? I want to know who's in the air above the river, where they're going, and where they've been."

Fulmar took off in such a steep climb that for a moment the noise blanketed any answer Tarrie Chernoff gave.

"Only one sled above the Jordan, sir, apart from that—other flight." She choked on her words and then recovered the impersonal reserve of a comm officer. "The sled does not acknowledge."

"They will," Paul assured her grimly. "Continue to monitor all traffic in that area."

Tubberman was just stupid enough to be obvious, but somehow Paul did not think that such stupidity was a trait of Stev Kimmer or whomever else Ted had talked into such an arrant abrogation of the democratic decision of the colony.

Tubberman was alone in the sled when Fulmar forced him to land in the riverside desolation of the ill-fated Bavaria Stake. He was unrepentant as he faced them, folding his arms across his chest and jutting his chin out defiantly.

"I've done what should have been done," he stated in pompous righteousness. "The first step in saving this colony from annihilation."

Paul clenched his fists tightly to his sides. Beside him, Emily was vibrating with a fury as intense as his own.

"I want the names of your accomplices, Tubberman," Paul said through his teeth, "and I want them now!"

Tubberman inhaled, bracing himself. "Do your worst, Admiral. I am man enough to take it."

The mock heroic attitude was so absurd to his auditors that one of the men behind Paul let out a short bark of incredulous laughter, which he quickly cut off. But the one burst of derision altered Paul's mood.

"Tubberman, I wouldn't let anyone touch a hair of your head," Paul said, grinning in a release of tension. "There are quite suitable ways to deal with you, plainly set out in the charter—nothing quite as crude or barbaric as physical abuse." Then he turned. "You men take him back to Landing in his sled. Put him in my office and call Joel Lilienkamp. He'll take charge of the prisoner." Paul had the satisfaction of seeing the martyred look fade from Tubberman's eyes, to be replaced by a mixture of anxiety and surprise. Turning on his heel, Paul gestured Emily, Fulmar, and the others back into their sled.

Tarrie reported no other vehicles in the area and apologized that traffic records were no longer kept. "Except for that . . . rocket thing, the pattern was normal, sir. Oh, and Jake's back. Did you want to speak to him?"

"Yes," Paul answered, wishing that Ongola were back in charge. "Jake, I want to know where Bart Lemos and Stev Kimmer are. And Nabhi Nabol." Beside him, Emily nodded approval.

By then, Fulmar had covered the short air distance between Bavaria and Oslo Landing. The remains of the launch platform were still smoking. While Paul went with the others to search the area for sled skids, Fulmar carefully prodded through the overheated circle beneath it, sniffing as he went.

"Shuttle fuel by the smell of it, Paul," he reported. "A homing capsule wouldn't take much."

"It would take know-how," Paul said grimly. "And expertise, and you and I know just how many people are capable of handling that sort of technology." He looked Fulmar square in the eye, and the man's shoulders sagged. "Not your fault, Fulmar. I had your report. I had others. I just didn't put the pieces together."

"Who'd have thought Ted'd pull such a crazy stunt? No one believes half of what he says!" Fulmar protested.

Emily and the others came back then from an inconclusive search. "There're a lot of skid marks, Paul," she reported. "And rubbish." She indicated a collapsed fuel sack and a handful of connectors and wires. Fulmar's look of desolation deepened.

"We're wasting time here," Paul said, curbing his irritation.

"Let's have Cherry and Cabot waiting in my office," Emily murmured as they climbed into the sled.

He's *proud* of what he did," Joel stormed when Paul and Emily called him into Emily's office on their return. "Says it was his *duty* to save the colony. Says we'll be surprised at how many people agree with him."

"He's the one who'll be surprised," Emily replied. Her jaw was set in a resolute line, and her lips curved in a curious smile, which her tired eyes did not echo.

"Yeah, Em, but what *can* we do to him?" Joel demanded in impotent indignation.

Emily poured herself a fresh cup of klah and took a sip before she answered. "He will be shunned."

"Who will be shunned?" Cherry Duff demanded in her hoarse voice, entering the room at that instant. Cabot Carter was right behind her, having escorted the magistrate from her office in reply to the summons.

"Shunned?" Carter's handsome face was enlivened by a smile that grew broader as he looked expectantly from Paul to Emily, then faded slightly as he saw the dour storesman.

Paul grinned back. "Shunned!"

"Shunned?" Joel exclaimed in a disgusted tone.

Emily gestured Cherry into the comfortable chair and motioned for the others to be seated. Then, at a nod from Paul, she gave a terse report that culminated in Tubberman's illicit use of the homing capsule.

"So we're to order Tubberman shunned, huh?" Cherry looked around at Carter.

"It's legal all right, Cherry," the legist replied, "since it is not a corporal punishment, per se, which is illegal under the terms of the charter."

"Refresh me on such a process," Cherry said, her tone doubly droll.

"Shunning was a mechanism," Emily began, "whereby passive groups could discipline an erring member. Religious communities resorted to it when someone of their sect disobeyed their peculiar tenets. Quite effective really. The rest of the sect pretended the offending member didn't exist. No one spoke to him, no one acknowledged his presence, no one would assist the shunned in any way or indicate that he—or she—existed. It doesn't seem cruel, but in fact the deprivation is psychologically destructive."

"It'll do," Cherry said, nodding in satisfaction. "An admirable punishment for someone like Tubberman. Admirable!"

"And completely legal!" Cabot concurred. "Shall I draft the announcement, Emily, or do you prefer to do it, Cherry?"

Cherry flicked her hand at him. "You do it, Cabot. I'm sure you learned all the right phrases. But do explain exactly what shunning entails. Not that most of us aren't so fed up with the man's rantings and rumors that they won't be delighted to have an official excuse to . . . ah . . . shun him! Shun him!" She tipped back her head and gave a hoot of outrageous laughter. "By all that's holy—and legal—I like that, Emily. I like that a lot!" In an abrupt switch of mood with no leavening of humor, she added, "It'll cool a lot of hotheads." She swept Paul and Emily with a shrewd look. "Tubberman didn't do it by himself. Who helped?"

"We've no proof," Paul began in the same minute that Joel said, "Stev Kimmer, Bart Lemos, and maybe Nabhi Nabol."

"Let's shun them, too," Cherry cried, banging the arm of her chair with her thin old hands. "Damn it, we don't need dissension. We need support, cooperation, hard work. Or we won't survive. Oh, flaming hells!" She raised both hands up high. "What'll we do if that capsule brings those blood-sucking FSP salvagers down on us?"

"I wouldn't bet on that," Joel answered her, rolling his eyes.

Cherry gave him a hard stare. "I'm relieved to know there is something you won't make book on, Lilienkamp. All right, so what *do* we do about Tubberman's accomplices?"

Cabot leaned over to touch her arm lightly. "First we have to prove that they were, Cherry." He looked expectantly at Paul and Emily. "The charter says that a person is judged innocent until proved guilty."

"We watch 'em," Paul said. "We watch 'em. Carter, compose that notice and see that it's posted throughout Landing, and that every stakeholder is apprised of the fact. Cherry, will you impose the sentence on Tubberman?" He held out his arm to assist her to her feet.

"With the greatest of satisfaction. What a superb way to get rid of a bore," she added under her breath as she marched forward. The unholy joy on her face brightened Joel Lilienkamp's mood as he followed them, rubbing his hands together.

The messenger was quite happy to bring a copy of the official notice to Bay and Wind Blossom, on duty in the large incubator chamber. The room was separated from the main laboratory and insulated against temperature changes and noise. The incubator itself stood on heavy shock absorbers, so that in the precarious early stages the embryos in their sacs could not be jarred by equipment moved around the main laboratory.

Although eggs within a natural womb, or even in a proper shell, could handle a great deal of trauma, the initial *ex utero* fertilization and alteration had been too delicate to risk the most minute jolt. Development was not yet canalized, nor was the new genetic structure balanced, and any variation in the embryos' environment would doubtless cause damage. Later, when the eggs were at the stage when naturally they would have been laid in a clutch, they would be transferred to the building where a warmed sand flooring and artificial sun lamps imitated the natural conditions in which dragonet eggs hatched. That point was several weeks ahead.

Special low-light viewing panels had been created, so no light filtered into the womblike darkness while observers had a clear view of the incubator's precious contents. A portable magnifier had been devised which could be set at any position on the incubator's four glass sides for very coarse and routine inspections. In the laboratories of First and Earth, each developing embryo would have been remotely monitored and recorded. But, in Pern's relatively primitive conditions, about which Wind Blossom constantly complained, the necessity for the avoidance of any toxic substances at all meant that no sensors could be allowed close to the embryos in the culture chambers.

Bay was jotting down Wind Blossom's assessment when the messenger delivered the notice. The lad was quite willing to explain any part of the shunning, but Bay shooed him off on his rounds.

"How extraordinary," Bay said when she had finished reading it aloud to Blossom. "Really, Ted has been quite a nuisance lately. Did you hear those rumors he was spreading, Blossom? As if that wretched Bitra had anything but her own plans in mind when she stole the *Mariposa.* Going for help, indeed!" She squinted loyally into the incubator at its forty-two hopes for their future. "But to send off a homing capsule when we most specifically voted against such an action."

"I am relieved," Wind Blossom said, sighing gently.

"Yes, he was beginning to upset you," Bay remarked kindly. She tried to tell herself that the woman was still grieving for her grandmother. There were moments recently, though, when Bay wanted to remind Blossom that it was not just the Yung family who had suffered a grievous loss. She had not, because Blossom had been rather volatile lately and might interpret such a comment as an aspersion on her ability to proceed with her grandmother's brilliant genetic-engineering program. As her mother's primary assistant, she was technically in charge of the program on file in the biology Mark 42 computer. Bay, too, had scanned it to familiarize herself with the procedure. Kitti Ping had left copious notes on how to proceed, anticipating those possible minor alignments, balancing, or other compensations that might be needed. She had apparently anticipated everything but her own death.

"You misunderstand me," Blossom replied, inclining her head in a gesture reminiscent of her grandmother correcting an erring apprentice. "I am relieved that the homing capsule has been sent. Now there is no blame to us."

Bay was not certain that she had heard correctly. "What under the suns do you mean, Blossom?"

Blossom gave Bay a long look, smiling faintly. "All our eggs are in one basket," she said with an inscrutable smile and moved the inspection lens to a new position.

When Pol and Phas Radamanth came to relieve them, Bay lingered. She and Pol did not have much time together anymore, and she did not look forward to another dull supper at the communal kitchen.

"You got a copy, I see," Pol said, indicating the shunning notice.

"Extraordinary that."

"More than time," Phas said, glancing up from Blossom's notations. "Let's hope he wasn't as incompetent a launcher as he was a botantist."

Bay stared in astonishment at the xenobiologist and Phas had the grace to look embarrassed.

"No one approves of Tubberman's actions, my dear," Pol assured her.

"Yes, but if they come . . ." Bay's gesture took in the incubator and the laboratory, and all that the colonists had managed to do with their new world.

"If it's any consolation," Phas said, "Joel Lilienkamp has not opened a book on an ETA."

"Oh!" Then she asked, "And what's happened to Ted Tubberman?"

"He was escorted back to his stake and told to remain there."

Pol could look quite fierce, she thought, when he wanted to. "What about Mary? And his young children?" she asked.

Pol shrugged. "She can stay or come. She's not shunned. Ned Tubberman was looking pretty upset, but he never was very close to his father, and Fulmar Stone thinks he's a very promising mechanic." He shrugged again and then gave his wife an encouraging smile.

Bay had no sooner turned to go than the ground under them shook. She instinctively lunged toward the incubator, and found Phas and Pol beside her. Even without the magnifier they could see that the amniotic fluid in the sacs was not rippling in response to the earthquake. The shock absorbers had proved adequate.

"That's all we need!" Pol cried, outraged. He stomped to the comm unit and dialed the met tower, slamming down the handset. "Engaged! Bay, reassure them." He gestured toward the first bunch of technicians heading anxiously to the door of the chamber. He dialed again and got through just as Kwan Marceau pushed his way into the room. "Are there going to be more shocks, Jake?" Pol asked. "Why weren't we warned?"

"It was a small one," Jake Chernoff replied soothingly. "Patrice de Broglie called it in but I am obliged to warn infirmary first in case surgery is in progress, and then your line was busy." That explanation placated Pol. "Patrice says there's a bit of tectonic plate action to the east, and there may be more jolts in the next few weeks. The incubator's on shocks anyway, isn't it? You don't have anything to worry about."

"Nothing to worry about?" Pol demanded. He jammed the handset back onto its stand.

There was a discreet knock on the door to the admiral's office, and when Paul answered with a noncommittal "Come in," Jim Tillek opened it. Emily smiled with relief. The master of Monaco Bay was always welcome. Paul leaned back in his swivel chair, ready for a break from the depressing inventory of airworthy sleds and serviceable flamethrowers.

"Hi, there," Jim said. "Just up to get my skimmer serviced."

"Since when have you needed assistance in that job?" Paul asked.

"Since all my spare parts at Monaco got reabsorbed by Joel Lilienkamp." Jim's drawl was cheerful.

"And pigs fly," Paul retorted.

"Oh, is that the next project?" Jim asked with a comic grin. He dropped into the nearest seat and laced his fingers together. "By the way, Maximilian and Teresa reported on the dolphin search Patrice requested. There are significant lava flows from the Illyrian volcano. It's only a small one, so don't be surprised if our easterlies bring in some black dust. It's *not* dead Thread. Just honest-to-Vulcan volcanic dust. I wanted you to know before another rumor started."

"Thanks," Paul said dryly.

"Logical explanations are always welcome," Emily added.

"I also dropped in to see our favorite patient." Jim pushed himself deeper into the chair and met Paul's eyes squarely. "He's raring to go and threatens to move into the second story of the met tower and run communications from there. Sabra threatens to divorce him if he does anything before he gets medical clearance. Myself, I told him he doesn't need to worry, as young Jake Chernoff's been doing a proper job of it. The boy won't even hazard a guess about the weather until he's run the satellite report twice and looked out the window."

Paul and Emily both smiled at his jocular account.

"Ongola *needs* to be back at work," Emily agreed.

"He's sure he'll never use his arm again. He'd do better

being so busy he doesn't think such negative thoughts." Jim cocked his head at Paul.

"According to the doctors," Emily said with a grateful smile, "Ongola *will* use that arm—even if he refuses to believe it—but the amount of mobility is still in question."

"He'll get it back," Jim said blandly. "Hey, is there any truth to the rumor that Stev Kimmer was involved with Tubberman?"

Paul pulled a face, and Emily shot him a glance. "I told you that was doing the rounds," she said.

Jim leaned forward, his expression eager. "Any truth to the one that he skitted out with one of the big pressurized sleds which has been seen near the Great Western Barrier where Kenjo staked his claim? Kimmer's a lot more dangerous than Ted Tubberman ever was."

Paul ran his thumb over his artificial fingers and stopped when he saw that Jim Tillek had noticed the nervous habit. "He is indeed. As the comm unit on that stolen sled was in working order when he lifted it, he will also know that he is wanted back here for questioning."

Jim nodded in solemn approval. "Has Ezra made any sense out of the reports of those probes Sallah . . ." He blinked, his eyes suspiciously wet.

"No," Paul said, clearing his throat. "He's still trying to translate them. The printout is unclear."

"Well, now," Jim said, "I've got a few hours to spare while my sled's serviced. I looked at hundreds of EEC survey team reports before I found a planet I liked the look of. Can I help?"

"A fresh eye might be useful," Paul said. "Ezra's been at it nonstop."

"Did I hear correctly," Jim asked gently, "that the *Mariposa* plunged directly into the eccentric?"

Paul nodded. "She made no informative comment." Avril's cryptic penultimate phrase, "It's not the . . ." still rang with some message that Paul felt he must unravel. "Look, Jim, do stop in and see if you can help Ezra. We need some good news.

Morale is still low after the murders, and having to shun Ted Tubberman and explain how he got his hands on that homing capsule have not improved the administration's image."

"Clever trick, though," Jim said, chuckling as he rose. "Keeps you from having to breach stake autonomy, and keeps that fool where he can't do more damage. I'll just amble over to Ezra's pod." He left the room with a backhanded wave at Emily and Paul.

Immeasurably cheered by his visit, they went back to the onerous tasks of scheduling crews for the upcoming Threadfalls and mustering teams to collect edible greenery for silage from places as yet untouched by the ravening organism.

"Look, Jim, I just can't find any other logical explanation for the destruction of the probes and *these*." Ezra Keroon waved a handful of probe pics, so blurred that no detail could be seen. "One, maybe two probes could malfunction. But I've sent off seven! And Sallah—" Ezra paused a moment, his face expressing the sorrow he still felt at her loss. "Sallah told us that there had been no damage report for the probe garage. Then we have the *Mariposa*. It did not hit the surface. Something hit it just about the same time one of the probes went bang!"

"So you prefer to believe that something down on the surface prevents inspection?" Jim Tillek asked wryly. He leaned back in his seat, easing shoulder muscles taut from hours of bending and peering through magnifiers. "I can't credit that explanation, Ez. C'mon, man. How can anything on that planet be functioning? The surface has been frozen. It can't have thawed appreciably in the time it's been swinging in to Rukbat."

"One does not have such regular formations on any unpopulated surface. I don't say they can't be natural. They just don't look natural. And I certainly won't make any guesses about what sort of creature made them. Then look at the thermal level here, here, and here." Ezra jabbed a finger at the pics he had been studying. "It's higher than I'd anticipate on a near-frozen surface. That much we got from the one probe that sent data back."

"Volcanic action under the crust could account for that."

"But regular *convex,* not concave, formations along the equator?"

Jim was incredulous. "You *want* to believe that plutonic planet could be the *source* of this attack?"

"I like that better than substantiating the Hoyle-Wickramansingh theory, I really do, Jim."

"If Arvil hadn't taken the gig, we could find out what that nebulosity is. Then we'd know for sure! Hoyle-Wickramansingh or little frozen blue critters." Jim's tone was facetious.

"We've the shuttles," Ezra said tentatively, tapping his pencil.

"No fuel, and there isn't a pilot among those left that I'd be willing to trust to do such a difficult retrieval. You'd have to match its orbital speed. I saw the dents on the *Mariposa*'s hull myself where the defense shields failed. Also, we didn't bring down any heavy worksuits that would protect a man out in a meteor storm. And if your theory's correct, he'll get shot down."

"Only if he gets too close to the planet," Ezra went on cautiously. "But he wouldn't have to, to get a sample of the trail. If the trail is nothing but ice, dirt, and rock, the usual cometary junk, we'd know then that the real menace is the planet, not the trail. Right?"

Jim eyed him thoughtfully. "It'd be dangerous either way. And there's no fuel to do it anyhow!" Jim opened his arms in a gesture of exasperation.

"There *is* fuel."

"There is?" Jim sat bolt upright, eyes wide with surprise.

Ezra gave him a wry smile. "Known only to a chosen few."

"Well!" Jim made his eyebrows twitch, but he grinned to show that he took no offense at having been excluded. "How much?"

"With a thrifty pilot, enough for our purpose. Or maybe, if we can find Kenjo's main cache, more."

"More?" Jim gawked. "Kenjo's cache? He scrounged fuel?"

"Always was a clever driver. Saved it from his drops, Ongola said."

Jim continued to stare at Ezra, amazed at Kenjo's sheer impudence. "So that's why Kimmer's nosing about the Western Barrier Range. He's out trying to find Kenjo's cache. For his own purposes or ours?"

"Not enough to get anyone's hopes up, mind you," Ezra continued, holding up a warning hand. "Maybe it's not too bad a thing that Tubberman sent off the homer. Because if it *is* the planet, we need help, and I'm not too proud to ask for it." Ezra grimaced. "Not that Kimmer said anything to anyone when he made off with the big sled and enough concentrated food and power packs to stay lost for years. Joel Lilienkamp was livid that anyone would *steal* from his Store. We don't even know how Stev found out about Kenjo's hoard. Except that he knew how much fuel the *Mariposa* had in her tanks eight years ago. So he must have figured out someone had saved fuel back when Kenjo made those reconnaissance flights." Then, as Jim opened his mouth, he added, "Don't worry about Kimmer taking off even if he finds fuel. Ongola and Kenjo disabled the shuttles some time back. Kimmer doesn't know where we stash the fuel sacks here. Neither do I."

"I'm honored—by your confidence and the cares you have so carefully laid on my bowed shoulders."

"You walked in here three days ago and volunteered your services," Ezra reminded him.

"Three days? Feels like three years. I wonder if my skimmer's been serviced." He rose and stretched again until the bones in his spine and joints readjusted with audible clicks. "So, shall we take this mess—" He gestured to the mass of photos and flimsies neatly arranged on the work surface. "—to the guys who have to figure out what we do with it?"

Paul and Emily listened, saying nothing, until both men had finished expressing their conflicting viewpoints.

"But when the planet is past us in the next eight or nine years, Threadfall will stop," Paul said, jumping to a conclusion.

"Depends on whose theory you favor," Jim said, grinning with good-natured malice. "Or how advanced Ezra's aliens are. Right now, if you buy his theory, they're keeping us at arm's length while the Thread softens us up."

Paul Benden brushed away that notion. "I don't credit that, Ezra. Thread was ineffective on the previous try. But the Pluto planet could be defending itself. I could live with that much of your theory based on the evidence."

Emily looked squarely at Jim. "How long will this gunge fall if it's from your cometary tail?"

"Twenty, thirty years. If I knew the length of that tail, I could give a closer estimate."

"I wonder if that's what Avril meant," Paul said slowly, "by 'it's not the . . . ' Did she mean that it wasn't the planet we had to fear, but the tail it brought from the Oort cloud?"

"If she hadn't taken the *Mariposa,* we'd have a chance of knowing." Emily's voice had a sharp edge.

"We still do," Ezra said. "There's enough fuel to send a shuttle up. Not as economical a vehicle as the *Mariposa* but adequate."

"Are you sure?" Paul's expression was taut as he reached for a calc pad on which he worked several equations. He leaned back, his face pensive, then passed the pad over to Emily and Jim. "It might just be possible." He caught and held Emily's gaze. "We have to know. We have to know the worst we can expect before we can plan ahead."

Ezra raised a warning hand, his expression wary. "Mind you, they can't get close to the planet! We've lost seven probes. Could be mines, could be missiles—but they blow up."

"Whoever goes will know exactly what and how big the risks are," Paul said.

"There's risk enough in just going up," Ezra said gloomily.

"I hate to sound fatuous, but surely there's one pilot who'd take the challenge to save this world," Paul added.

Drake Bonneau was approached first. He thought the scheme was feasible, but he worried about the risk of a shuttle that had certainly deteriorated from eight years' disuse. He then pointed out that he was married with responsibilities, and that there were other pilots equally as qualified. Paul and Emily did not argue with him.

"Marriage and dependent children will be the excuse of practically everyone," Paul told their private counselors, Ezra, Jim, and Zi Ongola, who had been permitted four hours of work a day by his reluctant medical advisers. "The only one still unattached is Nabhi Nabol."

"He's a clever enough pilot," Ongola said thoughtfully, "though not exactly the type of man on whom the future of an entire planet should ride. However, exactly the type if the reward could be made attractive enough for him to take the risk."

"How?" Emily asked skeptically.

Nabhi had already been reprimanded a dozen times and served Cherry Duff's sentences for social misdemeanors such as being caught "drunk and disorderly," several work delinquencies, and one "lewd advance." Lately he had somewhat redeemed himself by being a good squadron leader, and was much admired by the young men he led.

"He's a contractor," Ongola said. "If he should be offered, say, a charterer's stake rights, I think he might well go for it. He's griped about the disparity in land holdings often enough. That could sweeten him. He also fancies himself as a crack pilot."

"We've got some very good young pilots," Jim began.

"Who have had no experience in space with a shuttle." Ongola dismissed that notion. "Though it might be a good idea to choose one to go as copilot and give them the feel. But I'd rather trust Nahbi than a complete space novice."

"If we suggest that he was also our second choice, rather than our last one . . ." Emily remarked.

"We'd better get on with it, whatever we do," Ezra said. "I can't keep stalling questions. We need data and we need a sample of the stuff in that trail. Then we'll know for certain what our future is."

Bargaining with Nabhi began that afternoon. He sneered at the flattery and the appeal to his competence and demanded to know just how much the trip was worth in terms of a holding and other rights. When he demanded the entire province of Cibola, Paul and Emily settled down to their task. When Nabhi insisted on being granted charterer status, they agreed with sufficient reluctance to satisfy the man that he was ahead in the bargaining.

Then Emily nonchalantly mentioned that Big Island was now untenanted. She and Paul managed to suppress their relief when he immediately seized on the notion of occupying Avril's former property.

Nabhi said that he wanted the shuttle he had used during the ferrying operation and he specified the personnel who were, under his supervision, to handle the *Moth*'s recommissioning. He waved aside the fact that all the people he named were already heavily involved in crucial projects. He would only make the trip if he was satisfied that the long-disused shuttle checked out technically. But the other inducements were his immediately.

He then demanded Bart Lemos as his copilot, with the condition that Bart, too, would be given charterer status. Paul and Emily found that particularly unpalatable, but agreed reluctantly.

Nabol's attitude toward both admiral and governor immediately altered, becoming so arrogant and pompous that Emily had to struggle to contain her dislike of the man. His smile of triumph was only one degree less than a full sneer as he left their office with the signed charterer's warrant. Then he commandeered one of the speed shuttles, although it was needed for an imminent Threadfall, and went to inspect his new acquisition.

The admiral and the governor formally announced the venture, its aims, and its personnel. The news managed to outweigh every other topic of interest with one exception: the transfer of the twenty-seven mature eggs to their artificial hatching ground.

The full veterinary contingent assisted the biologists in that maneuver. Sorka Hanrahan and Sean Connell, in their capacities as advanced veterinary apprentices, had also done some of the early analysis and tedious documentation for the project, working under Kitti Ping's close supervision. It didn't take long to accomplish the transfer, but Sorka noticed that the amount of dithering was aggravating her lover. But the project meant more to him than his exasperation with worried biologists, and he suppressed his irritation. Finally the eggs were placed to the complete satisfaction of Wind Blossom, Pol, and Bay: in a double circle, seventeen on the inner ring, twenty on the outer, with the warm sand banked high around them to imitate the natural environment of dragonets.

"The whole thing could have been done in a third of the time," Sean muttered darkly to Sorka. "So much fuss is bad for the eggs." He scowled at the precise circles.

"They're much bigger than I thought they'd be," Sorka said after a moment's silence.

"Much bigger than *they* thought they'd be," Sean said in a scoffing tone. "I suppose we're lucky that so many survived to this stage—a credit to Kit Ping, considering all that had to be done to create them."

Sorka knew that it meant as much to Sean to be a part of the project as it did to her. They had, after all, been the first to discover one of the wild nests. Eager but tired, she was balancing on one of the edging timbers, keeping her feet off the uncomfortably warm sands of the artificial hatching ground.

Although the transfer was complete, the helpers had not yet dispersed. Wind Blossom, Pol, and Bay were deep in discussions with Phas, the admiral, and the governor, who had taken an official part in the removal. Sorka thought that Emily Boll particularly looked drawn and exhausted, but her smile remained warm and genuine. They, too, seemed reluctant to leave.

Most of the Landing population of dragonets had been in and out of the Hatching Ground, darting up to the rafters and vying to find roosting room. They seemed content to watch; none of them had been bold enough to examine the eggs closely. Sorka interpreted their little chirps as reverent, awed.

"Would they know what these are?" she asked Sean softly.

"Do we?" Sean retorted with an amused snort. He had both arms folded across his chest; he unlaced one to point to the nearest egg. "That's the biggest. I wonder if it's one of the golds. I've lost track of which was put where in that dance we just did. There were more males than females among the ones lost, and Lili's opened book on which of us get what."

Sorka gave the egg a long speculative look. She thought about whether or not it was a gold, and then decided, somewhat arbitrarily in her own mind, that no, it was not. It was a bronze. She did not tell Sean her conclusion. Sean tended to debate such issues, and that moment, surveying the first clutch of "dragons," was not a moment to spoil. She sighed.

Dragonets had become as important to her as horses. She readily admitted that Sean could make his fair behave better than she could hers. He could and did discipline his for effective use during Threadfall. But she knew that she *understood* any of them—hers, his, or those impressed by anyone else on Pern—better than he did, especially when they were injured fighting Thread. Or maybe her sensitivity, developed over the last couple of months along with her pregnancy, tended toward maternal caring. The doctor had said she was in excellent health and had found nothing in her physical profile to suggest problems. She could continue riding as long as she felt comfortable in the saddle.

"You'll know when you can't ride anymore," he had told

her with a grin. "And you'll have to curtail ground crew at five months. That's no time for you to be swinging the weight of a flamethrower about for hours on end."

Sorka had not yet found the proper moment to inform Sean of his impending fatherhood. She fretted about his reaction. They had saved enough work credits to make the Killarney holding a substantial one, but not with Thread falling. Sean had not even mentioned Killarney since the third Fall, but that did not mean he did not think about it. She saw the faraway look in his eyes from time to time.

She had thought he would mention Killarney when his father returned Cricket from his stud duties. But he had not. With everyone working double jobs just to keep essential services going, very few people had time to consider private concerns. Sean and Sorka spent what leisure moments they had keeping their horses fit, riding them out beyond the swath of destruction for an hour's grazing.

The main door opened to admit one of the security engineers, and there was an instant reaction from the gallery of winged watchers. Sean chuckled softly. "They don't need a security system in here," he murmured to Sorka. "C'mon, love, we've got surgery in five minutes."

With backward glances at the circles of mottled eggs, the two apprentices reluctantly went back to work. As they crossed one of the alleys, they had a clear view of the donks slowly moving the shuttle *Moth* into takeoff position.

"D'you think they'll make it?" Sorka asked Sean.

"They've been busy enough," he replied sourly. Neither Nabhi Nabol nor Bart Lemos had made himself popular since the sudden rise to charterer rank. "Still, I wouldn't be in their shoes for anything!"

She giggled. "Spacer Yvonne. You've never told me, Sean, did that help you on the drop?"

He gave her face a long and searching look, a slight smile tugging his lips. Then he put his arm about her and hauled her into his side. "All I could think about was proving to you I wasn't scared. But, by Jays, I was!" Then his expression changed and he halted, turning her roughly to him, both hands feeling across her stomach and pulling the bulky shipsuit taut across her body. He glared accusingly at her. "Why didn't you tell me you're pregnant?"

"Well, it's only just been confirmed," she said defiantly.

"Does everyone else know but me?" He was furious with her; for the first time in their years together, he was mad *at* her. His eyes were flashing and his hands rested hard across her thickening waistline.

"No one knows except the doctor, and he doesn't have to ground me for another three months." She pulled defensively at one hand to make him release her. "But there's Killarney and I know you think about it . . ."

"Your mother knows?"

"When do I have a chance to see her? She's minding half of Landing's babies, as well as my latest brother. You're the only other one who knows."

"Sometimes you baffle me, Sorka," Sean said, his anger abating. He shook his head. "Why wait to tell me? Killarney's a long way off in our future now. We're committed here. I thought you understood that." He put both hands on her shoulders and gave her a stern shake. "I've wanted to be the father of your children. I want you to have only mine. I want it to be now, too, Sorka love, but I didn't think I had the right to ask you to bring a child into the world the way it is." His voice fell into the special tender tone he always used when they were making love.

"No, it's the best time to have a child. Something for both of us to have," she said. She did not add "in case," but he knew what she was thinking and tightened his grip on her. His eyes compelled hers to look at him. The fury had been replaced by resolution.

"Immediately after surgery, we're going before Cherry Duff. This is going to be a two-parent child, or my name's not Sean Connell!"

Sorka burst out laughing and did not stop until they reached the surgery shed.

Ongola had ended up as arbiter on the reconditioning of the space shuttle *Moth*. Nabhi Nabol had been driving the refit crew demented, interrupting them at critical moments of repair, demanding to know if that circuit or this segment of hull had been checked. Despite the fact that he had a good working knowledge of the complexities of a shuttle, he delayed more than he assisted. The shuttle *Mayfly*, lying next to the *Moth*, had been sectioned off into offices for Ongola, Fulmar, and Nabhi, with a half-dozen comm lines so that Ongola could handle other commitments while on hand at the shuttle. His office was festooned with probe pics and survey maps, as well as with the various launch windows open to Nabhi. Nabhi would often come in and stand broodingly staring at the orbits, picking at his lower lip. Ongola ignored him.

The basic condition of the *Moth* had been surprisingly good: there had been practically no perishing of interior circuits or lines. But everything had to be double-checked. In that Ongola agreed with Nabhi. It put quite a burden on Fulmar's engineering team, but that was not where he disagreed with the autocratic Nabhi.

"I wouldn't care what he asked me to do," Fulmar told Ongola, "if he'd only ask politely. You'd think he was doing *me* a favor. Are you sure he's as good a driver as he thinks he is?"

"He is good," Ongola reluctantly admitted.

"I'd've preferred the mission in Bonneau's hands," Fulmar replied, shaking his head sadly. "But with that big stake, kids and all, I can't fault his refusal. It's just that—" He broke off, raising his big, work-stained hands in a helpless gesture.

"The mission has got to succeed, Fulmar," Ongola said, giving the man an encouraging clout on the shoulder. "And you're the best man to see that it does."

In the thirteenth week after Threadfall, the pattern suddenly shifted. As the squadrons reached the projected site, which was mainly over unoccupied lands, only the top of the squadron saw the leading edge. It was well north of their position: the gray shimmering stain on the horizon was all too easily identified.

"Hell and damnation!" Theo Force cried, ramming a call through to Ongola at Landing. "The damned stuff's shifted north, Zi. We'll need reinforcements."

"Give me the coordinates," Ongola said, issuing crisp orders and gesturing to Jake to get in touch with Dieter or Boris. "Go for it. We'll scramble another squadron or two to help. I'll alert Drake."

Boris was found, and made some quick calculations. "It's going to hit Calusa and Bordeaux. It seems to have shifted north by five degrees. That doesn't make sense. Why on earth would it shift so suddenly?"

There was no answer to his question. Ongola rang off. "Have you the week's roster there, Jake? Check where Kwan is today. I'll call Chuck Havers at Calusa."

Sue Havers answered the phone. After her initial shock at the news, she rallied. "We've several hours then, don't we? And it could just miss us? I hope so. I don't know where Chuck is working today. Thank you, Zi. And," she added, her voice less assured, "are you calling Mary Tubberman, or should I warn her?"

"We'll send Ned along." Ongola disconnected.

Shunning was very hard on the relatives. Ned was entitled to assist his mother and his younger brothers and sister in fighting Thread. If he chose also to assist his father in the emergency, there would be only family to witness it. Tubberman had been quick to clad his buildings with metal, so his stake was as safe as those precautions could make it. He would get no other help.

Ongola then contacted Drake and ordered him to avoid the Tubbermans' stake. Drake at first protested that they couldn't leave any Thread on any ground, shunned or not.

"Ned can protect that much with his mother's help, Drake, but we cannot assist Ted Tubberman."

"But it's Thread, man."

"That's an order, man," Ongola replied in a steely tone.

"Gotcha!"

Ongola then informed Paul Benden and Emily Boll of the pattern's alteration.

"Ezra will say that proves intelligence directs Fall," Paul remarked to Emily as they conferred.

"It's heads we lose, tails we lose, as far as I can see," Emily replied, heaving a sigh.

"It's as well we don't have to wait long to find out." Paul nodded toward the grid where the *Moth* was undergoing the final countdown. None of the technicians had been allowed to scramble for additional support squadrons. Their assignments on the shuttle had just become all-important.

Following the courtesy now well established, Drake Bonneau checked in at the Havers' stakehold on his way back from end of Fall which had just tipped Bordeaux across the Jordan River. He landed within sight of the Tubbermans' larger home.

"Ned and Mary were out with flamethrowers," Chuck told the squadron leader, "and then, for some insane reason, Ted drove them back into the house. There couldn't have been much damage, or we'd have seen results."

"Well, you're all right here," Drake said heartily.

"The ground crew arrived well in advance. But does anyone know why the pattern's shifted?" Sue asked. Weary with fighting, she needed some spark of reassurance.

"No," Drake replied cheerfully, "but we'll probably be told!"

He accepted a cup of the refreshing fruit drink that the oldest Havers girl brought him and his crew, then said good-bye. Drake had obeyed Ongola's order to bypass the Tubberman stake during Fall, but after what the Havers had said about Ted, he was curious. In his opinion, all Thread had to be destroyed, even if it fell on a shunned homesite. Thread did not care about human conflicts: it ate. Drake did not want to see a little burrow get started because of man-made restrictions.

Therefore, as he took off, he made a leisurely turn right over the Tubberman property. He saw Ned standing on the green patch surrounding the house. Ned waved and gesticulated rather wildly, at which point Drake felt obliged to follow orders and turn northwest towards Landing.

He was having a quick bite to eat in the dining hall when Ned Tubberman found him.

"You saw it, Drake, I know you did. You have to have seen it," Ned said, excitedly pulling at Drake's sleeve to pull him to his feet. "C'mon, you have to tell them what you saw."

Drake pulled his arm free. "Tell who what?" He forked up another mouthful of the hot food. Thread-fighting gave him an incredible appetite.

"Tell Kwan and Paul and Emily what you saw."

"I didn't *see* anything!" Then suddenly Drake had a flash of pure recall: Ned standing on a green square, a green square that was surrounded by scorched earth. "I don't believe what I saw!" He wiped his mouth, chewing absently as he absorbed that memory. "But Thread had just been across your place, and Chuck and Sue saw your father stop you flaming!"

"Exactly!" Ned grinned hugely and again pulled at Drake. The squadron leader rose and followed Ned out of the room. "I want you to tell them what you saw, to corroborate my statement. I don't *know* what Dad's done." The grin faded and some of the buoyancy drained from Ned Tubberman. "He says shunning works two ways. Mother told me that he locks himself away in his laboratory and won't let anyone near it. My brothers and sister go over to Sue's all the time, but Mother won't leave Dad, even if he isn't in the house much. She keeps the place ticking over."

"Your father's been experimenting with something?" Drake was confused.

"Well, he's got botanical training. He did say that until help came, the only defense was the planet itself." Ned slowed his pace. "And that patch of grass must have defended itself—somehow—against today's Fall, because it's still there!"

Drake did tell Kwan, Paul, Emily, and the hastily summoned Pol and Bay. Ned insisted that he had seen Thread fall on the ground-cover plants, had not seen them wither or be ingested, and that by the time Drake had overflown the stake, there was no evidence that Thread had ever fallen on that twelve-by-twenty-meter rectangle.

"I couldn't hazard a guess as to how he's done it," Pol finally said, looking to Bay for agreement. "Maybe he has been able to adapt Kitti Ping's basic program for use on a less complex life-form. Professionally I have to doubt it."

"But I saw it," Ned insisted. "Drake saw it, too."

There was a long silence, which Emily finally broke. "Ned, we do not doubt *you*, or Drake's verification, but as your father said, shunning works both ways."

"Are you too proud to ask him what he's done?" Ned demanded, his skin blanched under his tan, and his nostrils flaring with indignation.

"Pride is not involved," Emily said gently. "Safety is. He was shunned because he defied the will of the colony. If you can honestly say that he has changed his attitude, then we can discuss reinstatement."

Ned flushed, his eyes dropping away from Emily's tolerant gaze. He sighed deeply. "He doesn't want anything to do with Landing or anyone on it." Then he gripped the edge of the table and leaned across it toward the governor. "But he's done something incredible. Drake saw it."

"I did indeed see ground cover where there shouldn't've been any," Drake conceded.

"Could your mother present evidence on his behalf?" Paul asked, seeking an honorable way out for Ned's sake.

"She says he only talks to Petey, and Petey says he's sworn to secrecy, so she hasn't pushed him." Ned's face twisted with anguish for a long moment, then it cleared. "I'll ask her. I'll ask Petey, too. I can try!"

"This has not been easy for you either, Ned," Emily said. "All of us would like to see the matter happily resolved." She touched his hand where he still gripped the table edge. "We need everyone right now."

Ned looked her steadily in the eyes and gave a slow nod. "I believe you, Governor."

"Sometimes the duties to which rank entitles me are more than it's worth," Emily murmured to Paul as the hatch of the shuttle finally closed on Nabhi Nabol and Bart Lemos. She spoke quietly, because every young man in Nabhi's squadron had come to wish their leader good luck. She turned and smiled at them, leading the way off the grid to the safer sidelines, and waited dutifully with the technicians for the takeoff.

They waited and waited, until both admiral and governor were giving the meteorology tower anxious scrutiny. Just when both had decided that Nabhi was going to renege, as they had half suspected he would, they heard the roar of ignition and saw the yellow-white flame pouring out of the tubes.

"Firing well," Paul bellowed over the noise. Emily contented herself with a nod as she plugged her ears with her fingers.

She did not know much about the mechanics of shuttles, but the young men were grinning and waving their arms triumphantly. The look of relief on Fulmar's face was almost comical. Majestically the shuttle began its run up the grid, its speed increasing at a sensational rate. It became airborne, the engines thrusting it in an abrupt but graceful swoop up. The flame became lost in the blue of the sky as the observers shaded their eyes against the rising sun. Then the puffy contrail blossomed, billowing out as a tracer for the shuttle's path. The technicians who had made it possible cheered, and clapped one another on the back.

"Gawssakes, but it's good to get a bird up again," one of the men shouted. "Hey, what's wrong with them?" he added, pointing to several fairs of dragonets zipping at low level across the grid out of nowhere, crooning oddly.

"Who's having a baby?" Fulmar demanded.

Emily and Paul exchanged glances. "We are," she said, sliding quickly into the skimmer. "See? They're going straight to the Hatching Ground."

Looking up toward Landing, there was no doubt that fairs of dragonets were streaming in that direction. No one lingered on the grid. The roof of the Hatching Ground was covered with the crooning and chittering creatures. The cacophony was exciting rather than irritating. When the admiral and governor arrived, they had to make their way through the crowd to the open double doors.

"Welcome in nine-hundred-part harmony," Emily muttered to Paul as they made it to the edge of the warm sands. Their they halted, awed by the sense of occasion within.

Kitti Ping had left explicit instructions on who was to attend the birth day. Sixty young people between the ages of eighteen and thirty, who had already shown a sympathy for the dragonets, had the privilege of standing around the circle of eggs. Wind Blossom, Pol, Bay, and Kwan stood to one side on a wooden platform, their faces flushed and expectant.

The dragonets' song outside remaining softly jubilant while the crooning of those who had found roosting space inside sounded like subdued encouragement, almost reverent.

"They can't know what we expect for today, can they, Paul?"

"Young Sean Connell"—Paul pointed to where the young man stood beside his wife around the eggs—"would have you believe that they do. But then, they've always been attracted by birthing! After all, they protect their own young against attack."

A hush swept around the arena as a distinct crack was heard. One of the eggs rocked slightly, the motion drawing excited whispers.

Emily crossed her fingers, hiding them in the folds of her trousers. She noticed, with a slight grin, that others were doing the same. So much hung on the events of that day, on the first hatching and on what Nabhi Nabol was irrevocably committed to doing.

Another egg cracked and a third wobbled. The chorus became beguilingly insistent, striking an excited chord in everyone watching.

Then all of a sudden, one of the eggs cracked open and a creature emerged, damp from birth; it shook stubby wings and stumbled over its shell, squawking in alarm. The dragonets answered soothingly. The young people in the circle stood their ground, and Emily marveled at their courage, for that awkward creature was not the graceful being she had been expecting, a beast remembered from old legends and illustrations held in library treasuries. She caught herself holding her breath, and exhaled quickly.

The creature extended its wings; they were wider and thinner than she had expected. It was so spindly, so ungainly, and its very oddly constructed eyes were flashing with red and yellow. Emily felt a flush of alarm. The creature gave a desperate cry, and was answered reassuringly by the multivoiced choir above. It lurched forward, its voice pleading, and then the cry altered to one of joy, held on a high sweet note. It staggered another step and fell at the feet of David Catarel, who bent to help it.

He looked up with eyes wide with wonder. "He wants me!"

"Then accept him!" Pol bellowed, gesturing for one of the

stewards to come forward with a bowl of food. "Feed him! No, don't anyone else help you. The bond should be made now!"

Kneeling by his new charge, David offered the little dragon a hunk of meat. It bolted that and urgently cried for more, pushing at David's leg with an imperious head.

"He says he's very hungry," David cried. "He's talking to me. In my head! It's incredible. How did she do it?"

"The mentasynth works, then!" Emily murmured to Paul, who nodded with the air of someone not at all surprised.

"Ye gods, but it's ugly," Paul said in a very low voice.

"You probably weren't much to look at at birth either," Emily surprised herself by saying. She grinned at his quick glance of astonishment.

David coaxed his new friend out of the circle of people and toward the edge of the Hatching Ground, calling for more food. "Polenth says he's starving."

Bay had ordered plenty of red meat to be available, butchered from animals that had adapted well to the improved Pernese grasses. The young dragonets would require plenty of boron for growth in their first months, and would best absorb it from the flesh of cattle.

Another egg cracked, and a second bronze male made a straight-line dash to Peter Semling. A shrill voluntary came from Peter's fair of dragonets. There was a long wait before any more activity. A worried hum developed among the watchers. Then four more eggs abruptly shattered, two with unexpectedly dainty creatures, one golden and one bronze, who partnered themselves with Tarrie Chernoff and Shih Lao; the other two were stolid-looking browns who took to Otto Hegelman and Paul Logorides.

"Do they expect them all to hatch today?" Emily asked Paul.

"Let's go around to Pol and Bay," Paul said. They inched their way to the right, pausing to admire David Catarel's bronze, who was bolting down hunks of meat so fast that he seemed to be inhaling them. David looked ecstatic.

"Well, they could," Pol replied when they reached him. He was masking anxiety well. Wind Blossom was not, and barely acknowledged the quiet greetings of admiral and governor. "They were engineered within a thirty-six-hour period. The six that have hatched were from the first and second groups. We might have to wait. In our observations of wild dragonets, we know that laying the eggs can take several hours. I suspect the greens and golds may be like one of the Earth vipers, which can keep eggs within her body until she finds an appropriate place, or time, to lay them. We know that naturally clutched eggs do hatch more or less simultaneously. This," he said, pointing to the Hatching Ground, "is a concession to Kitti Ping's reverence for the ancestral species' habitat. Ah, another one's cracking." He consulted the flimsy in his hand. "One of the third group!"

"Six males, but only one female," Bay said quietly. "To be frank, I'd rather have more females. What do you think, Blossom?"

"One perfect male and one perfect female are all we need," Wind Blossom said in a tight, controlled voice. She had her hands hidden in her loose sleeves, but there were deep tension lines in her face and her eyes were clouded.

"Peter Semling's bronze looks sturdy," Emily said encouragingly. Wind Blossom did not respond, her gaze was fixed on the eggs. "Are they as you anticipated?" she asked, looking at Pol and Bay.

"No," Bay admitted, "but then it was Kitti who had the requisite image in her mind. If only . . ." She faltered. "Ah, another gold female. I believe that Kitti Ping made the choices gender imperative. For Nyassa Clissmann. And such charming creatures!"

Emily failed to see charm in the hatchlings, but she was glad to see so many live ones. But what had Kitti Ping had in her mind when she altered the dragonet ova? Those were not dragons of any kind Emily knew. And yet she had an unexpected vision of a sky full of the creatures, soaring and diving, breathing flame. Had Kitti Ping had such a vision?

"The shuttle!" Pol said suddenly. "Did I hear it take off?"

"Yes, he made it," Paul replied. "Ongola will keep us informed. We don't have enough fuel for a direct flight. The shuttle'll have to coast a week before it reaches the trail."

"Oh, I see." Then Pol refocused his attention on the eggs.

The crowd shifted as some people had to return to complete unfinished tasks and others moved in to take their places. Food was brought to the biologists and the leaders on their dais, and wooden benches to sit on. Wind Blossom remained standing. Food was also taken to the circle of hopeful dragon riders. The dragonets' encouragement did not abate. Emily wondered how they could keep it up.

It was dark before there was any further movement, and then all at once a brown and two golds cracked their eggs. Marco Galliani got the brown, and Kathy Duff and Nora Sejby the two golds. There was a good deal of cheering.

The crowd at the opening thinned, while the dragonets kept their posts and continued their encouraging song. Emily was becoming weary and she could see fatigue catching up with the others. She was half-asleep when Catherine Radelin-Doyle impressed her gold.

"Do they always go female to female?" Emily asked Pol. "And male to male?"

"Since the males are expected to be fighters and the females egg-carriers, Kitti made it logical."

"Logical to her," Emily said, a trifle bemused. "There aren't any blues or greens among them," she suddenly realized.

"Kitti programmed the heavier males, but I believe they're to carry sperm for the entire range. The greens will be the smallest, the fighters; the blues sturdier, with more staying power; the browns sort of anchor fighters with even more endurance. They'll have to fight four to six hours, remember! The bronzes are leaders and the golds . . ."

"Waiting at home to be egg-carriers."

Pol gave Emily a long look, his tired face reflecting astonishment at her sarcasm.

"In the wild, greens don't have good maternal instincts. The golds do," Bay put in, giving the governor an odd glance. "Kitti Ping kept as much natural instinct as possible. Or so her program reads."

"There!" Nabhi said, leaning back from the console, his swarthy face intense with an inner satisfaction. "Kenjo wasn't the only one who could save fuel."

Bart stared at him, surprised and confused. "Save it for what, Nabhi?" He spoke more sharply than he meant to, but he had been wound up with tension that would not ease. It was not that he did not trust Nabhi as a pilot—Nabhi was a good driver, or Bart would not have been talked into participating in the insane venture, not for the choicest land on Pern.

"To maneuver," Nabhi said. His mocking grin did nothing to ease Bart's disquiet.

"Where? You're not . . . you wouldn't be mad enough to try to land on the farking planet?" Bart clawed at the release straps, but Nabhi's indolent gesture of negation aborted the effort.

"No way. I came to get the pods or whatever." His smile then broadened, and Bart was amazed at the humor in it. "Our course is basically the same one Avril took." He turned his head and looked directly at his copilot.

"So?"

"They said the gig blew up." Nabhi's smile was pure malice. "Turn on the screens. There might be some interesting flotsam. Diamonds and gold nuggets and whatever else Avril took with her. No one needs to know what else we scooped up out of space. And it sure beats mining the stuff ourselves."

By midnight Pol and Bay decided to examine the remaining eggs and slowly did the rounds. Wooden platforms had been brought out for the candidates to rest on, since the heat in the sand was enervating. None of the chosen was willing to forgo the chance at impressing a hatchling by leaving the Ground.

When the two biologists returned, Pol was shaking his head and Bay looked drawn. She went immediately to Wind Blossom and touched her arm.

"The rest of the first group show no signs of life. But already the outcome is better than projected. We detected viable signs in the others. We can but wait. They were not all conceived at the same time."

Wind Blossom remained an unmoving statue.

Sean nudged Sorka in the ribs to wake her up. She had fallen asleep leaning against him, her cheek against his upper arm. She was instantly alert and aware of her surroundings. Sean pointed to the biggest of the eggs, which sat almost directly in front of them. He had taken that position at the outset, and finally, after his long vigil, the egg was rocking slightly.

"What time is it?" she asked.

"Nearly dawn. There's been no other movement. But listen to the dragonets. Listen to Blaze. She'll have no throat left!"

They had noted their own dragonets early during that long day, and Sorka had taken heart from their constant choral encouragements.

"That egg over there has been moving spasmodically for the last two hours," he said in a quiet tone. "The one beyond it rocked for a while, but it's stopped completely."

Sorka tried to contain a yawn, then gave in to the compulsion and felt better for it. She wanted to stretch, but another candidate was draped over her legs, fast asleep. Beyond, the other candidates began to wake.

At some point while Sorka had been dozing, the admiral

and the governor had left. Pol and Bay were leaning into each other, and Kwan's head was on his chest, arms limp in his lap. Wind Blossom had apparently not moved since she had taken up her watch.

"She's uncanny," Sorka said, turning away from the geneticist.

A single great crack startled everyone, and the egg before them parted into two ragged halves. The bronze hatchling walked out imperiously, lifted his head, and made a sound like a stuttering trumpet. Everyone came to attention. Sean was on his feet, and Sorka pushed at his legs to urge him on. She need not have worried. As he locked eyes with the hatchling, Sean gave a low incredulous groan and moved forward to meet the beast halfway. Their fair was bugling with triumph.

"Meat, quickly," Sorka called, beckoning to a sleepy steward. Hoping that the heat in the building had not soured the meat, she ran to meet the man, grabbed the bowl, and returned to thrust it into Sean's hands. She had never seen that utterly rapt look in his eyes before.

"He says his name is Carenath, Sorka. He knows his own name!" Sean transferred food from the bowl into Carenath's mouth as fast as he could shovel it. "More meat. Hurry, I need more meat."

Everyone in the Hatching Ground was wakened by his vibrant voice. Then the other egg broke open, and a golden female sauntered forth, chittering and looking about urgently. Sorka was too busy passing bowls of meat to Sean to notice until Betsy tugged at her arm.

"She's looking for you, Sorka. Look at her!"

Sorka turned her head and suddenly she, too, felt the indescribable impact of a mind on hers, a mind that rejoiced in finding its equal, its lifelong partner. Sorka was filled with an exultation that was almost painful.

My name is Faranth, Sorka!

"We have actually learned a great deal from eggs that didn't hatch," Pol told Emily and Paul when he, Wind Blossom, and Bay made their report two evenings later.

"So far, so good?" Paul asked hopefully.

"Oh, very good," Bay said enthusiastically, grinning and nodding her head vigorously. Wind Blossom managed a prim, set smile. The air of impenetrable gloom that had surrounded her on the Hatching Day had been exchanged for an aloof superiority.

"Then you do believe that the eighteen hatchings will all become viable adults?" Paul asked Wind Blossom.

She inclined her head. "We must await their maturity with patience."

"But they *will* be able to produce flame from phosphine-bearing rocks and go *between* as the dragonets do?" Paul asked her.

"I am, myself, much encouraged," Pol said, when Wind Blossom said nothing. "Bay is, too, by the way in which mentasynth has provided a strong empathic bond and telepathic communication."

"A genuine mind-to-mind contact," Bay added with a smile of satisfaction. "Especially strong for Sorka and Sean."

"The dragons were *designed*," Wind Blossom added pompously, "to make Impression with other than their own ancestral species. In that much, the program has succeeded." She held up her hand. "We must contain impatience and strive to achieve the perfect specimen."

"The stabilization of Impression to another species was the most important aspect," Pol said, his brows creasing slightly. "After all, the dragonets have teleported as naturally as they breathe."

"The *dragonets* have," Wind Blossom said coolly. "We have yet to see if the dragons can."

"Kitti Ping did not alter those capabilities, you know. They will, of course, have to be refined and controlled," Pol went on. He did not like Wind Blossom's attitude, her refusal to concede the triumphs already achieved. "I must say, I am very glad that the young Connells both Impressed. With their veterinary training and their general competence, not to mention their proven ability to discipline their dragonet fairs, we couldn't ask for better mates."

Wind Blossom made a slight noise, which the listeners took as disapproval.

"They're qualified," Bay said with unexpected heat. "Someone must make the beginning."

"Their progress must be strictly monitored," Wind Blossom said, "so that we will know what mistakes must be avoided the next time."

"Next time?" Emily blinked in surprise and noticed that Bay and Pol were reacting similarly.

"I do not yet know if these creatures will perform on the other design levels, either natural or imposed." Her sepulchral tone indicated that she had grave doubts.

"How can you not be encouraged—" Pol began with some heat.

A decisive gesture of dismissal cut him off, and he stared at Wind Blossom.

"I will begin anew," Wind Blossom informed them in a tone that almost implied martyrdom. Pol and Bay regarded her in astonishment. "With what we learned from the post mortem examinations, I cannot be sure that any of the living will be fertile or reproduce. More importantly—reproduce themselves! I must try again, and again, until success is assured.

This experiment is only begun."

"But, Wind Blossom—" Pol began, astounded.

"Come, you shall assist me." With an imperious gesture, she swept from the room.

Neither the veterinarians nor the xenobiologists had any criteria by which to judge the health of eighteen representatives of a new species. But the dragons' hearty appetites, the vibrant color of their suedelike hides, and the ease of their physical exertions—which consisted mainly of eating and exercising their wings—were taken as measures of well-being. In the first week of life, each had grown at least a handspan taller and had filled out; they looked considerably more substantial. And as the toughness of their transparent wings became more and more evident, those who had worried about their fragility were relieved.

Fascinated, the official medical support group watched as the two Connells bathed and oiled their ten-day-old dragons. Large shallow bathing pools of siliplas had been erected near the homes of all the dragonmates. Faranth was coyly aware of the admiring glances.

"She's preening, Dad," Sorka said, amused, as she poured oil on a scaly patch between the dorsal ridges. "Is that the itchy spot, Farrie?"

My name is Faranth and that is that *itchy spot,* Faranth said in tones that went from reproof to relief. *Another is starting on my hind leg.*

"She doesn't like to be called by a nickname," Sorka said tolerantly, grinning at her father. "But jays, she takes scrubbing." A bristle brush had been made for the purpose, firm enough to rub in oil but not harsh enough to mar the tender, smooth hide.

Suddenly everyone was drenched as Carenath, sweeping his glistening wings forward in the low bath, showered them with water.

"Carenath, behave yourself!" Sorka and Sean spoke in the same sharp tone.

I am already clean, you polka-dotted idiot, Faranth said in an excellent mimicry of one of Sorka's favorite admonitions. *I was* nearly *dry, and now my oiling has to be done again.*

Sean and Sorka laughed and then hurriedly explained to the drenched men that they were amused by what Faranth had said, not by Carenath's playfulness. Sean gestured to the dragonets that perched on the rooftree, obviously watching everything below them. Almost instantly, the soaked observers had towels dropped about them.

"Handy critters, Sean," Red Hanrahan said, drying his face and hands and mopping his clothing.

"Very useful with young dragons, too, Red," Sean replied. "They fish constantly for these walking appetites."

Am I that much trouble to you? Carenath sounded aggrieved.

"Not at all, pet," Sean quickly assured him, lovingly caressing the head that was tilted wistfully. "Don't be silly. You're young, you have a good appetite, and it's our job to keep you fed."

Red was beginning to get accustomed to the sudden non sequiturs from his daughter and son-in-law, but the others were startled. Faranth butted at Sorka for reassurance and when she received it, her eyes settled to the blue of contentment.

"Can't they be ridden yet? And hunt for themselves?" Phas Radamanth asked.

"You don't attempt to ride a foal, even a good big one," Sean replied, brushing oil on the rough patch on Carenath's broad back. "Kitti Ping's program suggests waiting a full year before we attempt it."

"Can we wait long enough for them to mature?" Threadfall and the need to fight it was never far from anyone's mind.

"I've never rushed a horse," Sean said, "and I'm not about to start with my dragon. However, at the rate they're growing, and if we can be sure that their skeletal structure—it's boron-silicate, you know, which is tougher than our calcareous material—is developing properly, I think they'll be capable of manned flight as scheduled." Sean grinned. "Jays, what times we'll have then, old fella, won't we?"

The tenderness, the concern, and the deep affection in Sean's voice were almost embarrassing to hear. Red looked at his son-in-law in surprise. So Impression had affected young Connell, as it had changed all the dragonmates. Even Sorka, who had always been caring and capable, seemed somehow strengthened and exuded a radiance that could not all be attributed to her pregnancy.

Young David Catarel had altered in the most spectacular way. Badly scarred mentally as well as physically by that First Fall and Lucy Tubberman's tragic death, the young man had retreated into a wallow of self-disgust and needless guilt. Not even intensive therapy had broken through the stubborn facade. David fought Thread with a vindictive intensity that was frightening to watch. Only when he had seen how useful dragonets were in ground-crewing had he tolerated their wistful affection.

The renaissance of his personality had begun the moment Polenth nudged his knee. An openly smiling, ecstatic David Catarel had left the hatching sands, solicitously and deftly assisting the staggering little dragon. The changes in the other youths had been felicitous as well, though Catherine Radelin-Doyle's tendency to giggle at some unheard comment from her golden mate could be disconcerting. Shih Lao, who had Impressed bronze Firth, also went about with smiles on his once pensive face, Tarrie Chernoff had stopped apologizing for any minor accident or inconsistency, and Otto Hegelman's stutter had completely disappeared.

"They're credits to you both," Caesar Galliani said to Sean and Sorka. "Though Marco's Duluth, if I say so myself, looks equally as well."

Sean grinned at the Roma stakeholder. "He does, indeed. As long as they're eating, sleeping—"

"Being bathed, cosseted, oiled, and scratched, they have *nothing* to complain of," Sorka finished, giving Faranth's nose a final swipe. "There now, love, why don't you curl up and go to sleep?"

Carenath's not finished, Faranth complained even as she was moving to the sun-warmed plascrete she preferred as her couch. *I like him to lean against. I'm a little hungry.*

Sorka put her fingers between her front teeth and gave a piercing whistle. The dragonets instantly disappeared.

All clean, Carenath cried, hopping out of the bath. Warned by Sean, he did not shake himself all over his audience. Carefully he extended his wet glistening wings, holding them aloft in the slight breeze while Sean, with Sorka's help, mopped his underparts dry.

"D'you need anything, Sean, while we're here?" Red asked.

"Nope," Sean grunted as he bent to dry the claw sheaths. The claw design was one of the few physical modifications that Kitti Ping had made from dragonet to dragon. The fingerlike claws would be more useful, she had thought, for grabbing running animals than the dragonets' pincer-type arrangement. "As soon as they've had their snack, we'll have one, too."

"Amazing couple," Phas Radamanth said, smiling up at Red. "Now if that bronze is fertile, and the gold willing, we'll have our next generation."

"Let's not rush too far ahead in our hopes," Caesar said, looking back over his shoulder at the scene. "Wind Blossom strongly advocates caution about this first batch."

"Her *grandmother* bioengineered them." Phas spoke firmly, stopping in his tracks.

"Well, she also produced imperfect ones that didn't hatch."

"Eighteen was a very good result, and we learned a great deal from dissecting the aborts," Phas said.

They were just turning away when the air filled with dragonets, each carrying a fair-sized packtail in its claws. The dragons lifted their heads, opened their mouths, and took the offerings as rightful homage. The men grinned and continued their morning round.

Once Faranth and Carenath had their snack, they were quite willing to curl up together, Carenath with his triangular head neatly placed on his outstretched forelegs. Faranth draped her head and neck over his forequarters, her tail twitching occasionally just in front of his muzzle, her wings sagging slightly from their folded position on her back. Both freshly oiled hides gleamed in the sun.

"I will be glad when they *can* hunt for themselves," Sean murmured to Sorka as they wearily settled on the ground in the shade of the east wall of their home.

"Meanwhile," Sorka said, reaching for a water jar, "we couldn't manage it without the fair." She sent strong feelings of gratitude to Duke, Emmett, Blazer, and the others. Their response, muted in deference to the somnolent dragons, was clearly "You're welcome."

"The requirements of dragons were never considered by Landing's architects," Sean remarked as he took the water jar in turn. Washing dragons was thirsty business. "When they get bigger, something will have to be done. There aren't enough places to house people in Landing anymore, much less dragons."

"D'you think they'd be comfortable in some of Catherine's caves? She mentioned it again yesterday."

"Yes, so she did. Then she giggled."

The two Connells exchanged amused and tolerant grins. The human dragonmates had abruptly found themselves a group set apart, by occupation and dedication, as well as by the subtler changes within them. Though they had the unqualified support and help of every member of the medical, veterinary, and biological teams, they found that talking minor problems over among themselves brought better results. One had to *be* a dragonmate to appreciate the problems—and the joys!

Sorka noted with quiet pride that it was Sean's opinion that seemed to be sought most frequently by the others. And she agreed. He had always been sensible about animals. But, she realized, she could not really call the dragons "animals." They were too . . . human. Even their voices: Carenath's voice sounded just like Sean's light baritone being spoken through a long tunnel. And Sorka suspected that Faranth's voice was a version of her own.

From the moment they had brought the two hatchlings to Irish Square, Sorka had realized that she heard both Faranth and Carenath, while Sean heard only Carenath. That Sorka could hear both did not seem to distress either dragon. They were amenable to everything in life as long as they had full bellies and oiled hides. Then, as Sean's bond with the bronze developed, Sorka heard fewer private exchanges. She, too, had learned, as she suspected each dragonmate had, to communicate telepathically on a private band.

"I'd say they'll be ready to hunt in another week or two—if we can use a small corral to pen the beasts." Sean found her hand and squeezed it, then laid his hand over her belly. "All this won't harm our child, will it?"

Sorka felt guilty. Lately, she had not had time to think about her condition: there was always something to be done for Faranth, or for one of the other young dragons. And she and Sean were still on duty at the dragonet clinic, treating those injured fighting Thread.

"The doctor said I was healthy and could ride . . ." Sorka groaned. "Will *we* be able to teach them to fly *between,* Sean?" Her voice was low, and she clutched his hand apprehensively.

"Now, dear heart, we'll be able for what we have to do." The unknown clearly did not faze Sean anymore.

"But, Sean . . ."

"If *we* know where we're going, *they* will. They'll see it in our minds. They see everything else. What makes you think directions will be difficult?"

"But we don't even know how the dragonets do it!"

Sean shrugged, grinning down at her. "No, we don't. But

if the fire-lizards are capable of the teleportation, the dragons will be, too. Kitti Ping did not tamper with that. Let's not fret ourselves. We won't fret them."

She eyed him sourly, then shook her finger at him. "Then *you* stop worrying about it!"

Laughing, his blue eyes sparkling at her shrewd hit, he took her hand and pulled her into his embrace. She nestled there, taking strength from him and returning it. Although Sorka had never before felt so in charge of herself, so dynamic, there were moments when she was assailed with the fear that she might fail Faranth in some small but essential way. She expressed that to Sean.

"No, you won't," he said, smoothing her sweat-damp hair back from her face. "No more will I Carenath. They're ours, and we belong to them." He turned her face up to look at him, his eyes so intense with love and assurance that her breath caught. Sean embraced her again tightly. "Ever since we dropped to this planet, Sorka, this has been our destiny. Or why else were we the first to find the fire-lizards? Out of all the people exploring the world, why did the fire-lizards come to us? Why did the last of Kitti Ping's creation search *us* out of the crowd? No, believe in yourself, in us and our dragons." He held her a moment longer and then released her. "I think we have to give Cricket and Doove to your father. Brian gets along with Cricket very well."

Sorka had known that some decisions had to be made about their horses, both of whom had from the start been terrified of the wobbling dragons. Red and Brian had taken the horses up to the main veterinary barn. Sorka thought briefly of all the grand moments she had experienced on the bay mare's back, most of them shared with Sean and Cricket. But their dragons had become all-important.

"Yes," she heard herself saying with no further twinge of regret. "I never thought there'd come a day when I wouldn't have time for horses." She looked lovingly at the sleeping figure of Faranth and grinned at the bulge in the golden belly, which would all too quickly disappear. "I'll fix us something to eat."

Sean kissed her on the forehead. His new willingness to display affection was one of the fringe benefits from Carenath, and Sorka loved him more than ever. She leaned against him, inhaling his manly smell mixed with the herbal dragon oil.

"Make sandwiches, love," Sean advised. "Here comes Dave Catarel at the trot. If Polenth's asleep, the others will be along, too."

"They've got it," Ongola informed Paul when the admiral answered the comm unit in Emily's quarters, where he was anticipating one of Pierre's excellent dinners. Emily had taken pity on him as Ju had gone back to check on their Boca holding the previous day. "Nabhi just called in. Bart Lemos got a scoopful. Although . . ."

"Although what?" Paul asked, exchanging glances with Emily.

"Although it took them a long time," Ongola finished on a troubled sigh. "They should have been well up in the trail before now." Ongola sounded puzzled. "They have what we need, that's the important thing: the pods. The fax are being relayed to the interface right now. Ezra and Jim should have an analysis sometime tomorrow."

"Are you still at the *Moth?*" Paul asked, frowning. Ongola was not completely recovered from his injuries, and Paul was proprietary in his concern for him. Ongola would be a key man in the coming struggle for autonomy and survival.

"Yes, but Sabra's brought me dinner." Ongola was indulging in one of his rare chuckles as he signed off.

"They've got what we need," Paul told Emily as he reseated himself. "Now I can enjoy this dinner."

The first rumblings occurred the next morning, early enough to rattle many people in their beds. Only the young dragons were unperturbed, sleeping through the commotion made by the excited, frightened humans.

"Will this planet never let up on us?" Ongola demanded as he untangled himself from his bedsack and fumbled for the comm unit set.

"Was that an earthquake?" Sabra asked sleepily. She had left the children with a friend so that she and Ongola could have a few hours together. Sabra felt she needed that comfort almost as much as Ongola must. And she had signed on a charter promising order and tranquility!

"Go back to sleep," Ongola told her as he dialed. "What does Patrice say, Jake?" he asked his efficient assistant.

"He says the gravity meters have all been registering a disturbance in lava chambers along the island ring. He doesn't know what's going to blow, but the display suggests that something has to. He's trying to guess the most likely escape point."

Ongola's next call was to Paul, at home.

"No rest for the weary, huh?" Paul asked in a resigned tone.

"Volcanic disturbance all along the chain."

"Chain, my foot! That rumble was right under my ear, Ongola, and we do have three volcanoes looming over us."

Ongola was so accustomed to the great peaks that he had forgotten that they, also, could pose a threat; though the experts had all agreed that the last eruption of Mount Garben had occurred a millennium ago.

By midmorning Patrice relieved the worst fears by his announcement that a new volcano was erupting out of the sea beyond the eastern tip of Jordan Province. Young Mountain, which had been monitored for the past eight years, was throwing up a cloud of smoke, gas, and some ash, but magma pressure did not seem to be building there.

A second underground churning startled people midafternoon. When Patrice arrived, parking his sled in Administration

Square and going in to consult with Paul and Emily, an anxious crowd quickly gathered to await the result of that meeting. Finally the colony's two leaders appeared on the porch with Patrice, who was smiling and waving fax in both hands.

"A new volcano to be named. Like Aphrodite rising from the sea, but I don't necessarily insist on that name," he shouted.

"Where?"

"Beyond the easternmost tip of Jordan, safely away from us, my friends." He held up the largest photo so that the roiling seas and the protruding tip of the smoking peak could be seen by all.

"Yeah, but that's still the same little tectonic plate we're on, isn't it?" one man shouted. He pointed back over his shoulder at the lofty peak of Mount Garben. "That one could go again. Couldn't it?"

"Of course it could," Patrice answered easily, shrugging his shoulders. "But it is very unlikely in my opinion. It shot its head off thousands of years ago. There has been no evidence of activity here. It's an old one, that volcano. The young ones have more to say, and are saying it. Do not panic. We are safe at Landing." He sounded so certain that the anxious murmurings abated and the crowd dispersed.

All through the day there were sporadic growlings, as Telgar called them. Wandering at random through Landing, he had made himself available to anyone who wished to be reassured. It was the first time since Sallah's death that Telgar had circulated socially. That night, a large proportion of Landing's population gathered in Bonfire Square, and the blaze was built up to an unusual, almost defiant size.

"Our beautiful Pern has popped a pimple on her face," Telgar said with a hint of his former joviality, talking to a group of young people. "She's not so old that her digestion is perfect. And we have been disturbing her with our borings and diggings."

When he moved off, one of the apprentice geologists followed him. "Look, Tar-Telgar," the young man began earnestly. "We're not on basement rock here in Landing."

"That is very true," Telgar replied with a slight smile. "Which is why we are rocking a little. But I am not concerned."

The apprentice flushed. "Well, there's a wide, long strip of basement rock in the northern continent, along the western mountain range."

"Ah, how well you have studied your lessons," Telgar commented. He nodded equably to Cobber Alhinwa and Ozzie Munson, who had just joined them. "Ah, have a glass with us."

Embarrassed by having stated the obvious, the young man hastily excused himself.

"So people are talking of basement rock," Cobber said, and beside him Ozzie smirked.

"I know, you know, and he knows, but we have had enough of insecurity today. The basement rock will not shift. As you know, I have given my opinion to Paul, Emily, and Patrice." Telgar looked beyond the big miner to a distant view that only his eyes saw. Cobber and Ozzie exchanged meaningful glances. The set, pained look on Telgar's face meant that he was remembering something about Sallah.

Cobber nudged Ozzie and leaned conspiratorially toward Telgar. "Are we all to go look at some basement rock now, Telgar?"

The next morning a rumble of a different kind finally roused Paul as Ju reached across him for the handset.

"For you," she mumbled sleepily, dropping it on the bedsack and rolling over again.

Paul fumbled for it and cleared his throat. "Benden."

"Admiral," Ongola said urgently, "they've begun reentry, and Nabhi's on a bad course."

Paul pulled loose the fasteners of the bedsack and sat bolt upright. "How could he be?"

"*He* says he's green, Admiral."

"I'm coming." Paul had an irrational desire to slam the handset down and go back to sleep beside his wife. Instead he dialed Emily, who said she would join him at the met tower. Then he alerted Ezra Keroon and Jim Tillek.

"Paul?" Ju asked sleepily.

"Sleep on, honey. Nothing to worry you."

He had tried to keep his voice low and was sorry to have disturbed her. In the second semester of a new pregnancy, Ju needed more sleep. They had stayed up late talking, regretfully aware that they must set the example and close down their stake. The constant drain of Threadfall was having a devastating effect on supplies and resources. Joel particularly fretted over the dwindling efficiency of the power packs. According to Tom Patrick, the psychological profile of Landing's population was, in the main, encouraging, although therapy and medication were increasingly required to keep distressed people functioning. Somehow Paul could not bring himself to hope that Nabhi Nabol and Bart Lemos had brought back something as vital as encouragement.

Yesterday Ezra and Jim had produced the latest analysis of the eccentric's orbit. It was as wayward, in Jim Tillek's phrasing, as a drunken whore on a Saturday night at a space facility in the Asteroid Belt. What had looked to be a reasonable, predictable elliptical orbit through Rukbat's system proved to be even more bizarre, at an angle to the ecliptic. The planet would wobble into the vicinity of Pern every two hundred and fifty years, though Ezra had made extrapolations that provided some variations of its course, due to the effect of other planets in the system. During some of its orbits, it looked as if the eccentric and its cloud of junk would miss Pern.

"The most singular planet I've ever tried to track," Ezra had said apologetically, scratching his head as he summed up his report.

"Natural orbit?" Jim had asked, with a sly grin at the astronomer.

Ezra had given him a long scornful look. "There's nothing natural about that planet."

Although Thread had shifted five degrees to the north in the current—third—round of Falls, the admiral no longer held much hope for Ezra's theory that the Falls were deliberate, a softening-up procedure by some sentient agency. If that had been the case, he argued, the Falls ought to have accelerated in frequency and density after the wild planet swung to its nearest spatial point to Pern. But Thread had continued to drop in mindless patterns, each consistent with the northern shift. Mathematical calculations, checked and double-checked by Boris Pahlevi and Dieter Clissmann, concurred with Ezra's depressing conclusion. The eccentric would swing away from Pern and the inner system, only to swing back again in two hundred and fifty years.

The fax Bart had flashed back to Pern had shown the trail of debris to be endless.

"All the way to the edge of the system," Ezra declared in total capitulation. "The planet pierces the Oort cloud and drags the stuff down with it. Hoyle and Wickramansingh's theory has been vindicated in the Rukbat system."

"Aren't we lucky?" Jim added. "The junk could still be just ice and rock. We won't know for sure until we see what Bart Lemos scooped up out there." Jim was not at all happy that his theory was right. He would almost prefer a sentient intelligence somehow surviving on the eccentric planet. You could usually deal with intelligence. His theory made it tough on Pern.

In the cold light of a new morning, Paul dressed quickly, toeing his feet into his boots and closing the front of his shipsuit. He combed his hair neatly back and then stumbled into the predawn light. He used the skimmer—it would be quieter than him puffing and jogging down to the tower. He tried to practice what he preached in matters of conservation, but that morning he did not wish to be heard passing by.

The last few days, with the *Moth* overdue, had been hard on him. Waiting had never been his forte: decision and implementation were where he shone. Emily had proved once again the staunch, unswerving, resolute governor of herself and her subordinates. She was the best sort of complement to his strengths and flaws.

He saw lights over in Irish Square and, through the lines of dwellings, he caught a glimpse of fluttering wings as the young Connells gave their dragons the early morning meal. In the next square, Dave Catarel was up, too, feeding his young bronze.

At the thought of those young people committed to survival on Pern, Paul felt a sudden surge of confidence that he and Emily would bring everyone through. By all that was holy, they would! Had he not gone through bleaker days before the Battle at Purple Sector? And Emily had been blockaded for five years, emerging with a healthy functioning population despite a shortage of raw materials.

The tower was still dark as Paul parked his skimmer behind it. The windows were shuttered, but the main door was ajar. He went up the stairs as quietly as he could. Lately, with the dormitories so crowded, off-duty communications personnel slept on the ground floor. All of Landing was crowded—with refugees, Paul made himself add. People had even begun to make homes out of some of the Catherine Caves. That may have originated from some atavistic urge, but caves *were* Threadproof, and some of them were downright spacious. Caves might be a good place to lodge the fast-growing dragons, too.

As he reached the top floor, his eyes went immediately to the big screen, which showed the *Moth*'s position above Pern, relayed from the moon installation.

"He has not corrected his course once," Ongola said, swinging his chair toward Paul. He motioned for Jake to vacate the second console chair. The young man's eyes were black holes of fatigue, but Paul knew better than to suggest that Jake stand down until the shuttle was safely landed. "He ought to have fired ten minutes ago. *He* says he doesn't need to."

Paul dropped to the chair and toggled in the comm unit. "Tower to *Moth,* do you read me? Benden here. *Moth,* respond."

"Good morning, Admiral Benden," Nabhi replied promptly and insolently. "We are on course and reentering at a good angle."

"Your instrumentation is giving you false readings. Repeat, you are getting false readings, Nabol. Course correction essential."

"I disagree, Admiral," Nabhi replied, his tone jaunty. "No need to waste fuel! Our descent is on the green."

"Correction, *Moth!* Your descent is red and orange across our board and on our screen. You have sustained instrument malfunction. I will give you the readings." Paul read the numbers off from the calculator pad that Ongola handed to him. He was sure he heard a startled gasp in the background.

But Nabhi seemed undisturbed by Paul's information, and he did indeed report readings consonant with a good reentry.

"I don't believe this," Ongola said. "He's coming in from the wrong quadrant, at too steep an angle, and he's going to crash smack in the center of the Island Ring Sea. Soon."

"Repeat, *Moth,* your angle is wrong. Abort reentry. Nabol, take another orbit. Sort yourself out. Your instruments are malfunctioning." Fardles, if Nabol could not feel the wrongness of that entry, he was nowhere near the driver he thought himself.

"I'm captain of this ship, Admiral," Nabol snapped back. "It's your screen that's malfunctioning . . . Whadidya say, Bart? I don't believe it. You've got to be wrong. Give it a bang! *Kick it!*"

"Yank your nose up and fire a three-second blast, Nabol!" Paul cried, his eyes on the screen and the speed of the incoming shuttle.

"I'm trying. Can't fire. No fuel!" Sudden fear made Nabol's voice shrill.

Paul heard Bart's cries in the background. "I told you it felt wrong. I told you! We shouldn't've . . . I'll jettison. They'll have that much!" Bart shouted. "If the farking relay'll work."

"Use the manual jettison lever, Bart," Ongola yelled over Paul's shoulder.

"I'm trying, I'm trying . . . She's heating up too fast, Nabhi. She's heatin—"

Horrified, Paul, Ongola, and Jake watched the dissolution of the shuttle. One stubby wing sheared off and the shuttle began to spin. The tail section broke off and spun away on a different route, burning up in the atmosphere. The second wing followed suit.

"It'll hit the sea?" Paul asked in a bare whisper, trying to calculate the impact of that projectile on land. Ongola nodded imperceptibly.

Like an obituary, the relay screen lit up with a glorious sunlit spread of many bits and one larger object, disappearing into many faint pricks of glitter.

A team of dolphins were sent out to the Ring Sea to find the wreck. Maxmilian and Teresa reported back a week later, tired and not too happy to tell humans that they had seen the twisted hulk wedged into a reef in waters too deep for them to examine closely. All the dolphins were still searching the Ring Sea for the jettisoned scoop.

"Tell them not to bother," Jim Tillek muttered dourly. "There's unlikely to be anything left to analyze. We know that the junk goes back in a years' long tail. We're stuck with it. Hail Hoyle and Wickramansingh!"

"Ezra?" Emily asked the solemn astronomer.

Keroon's butterscotch-colored skin seemed tinged with gray, and he looked bowed by his responsibilities. He heaved a heavy, weary sigh and scratched at the back of his head. "I have to concede that Jim's theory is correct. The contents of the pod would have been the final proof, but I, too, doubt the scoop survived. Even if it did, it could take years to find it in such a vast area. Years also apply to that trail, I fear. We won't be able to judge until the end of that tail comes in sight."

"And where does that leave us?" Paul asked rhetorically.

"Coping, Admiral, coping!" Jim Tillek replied proudly. With a twitch of his sturdy shoulders, he had thrown off his doomsday expression and instead challenged them all. "And we've Thread falling in two hours, so we'd better stop worrying about the future and attend to the present. Right?"

Emily looked at Paul and managed a tentative smile, which she also turned on Zi Ongola, who was watching them impassively.

"Right! We'll cope." She spoke in a firm, resolute voice. Surely we can hold out for ten years, she thought to herself, if we're very careful. She wondered why no one mentioned the homing capsule. Perhaps because no one had much faith in Ted Tubberman. "We've got to."

"Until those dragons start earning their keep," Paul said. "But this settlement must be restructured." Emily and he had been discussing redispositions for days. They had been waiting for the right moment to broach the subject to the others of the informal Landing council.

"No," Ongola said, surprising everyone. "We must resettle completely. Landing is no longer viable. It used to be sort of a link with our origins, with the ships that brought us here. We no longer require that sense of continuity."

"And most especially," Jim picked up the thoughts, "not with volcanoes popping up and spouting off in this vicinity." Jim shifted in his chair, settling in to discuss basics. "I've been listening to what people are saying. So has Ezra. Telgar's notion about moving to that cave system on basement rock in the north is gaining strength. The cave complex is big enough to house Landing's population—plus dragons! We're not out of raw materials to make plastic and metal for housing. But making it takes time away from the essential task of fighting Thread and keeping us alive. Why not use a natural structure? Use our technology to make the cave system comfortable, tenable, and totally safe from Thread?"

Emily did not even pause to take a breath. "Just what Paul and I have been discussing. There's enough fuel, I believe, to transport some of the heavier equipment by shuttle. Then we can use the metal in situ. Jim, the Pern Navy is about to be commissioned."

Paul grinned at Emily. It was much easier when people made up their own minds to do what their leaders had decided was best for them.

PART THREE
Crossing

11.18.08 Pern

"Holiest of holies," Telgar murmured respectfully as he held his torch high and still could not illuminate the ceiling. His voice started echoes in the vast chamber, repeating and repeating down side corridors until finally the noise was absorbed by the sheer distance from its source.

"Oh, I say, mate, this is one big bonzo cave," Ozzie Munson said, keeping his voice to a whisper. His eyes were white and wide in his tanned, wind-seared face.

Cobber Alhinwa, who was rarely impressed by anything, was equally awed. "A bleeding beaut!" His whisper matched Ozzie's.

"There are hundreds of ready-made chambers in this complex alone," Telgar said. He was unfolding the plassheet on which he and his beloved Sallah had recorded their investigations of eight years earlier. "There are at least four openings to the cliff top which could be used for air circulation. Channel down to water level and install pumps and pipe—I came across big reservoirs of artesian water. Core down to the thermal layer and, big as it is, this whole complex could be warmed in the winter months." He turned back to the opening. "Block that up with native stone and this would be an impregnable fort. No safer place on this world during Threadfall. Further along the valley, there are surface-level caves near that pasture land. Of course, it would have to be seeded, but we still have the alfalfa grass propagators that were brought for the first year.

"At the time there was no need to investigate thoroughly, but the facilities exist. As I recall when we overflew the range above us, we discovered a medium-size caldera, well pocked with small cliffs, about a half-hour's flight from here. We didn't think to mark whether it was accessible at ground level. It might be ideal for dragon quarters, so accessibility isn't a problem, provided they do fly as well as dragonets."

"We seen a couple old craters like that," Ozzie said, consulting the battered notebook that habitually lived in his top pocket. "One on the east coast, and one in the mountains above the three drop lakes, when we was prospecting for metal ores."

"So," Cobber began, having recovered from his awe, "the first thing is cut steps to this here level." He walked to the edge of the cave and looked down critically at the stone face. "Maybe a ramp, like, to move stuff up here easy like. That incline over there's nearly a staircase already." He pointed to the left-hand side. "Steps neat as you please up to the next level."

Ozzie dismissed those notions. "Naw, those Landingers will want their smart-ass engineers and arki-tects to fancify it for them with the proper mod cons."

Cobber settled a helmet on his head and switched on its light. "Yeah, else some poor buggers get all closet-phobic."

"Claustrophic, you iggerant digger," Ozzie corrected him.

"Whatever. Inside's safest with that farking stuff dropping on ya alla time. C'mon, Oz, let's go walkabout. The admiral and the governor are counting on our expertise, y'know." He gave an involuntary grunt as he settled the heavy cutter on his shoulder and strode purposefully toward the first tunnel.

Ozzie put on his own helmet and picked up a coil of rope, pitons, and a rock hammer. Thermal and ultraviolet recorders, comm unit, and other mining hand-units were attached to hooks on his belts. Lastly, he slung one of the smaller rock cutters over his shoulder. "Let's go test some claustrophia. We'll start left, right? I'll give ya a holler in a bit, Telgar."

Cobber had already disappeared in the first of the left-hand openings as Ozzie followed him. Alone, Telgar stood for a long moment, eyes closed, head back, arms slightly away from his body, his palms turned outward in supplication. He could hear the slight noises of disturbed creatures and the distorted murmur of low conversations from Ozzie and Cobber as they made their way past the first bend in the tunnel.

There was nothing of Sallah in that cave. Even the place where they had built a tiny campfire had been swept bare to the fire-darkened stone. Yet there she had offered herself to him, and he had not *known* what a gift he had received that night!

The sudden high-pitched keening of the stone cutter shattered all thought and sent Telgar about the urgent business of making the natural fort into a human habitation.

The hum roused Sorka and she tried to find a more comfortable position for her cumbersome body. Fardles, but she would be grateful when she could finally sleep on her stomach again. The humming persisted, a subliminal sound that made a return to sleep impossible. She resented the noise, because she had not been sleeping at all well during the past few weeks and she needed all the rest she could get. Irritably she stretched out and twitched aside the curtain. It could not be day already. Then, startled, she clutched the edge of the curtain because there *was* light outside her house—the light of many dragon eyes, sparkling in the predawn gloom.

Her exclamation disturbed Sean, who stirred beside her, one hand reaching for her. She shook his shoulder urgently.

"Wake up, Sean. Look!" Whichever way she turned, she felt a sudden stab of pain in her groin so unexpected that she hissed.

Sean sat bolt upright beside her, his arms around her. "What is it, love? The baby?"

"It can't be anything else," she said, laughter bubbling out of her as she pointed out the window. "I've been warned!" She could not stop giggling. "Go look, Sean. Tell me if the fire-dragonets are roosting! I wouldn't want them to miss this, any of them."

Grinding sleep out of his eyes, Sean struggled to alertness. He half glared at her for her ill-timed levity, but annoyance was replaced by concern when her laughter turned abruptly into another hissing intake of breath as a second painful spasm rippled across her distended belly.

"It's time?" He ran one hand caressingly across her stomach, his fingers instinctively settling on the band of contracting muscle. "Yes, it is. What's so funny?" he added. She could not quite see his face in the dim light, but he sounded solemn, almost indignant.

"The welcoming committee, of course! All of them. Faranth, love, are all present and accounted for?"

We are here, Faranth said, *where we should be. You are amused.*

"I am very amused," Sorka said, but then another contraction caught her, and she clutched at Sean. "But that was not at all amusing. You'd better call Greta."

"Jays, we don't need her. I'm as good a midwife as she is," he muttered, shoving feet into the shoes under their bed.

"For horses, cows, and nanny goats, yes, Sean, but it is expected for humans to assist humans . . . oooooh, Sean, these are very close together."

He rose to his feet, pausing to throw the top blanket across his bare shoulders against the early morning's chill, when there was a discreet knock at the door. He cursed.

"Who is it?" he roared, not at all pleased at the idea that someone might have come to summon him for a veterinary emergency right then.

"Greta!"

Sorka started to laugh again, but that became very difficult to do all of a sudden, and she switched to the breathing she had been taught, clutching at her great belly.

"How under the suns did you know, Greta?" she heard Sean ask, his voice reflecting his astonishment.

"I was called," Greta said with great dignity, gently pushing him to one side.

"By whom? Sorka only just woke up," Sean replied, following Greta back to their room. "She's the one who's having the baby."

"Not always the first to know when labor commences," Greta said in a very calm, almost detached manner. "Not in Landing. And certainly not with a queen dragon listening in on your mind." She flicked on the lights as she entered the room and deposited her midwifery bag on the dresser. She had been a gangly girl who had turned into a rangy woman with hair and skin the same coffee color and a dusting of freckles across the bridge of her nose. Her eyes, very brown in her kindly face, missed few details.

"Faranth told you?" Sorka was astonished. A dragon speaking to someone outside of their group was unheard of.

"Not exactly," Greta replied with a chuckle. "A fair of fire-dragonets flew in my window and made it remarkably plain that I was needed. Once I got outside, it wasn't hard to figure out whose baby was coming. Now, let me see what's going on here."

I told them to get her, Faranth told Sorka in a smugly complacent tone of voice. *You like her.*

As Sorka lay back for Greta's examination, she tried to figure that out. She liked her doctor, too, and had no qualms about him attending her delivery. How had Faranth sensed that she really had wanted Greta in attendance? Could Faranth possibly have sensed that she had always been friendly with Greta? Or was it some connection the golden dragon had made because Sorka had assisted Greta in the birth of Mairi Hanrahan's latest, Sorka's newest baby brother? But for Faranth to recognize an unconscious preference . . .

Sean slid cautiously onto the other side of the bed and reached for her hand. Sorka gave him a squeeze, laughter still bubbling up in her. She had so hated the last few weeks when her body had not seemed to be her own, when all its controls seemed to have been assumed by the bouncing, kicking, impertinent, restless fetus that gave her no rest at all. Her laughter was sheer elation that all of *that* was nearly over.

"Now, let me have a look . . . another contraction?"

Sorka concentrated on her breathing, but the spasm was far more painful than she had anticipated. Then it was gone, pain and all. She felt sweat on her forehead. Sean blotted it gently.

You are hurting? Faranth's voice became shrill.

"No, no, Faranth. I'm fine. Don't worry!" Sorka cried.

"Faranth's upset?" Keeping her hand tight in his, Sean crouched to see out the window to the dragons waiting there. "Yes, she is! Her eyes are gaining speed and orange."

"I was afraid of that!" Mutely Sorka appealed to Sean. Expressions flitted across his face. If she read them correctly, he was annoyed with Faranth, indecisive—for once—about what to do, and anxious for her. Then tender concern dominated his face as he looked down at her, and she felt that she had never loved him more than at that moment.

"A pity we can't have your dragon heat a kettle of water to keep her out of mischief," Greta remarked, her strong capable hands finishing the examination. She gave Sorka's distended belly a gentle pat. "We'll take care of her fussing you right now. Can you turn on one side? Sean, help her."

"I feel like an immense flounder," Sorka complained as she struggled to turn. Then Sean, deftly and with hands gentler than she had ever known, helped her complete the maneuver. She had just reached the new position when another mighty spasm caught her, and she exhaled in astonishment. Outside Faranth trumpeted a challenge. "Don't you dare wake everyone up, Faranth. I'm only having a baby!"

You hurt! You are in distress! Faranth was indignant.

Sorka felt a slight push against the base of her spine, the coolness of the air gun, and then a blessed numbness that spread rapidly over her nether region.

"Oh, blessed Greta, how marvelous!"

You don't hurt. That is better. Faranth's alarm subsided back into that curious thrumming of dragons, and Sorka could identify her voice in the hum as clearly as she heard the noise intensify. Oddly enough, the humming was soothing—or was it simply that she no longer had to anticipate that painful clutching of uterine muscles?

"Now, let's get you to your feet for a little walking, Sorka," Greta said. "You're already fairly well dilated. I don't think you're going to be any time delivering this baby, even if you are a primipara."

"I'm numb," Sorka said by way of apology as Greta got her to her feet. Then Sean was on her other side.

He had gotten dressed, but Sorka, trying to watch where her nerveless feet were going, noticed that he did not have his socks on. She thought that endearing of him. Odd the difference between his hands and Greta's—both caring, both gentle, but Sean's loving and worried.

"That's a girl," Greta said encouragingly. "You're doing just fine, three fingers dilated already. No wonder the fairs were alerted. And you're not the only one exciting them tonight." Greta chuckled as they began to retrace their steps across the lounge, up the short hall, and into the bedroom. "It's the walking that's important . . . ah, another contraction. Very good. Your breathing's fine."

"Who else is delivering?" Sorka asked because it helped to concentrate on things other than what her muscles were doing to her.

"Fortunately, Elizabeth Jepson. A new baby will help her get over the loss of the twins."

Sorka felt a pang of grief. She remembered the two boys as mischievous youngsters on the *Yoko,* and recalled how she had envied her brother, Brian, for having friends his own age.

"It's funny that, isn't it?" Sorka said, speaking quickly. "People having two complete families, almost two separate generations. I mean, this baby will have an uncle only six months older. And be part of an entirely different generation . . . really."

"One reason why we have to keep very careful birth records," Greta said.

Sean grunted. "We're all Pernese, that's what matters!"

Sorka's water burst then, and outside the humming went up a few notes and deepened in intensity.

"I think I'd better check you, Sorka," Greta said.

Sean stared at her. "Do you deliver to dragonsong?"

Greta gave a low chuckle. "They've an instinct for birth, Sean, and I know you vets have been aware of it, too. Let's get her back to the bed."

Sorka, involved in the second phase of childbirth, found the dragonsong both comforting and soothing: it was like a blanket of sound shimmering about her, enfolding and uplifting and comforting. The sound suddenly increased in tempo, rising to a climax. Sean's hands grasped hers, giving her his strength and encouragement. Every time she felt the contractions, painless because of the drug, he helped her push down. The spasms were becoming more rapid, almost constant, as if matters had been taken entirely out of her control. She let the instinctive movements take over, relaxing when she could, assisting because she had no other option.

Then she felt her body writhe in a massive effort, and when it had been expended, she felt a tremendous relief of all pressures and pullings. For one moment, there was complete silence outside, then she heard a new sound. Sean's cry of triumph was lost in the trumpeting of eighteen dragons and who knew how many fire-dragonets! Oh dear, she thought distractedly. They'll wake up the whole of Landing!

"You have a fine son, my dears," Greta said, her voice ringing with satisfaction. "With a crop of thick red hair."

"A son?" Sean asked, sounding immensely surprised.

"Now, don't tell me, after all my hard work, Sean Connell, that you wanted a daughter?" Sorka demanded.

Sean just hugged her ecstatically.

"Sometimes I feel as if everyone's forgotten all about us," Dave Catarel said to Sean as they watched their two bronzes hunting. Sean, his eyes on Carenath, did not reply.

Although all the dragons were well able to fly short distances and had proved capable of hunting down wild wherries, their human partners grew anxious if they flew out of sight. Nor was it always possible to use a sled or a skimmer to accompany them. As a compromise, Sean had talked Red into giving them the culls or injured animals from the main herds. He and the others had rigged a Threadfall shelter for the mixed herd in one of the caves, and each took turns on the succession trays that supplied their fodder.

The young dragons were strong and flew well. But, erring on the side of caution, the veterinary experts had decided that riding should not be attempted until the full year had passed. Sean had railed privately to Sorka about such timidity, but she had talked him out of defiance, reminding him how much they stood to lose in forcing the young dragons. Fortunately the decision had been reached without consultation with Wind Blossom, which made it easier for Sean to accept what he called 'sheer procrastination.' He did not like her proprietary attitude toward the dragons. She continued to exercise Kitti Ping's program, though without the same success. Her first four batches had not produced any viable eggs, but seven new sacs in the incubator looked promising.

The odds in Joel Lilienkamp's book favored the success of the first Hatching, but only marginally. Sean was privately determined to upset such odds, but he also would not risk official censure or jeopardize the young dragons.

"I really cannot repose the same confidence in Wind Blossom as I did in Kitti Ping," Paul had told Sean and Sorka in a private conference, "but we would all breathe more easily if we could see some progress. Your dragons eat, grow, even fly to hunt. Will they also chew rock?" Paul began to tick off the points on his left hand. "Carry a rider? And preserve their valuable hides during Threadfall? The power pack situation is getting tight, Sean, very tight indeed."

"I know, Admiral," Sean had replied, feeling grim and defensive. "And eighteen fully functional dragons are not going to make fighting Thread all that much easier."

"But self-reproducing, self-sustaining Thread fighters will make one helluva lot of difference in the long run. And it's the long run, frankly, Sean, Sorka, that worries me."

Sean kept his opinion about Wind Blossom to himself. Part of it was loyalty to Carenath, Faranth, and the others of the first Hatching; a good deal stemmed from his lack of confidence in Wind Blossom, where he had had every faith in her grandmother. After all, Kit Ping had been trained at the source, with the Eridani.

As he watched the grace of Carenath, swooping to snatch a fat wether from the stampeding flock, his faith in these amazing creatures was reinforced.

"He really got some altitude there," David said with ungrudging praise. "Look, Polenth's dropped his wings now. He's going for that one!"

"Got it, too," Sean replied in a return of compliment.

Maybe they were all being too cautious, afraid of pushing down the throttle and seeing the result. Carenath flew strongly and well. The bronze was nearly the same height in the shoulder as Cricket, though the conformation was entirely different, Carenath being much longer in the body, deeper in the barrel, and stronger in the hindquarters. In fact, the dragons already were much stronger than similar equines, their basic structure much more durable, utilizing carborundums for strength and resilience. Pol and Bay had gone on about the design features of dragons as if they had been new sleds, which indeed, Sean thought wryly, was what they were intended to replace. According to the program, dragons would gradually increase in size over many generations until they reached the optimum. But in Sean's eyes, Carenath was just right.

"At least they eat neatly," Dave said, averting his eyes from the two dragons who were rending flesh from the carcasses of their kills. "Though I wish they didn't look like they enjoyed it so much."

Sean laughed. "City-bred, were you?"

Dave nodded and smiled weakly. "Not that I wouldn't do anything for Polenth. It's just that it's one thing on three-D, another to watch it live and *know* that your best friend prefers to hunt living animals. What did you say, Polenth?" Dave's eyes took on that curious unfocused look that people had when being addressed by their dragons. Then he gave a rueful laugh.

"Well?" Sean prompted him.

"He says anything's better than fish. He's meant to fly, not swim."

"Good thing he has two bellies," Sean remarked, seeing Polenth devouring the sheep, horns, hooves, fleece, and all. "The way he's squaffing down the wool, he could start a premature blaze when he starts chewing firestone."

"He will, won't he, Sean?" Dave's earnest plea for reassurance worried Sean. The dragonmates could not doubt their beasts for a moment, not on any score.

"Of course he will," Sean said, standing up. "That's enough, Carenath. Two fills your belly. Don't get greedy. There are more to be fed here today."

The bronze had been about to launch himself into the air again, aiming toward the rise into the next valley where the terrified flock had stampeded.

I would really like another one. So tasty. So much better than fish. I like to hunt. Carenath sounded a trifle petulant.

"The queens hunt next, Carenath."

With a peevish swing of his head, Carenath began to amble back down to Sean, spreading his wings to balance himself. Dragons looked odd when they walked, since they had to crouch to their shorter forelegs; some of them fell more easily into a hop-skip gait, dropping to the forequarters every few steps or using their wings to provide frontal lift. Sean disliked seeing the dragons appear so ungainly and unbalanced.

"See you later," he said to David as he and Carenath turned to walk back to the cave they inhabited.

The dragons had quickly outgrown the backyard shelters and, in many cases, the patience of neighbors, some of whom worked night shifts and slept during daylight hours. Dragons were a vocal lot for a species that could not speak aloud. So dragons and partners had explored the Catherine Caves for less public accommodations. Sorka had at first worried about living underground with their baby son, Michael, but the cave-site Sean had chosen was spacious, with several large chambers—their new home actually had far more space than did the house in Irish Square. Faranth and Carenath were delighted. There was even a shelf of bare earth above the cave entrance where dragons could sunbathe, the leisure activity they enjoyed even above swimming.

"We are all much better suited here," Sorka had exclaimed in capitulation, and had set about making their living quarters bright with lamps, her handwoven rugs, fabrics, and pictures that she had cadged from Joel.

But the new quarters had proved to be more than just a physical separation, Sean realized as he and Carenath trudged along. Dave Catarel had put his finger on it in his wistful comment about being forgotten.

This walk is long. I would rather fly on ahead, Carenath said, doing his little hop-skip beside Sean. Once again Sean thought that his brave and lovely Carenath looked like a bad cross between a rabbit and kangaroo.

"You were designed to fly. I'll be happy when we both fly."

Why do you not fly on me, then? I would be easier to ride than that scared creature. Carenath did not think much of Cricket as a mount for his partner.

Scared creature, Sean thought with a chuckle. Poor Cricket. How easy it would be to swing up to Carenath's back and just take off! The notion made the breath catch in his throat. To fly *on* Carenath, instead of shuffling along on the dusty track. The adolescent year for the dragons was nearly over. Sean looked about in deep speculation. Let Carenath drop off the highest point, and he would have enough space to make that first, all-important downsweep of his wings . . .

Sean had spent as much time watching how fire-lizards and dragons handled themselves in the air as he once had patiently observed horses. Yes, a drop off a height would be the trick.

"C'mon, Carenath. I'm glad I didn't let you fill your belly. C'mon, right up to the top."

The top? The ridge? Sean heard comprehension color the dragon's mind, and Carenath scrambled to the height in a burst of speed that left Sean coughing in the dust. *Quickly! The wind is right.*

Rubbing dust particles out of his eyes, Sean laughed aloud, feeling elation and the racing pulse of apprehension. This is the sort of thing you do *now,* at the right time, in the right place, he thought. And the moment was right for him to ride Carenath!

There was no saddle to vault to, no stirrup to assist Sean to the high shoulder. Carenath dipped politely, and Sean, lightly stepping on the proferred forearm, caught the two neck ridges firmly and swung over, fitting his body between them.

"Jays, you were designed for me," he said with a triumphant laugh, and slapped Carenath's neck in affection. Then he grabbed at the ridge in front of him.

Carenath was perched on the very edge of the ridge, and Sean had an awesome view of the bottom of the rockstrewn gorge. He swallowed hastily. Flying Carenath was not at all the same thing as riding Cricket. He took a deep breath. It was also not the time for second thoughts. He took a compulsive hold with legs made strong from years of riding and shoved his buttocks as deeply into the natural saddle as he could.

"Let's fly, Carenath. Let's do it now!"

We will fly, Carenath said with ineffable calm. He tilted forward off the ridge.

Despite years of staying astride bucking horses, sliding horses, and jumping horses, the sensation that Sean Connell experienced in that seemingly endless moment was totally different and completely new. A brief memory of a girl's voice urging him to think of Spacer Yves flitted through his mind. He was falling through space again. A very short space. What sort of a nerd-brain was he to have attempted this?

Faranth wants to know what we are doing, Carenath said calmly.

Before Sean's staggered mind registered the query, Carenath's wings had finished their downstroke and they were rising. Sean felt the sudden return of gravity, felt Carenath's neck under him, felt the weight and a return of the confidence that had been totally in abeyance during that endless-seeming initial drop. The power in those wing sweeps drove his seat deeper between the neck ridges as Carenath continued to beat upward. They were level with the next ridge, the floor of the gorge no longer an imminent crash site.

"Tell Faranth that we're flying, of course," Sean replied. He would never admit it to Sorka—he could barely admit it to himself—but for one moment he had been totally and utterly terrified.

I will not let you fall, Carenath's tone chided him.

"I never thought you would." Sean forced his body to relax, forced his long legs down and around Carenath's smooth neck, but he took a firmer grip on the neck ridge. "I just didn't think I'd stay aboard you for a minute there."

Carenath's wings swept up and down, just behind Sean's peripheral vision. He felt their strong and steady beat even if he did not see them. He could feel the air pressure against his face and his chest. There was nothing around him but air, open, empty, and absolutely marvelous.

Yes, once he got the hang of it, flying his dragon was the most marvelous sensation he had ever had.

I like it, too. I like flying you. You fit on me. This goes well. Where shall we go? The sky is ours.

"Look, we better not do much of this right now, Carenath. You just ate, and we're going to have to think this thing through. It's not enough to fall of a ridge. Oooooooh—" he cried inadvertently as Carenath banked and he saw the wide-open, dusty, Thread-barren ground far, far beneath him. "Straighten up!"

I wouldn't let you fall! Carenath sounded nearly indignant, and Sean freed one hand to give him a reassuring slap. But he quickly replaced his hand on the ridge. Jays, a rider can't fly Thread hanging on for dear life!

"You wouldn't let me fall, my friend, but I might let me!"

Trying to quell his rising sense of panic, Sean hazarded a glance at the ground. They were nearly to the rank of caves that had become their home. Sean could see Faranth on the height where she must have been sunning herself. She was sitting on her haunches, her wings half-spread. In a few sweeps of Carenath's powerful wings, they had covered a distance that ordinarily took a half hour of up-hill–down-dale slogging.

Faranth says that Sorka says that we had better come down right away. Right away! Carenath's tone was defiant, begging Sean to contradict the golden dragon and anything that shortened their new experience. *We are flying together. It is the right thing to do for dragons and riders.*

"It's a fantastic thing to do, Carenath, but as we are now home, can you land us, say, by Faranth? Then you can tell her just how we did it!"

Sean did not care if Sorka had hysterics over his spontaneous and totally unplanned flight. He had done it, they had succeeded, and all was well that ended well. The dragons of Pern finally had riders! That would change the odds in Joel's book!

The other seventeen riders, including Sorka, once Faranth had reassured her about Carenath's prowess, were delighted at their tremendous advance. Dave wanted to know why Sean had been so precipitous.

"Couldn't you have waited for me? Polenth and I were just behind you. You scared the living wits out of me for a moment, you know."

Sean clasped Dave's arm in tacit apology. "It was what you'd said about being forgotten, Dave. I just had to try, but I didn't want to endanger anyone else in case I was wrong." Sean caught Sorka frowning at him and pretended to flinch. "I was all right, love. You *know* that! But—" He glared warningly at the others seated on the rugs around him. "We've got to go about this in a logical and sensible way, folks. Flying a dragon's not like riding a horse."

His glance held Nora Sejby's. She certainly was not the sort of person he would have said would Impress a dragon, but Tenneth had chosen her, and they would have to make the best of it. Nora was accident-prone, and Tenneth had already hauled her partner out of the lake and prevented her from falling into the crevices and holes that pitted the hills around the Catherine Caves. On the other hand, Nora had been sailing across Monaco Bay since she was strong enough to manage a tiller and she had checked out on both sleds and skimmers.

"For one thing, there's all this open air around you. Falling is down onto a hard and injurious surface," Sean made appropriate gestures, smacking one hand into the palm of the other and startling Nora with the noise.

"So?" Peter Semling said. "We use a saddle."

"A dragon's back is full of wing," Sorka replied dryly.

"You ride forward, sitting your butt in the hollow between the last two ridges," Sean went on, grabbing for a sheet of opaque film and a marker. He made a quick sketch of a dragon's neck and shoulders, and the disposition of two straps. "The rider wears a stout belt, wide like a tool belt. You strap yourself in on either side, and the safety harness goes over your thigh for added security. And we're going to need special flying gear and protective glasses—the wind made my eyes water, and I wasn't even aloft all that long."

"What did it really feel like, Sean?" Catherine Radelin asked, her eyes shining in anticipation.

Sean smiled. "The most incredible sensation I've ever had. Beats flying a mechanical all hollow. I mean . . ." He raised his fists, tensing his arms into his chest and giving his hands an upward thrusting turn of indescribable experience. "It's . . . it's between you and your dragon and . . ." He swung his arms out. "And the whole damned wide world."

He made a less dramatic presentation at the impromptu meeting where he was asked to account for such risk-taking. He would rather have reported privately, to maybe Admiral Benden or Pol or Red, but he found himself facing the entire council.

"Look, sir, the risk was justified," he said, looking quickly from the admiral to Red Hanrahan. His father-in-law had been both furious and hurt by what he considered a betrayal. Sean had not anticipated that. "We were almost to the ridge when I suddenly knew I had to prove that dragons could fly us. Sir, all the planning in the world sometimes doesn't get you to the right point at the right time."

Admiral Benden nodded wisely, but the startled expression on Jim Tillek's blunt face and Ongola's sudden attention told Sean that he had said something wrong.

"I could risk my own neck, sir, but no one else's," he went on, "so we've got to take our time getting some of the other riders ready to fly. I've done a lot of riding and sled-driving, but flying a dragon's not the same thing, and I'm not about to go out again until Carenath's got some safety harness on him. And me."

Joel Lilienkamp leaned forward across the table. "And what will that require, Connell?"

Sean grinned, more out of relief than amusement. "Don't worry, Lili, what I need is what Pern's got plenty of—hide. I found a use for all that tanned wher skin you've got in Stores. It's plenty tough enough and it'll be easier on dragons' necks than that synthetic webbing used in sled harnesses. I've made some sketches." He unfolded the diagrams, much improved on by his discussions with the other dragonmates. "These show the arrangement of straps and the belts we'll need, the flying suits, and we can use some of those work goggles plastics turns out."

"Flying suits and plastic goggles," Joel repeated, reaching for the drawings. He examined them with a gradually less jaundiced attitude.

"As soon as I can rig the flying harness for Carenath, Admiral, Governor, sirs," Sean said, politely including all assembled and adding a tentative grin at Cherry Duff's deep scowl, "you can see just how well my dragon flies me."

"You were informed, weren't you," Paul Benden said, and Sean saw him rubbing the knuckles of his left hand, "that there're new eggs on the Hatching Sands?"

Sean nodded. "Like I told you, Admiral, eighteen are not enough to take up much slack. And it'll be generations before there're enough."

"Generations?" Cherry Duff exclaimed in her raspy voice, swinging in accusation on the veterinary team. "Why weren't we told it'd take generations?"

"Dragon generations," Pol answered, smiling slightly at her misinterpretation. "Not human."

"Well, how long's a dragon generation?" she demanded, still affronted. She shot a disgusted scowl at Sean.

"The females should produce their first independent clutches at three. Sean has proved that a male dragon can fly at just under a year—."

Cherry brought both hands down on the table, making a sharp, loud noise. "Give me facts, damn it, Pol."

"Then, four to five years?"

Cherry pursed her lips in annoyance, a habit that made her look even more like a dried prune, Sean thought idly.

"Humph, then I'm not likely to see squadrons of dragons

in the sky, am I? Four to five years. And when will they start flaming Thread? That was their design function, wasn't it? When will they start being useful?"

Sean was fed up. "Sooner than you think, Cherry Duff. Open a book on it, Joel." With that he strode from the office. It galled him to the bone to have to take a skimmer back to Sorka and the others who waited to hear what had happened.

Ten days later, when Joel Lilienkamp himself brought them the requisitioned belts, straps, flying kit, and goggles, flight training on the Dragons of Pern began in earnest.

Landing had grown accustomed over the past year and a half to the grumblings and rumblings underfoot. On the morning of the second day of the fourth month of their ninth spring on Pern, early risers sleepily noted the curl of smoke, and the significance did not register.

Sean and Sorka, emerging from their cave with Carenath and Faranth, also noticed it.

Why does the mountain smoke? Faranth wanted to know.

"The mountain *what?*" Sorka demanded, waking up enough to absorb her dragon's words. "Jays, Sean, look!"

Sean gave a long hard look. "It's not Garben. It's Picchu Peak. Patrice de Broglie was wrong! Or was he?"

"What on earth do you mean, Sean?" Sorka stared at him in amazement.

"I mean, there's been all this talk of basement rock, and shifting Landing to a more practical base, with a special accommodation for dragons and us . . ." Sean kept his eyes on the plume curling languidly up from the peak, dwarfed beside the mightier Garben but certainly as ominous. He shrugged. "Not even Paul Benden can make a volcano erupt on cue. Come, we can get breakfast at your mother's. Let's stuff Mick in his flying suit and go. Maybe your dad will have received some official word." He scowled. "We're always the last ones to get news.

I've got to convince Joel to release at least one comm unit for the caves."

Sorka got their wriggling son into his fleece-lined carrying sack before she shrugged into her jacket and crammed helmet and goggles onto her head. Sean carried Mick out to Faranth. With an ease grown of practice, Sorka ran the two steps to her dragon's politely positioned foreleg and vaulted astride. Sean handed her a protesting bundle to sling over her back and then turned to mount the obliging Carenath.

The dragons leapt upward from the ledge before the cave, giving themselves enough airway to take the first full sweep. Over the last few weeks, dragon backs had strengthened and muscled up. They had managed flights of several hours' duration. Riders, even Nora Sejby—Sean had contrived a special harness that made her feel securely fastened to Tenneth—were improving. Long discussions with Drake Bonneau and some of the other pilots who had both fighter experience in the old Nathi War and plenty fighting Thread had improved the dragonriders' basic understanding of the skills needed. And practice had encouraged them.

Three weeks before, Wind Blossom's latest attempt had hatched. The four creatures who had survived had not been Impressed by the candidates awaiting them, although the creatures ate the food presented. Indeed, the poor beasts turned out to be photophobic, but Blossom, much to the disgust of Pol and Bay and against their advice, had insisted on special darkened quarters for the beasts, for the purpose of continued examination of that variant.

Even the fire-lizards were more useful, Sean thought, as the two fairs erupted into the air about them, bugling a morning welcome in their high, sweet voices. Now, if the dragons could only prove capable of *that,* Sean thought enviously. But how do you teach a dragon to do something you do not yourself understand? The dragons got smarter every day and they were fast learners, but it was impossible to explain telekinesis to them or ask them to teleport the way the fire-lizards did. Kitti Ping had called it an instinctive action. Nowhere in the genetics program that Sean had memorized did he find any words of wisdom on how to instruct a dragon to use his innate instinct.

And it was not the sort of exercise one did on a spontaneous basis. First, they would try to chew firestone and make flame. They knew where the fire-lizards got the phosphine-bearing rock; Sean had even watched the browns and Sorka's Duke selecting the pieces to chew and the careful way they concentrated while they chewed. The fire-lizards had learned to produce flame on demand, so Sean felt easy about teaching the dragons that. But going *between* one place and another . . . that was scary.

Flame of a different kind obsessed Landing's counselors three days later.

"What people want to know, Paul, Emily," Cherry Duff said, turning her penetrating stare from admiral to governor, "is how much warning you had of Picchu's activity."

"None," Paul said firmly. Emily nodded. "Patrice de Broglie's reports have not been altered. There's been a lot of volcanic activity all along the ring, as well as that new volcano. You've felt the same shakes I have. Landing and all stakeholders have been apprised of every technical detail. This is as much of an unpleasant surprise to us as it is to you!" Then Paul's stern expression altered. "By all that's holy, Cherry, all that black ash gave me as much a fright yesterday as it did everyone else."

"So?" Cherry demanded, her attitude unsoftened.

"Picchu is officially an active volcano!" Paul spread his hands, looking past Cherry to Cabot Francis Carter and Rudi Shwartz. "And officially, it's likely to continue to spout smoke and ash. Patrice and his crew are up at the crater now. He'll give a full public report this evening at Bonfire Square."

Cherry gave him a long hard stare, her black eyes piercing, her face expressionless. Then she snorted. "I believe him, but that doesn't mean I like it—or the obvious prognosis. Landing moves, doesn't it?"

Emily Boll nodded solemnly.

"And your next statement," Cherry went on in her hard voice, "is that you have prepared a place for us!"

Paul burst into guffaws, though Emily muffled her laughter when she saw how such levity affronted Rudi Shwartz.

"You had no right," Paul said, controlling his laughter, "to steal that line from Emily, Cherry Duff! Damn it, we were working on the official announcement when you barged in. And you fardling well know we've been rushing to complete the northern fort. Landing couldn't continue much longer as a viable settlement even if Picchu hadn't started showering us with ash. That doesn't, of course, mean," he put in quickly, holding up his hand to forestall Cabot's explosion, "that stakeholders will be asked to leave their lands. But the administration of this planet will have to be in the most protected situation we can contrive. Plainly Landing has outlived its usefulness. It was never intended as a permanent installation."

Emily took up the discussion then, passing to each of the delegation copies of the directive she and Paul had been drafting. "The transfer is being organized much as our space journey here. We have the technicians and the equipment to make a northern crossing as easy as possible. We have enough fuel to power two of the shuttles to transport equipment too bulky to fit on any of Jim's ships. It'll be a one-way trip for the shuttles: they'll be dismantled for parts. When there's time, we can send a crew back to scavenge the other three. Joel Lilienthal has been working on priority shipments for the big sleds, taking as few as possible from the fighting strength."

"Speaking of fighting strength, has that young upstart taught them any new tricks?" Cherry demanded imperiously, looking down her long nose at Paul. "Speaking of eruptions, as we were, how are those beasts of Kitti Ping's progressing? I see them flitting around all the time. Mighty pretty they look in formation, but are they any good in battle?"

"So far," Paul began cautiously, "they've matured well beyond the projections. The young Connells have proved splendid leaders."

"They were the best ground-crew leaders I had," Cabot Carter said, disgruntled.

"They'll be superior as aerial fighters," Paul went on, overriding the legist's unspoken criticism. "Self-perpetuating, too, unlike sleds and skimmers."

"D'you know that for sure?" Cherry demanded in her raspy voice. "Blossom's experiments aren't all that successful."

"Her grandmother's are," Paul replied with a firm confidence he hoped would reassure Cherry. "According to Pol and Bay, the males are producing their equivalent to sperm. Genetic analysis has started but will take months. We might have direct proof of dragon fertility by then, as the gold females mature later." Paul tried not to sound defensive, but he wanted to counter the very bad publicity surrounding Wind Blossom's brutes. Especially when the young dragonriders were trying so very hard to perfect themselves for combat against Thread. Though it was not public knowledge, Sean and his group had already served as messengers and had transported light loads efficiently.

Paul had a report on his desk from Telgar and his group. They had done a survey of the old crater above the fort hold, with its myriad bubble caves and twisting passages, and had pronounced it a suitable accommodation for the dragons and their riders. Telgar had a team working to make the place habitable, while they still had power in the heavy equipment. A stream was being dammed up for a dragon-sized bathing lake, water piped into the largest of the ground-level caverns for kitchen use, and a chimney hole had been bored for a large hearth complex.

Obviously, that would be the pattern for future human habitation on Pern, and for some, accustomed to sprawling living space, it would take some getting used to. But it was the best way to survive!

"Pol?"

It took a moment for the biologist to identify the anxious voice. "Mary?" His response was equally tentative, but he pulled at Bay's sleeve to attract her attention away from the monitor she was frowning at. "Mary Tubberman?"

"Please don't turn an old friend away unheard."

"Mary," Pol said kindly, "*you* weren't shunned." He shared the earpiece with Bay, who nodded in vigorous approval.

"I might as well have been." The woman's tone was bitter, then her voice broke on a tremulous note and both Bay and Pol could hear her weeping. "Look, Pol, something's happened to Ted. Those creatures of his are *loose*. I've pulled down the Thread shutters, but they're still prowling about and making awful noises."

"Creatures? What creatures?" Pol locked glances with Bay. Beyond them, their dragonets roused from a doze and chirped in empathic anxiety.

"The beasts he's been rearing." Mary sounded as if she thought Pol knew what she was talking about and was being deliberately obtuse. "He—he stole some frozen in-vitros from veterinary and he used Kitti's program on them to make them obey him, but they're still . . . things. His masterpiece does nothing to stop *them*." Again her bitterness was trenchant.

"What makes you think something has happened to Ted?" Pol asked, picking up on the words Bay mouthed to him as she gestured urgently.

"He would never let those animals *loose,* Pol! They might harm Petey!"

"Now, Mary, calm down. Stay in the house. We'll come."

"Ned's not in Landing!" Her tone became accusatory. "I tried his number. He'd believe me!

"It's not a question of belief, Mary." Bay pulled the mouthpiece around to speak directly into it. "And anyone can come assist *you.*"

"Sue and Chuck won't answer."

"Sue and Chuck moved north, Mary, after that first bad rock shower from Picchu." Bay was patient with her. The woman had a right to sound paranoid, living in seclusion as she had for so long, with an unbalanced husband and so many earthshocks and volcanic rumblings.

"Pol and I are coming down, Mary," Bay said firmly. "And we'll bring help." She replaced the handset.

"Who?" Pol demanded.

"Sean and Sorka. Dragons have an inhibiting effect on animals. And that way we don't have to go through official channels."

Pol looked at his wife with mild surprise. She had never criticized either Emily or Paul, obliquely or bluntly.

"I always felt someone should have investigated the report Drake and Ned Tubberman made. So did they. Sometimes priorities get lost in the shuffle around here." She wrote a hasty note which she then attached to her gold dragonet's right foot. "Find the redhead," she said firmly, holding the triangular head to get Mariah's full attention. "Find the redhead." Bay walked with her to the window and opened it, pointing firmly in Sorka's direction. She filled her mind with an image of Sorka, leaning against Faranth. Mariah chirped happily. "Now, off with you!" Then, as the dragonet obediently flew off, Bay ran a finger over the black grime that was once again settling on the windowsill she had swept earlier. "I'll be glad to move north. I'm so eternally tired of black dust everywhere. Come on, Pol, we'd better get dressed warmly."

"You volunteered to help Mary because it gives you a chance to ride a dragon again," Pol said, chuckling.

"Pol Nietro, I have long been concerned about Mary Tubberman!"

Fifteen minutes later, two dragons came swooping over the rise to settle on the road in front of their house.

"They are so graceful," Bay said, making certain her headscarf was tied, as much against the prevailing dust outside as in hopes of riding. As she left the house, Mariah circled down and settled to the plump shoulder with a chirrup of smug satisfaction. "You're marvelous, Mariah, simply marvelous," Bay murmured to her little queen as she marched right up between Faranth and Carenath. However, it was Sorka she addressed. "Thank you for coming, my dear. Mary Tubberman just contacted us. There's trouble at Calusa. Creatures are loose, and Mary thinks something has happened to Ted. Will you take us there?"

"Officially, or unofficially?" Sean asked as Sorka glanced over at her mate.

"It's all right to help Mary," Bay said, looking for support from Pol, who had just come up to the dragons, his glance as admiring as ever. "And with who knows what sort of beast . . ."

"Dragons are useful," Sorka replied with a grin, arriving at her own decision. She beckoned to Bay. "Give the lady your leg, Faranth. Here's my hand."

With Faranth's assist, Bay was agile enough to settle herself quietly behind Sorka. She would never admit that she was pinched fore and aft between the ridge. Mariah gave her usual squeak of protest.

"Now, Mariah, Faranth's perfectly safe," Bay said, and looked over to see that Pol was settling behind Sean. The young dragonrider's grin was very broad as he winked at Bay. Well, this time it really is an emergency, she told herself. A woman trapped in her home with small children and unidentifiable menaces prowling outside.

"Hang on tight now," Sean said as always. He pumped his arm in the signal to launch.

Bay suppressed an exclamation as Faranth's upward surge pushed her painfully against the stiff dorsal ridge. Her discomfort lasted only a moment, as the golden dragon leveled off and veered leisurely to her right. Bay caught her breath. She would never get accustomed to this; she didn't want to. Riding a dragon was the most exciting thing that had happened to her since . . . since Mariah had first risen to mate.

Calusa was not a long trip by air, but the flight was tremendously exhilarating. The dragons hit one of the many air currents that were the result of Picchu's activity, and Bay clutched at Sorka's belt, stuffing her fingers to the knuckle in the belt loops. Flying on a dragon was so much more immediate an activity than going in the closed sled or skimmer. Really much more exhilarating. Bay turned her head so that Sorka's tall, strong body shielded her from the worst of the airstream and the dust from Picchu that seemed to clog the air even at that altitude.

The journey gave Bay time to ponder what Mary had said about "beasts." Red Hanrahan had reported a late-night entry into the veterinary laboratory. A portable bio-scan had been missing without being logged out, but as the bio lab was always borrowing vet equipment, the absence was dismissed. Later someone had noticed that the order in which the frozen ova of a variety of Earth-type animals were stored had been disarranged. It *could* have happened during the earthquakes.

Ted Tubberman had been very busy in his discontent, Bay thought grimly. One of the strictest dictums of her profession as a microbiologist was a strict limitation of genetic manipulation. She had actually been surprised, if relieved, that Kitti Ping Yung, as the senior scientist on the Pern expedition, had permitted the bioengineering of the fire-dragonets. Had Kitti Ping any idea of what a marvelous gift she had bestowed on the people of Pern?

But for Ted Tubberman, disgruntled *botanist*, to tinker with ova—and he *had not* at all understood the techniques or the process—to make independent alterations was intolerable to her, both professionally and personally. Bay knew herself to be a tolerant person, friendly and considerate, but if Ted Tubberman was dead, she would be tremendously relieved. And she would not be the only one. Just thinking about the man produced symptoms of agitation and pure fury which made Bay lose her professional detachment, and that annoyed her even more. There she was on dragonback, a marvelous opportunity for peaceful reflection, with only the noise of the wind in her ears, with all Jordan spread below her, and she was wasting contemplative time on Ted Tubberman. Bay sighed. One had so few moments of total relaxation and privacy. How she envied young Sorka, Sean, and the others.

She was astonished to see Calusa in the next valley. It was a sturdy complex, built by the Tubbermans as headquarters for their stake acres. The galvanized roofs of the main buildings had grown to a dull dark gray from the repeated showers of volcanic ash that Picchu Peak deposited wherever the wind blew. But Bay had scarcely had time to notice that when Sorka's cry of astonishment blew back to her.

"Jays, that building's a shambles!" Sorka pointed to her right, and Faranth abruptly turned in response to an unspoken request. The dorsal ridge bit into the soft flesh of Bay's crotch, and she gripped Sorka's belt more tightly.

"Look!" Sorka was directing her gaze downward.

Seventy-five meters from the main house, there was a roofed compound with separate enclosures along an L passageway, forming two sides of a fenced-in area. One of the outside walls and several of the interior partitions were smashed, and a corner of the roofing had burst outward. Bay could not recall if there had been any more earthshocks reported in that area to cause such structural damage. No other building was damaged.

As the dragon once more changed direction, Bay grabbed

at Sorka, felt the girl's reassuring fingers on hers, and then they were down.

"I do like riding Faranth. She's so very graceful and strong," Bay said, tentatively patting the warm hide of the dragon's neck.

"No, don't dismount," Sorka said. "Faranth says there's something prowling in there. The dragonets will have a look. Whoops!"

The air was suddenly full of the chitterings and chatterings of angry dragonets. Bay's Mariah shrieked in her ear.

"Now, now, it's all right. Faranth won't let anyone harm you." Bay held up her arm for her gold, but Mariah joined the investigating fairs. Bay was astounded to realize that the dragon was growling, a sensation she could also feel through her body contacts. Faranth turned her impressive head toward the compound, the many facets of her eyes gleaming with edges of red and orange.

A piercing yowl was clearly audible and then there was silence. The excited fairs swirled back over the two dragonriders' heads, chittering and clattering with their news. Faranth looked up, her eyes wheeling as she absorbed the dragonets' images.

"There's some kind of very large spotted beast out there," Sorka told Sean. "And something else that is even larger but silent."

"We'll need trank guns, then," he said. "Sorka, have Faranth call up some reinforcements. Marco and Duluth, if possible; Dave, Kathy—we may need a medic. Peter's Gilgath is sturdy, Nyassa won't panic, and ask for Paul or Jerry. I think we should evacuate Mary and the two children until the beasts can be captured."

Her ordeal ended, Mary Tubberman wept copiously on Bay's shoulder. Her son, Peter, usually a cheerful seven-year-old, watched poker-faced and taut with anxiety. His two little sisters clung together on a lounger and would not respond to

Pol's efforts to comfort them, though he was generally very deft with children. Mary did not resist the suggestion that she move to a safer location.

"Dad's dead, isn't he?" Petey asked, stepping right up to Sean.

"He could be out trying to recapture the beasts," kind-hearted Bay suggested. The boy gave her a scornful look and went off down the corridor to his room.

The dragon reinforcements arrived with the trank guns. Sean was pleased to see them landing in the order they had been drilled in. Sean gave Paul, Jerry, and Nyassa the trankers and sent them off on their dragons to see if they could find and disable the escaped animals.

Leaving Sorka to help the Tubbermans assemble their gear, Sean and the others, armed with the pistols, cautiously approached the wrecked compound. Inside the building, the reek of animal was heavy and mounds of recent dung littered the place. They found Ted Tubberman's mauled and gnawed body pitifully sprawled outside his small laboratory.

"Fardles, nothing we have kills like that!" David Catarel exclaimed, backing out of the corridor.

Kathy knelt by the corpse, her face expressionless. "Whatever it was had fangs and sharp claws," she remarked, slowly getting to her feet. "His back was broken."

Marco grabbed up an old lab coat and some toweling from a rail and covered the corpse. Then he picked up the remains of a chair, made of one of the local pressed vegetable fibers that were used for interior furnishings. "This'll burn. Let's see if we can find enough to cremate him here. Save a lot of awkwardness." He waved in the direction of the main house. Then he shuddered, clearly unwilling to move the mangled body.

"The man was insane," Sean said, poking a rod into the dung pats in one enclosure. "Developing big predators. We've enough trouble with wherries and snakes!"

"I'll go tell Mary," Kathy murmured.

Sean caught her arm as she went by. "Tell her he died quickly." She nodded and left.

"Hey!" Peter Semling picked up a covered clipboard from the littered floor of the laboratory. "Looks like notes," he exclaimed, examining the thin sheets of film covered with notations in a cramped hand. "This is botanical stuff." He shrugged, held it out to Kathy, and picked up another. "This is . . . biological? Humph."

"Let's collect any notes," Sean said. "Anything that would tell us what kind of creature killed him."

"Hey!" Peter said again. He flipped the cover back on a portable bio-scan, complete with monitor and keyboard. "This looks like the one that went missing from the vet lab a while back, along with some AI samples."

Meticulously they gathered up every scrap of material, even taking an engraved plate with the cryptic message *Eureka, Mycorrhiza!* which had been nailed to the splashboard of the sink unit. Dave carried out several sacks to be brought back to Landing. Then Sean and Peter collected enough flammable materials to make a pyre that could be lit once Mary and the children had gone.

"Sean!" David Catarel called. He was hunkered down by a wide green swath that was the only living thing in the raddled and ash-littered plot, though its color was dimmed by the pervasive black ash. "How many Falls has this area had?" he asked, glancing about. He ran his hand over the grass, a tough hybrid that agro had developed for residence landscaping before Thread had fallen.

"Enough to clear this!" Sean knelt beside him and pulled up a hefty tuft. The dirt around the roots contained a variety of soil denizens, including several furry-looking grubs.

"Never seen that sort before," David remarked, catching three deftly as they dropped. He felt in his jacket pocket, extracted a wad of fabric, and carefully wrapped the grubs. "Ned Tubberman was yakking about a new kind of grass surviving Fall down here. I'll just take these back to the agro lab."

Just then Sorka, Pol, Bay, and Peter, each loaded with bundles, came out of the main house. Sean and Dave began to load the eight dragons.

"We can make another run for you, Mary," Sorka suggested tactfully when the woman joined them with two stuffed bed-sacks.

"I don't have much besides clothes," Mary said, her glance flicking to the compound. "Kathy said it was quick?" Her anxious eyes begged confirmation.

"Kathy's the medic," Sean assured her smoothly. "Up you go now. David and Polenth will take you. Mount up. You kids ever ridden a dragon before?"

Sean made a game of it for them and passed quickly over the awkwardness of the moment. He saw them all off before he and Pol ignited the funeral pyre. Then they took off in yet another shower of the volcanic dust which would eventually bury Landing.

I can't break Ted's personal code!" Pol exclaimed in exasperation, throwing the stylus down to a worktop littered with clipboards and piles of flimsies. "Wretched, foolish man!"

"Ezra loves codes, Pol," Bay suggested.

"Judging by the DNA/RNA, he was experimenting with felines, but I cannot imagine why. There're already enough running wild here at Landing. Unless—" Pol broke off and pinched his lower lip nervously, grimacing as his thoughts followed uneasy paths. "We *know*—" He paused to bang the table in emphasis. "—that felines do not take mentasynth well. *He* knew that, too. *Why* would he repeat mistakes?"

"What about that other batch of notes?" Bay asked, gesturing to the clipboard lying precariously on the edge.

"Unfortunately, all I can read of them are quotations from Kitti's dragon program."

"Oh!" Bay cocked her jaw sideways for a moment. "He had to play creator as well as anarchist?"

"Why else would he refer to the Eridani genetic equations?" Pol slapped the worktop with his hand, frustrated and anxious, his expression rebellious. "And what did he hope to achieve?"

"I think we can be grateful that he hadn't tried to manipulate the fire-dragonets, though I suspect he was practicing on the ova he appropriated from the vet frozen storage."

Pol rubbed the heels of his hands into his tired eyes. "We can be grateful for small mercies there. Especially when you consider what Blossom has done. I shouldn't have said that, my dear. Forget it."

Bay permitted herself a scornful sniff. "At least Blossom has the good sense to keep those wretched photophobes of hers chained. I cannot think why she persists with them. She's the only one they like." Bay gave a shudder of revulsion. "They positively fawn on her."

Pol snorted. "That's why," he said absently, riffling through the notes on the undecipherable clipboard. "What I don't understand is why he chose the large felines?"

"Well, why don't we ask Petey? He helped his father in the compound, didn't he?"

"You are the essence of rationality, my dear," Pol said. Pushing himself out of the chair, he went over and laid an affectionate kiss on her cheek, ruffling her hair. She was admonishing him when he punched the commcode for Mary Tubberman's quarters. Both he and Bay had been visiting her daily to help her settle back into the community. "Mary, is Peter available?"

When Peter answered, his tone was not particularly encouraging. "Yeah?"

"Those large cats your father was breeding? Did they have spots or stripes?" Pol asked in a conversational tone.

"Spots." Peter was surprised by the unexpected question.

"Ah, the cheetah. Is that what he called them?"

"Yeah, cheetahs."

"Why cheetahs, Peter? I know they're fast, but they wouldn't be any good hunting wherries."

"They were great going after the big tunnel snakes." Peter's voice became animated. "And they'd come to heel and do everything Dad told them—" he broke off.

"I expect they did, Petey. Several ancient cultures on Earth bred them to hunt all manner of game. Speediest things on four legs!"

"Did they turn on him?" Peter asked after a moment's silence.

"I don't know, Petey. Are you coming to the bonfire tonight?" Pol asked brightly, feeling that he could not leave the conversation on such a sour note. "You promised me a rematch. Can't have you winning every chess game." He received a promise for that evening and disconnected. "From what Petey said, it would appear that Ted used mentasynth on cheetahs to enhance their obedience. He used them to hunt tunnel snakes."

"They turned on him?"

"That seems likely. Only why? I wish we knew how many ova he took from vet. I wish we could decipher these notes and discover if he only used mentasynth or if he implemented any part of Kitti's program. Be that as it may—" Pol exhaled in frustration. "We have an unknown number of predatory animals loose in Calusa. Loose in Calusa!" Pol let out a derisory snort for his inadvertent rhyming. "I wonder if Phas Radamanth has had any luck deciphering the notes on those grubs. *They* could be useful."

Patrice de Broglie burst into Emily's office. "Garben's getting set to blow. We've got to evacuate. Now!"

"What!" Emily rose to her feet, the flimsies she was studying slipping out of her hands to scatter on the floor.

"I've just been to the peaks. There's a change in the sulfur-to-chlorine ratio. It's Garben that's going to blow." He slapped his hand to his forehead in a self-accusatory blow. "Right before my eyes, and I didn't see it."

Alerted by Emily's cry, Paul came through from the adjoining office. "Garben?"

"You've got to evacuate immediately," Patrice cried, his expression contorted. "There've even been significant increases in mercury and radon from the damned crater. And we thought it was leaking from Picchu."

"But it's Picchu that's smoking!" Stunned, Paul struggled to keep his cool. He reached for the comm unit just as Emily did. She grabbed it first, and he jerked his fingers back and let her contact Ongola.

"That Garben is as sly a mountain as the man we named it for. Volcanology still isn't a precise science," Patrice said, rolling his eyes in frustration as he paced up and down the small office. "I've sent a skimmer up with the correlation spectrometer to check on the content of the fumarole emissions that just started in the Garben crater," Patrice went on. "I brought down samples of the latest ash. But that rising sulfur-to-chlorine ratio means the magma is rising."

"Ongola," Emily said. "Sound the klaxon. Volcano alert. Recall all sleds and skimmers immediately. Yes, I know there's Threadfall today, but we've got to evacuate Landing *now,* not later. How long do we have, Patrice?

He shrugged in exasperation. "I cannot give you the precise moment of catastrophe, my friends, nor which way it will spew, but the wind is a strong nor'easterly. Already the ash increases. Had you not noticed?"

Startled, governor and admiral glanced out the window and saw that the sky was gray with ash that obscured the sunlight, and that Picchu's smoking yellow plume was broader than usual. A similar halo was beginning to grow about Garben's peak.

"One can even become accustomed to living beneath a volcano," Paul remarked with dry humor.

Patrice shrugged again and managed a grin. "But let's not,

my friends. Even if the pyroclastic flow is minimal, Landing will soon be covered with ash at the rate it's now falling. As soon as we've decided possible lava flow paths, I'll inform you, so you can clear the most vulnerable areas first."

"How fortunate we already have an evacuation plan," Emily remarked, selecting a file and bringing it up on the terminal. "There!" She ran the sequence to all printers, on emergency priority. "That's going to all department heads. Evacuation is officially under way, gentlemen. What a nuisance to have to do it at speed. Something is bound to be forgotten no matter how carefully you plan ahead."

Trained by repeated drills, the population of Landing reacted promptly to the klaxon alert by going to their department heads for orders. A brief flurry of panic was suppressed, and the exercise went into high gear.

The sky continued to darken as thick black clouds of ash rolled up, covering the peaks of the now active volcanoes that had once appeared so benign. White plumes rose from Garben's awakened fumaroles and from crevasses down its eastern side. Morning became twilight as the air pollution spread. Handlamps and breathing masks were issued.

In charge of the actual evacuation, Joel Lilienkamp supervised from one of the fast sleds, keeping the canopy open so that he could bawl orders and encouragement to the various details and make on-the-spot decisions. The laboratories and warehouses nearest the simmering volcano were being cleared first, along with the infirmary, with the exception of emergency first aid and burn control. The donks trundled everywhere, depositing their burdens at the grid or carrying them on down to temporary shelter in the Catherine Caves.

Patrice's group had already calculated areas of high and low pyroclastic hazard. Warnings had been sent as far east as Cardiff, west to Bordeaux, and south to Cambridge. Already favored with a heavy fall of ash, Monaco was also in range of moderate pyroclastic missile danger. Every boat, ship, and barge was mobilized in the bay, to be loaded and sent off to stand beyond the first Kahrain peninsula.

The last sacs of fuel were emptied into the tanks of the two remaining shuttles. Most of the dragonriders were put to herding the livestock toward the harbor. For the first time, no one assembled to fight Thread at Maori Lake—a more deadly fall threatened.

No one had time to cheer as Drake Bonneau lifted the old *Swallow,* with its cargo of children and equipment, just as daylight receded from the plateau. The technicians moved immediately to the *Parrakeet*. Ongola and Jake, monitoring in the tower, took advantage of the respite to eat the hot food that had been sent up to them. The communications equipment had been placed on trolleys and could be quickly shifted if the tower was threatened.

"*Swallow* looks good," Ezra called in from the interface chamber where he was monitoring the flight. He had spent much of that day erecting a shield of heatproof material around the chamber, not quite ready to accept Patrice's hurried assurance that the room's location did not intersect any channels of previous lava flows. Unfortunately the interface with the orbiting *Yokohama* could not be disconnected, relying as it did on a fixed beacon to the receiver on the *Yoko*. Since the setting on the *Yoko* could no longer be altered to a new direction, there was no point in taking the interface and reassembling it.

That night, the air was choking with sulfur fumes and full of gritty particles, and Patrice warned that the buildup was reaching the critical point. White plumes from both Picchu and Garben, ominously rooted in a muted glow from peak and crater, were visible even against the dark sky, casting an eerie light over the settlement.

Drake Bonneau reported that he was safely down after a difficult flight. "Damn crate nearly shook apart, but nothing was damaged. None of the kids so much as bruised, but I don't think any of them will develop a yen for flying. Hard landing, too, plowed a furrow when we overshot the mark. We'll need the rest of the day to clear the site for the *Parrakeet*. Tell Fulmar to check the gyros and the stabilizing monitors. I'll swear we had tunnel snakes in the *Swallow*'s."

There was a constant stream of vehicles down to the harbor, as the bigger ships and barges were loaded with protesting animals prodded into stalls erected on deck. Crates of chickens, ducks, and geese were strapped wherever they could be attached, to be off-loaded at the Kahrain cove, safely out of the danger zone. With any luck, most of the livestock would be evacuated. Skimming over the harbor, Jim Tillek managed to be everywhere, encouraging and berating his crews.

By nightfall, Sean called a halt for dragonriders ferrying people and packages to the Kahrain cove. "I'm not risking tired dragons and riders," he told Lilienkamp with some heat. "Too risky, and the dragons are just too young to be under this sort of stress."

"Time, man, we don't have time for niceties!" Joel replied angrily.

"You handle the exodus, Joel, I'll handle my dragons. The riders will work until they drop, but it's bloody stupid to push young dragons! Not while I can prevent it."

Joel gave him an angry, frustrated glare. The dragons had been immensely useful, but he also knew better than to put them at risk. He gunned the sled away, perched behind the console like a small, ash-covered statue.

Sean and the other riders did work until they dropped. Each dragon then curled protectively about his rider as they slept. No one had time to notice that there were few dragonets about.

Then, all too soon, Joel was there again, exhorting them from the air, and they rejoined the Herculean efforts of the people around them.

Suddenly, the klaxon sounded a piercing triple blast. All activity ceased for the message that followed.

"She's going to blow!" Patrice's almost triumphant shout echoed throughout Landing.

Every head turned toward Garben, its peak outlined by the eerie luminosity from its crater.

"Launch the *Parrakeet!*" Ongola's stentorian voice broke the awed, stunned silence.

The engines of the shuttle were drowned by the rumbling earth and an ear-splitting roar of tremendous power as the volcano erupted. The attentive stance of observers broke as people scrambled to complete tasks at hand, shouting to one another above the noise. Later, those who watched the peak fracture and the red-hot molten lava begin to ooze from the break said that everything appeared to happen in slow motion. They saw the fissures in the crater outlined by orange-red, saw the pieces blowing out of the lip, even saw some of the projectiles lifting out of the volcano and could track their dizzying trajectory. Others averred that it all happened too fast to be sure of details.

Bright red tongues of lava rolled ominously up and over the blasted lip of Garben, one flow traveling at an astonishing rate directly toward the westernmost buildings of Landing.

In that dawn hour, the wind had dropped, saving much of the eastern section of Landing from the worst of the shower of smaller rocks and hot ash. The larger, devastating projectiles that Patrice had feared did not appear. But the lava was sufficiently frightening a menace.

The *Parrakeet,* laden with irreplaceable equipment, pierced the western gloom, her engine blasts visible, if not audible, as she drove northwest and out of danger.

At the sound of the klaxon, the dolphins began to tow heavily laden small boats out of Monaco Bay, a flotilla of vessels not ordinarily suitable for any prolonged sea travel. The dolphins had assured humans that they would get their charges safely to the sheltered harbor beyond the first Kahrain peninsula. *Maid* and *Mayflower,* which were not fully loaded, left the harbor to wait outside the estimated fallout zone until they could return for the last of their cargoes. Jim, on board the

Southern Cross, shepherded barges and luggers along the coast on their long journey to Seminole, from where they would make the final run north.

Sleds and skimmers streamed between Landing and Paradise River Hold as the nearest safe assembly point. Traffic there was chaotic, as vital supplies were kept available and loads were shunted to designated areas of the beach. Landing was being cleared of all that could be reused in the new northern hold.

Thick sulfur-smelling ash began to cover Landing's buildings. Some of the lighter roofs collapsed under the load, and observers could hear the plastic groaning and shifting. The air was almost unbreathable with traces of chlorine. Everyone used the breathing masks without complaint.

By midafternoon, a haggard Joel Lilienkamp dropped his battered sled on the lee side of the tower beside Ongola's. He waited a moment to gather enough strength to thumb open the comm unit.

"We've cleared all we can," he said in gasps, his voice raspy from the acrid airborne fumes. "The donks are parked in the Catherine Caves until we can strip 'em down for shipment. You can leave now, too."

"We're coming," Ongola replied.

Moments later he appeared, slowly angling a heavy comm package on a grav unit past the door. Jake came next, similarly encumbered. Paul followed, guiding two more components.

"Need a hand?" Joel asked automatically, though the way he slumped at the console made it hard to believe that he had any more energy to spare.

"One more trip," Ongola said when they had positioned the equipment in his sled. "Is your power pack up to a load?" he asked Joel.

"Yup. My last fresh unit."

As Ongola and Jake went back into the tower, Paul went to the flagstaff and, with a bleak expression on his face, solemnly lowered the singed tatters of the colony's flag. He made a ball of it, which he stuffed underneath the seat he took on the sled. He gave the supply master one long look. "Want me to drive, Joel?"

"I got you here, I'll take you out!"

Paul dared not look back at the ruins of Landing, but as Joel veered east and then north in a wide sweep, the admiral saw that he was not the only one with tears coursing down his cheeks.

A stiff nor'easterly wind kept the Kahrain cove clear of ash and the acrid taint of Garben's eruption. The gray pall spread over the eastern horizon as the volcano continued to spew lava and quantities of ash. Patrice and a skeleton team remained to monitor the event after Landing was abandoned.

"We hunt this morning," Sean said to the other riders.

They had found a quiet cove up the beach from the main evacuation camp. None of the dragons sprawled in the warm sun had a very good color, and privately Sean worried that their maturing strengths had been overtaxed. He decided stoutly that there was nothing wrong that a good meal would not restore. He looked around for fire-lizards and swore under his breath. "Damn them! We *need* all we've got. Four queens and ten bronzes can't possibly catch enough packtail to feed eighteen dragons! Surely they've seen volcanoes erupt before."

"Not on top of them," Alianne Zulueta replied. "I couldn't reassure mine. They just left!"

"Red meat would be better than fish—more iron," David Catarel suggested, his eyes on his pale bronze Polenth. "There's sheep here."

"Hold it," Marco Galliani said firmly, raising both hands in restraint. "My father's shipping them on to Roma as soon as sleds are free. Prime breeding stock."

"So are dragons." Sean rose, an odd grin on his face. "Peter, Dave, Jerry, come with me. Sorka, you run interference—if there is any."

"Hey, wait a minute, Sean," Marco began, dual loyalties in conflict.

Sean grinned slyly, laying a finger along his nose. "What the eye doesn't see, Marco, the heart won't grieve."

"It's for your dragon, man," Dave muttered as he passed him.

An hour later, several dragons disappeared in a westerly direction, skimming the treetops. The other riders were so conspicuous in their efforts to help the crew struggling to organize the chaos on the beach that no one would have noticed that the riders were not all present at any one time. By noon, seventeen brightly hued, sated dragons lolled on the strand. One sat patiently on the headland while fire-dragonets dove into the sea, fishing for packtail.

Caesar and Stefano Galliani, taking a poll count as their sheep were loaded, discovered that the tally was short by some thirty-six animals, including one of the best rams. Caesar called on the dragonriders to search the area and herd the missing sheep back to the shore.

"Useless things, always wandering off," Sean agreed, nodding sympathetically at the frustrated and puzzled Gallianis. "We'll give a look."

When Sean reported back an hour later, he suggested to Caesar that the sheep must have dropped into some of the many potholes in the area. Reluctantly the Gallianis took off with the depleted flock. The big transport sleds had schedules to keep, and shipment could not be postponed.

As the last of the sleds departed, Emily came over to Sean. "Are your dragons fit for duty?"

"Anything you say!" Sean agreed so amiably that Emily shot him a long look. "The fire-lizards worked hard all morning to feed the dragons." He gestured toward the cove where Duluth was accepting a packtail from a bronze.

"Fire-lizards?" Emily was momentarily baffled by "lizards,"

then remembered that Sean tended to use his own name for the little creatures. "Oh, yes, then your fairs have returned?"

"Not all of them," Sean said ruefully, and then added quickly, "but enough of the queens and bronzes to be useful."

"The eruption scared them all, didn't it?"

Sean gave a snort. "The eruption scared all of us!"

"Not out of our wits, it would seem," Emily said with a crooked smile. "At least nobody acted as foolish as sheep, did they?" Sean pretended neither innocence nor understanding; he returned her look until she broke eye contact. "If your dragons have lost the taste for fish, hunt wherries. That eruption whittled down our herds quite enough, thank you." Sean inclined his head, still noncommittal. "There's so much to be done, and done quickly." Consulting the thick sheets on her clipboard, she paused to rub her forehead. "If only your dragons were fully functional . . ." Then she shot him a penitent smile. "Sorry, Sean, that's an egregious comment."

"I, too, wish we were, Governor," Sean replied without prejudice. "But we're not sure *how* it's done. Not even what to tell them to do." He blotted the sweat from his forehead and neck, a sweat not entirely provoked by the hot sun.

"A point well made and a matter we must look into, but not here and now. Look, Sean, Joel Lilienkamp's worried about the supplies still at Landing. We're shifting loads out of here as fast as we can." She swept her arm over the mounds of color-coded crates and foam-covered pallets. "The orange stuff has to be protected from Threadfall, so it has to go north as fast as possible to be stored in the Fort Hold. We still have to try to save what's left at Landing before the ash covers it."

"That ash burns, Governor. Burns as easily through dragon wings as—" Sean broke off, staring fixedly toward the western beach, one hand coming up in a futile gesture of warning. Emily twisted around to see what had prompted his concern.

The dragon's trumpet of alarm was faint and thin on the hot air. The driver of the sled on collision course with the creature seemed unaware that he was descending onto another flyer. Then, just before the sled would have hit, dragon and rider disappeared.

"Instinct is marvelous!" Emily exclaimed, her face lit with both relief at the last-minute evasion and joy that a dragon had displayed that innate ability. She looked back to Sean and her expression changed. "What's the matter, Sean?" She glanced quickly up at the sky, a sky empty of both dragonpair and the sled, which was lost in the many coming and going on the Kahrain cove. "Oh no!" Her hand went to her throat, which seemed to close as she felt the wrenching of fear in her guts. "No. Oh no! Shouldn't they be visible again now? Shouldn't they, Sean? Isn't it supposed to be an instantaneous displacement?"

Distressed, she reached out to clasp his arm, giving him a little shake to attract his attention. He looked down at her, and the anguished expression in his eyes gave her an answer that altered fear to grief. She turned her head slowly from side to side, trying to deny the truth to herself.

Just as one of the cargo supervisors came striding up to her, a sheaf of plasfilm in his hand and an urgent expression on his face, the most appalling keen rose into the air. The dissonant noise was so piercing that half the people on the beach stopped to cover their ears. In the same moment as the unbearable sound mounted steadily, the air was full of fire-dragonets, each adding its own shrill voice to swell the sound of lament.

The other dragons rose, riderless, to fly past the point where one of their number and his human partner had lost their lives. In a complex pattern that would have thrilled watchers on any other occasion, the fire-dragonets flew around their larger cousins, emitting their weird counterpoint to the deeper, throbbing, mournful cry of the dragons.

"I'll find out how that could have happened. The driver of that sled—" Emily stopped as she saw the terrible expression on Sean's face.

"That won't bring back Marco Galliani and Duluth, will it?" He whipped his hand sideways in a sharp, dismissive cut. "Tomorrow we will fly wherever you need us for whatever we can save for you."

For a long long moment Emily stood looking after him until the image of the sorrowing young man was indelibly imprinted in her mind. In the sky, as if escorting him back to the dragonriders' camp, the graceful beasts wheeled, dipped, and glided westward to their beach.

Whatever pain Emily felt, it could be nothing, she realized, to the sense of loss that would be experienced by the dragonriders. She scrubbed at her face, at a chin that trembled, determinedly swallowed the lump in her throat, and irritably gestured for the cargo supervisor to approach her.

"Find out who drove that sled and bring him or her to my tent at noon. Now, what's on your mind?"

"Marco and Duluth disappeared, just the way the fire-lizards do," Sean said, his voice oddly gentle.

"But they *didn't* come back," Nora cried out in protest. She started to weep afresh, burying her face in Peter Semling's shoulder.

The shock of the unexpected deaths had been traumatic. The dragons' lament had subsided over the afternoon. By evening, their partners had coaxed them to curl up in the sand and sleep. The dragons seen to, the young people hunched about a small fire, dispirited and apathetic.

"We have to find out what went wrong," Sean was saying, "so that it can never happen again."

"Sean, we don't know even know what Marco and Duluth were doing!" Dave Catarel cried.

"Duluth was exhibiting an instinctive reaction to danger," a new voice said. Pol Nietro, Bay beside him, paused in the light thrown by the fire. "An instinct he was bred to exercise. May we offer condolences from all those connected with the dragon program. We—Bay and I—why, all of you are like family to us." Pol awkwardly dabbed at his eyes and sniffed.

"Please join us," Sorka said with quiet dignity. She rose and drew Bay and Pol into the firelight. Two more packing crates were hauled into the circle.

"We have tried to figure out what went wrong," Pol continued after he and Bay had settled down wearily.

"Neither looked where he was going," Sean said with a heavy sigh. "I was watching. Marco and Duluth took off from the beach and were rising just as the sled driver made an approach turn. He wouldn't have seen Marco and Duluth coming up under him. Dragons aren't fitted with proximity warning devices." Sean raised both hands in a gesture of helplessness. "I have it from very good authority that the sled driver had turned his alarm off because the constant noise in so much traffic was getting on his nerves."

Pol leaned toward him. "Then it is more important than ever that you riders teach your dragons discipline." A ripple of angry denial made him hold up his hands. "That is not meant to sound censorious, my dear friends. Truly I mean to be constructive. But obviously now is the moment to take the next step in training the dragons—training them to make proper use of the instinct that ought to have saved both Marco and Duluth today."

The comment raised murmurs, some angry, some alarmed. Sean held up his hand for silence, his tired face lit by the jumping tongues of flame. Next to him, Sorka was keenly aware of the muscles tightening along his jawline and the stricken look in his eyes.

"I believe we've been thinking along the same lines, Pol," he said in a taut voice that told the biologist just how much strain the young dragonrider was under. "I think that Marco and Duluth panicked. If only they'd just come back to the place they'd left, the farking sled was gone!" His anguish was palpable. He took a deep breath and continued in a level, almost emotionless tone. "All of us have fire-lizards. That's one of the reasons Kit Ping chose us as candidates. We've all sent them with messages, telling them where to go, what to do, or who to look for. We should be able to instruct the dragons to do the same thing. We know now, the hard way, that they can teleport, just as the fire-lizards do. We have to guide that instinct. We have to discipline it, as Pol suggested, so panic doesn't get us the way it got Marco."

"Why did Marco panic?" Tarrie Chernoff asked plaintively.

"I'd give anything to know," Sean said, the edge of anguish returning to his voice. "One thing I do know. From now on, no rider takes off without checking what's in his immediate airspace. We must fly defensively, trying to spot possible dangers. *Caution,*" he said, stabbing his index finger into his temple, "should be engraved on our eyeballs." He spoke rapidly, his tone crisp. "We know that the fire-lizards do go wherever it is they go, *between* one place and another, so let's stop taking that talent of theirs for granted and *watch* exactly what they do. Let's scrutinize their comings and goings. Let's send them to specific places, places they haven't been before, to see if they can follow our mental directions. Our dragons hear us telepathically. They understand exactly what we're saying—not like the fire-lizards—so if we get used to giving precise messages to the fire-lizards, the dragons ought to be able to operate on the same sort of mental directions. When we understand as much of fire-lizard behavior as we can, *then* we will attempt to direct our dragons."

The other riders murmured among themselves, Sean watching them with narrowed darting glances.

"Wouldn't that risk our dragonets?" Tarrie asked, stroking the little gold that had nestled in the crook of her arm.

"Better the dragonets than the dragons!" Peter Semling said firmly.

Sean gave a derisive snort. "The fire-lizards're very good at taking care of themselves. Don't misunderstand me—" He held up a hand against Tarrie's immediate protest. "I appreciate them. They've been great little fighters. Jays, we'd never have fed the hatchlings without their help, but—" He paused to look around the circle. "—they have got a well-developed survival mechanism or they wouldn't have lasted through the first pass of that Oort cloud. Whenever that was. As Peter said, it's a lot safer to experiment with the fire-lizards than another dragonpair."

"You've made some very good points there, Sean," Pol said, beginning to take heart himself, "though I trust you mean to use the gold and bronze fire-dragonets. They have always seemed more reliable to Bay and myself."

"I had. Especially since the blues and greens all scarpered off after the eruption."

"I'm game to try," Dave Catarel said, throwing his shoulders back and straightening up, sending a challenging look at the others. "We've got to try something. Cautiously!" He shot Sean a quick glance.

A slow smile broke across Sean's face as he reached across the fire to grasp Dave's hand.

"I'm willing, too," Peter Semling said. Nora tentatively agreed.

"It sounds eminently sensible to me," Otto said, nodding vigorously and looking about him. "It is, after all, what the dragons were bred to do, escape from the danger of Threadfall as the mechanical sleds cannot."

"Thanks, Otto," Sean said. "We all need to think positively."

"And cautiously," Otto amended, raising one finger in warning.

Stirred from their apathy, the riders began murmuring to one another.

"Do you remember, Sorka," Bay said, leaning toward her urgently, "when I sent Mariah to you the day we were called to Calusa?"

"She brought me your message."

"She did indeed, but all I told her was to find the redhead by the caves." Bay paused significantly. "Of course, Mariah has known you all her life and there aren't *that* many redheads in Landing, or on the planet." Bay knew she was babbling, which was something she rarely did, but then she rarely broke down in tears, either, and when she had heard the dreadful news, she had cried for nearly an hour, despite Pol's comforting. As Pol had said, it had been like losing family. Without a terminal to consult for possible solutions, they had spent two frantic hours searching for the crate in which they had packed all their written notes of the dragon program, wanting to have some positive suggestion with which to comfort the young people. "But Mariah did find you with no trouble that day, and you were at our house in minutes. So it can't have taken her very long to do it."

"No, it didn't," Sorka said thoughtfully. She looked around the circle of fire-lit faces. "Think of how many times we told the dragonets to get us fish for the hatchlings."

"Fish are fish," Peter Semling remarked, absently prodding the sand with a branch.

"Yes, but the dragonets knew which ones the dragons like best," Kathy Duff said. "And it takes them no time at all from the moment we issue the command. They just wink out and a couple of breaths later they're back with a packtail."

"A couple of breaths," Sean repeated, looking out to the darkness, his stare fixed. "It took more than a couple of breaths for any of our dragons to realize that . . . Marco and Duluth were not coming back. Can we infer from that that it also only takes a couple of breaths for dragons to teleport?"

"Cautiously . . ." Otto held up his finger again.

"Right," Sean went on briskly, "this is what we do tomorrow morning at first light." He reached over and took Peter's stick, and drew a ragged coastline in the sand. "The governor wants us to ferry stuff out of Landing. Dave, Kathy, Tarrie, you've all got gold fire-lizards. You make the first run. When you get to the tower, send your fire-lizards back here to me and Sorka. Bay, do you and Pol have to be anywhere else tomorrow?"

Bay gave a derisory sniff. "The pair of us are useless until we get our systems going again at Fort Hold. And we have to wait for transport. We'd be delighted to help you, any way we can!"

"We'll time the fire-lizards. Only, we've got to have handsets to do it on the mark."

"Let me scrounge those," Pol offered.

Sean grinned with real humor. "I was hoping you'd volunteer. Lilienkamp wouldn't deny you, would he?"

Pol shook his head emphatically, feeling much better than he had all afternoon, vainly searching for mislaid documentation during the nadir of his grieving.

"Well then, Bay and I will leave you now," Pol said, rising and giving her a helpful hand to her feet. "To scrounge handsets. How many? Ten? We'll meet you here at dawn, then, with handsets." He made a bow to the others, noting that only Bay understood his whimsy. "Yes, at dawn, we'll begin our scientific observations."

"Let's all get some sleep, riders," Sean said. He began to scoop sand over the dying flames.

With a handset to his ear, Pol dropped his finger as Bay, Sean, and Sorka set the mark on their wrist timers. Keeping index fingers hovering over the stop pin, they all looked up toward the eastern sky, Bay squinting against the sunglare from the smooth sea.

"Now!" Four voices spoke and four fingers moved as a fire-dragonet erupted into the air over their heads, chirping ecstatically.

"Eight seconds again," Pol exclaimed happily.

"Come, Kundi," Sorka said, holding up her arm as a landing spot. Dave Catarel's bronze cheeped, cocking his head as if considering her invitation, but he veered away as Duke, Sorka's bronze, warned him off. "Don't be ugly, Duke."

"Eight seconds," Sean said admiringly. "That's all it takes them to travel fifty-odd klicks."

"I wonder," Pol mused, tapping his stylus on the clipboard with its encouraging column of figures. "The figure doesn't vary no matter who we send which direction. How long would it take them to go to say, Seminole or the Fort Hold in the north?" He looked with bright inquiry at the others.

Sean began to shake his head dubiously, but Sorka was more enthusiastic.

"My brother, Brian, is working at the fort. Duke knows him as well as he knows me. And I've seen plenty of fax of the place. He'd go to Brian." As if understanding that he was being discussed, Duke circled in to land on Sorka's shoulder. She laughed. "See, he's game!"

"He may come when he's called," Sean said, "but will he go where he's sent? Landing's one thing—they all know it well."

"We can only try and see," Pol remarked firmly. "And this is a good hour to reach Brian at the Fort Hold." He punched the comm unit. "What a boon that the tower's functional. Ah, yes, Pol Nietro speaking. I need an urgent word with Brian Hanrahan . . . I said urgent! This is Pol Nietro. Get him for me! Idiots," he murmured in an aside. "'Is this call important?'"

Brian was found and was surprised to hear from his sister. "Look, what's this all about? You don't just scream priority around here. I can assure you that Mother's taking good care of Mick. She dotes on him."

His slightly aggrieved voice was clear to the others, and Sorka was taken aback by his uncooperative response. Sean took the handset from her.

"Brian, Sean here. Marco Galliani and his dragon Duluth died yesterday in an unfortunate accident. We're trying to prevent a recurrence. We're only asking for a few minutes of your time. And this is a priority."

"Marco and Duluth?" Brian's tone was chastened. "Jays, we hadn't heard anything. I'm sorry. What can I do?"

"Are you outside? Someplace where you can be easily spotted from the air?"

"Yes, I am. Why?"

"Then tell Sorka exactly where you are. I'm handing you over to her."

"Hell and damnation, Sorka, I'm sorry I dumped on you. So I'm outside. Have you seen the recent fax? Well, I'm approximately twenty meters from the new ramp. At the vet caves. They finally carved us some more headroom, and there's a huge pile of rock about a meter from me and nearly as high. What do I do now?"

"Just stand there. I'm sending Duke to you. When I say 'mark,' set your timer."

"Come on, now, sis," he began in patent disbelief, "you're in Kahrain Cove, aren't you?"

"Brian! For once in your life, don't argue with me."

"All right. I'm ready to mark the time." He still sounded aggrieved.

Sorka held her arm high, ready to pitch Duke into the air. "Go to Brian, Duke. He's at the new place! Here!" She screwed her eyes shut and concentrated on an image of Brian standing on the site he had described. "Go, Duke."

With a startled squawk, Duke launched himself into the air and vanished.

"Mark!" Sorka cried.

"Hey, I can hear you loud and clear, sister. You don't need to roar. I don't know what good this is going to do. You can't imagine for one minute that a fire-dragonet could possibly—Jays!" Brian's voice in her ear faded into astonishment. "I don't bloody believe it. Shit. I forgot to mark time."

"That's all right," Sorka said, nodding her head with delight, "we used your 'jays' to mark!"

Pol was jumping up and down, holding his wrist chrono and shouting, "Eight seconds! *Eight seconds!*"

He grabbed Bay by the waist and danced around her. Sean lifted Sorka from her feet and kissed her soundly while Mariah and Blazer led an augmented fair of fluting fire-dragonets in a dizzy aerial display.

"Eight seconds to the fort, only eight seconds," Pol gasped, reeling to a standstill, Bay clinging to him.

"That doesn't make much sense, does it?" Bay said, panting, one hand on her heaving chest. "The same time to go fifty klicks or nearly three thousand."

"Hey, Sorka," came Brian's plaintive voice. She put the handset to her ear again, mopping the sweat off her forehead against her sleeve. "I really gotta go, only what am I supposed to do with Duke now you've got him here?"

"Tell him to come back to me. And give us the mark when he disappears."

"Sure, right. On the mark, now . . . Duke, find Sorka! Sorka! Find—he's gone. Shit! Mark!"

On the beach at Kahrain Cove, four fingers pressed sweep hands, four pairs of eyes turned westward to the hot afternoon skies, and four voices counted the seconds.

"Six . . . seven . . . eight . . . He did it!"

Their elation had new confidence as Duke, cheeping happily, settled back to Sorka's shoulder and rubbed a cold muzzle against her cheek.

"Well, this has been most satisfying and productive," Bay said, beaming broadly.

"Report it to Emily, will you, Bay?" Sean asked, tucking his hand under Sorka's elbows. "We'd better go do our share of the donk work today."

So the Galliani boy's death proved to be a catalyst?" Paul Benden asked Emily as they conferred that evening by comm unit.

"Pol and Bay are much encouraged," Emily replied, still unaccountably saddened by the tragedy. She was tired, she knew, and while she spoke to Paul, hoping for the consolation of any sort of good news from the northern continent, half her mind was still on things that *had* to be organized.

"Telgar's group has made a tremendous effort, Em. The quarters are magnificent. You wouldn't know you were twenty or thirty feet in solid rock. Cobber and Ozzie have penetrated several hundred feet down on seven tunnels. There's even an eyrie for Ongola's communications equipment, cut high up in the cliff face. This place is big enough to house the entire population of Landing."

"Not everyone wants to live in a hole in the ground, Paul." Emily spoke for herself.

"There are quite a few ground-level caverns, immediate access," he replied soothingly. "You wait. You'll see. And when are you coming over? I've got to put in an appearance at the next Fall or they'll fire me."

"Don't you wish it!"

"Emily." Paul's flippant tone turned serious. "Let Ezra take over from you. He and Jim can liaise on shipments. Others can handle transportation and sled and skimmer maintenance. Pierre should be here to supervise the catering arrangements. He's got the biggest kitchen unit on Pern."

"That would be a welcome change from the largest single barbecue pit! It's the dragons that I worry about, Paul."

"I think they have to sort it out themselves, Emily. From what you reported, I believe they will."

"Thank you, Paul," she replied fervently, heartened by the absolute confidence in his voice. "I'll reserve a seat on the evening sled tomorrow."

After the excitement of sending Duke north, directing fire-dragonets back and forth between Kahrain and Landing was anticlimactic, but it helped to pass the tedium of the long journey. On the way back, Sean had the dragonriders practice flying in both close and loose formations and, more importantly, learning how to identify and benefit from the helpful airstreams.

Their campfire that night was bigger, and Pol and Bay slipped into its light to discuss observations about the fire-dragonets and how to apply them to the dragons. There had been no real need for Sean to promote caution as a byword: Marco and Duluth were still very much in everyone's mind. To counter any morbidity, Sean suggested that they get more formation practice the next day, practice that would stand them in good stead during Threadfall.

"If you know where you are in relation to other wing riders, you'll always know where to come back to," he said, stressing the last word.

"Your dragons are so young," Pol went on, seeing the favorable reaction, "in terms of their species. The fire-dragonets do not appear to suffer from degeneration. In other words, they don't age as we do physiologically."

"You mean, they could go on living after we die?" Tarrie asked, amazed. She glanced around toward Porth, a darker bulk against the shadowy vegetation.

"From what we've discerned, yes, Tarrie," Pol replied.

"Our major organs degenerate," Bay went on, "although modern technology can effect either repair or replacement, permitting us long, and useful, life spans."

"So they're not likely to get sick or to ail?" Tarrie brightened at that prospect.

"That's what we *think*," Pol answered, but he held up a warning finger. "But then we haven't *seen* any elderly dragonets."

Sean gave a snort, which Sorka softened with a laugh. "We've really only *our* generation to judge by," she said. "At that, we only get to treat our own, who trust us, and that's usually for scoring or scorching, or an occasional hide lesion. I find it comforting to know that dragons should be as long-lived."

"So long as *we* don't make mistakes," Otto Hegelman said gloomily.

"So, we *don't* make mistakes!" Sean's tone was decisive. "And so that we don't make mistakes, tomorrow let's split up into three sections. Six, six . . . and five. We need three leaders."

Although Sean had left the choice open, he was nominated at once. Dave and Sorka were selected after a minimum of discussion.

Later, when Sean and Sorka had made themselves comfortable on the sand between Faranth and Carenath, she gave him a long hug and kissed his cheek.

"What's that for?"

"Giving us all hope. But Sean, I'm worried."

"Oh?" Sean stroked her hair away from his mouth and inched his left shoulder into a new hollow.

"I think we oughtn't to wait too long before we try to teleport."

"My thoughts entirely, and I'm grateful to Pol and Bay for their comments on dragon longevity. Cheered me up, too."

"So, as long as *we* keep our wits, we'll keep our dragons." She snuggled against him.

"I wish you'd kept your hair long, Sorka," he muttered, pushing another curl out of his mouth. "I didn't eat so much of it then."

"Short hair's easier under a riding helmet," she replied in a sleepy sort of mumble. Then they both slept.

Although they could see the diminution of the parcels and plastic-cocooned equipment at Landing, cargo did not move out of Kahrain Cove as quickly. That second evening, when Sean was helping his wing riders unload, he caught sight of one of the cargo supervisors seated at a makeshift desk peering at the small screen of a portable unit.

"We'll finish off transferring from Landing by tomorrow, Desi," Sean assured the man.

"That's great, Sean, great," Desi said curtly, with a dismissive wave.

"What the hell's the matter, Desi?" Sean asked.

The edge in his voice caused Desi to look up in surprise. "What's the matter? I've got a beachful of stuff to shift and no transport." Desi's face was so contorted with anxiety that Sean's rancor dissolved.

"I thought the big sleds were coming back."

"Only when they're recharged and serviced. I wish they'd mentioned that earlier." Desi's voice rose in a quaver of frustration. "All my schedules . . . gone. What'm I to do, Sean? We'll be under Threadfall again here soon and all that stuff—" He flourished a sweat-grimed rag at the bulk of orange cartons. "—is irreplaceable. If only—" He broke off, but Sean had a good idea what the man had almost said. "You've done great, Sean, great. I really appreciate it. How much did you say is still to be shipped forward?"

"We'll have cleared it tomorrow."

"Look, then, the day after . . ." Desi rubbed at his face again, trying to hide his flush of embarrassment. "Well, I heard from Paul. He wants you riders to start making your way to Seminole, and cross to the north from there. And . . ." Desi screwed up his face again.

"You'd like us to take some of the orange out of danger?" Sean felt resentment welling up again. "Well, I suppose that's better than being good for nothing at all." He strode off before his temper got the better of him.

Faranth and Sorka come, Carenath said in a subdued tone. Sean altered his course to their point of arrival. He could not fool Sorka, but he could work off some of his fury during the unloading.

"All right, what happened?" Sorka said, pulling him to the seaward side of her golden queen, where they were shielded from the other riders, who were still sorting packages into the color-coded areas.

Sean set his fist violently into the palm of his other hand several times before he could put words to the humiliation.

"We're considered nothing but bloody pack animals, donks with wings!" he said finally. He did remember to keep his voice down, though he was seething.

Faranth turned her head around her shoulder, regarding

the two riders, hints of red beginning to gleam through the blue of her eyes. Carenath shoved his head over her back. Beyond them, Sean heard the other dragons muttering. The next thing he knew, he and Sorka were surrounded by dragons, and their riders were weaving into the central point.

"Now, see what you've done," Sorka said with a sigh.

"What's the matter, Sean?" Dave asked, squeezing past Polenth.

Sean took a deep breath, burying anger and resentment. If he could not control himself, he could not control others. There were flares of the yellow of alarm in the dragons who looked down at him. He had to quiet them, himself, and the other riders. Sorka was right. He had done something he had better quickly undo.

"We seem to be the only available aerial transportation unit," he said, managing a sort of a smile. "Desi says all the big sleds are grounded until they've been serviced."

"Hey, Sean," Peter Semling protested, jerking his thumb over his shoulder at the masses of material on the beach. "We can't shift all that!"

"No way." Sean made a decisive cut with his hands. "That's not been laid on us. When we've cleared Landing, Paul wants us to fly across to Seminole and make the final crossing north from there. That's okay." He gave a genuinely rueful smile. "But Desi would like us to take some of the irreplaceable stuff with us."

"So long as everyone understands we're not in the freight business," Peter said in an aggrieved tone that echoed Sean's sentiments.

"That's not at issue, Pete," Sean said firmly. "We're coming along as dragonriders, coming along fine. But Desi's caught between a rock and a hard place and he needs us."

"I just wish we were needed for what we're supposed to do," Tarrie remarked.

"Once we've fulfilled our commitment here," Sean said,

"we concentrate on that, and that alone. I mean to see us all teleporting by the time we reach Seminole."

"To places we've never seen?" asked the practical Otto.

"No, to the places we've just been. Look on our flight to Seminole as a chance to see the most important stakes in the south," Sean replied in a bracing tone. He was surprised to find himself believing it. "We'll need such reference points to teleport when we're fighting Thread." Sorka's face was glowing with pride as he managed not only to turn around his own anger but to restate the dignity of their future. Above their heads, the yellow was fading from dragon eyes. "I can smell food. I'm hungry. Let's go eat. We've earned it."

"We're going to have to hunt the dragons before we go skiting across the continent," Peter said, jerking his chin toward the animal enclosures.

Sean shook his head, smiling as he remembered Emily's oblique warning. "Can't go to that well twice, Pete. Tomorrow, we'll hunt the critters that got through the roundup in the Landing area." He began to push through the ring of dragons. "Food tomorrow, Carenath," he said, affectionately clouting the bronze as he passed him.

Fish? Carenath queried in a tone that carried dismay.

"Meat. Red meat," Sean said. He laughed when some of the dragons bugled gratefully. "But this time we won't kidnap it for you." Then he put an arm around Sorka and started up the beach to the cooking fires.

The next day, as the three wings of dragonriders crossed the Jordan River, they spread out in three different directions, bypassing the ash-covered settlement and heading south and east at low levels.

Faranth says that she has found running meat, Carenath reported to his rider. *Have we?*

Sean had his binoculars trained on a little valley. They were north of the path of the two Threadfalls that had dropped on that area, so there was vegetation to attract grazers.

"Tell her we've hit pay dirt, too."

Not meat? Carenath asked wistfully.

Sean grinned, and slapped his dragon's shoulder. "Yes, meat, by another name. And all you can eat this time," he added as the small mixed herd of sheep and cattle stampeded to escape the danger above them. He signaled to the rest of his wing in the exaggerated arm gestures that they had been rehearsing. Since the dragons could communicate with one another, the riders had chosen not to use handsets. But Sean had retained those Pol had scrounged. Although too valuable to risk dropping from a height, the handsets were too useful to be surrendered. "Land me on that ridge, Carenath. There's enough room there for the others."

Porth says they've enough for all of us, Carenath reported as he touched down gracefully and dipped his shoulder for Sean to dismount.

"Tell Porth we're grateful, but you'd better hurry to catch that lot," Sean advised. The herd was making all possible speed down the valley. He had to shield his face from the gravel and omnipresent ash thrown up by Carenath's abrupt departure. Bright streaks followed the bronze. "Welcome back," Sean said derisively as he distinguished blues and greens among the small colorful fire-lizard bodies following Blazer as she led the way.

The rest of his wing soon joined him. Even Nora Sejby managed a creditable landing on Tenneth; she was improving all the time. He worried more about Catherine Radelin-Doyle: she had not giggled with Singlath since the tragedy. Nyassa, Otto, and Jerry Mercer completed his wing. Once their dragons followed the hunt, Sean turned his glasses on Carenath in time to see the bronze swoop and grab a steer neatly without slowing his forward motion.

"Nice catch, Carenath!" Sean passed the binoculars to Nyassa to check on Milath.

"Seemed to me there were quite a lot of cattle in that bunch," Jerry said, pulling off his helmet and ruffling his sweat-damp hair. "What'll happen to them?"

Sean shrugged. "The best stock went north. These'll survive, or they won't."

"Sean, look who's come to dinner!" Nyassa pointed northward at the unmistakable outline of five wherries. "Go to it!" she added as she caught a glimpse of fire-dragonets launching an attack on the intruders. "Wait your turn!"

"I brought some lunch," Catherine said, twisting out of her backpack. "We might as well take a meal break, too."

Sean called a halt to the hunt when each dragon had consumed two animals. Carenath complained that he had eaten only one big one, so he needed two of the smaller kind. Sean replied that Carenath's belly would be so full that he would be unable to fly, and they still had work to do. The dragons grumbled, Carenath ingenuously remarking that Faranth wanted another meal, too, but Sean was adamant, and the dragons obeyed.

Sean re-formed the wing once they were aloft.

"All right, Carenath," he said, thinking ahead with relief to the last loads at Landing. "Let's get back to the tower as fast as we can and get this over with!"

He raised his arm and dropped it.

The next instant he and Carenath were enveloped in a blackness that was so absolute that Sean was certain his heart had stopped.

I will not panic! he thought fiercely, pushing the memory of Marco and Duluth to the back of his mind. His heart raced, and he was aware of the stunning cold of the black nothingness.

I am here!

Where are we, Carenath? But Sean already knew. They were *between*. He focused intense thoughts on their destination, remembering the curious ash-filtered light around Landing, the shape of the meteorology tower, the flatness of the grid beyond it, and the bundles awaiting them there.

We are at the tower, Carenath said, somewhat surprised. And in that instant, they were. Sean cried aloud with relief.

The he went wide-eyed with sudden terror. "Jays! What have I done?" he shrieked. "Where are the others, Carenath? Speak to them!"

They're coming, Carenath replied with the utmost calm and confidence, hovering above the tower.

Before Sean's unbelieving eyes, his wing suddenly materialized behind him, still in formation.

"Land, Carenath, please, before I fall off you," Sean said in a whisper made weak by the unutterable relief he felt.

As the others circled in to land, Sean remained seated on Carenath, reviewing everything, half in wonder, half in remembered terror at the unthinkable risk that had just been unaccountably survived.

"Keeeeyoooo!" Nyassa's yodel of triumph brought him up short. She was swinging her riding helmet above her head as Milath landed beside Carenath. Catherine and Singlath came in on the other side, Jerry Mercer and Manooth beyond them, and Otto and Shoth beside Tenneth and Nora.

"Hip, hip, hooray!" Jerry led the cheer while Sean stared at them, not knowing what to say.

It was easy, you know. You thought me where to to go, and I went. You did tell me to go as fast as possible. Carenath's tone was mildly reproving.

"If that is all there is to it, what took us so long?" Otto asked.

"Anyone got a spare pair of pants?" Nora ask plaintively. "I was so scared I wet myself. But we did it!"

Catherine giggled. The sound brought Sean to his senses, and he allowed himself to smile.

"We were ready to try!" he said, shrugging nonchalantly as he unbuckled his riding straps. Then he realized that he, too, would need to find a clean pair of pants.

"I said, we'll maintain silence about Emily's condition," Paul said sternly, glaring at Ongola, Ezra Keroon, and the scowling Joel Lilienkamp. He did *not* want Lilienkamp taking book on whether or not Emily Boll would recover from her multiple fractures. He moderated his expression as his eyes rested on the bent head of Fulmar Stone, who kept pulling with agitated fingers at a wad of grease-stained rag. "As far as Fort Hold is concerned, she's resting comfortably. That is the truth, according to the doctor and all the support systems monitoring her condition. For outside inquiries, she's busy—shunt the call to Ezra."

Abruptly Paul pushed himself to his feet and began to pace his new office, the first apartment on the level above the Great Hall. Its windows gave an unimpeded view of the ordered rows of cargo and supplies that filled that end of the valley. Eventually all those goods would be stored in the vast subterranean caverns of Fort. So much had to be done, and he sorely missed Emily's supportive presence.

He caught himself fingering the prosthetic fingers and jammed both hands into his pockets. His position had required him to contain his distress in order to avoid alarming people already under considerable tension. But before his close and trusted friends, he could give vent to the anxieties that they all shared.

The disastrous failure of the big sled's gyros and its subsequent crash had been visible to the inhabitants of Fort Hold, but few had known that the governor had been a passenger that night. They could be honest about the severity of the pilot's injuries, for he would recover easily from two broken arms and numerous lacerations. None of the other passengers had been severely hurt, and those who rescued the injured had not recognized Emily, her face bloodied by the head wound. At least until she was convalescing, Paul would not allow the facts to be common knowledge. Following so closely after the exodus from Landing, that crash, with the loss of some irreplaceable medical supplies as well as the sled itself, had to be minimized to sustain morale.

"Pierre agrees," Paul went on. He could feel the resistance from the others, the unspoken opinion that suppression would undermine his credibility. "Even insists on it. It's what Emily would want." In his pacing, Paul inadvertently glanced out the deep-set window and averted his eyes from the view of the scar that the sled had gouged two days ago. "Ezra, get someone to smooth that over, will you? I see it every time I look out the window."

Ezra murmured a response and made a note.

"How long can we expect Emily's state to be kept a secret?" Ongola asked, his face craven with new worry lines.

"As long as we have to, dammit, Ongola! We can at least spare people one more worry, especially when we haven't got a positive prognosis." Paul drew in a deep breath. "The head wound wasn't serious—no skull fracture—but it was a while before she was removed from the sled. The trauma wasn't treated quickly enough, and we don't have the sophisticated equipment to relieve the shock of multiple fracture. She must be given time and rest. Fulmar—" Paul swung to the engineer. "There will be a transport sled ready to go south today, won't there? I can't keep stalling Desi."

"All that orange-coded stuff is irreplaceable," Joel added, rearranging himself in the chair. "Not that we've got half the stuff moved inside here yet, but it'd be a sight more protectable in our front yard than on some frigging beach half a world away. Otherwise, you're going to have to send Keroon back for it. And I'll figure out a new schedule of priorities. You couldn't make that two sleds to go, could you, Fulmar?"

Fulmar looked up at him with eyes so reddened by strain and grief that even the doughty storesman recoiled in dismay. He knew that Stone's crews had been working impossible hours to service the big transport sleds. Joel would admit only to himself that more of the blame of that crash could be attributed to Stores than to maintenance. But what could he do with one emergency after another dumping on him?

"Whenever you can, Fulmar," Joel said in a gentler tone. "Whenever they're ready." He walked out of the room without a backward glance.

"We're doing our best, Admiral," Fulmar said wearily, struggling to his feet. He looked at the rag in his hands, perplexed to see it in tatters, and then jammed it into his hip pocket.

"I know, man, I know." Placing his arm across Fulmar's hunched shoulders, Paul guided the man to the door, giving him a final appreciative squeeze. "In all that spare time you have, Fulmar, run up a list of servicing dates on the smaller craft. I've got to know how many I'll have for this Fall.

"The accident was no one's fault," Paul said, returning to his desk and slumping down into his chair. "There's Fulmar, blaming himself for not insisting on servicing earlier. For that matter, I shouldn't have urged Emily to come north. The cargo was inadequately secured in the cabin. However, gentlemen, it is folly to read more into such an accident than bad timing and a lousy concatenation of circumstances. We evacuated Landing in reasonable order. A place had been prepared for us, and we've got to mobilize enough personnel and machines to fight Thread." He no longer hoped for support from either dragonets or dragons.

"You did *what?*" Sorka cried, her skin blanching then flushing brightly in fury. Faranth, her eyes whirling orange in sympathy with her rider, lowered her head. Carenath bugled alarm.

Sean grabbed Sorka by the arms, obscurely irritated by her reaction. He had managed to get the others to wait until Sorka's wing had landed before broadcasting their feat.

"Look, it wasn't something I planned, Sorka! Jays, it was the last thing in my head. I just told Carenath to get back to Landing as fast as possible. He did!"

It was really very simple, Carenath said modestly. *I've told Faranth. She believes me.* He swiveled his head to cast a reproachful look on Sorka.

"How . . . how . . . did the others know?" Fear returned to shadow her eyes. She ignored the general carry-on about her as Sean's wing cavorted with her riders, babbling the good news and going into specific detail at the top of their lungs.

He told them, Faranth replied, an edge to her tone.

"We've spent two hours figuring that out." Sean smiled, hoping to coax a smile from Sorka. Putting his arm about her shoulders, he drew her back to the others. "I think," he said, choosing his words carefully, "we were all scared shitless by Marco and Duluth dying like that. Now we know, firsthand, why Marco panicked. Sorka, it's like nothing you've ever seen, and you can't feel anything, even your dragon between your legs. Otto called it total sensory deprivation."

It is between, Carenath said in an almost didactic tone. He and Faranth followed their riders back to the mass of netted bundles which would be their final load. The dragons of Sean's wing were sitting on their haunches in a loose circle, occasionally shaking themselves to dislodge windblown ash. Faranth made a noise low in her throat, which made Sean grin. The golden queen was as skeptical as her rider.

"Can Faranth tell me how far away Dave's wing is?" he asked Sorka.

They are in sight now, Carenath said just as Sorka replied, "Faranth says they're in sight now." She pointed northeast.

"Polenth says that they hunted well. Meat!" Sorka gave a brief smile, and Sean decided that she was halfway to forgiving him.

There was of course renewed astonishment and rueful congratulations when Dave and his wing riders heard the news.

"Okay then," Sean said, mounting a carton to address them all. "This is what we do, riders. We teleport to Kahrain Cove. We know its aerial aspect as well as we know Landing's. So it's the perfect test. Carenath insists that he told the other dragons where they were going, but I'd prefer that you riders tell your own dragons where to go. I think that has to be as much part of our preflight drill as strapping on and checking the immediate airspace." He grinned at them.

"What're we going to tell *them*?" Dave asked, jerking a thumb in a northerly direction.

"Emily's gone to join the admiral. Pol and Bay were supposed to get the first sled back." Sean paused, looking around again, and then gave Sorka a long look. She nodded slowly in approval. "I think we keep this to ourselves for the time being. We'll spring the finished product on them, fighting-ready dragons! It's one thing to send a fire-lizard north on the strength of fax, but I sure wouldn't want to risk Carenath going someplace *I've* never been." Sean took another deep breath, having gauged the favorable reaction. "Desi said we're to make our way along the coast to Seminole. That'll give us time to practice teleporting between where we are and where we've been. That way we'll know exactly how to get back to any of the major stakes when we need to fight Thread over them."

"Yeah, but the dragons don't flame yet," Peter Semling pointed out.

"There's phosphine-bearing rock all along the coast. We've all watched the fire-lizards chew rock. That's the easiest part of this whole thing," Sean replied dismissively.

"It's one thing to go from one place to another," Jerry began slowly. "We've *done* it now. We go from here—" He stabbed his left index finger. "—to there." He held up his right finger. "And the dragons do the work. But dodging Thread, or a sled—" He broke off.

"Duluth caught Marco off-balance. He panicked." Sean spoke quickly and confidently. "Frankly, Jerry, that place *between* scared me, and I'll lay book the rest of us were scared. But now we know, we adapt. We'll plan emergency evasive tactics." Sean pulled the knife out of his boot cuff and hunkered down. "Most of us have flown sleds or skimmers in Threadfall, so we've seen *how* the junk drops . . . most of the time." He drew a series of long diagonal stripes in the ash. "A rider sees he's on a collision course with Thread . . . here—" He dug his point in. "—and *thinks* a beat forward." He jumped the point ahead. "We'll have to practice skipping like that. It's going to take quick reflexes. We see fire-lizards using such tactics all the time—wink in, wink out—when they're fighting Thread with ground crews. If they can, dragons can!"

The dragons bugled in answer to the challenge, and Sean grinned broadly.

"Right?" Sean's question dared the riders.

"Right!" They all replied enthusiastically, and fists were brandished to show staunch determination.

"Well, then." Sean stood up, bringing his hands together with an audible smack. Ash sifted off his shoulders. "Let's load up and teleport ourselves back to Kahrain."

"What if someone sees us, Sean?" Tarrie asked anxiously.

"What? The flying donks doing what they were designed to do?" he asked sarcastically.

"Obviously," Paul told the worried pilots, "we're not going to be able to protect as much land with such a depleted aerial coverage."

"Damn it, Admiral," Drake Bonneau said, twisting his face into a frown. "We were supposed to have enough power packs to last fifty years!"

"We did." Joel Lilienkamp jumped to his feet once again.

"Under normal usage. They have *not* had what anyone could possibly term normal usage, or even normal maintenance. And don't blame Fulmar Stone and his crew. I don't think they've had a full night's sleep in months. The best mechanics in the world can't make sleds operate on half-charged or badly charged packs." Glaring belligerently around him, he sat down hard, and the chair rocked on the stone floor.

"So it really is a case of taking the greatest care of the sleds and skimmers we have left, or have no aerial vehicles at all in a year?" Drake asked plaintively.

No one answered him immediately.

"That's it, Drake," Paul finally replied. "Burn a swath around your homes and what vegetable crops you've managed to save, keep the home stake clear . . . and thank whatever agency you will that hydroponics are available."

"Where're those dragons? There were eighteen of them," Chaila said.

"Seventeen," Ongola corrected her. "Marco Galliani died at Kahrain, with the brown, Duluth."

"Sorry, forgot that," Chaila murmured. "But where are the others? I thought they were to take up when vehicles failed."

"They're en route from Kahrain," Paul replied.

"Well?" Chaila prompted pointedly.

"The dragons are not yet a year old," Paul said. "According to Wind Blossom"—he noted the subtly disapproving reaction to her name—"Pol, and Bay, the dragons will not be mature enough to be fully . . . operational . . . for another two or three months."

"In two or three months," someone called out bitterly, "there'll have been between eighteen and twenty more uncontained Falls!"

Fulmar rose, turning to the back of the chamber. "We will have three completely reconditioned sleds back on line in three weeks."

"I heard there were more creatures hatched," Drake said. "Is that true, Admiral?"

"Yes, that's true."

"Are *they* any good?"

"Six more dragons," Paul said, more heartily than he felt.

"Removing six more young people from our defensive strength!"

"Giving us six more potential self-maintaining, self-propagating fighters!" Paul rose to his feet. "Consider the project in the right perspective. We have got to have an aerial defense against Threads. We have bioengineered an indigenous life-form to supply that critical need. They will!" He laced his voice with conviction. "In a few generations—"

"Generations?" The cry elicited angry murmurs from an audience already unnerved by an unpalatable briefing.

"Dragon generations," Paul said, raising his voice over the reactions. "The fertile females are mature enough to reproduce when they're two and a half or three years. A dragon generation is three years. The queens will lay between ten to twenty eggs. We've ten golds from the first Hatching, three from this second one. In five, ten years, we'll have an invincible aerial defense system to combat the intruder."

"Yeah, Admiral, and in a hundred years there won't be any space for humans left on the planet!" The suggestion was met with a ripple of nervous laughter, and Paul smiled, grateful to the anonymous wit.

"It won't come to that," he said, "but we will have a unique defense system, bioengineered to our needs. And useful in other ways. Desi tells me the dragonriders have been delivering supplies to the stakes as they make their way here to Fort. Meanwhile, you have your orders."

Paul Benden rose and left quickly, Ongola right behind him.

"Damn it, Ongola, where the hell are they?" Paul exclaimed when they were alone.

"They check in every morning. Their progress is good. We can't ask more of an immature species. I heard Bay tell you that she and Pol both worried that the dragons had been dangerously extended during the evacuation."

Paul sighed. "Not that there is any other way for them to get here, with the transport situation." He started down the winding iron stairs that went from the executive level to the underground laboratory complex. "Wind Blossom's staff has to be reassigned. We don't have time, personnel, or resources for further experimentation no matter what she says."

"She's going to want to appeal to Emily!" Ongola replied.

"Let's devoutly hope that she can! Any news from Jim this morning?" Paul had reached the state of mind at which he was so saturated with bad news that he did not feel additional blows so keenly. The previous day's news, that Jim Keroon's convoy, sailing past Boca, had been caught in a sudden tropical storm that capsized nine craft, had seemed almost inconsequential.

"He reports no loss of life," Ongola said reassuringly, "and all but two of the boats have been refloated and can be repaired. The dolphins are recovering cargo. There is some heavy stuff, though, that divers will have to locate. Fortunately, they were in shallow water, and the storm didn't last long." Ongola hesitated.

"Well, let me have it," Paul said, pausing on a landing.

"There were no manifests, so there's no way of checking that they've recovered everything."

Paul regarded Ongola stolidly. "Does he have any idea how long that's going to hold him up?" Ongola shook his head. "All the more reason, then, to reassign Wind Blossom's personnel," Paul said then. "When that's done, I'll have a word with Jim. It's incredible that he's got such an ill-assorted flotilla as far as he has! Through fog, Fall, and storm!"

Ongola agreed fervently.

While Carenath concentrated very carefully on chewing, Sean stood slightly to one side trying not to be anxious. Firedragonets flitted around the dragons, chirping what was obviously encouragement. Duke and some of the other bronzes had found pebbles that they masticated in demonstration.

The dragons and their riders had located the necessary phosphine-bearing rock on an upland plateau halfway between the Malay River and Sadrid. Over the past few days, the confidence of the riders had improved as time and again they were able to teleport to and from given landmarks. Otto Hegelman had suggested that each rider keep a log, noting down reference points for later identifications. The notion had been enthusiastically adopted, although it was immediately necessary for them to request writing materials at the Malay River Stake. They had been surprised to find only children there, with Phas Radamanth's sixteen-year-old daughter in charge.

"Everyone's out fighting Thread, you know," she said, cocking her head at them in what Tarrie later said was pure insolence.

"Desi gave us supplies for you," Sean replied, stifling his resentment of her implied criticism and the current menial status of dragonriders. He gestured for Jerry and Otto to bring the cargo net into the house. "Would you have any notebooks we could have?"

"What for?"

"We're doing a coastline survey," Otto said pompously.

The girl looked surprised, then her face relaxed into a less antagonistic expression. "I guess so. There's all that sort of stuff in the schoolroom over there. Who has time for lessons these days?"

"You're most kind," Jerry said, giving her a quick bow and a broad grin as they withdrew.

The incident had reinforced the riders' determination to accomplish their purpose during their westward journey.

"It isn't as if you can chew for him, Sean," Sorka said, holding out another piece to Faranth. "How much do they need to eat?"

"Who knows how much stoking it takes to start a dragon's

fires?" Tarrie sang out cheerfully. "I'd say this—" She hefted the stone in her hand. "—is comparable to the pebble-size I used to feed my gold dragonet. Isn't it, Porth?"

The queen obediently lowered her head and took the offering.

"The dragonets chew at least a handful before they can flame," Dave Catarel said, but he was watching Polenth dubiously as the bronze worked his jaws with the same solemn contemplative look the others had. "Look, Sorka, your fair's setting the example!"

Duke let go a fine long plume of fire, while Blazer took to the air, scolding him.

Just then Porth let out a squawk, her mouth opened, and a green-stained rock fell to the ground, just missing Tarrie's foot. Porth snapped her mouth shut and moaned.

"What did she do?" Dave asked.

"She says she bit her tongue," Tarrie replied. She patted Porth's shoulder sympathetically. "She did, too. Look!" The green ichor on the rock glistened in the sunlight. "Should I look, Sorka? She might have done herself damage."

"What does Porth say?" Sorka asked with professional detachment. She could not recall ever having had to deal with self-inflicted dragonet bites.

"It hurts, and she'll wait until it doesn't before she chews any more rock." Tarrie retrieved the offending piece and put it back in the pile they had gathered.

There was another draconic exclamation of pain, and Nora's Tenneth followed Porth's bad example. Sean and Sorka exchanged worried glances and continued to offer the firestone to their dragons.

Suddenly Polenth burped, and a tiny flame leapt beyond his nose. The startled bronze jumped backward.

"Hey, he did it!" Dave cried proudly. "Phew!" he added, waving the air from his face. "Stand upwind, folks. That stinks."

"Watch it!" Sean leapt sideways as Carenath belched, surprising everyone with a respectable tongue of flame that just missed searing his rider. Overhead the fire-lizards flew in congratulatory circles, alternately chirping or expelling flame, their eyes whirling bright blue with approval.

"Upwind and to one side, riders!" Sean amended. "Try it again, Carenath!" Sean offered a larger chunk.

"Jays, that's awful!" Tarrie said as the wind blew the overpowering stench of the fire-making stone straight into her face. Choking, she ducked around Porth to escape it.

"Where there's fire, there's smell," Jerry quipped. "No, Manooth, turn your head that way!"

Just as the brown dragon obeyed, a blast of flame erupted from his mouth and seared into charcoal one of the scrawny bushes that dotted the plateau.

Jerry pounded his dragon's shoulder in exultation. "You did it! Manooth! Master blaster!"

The others returned to stoking their dragons with renewed enthusiasm. An hour later, all the males had produced flame, but none of the females had; though the golds had chewed and chewed, one after the other they had regurgitated an awful gray pastelike substance.

"As I recall the program," Sean said as the gold riders stood disconsolately about, "the queens aren't mature until they're nearly three. The males are . . . well . . ." Sean cast about for a diplomatic phrase.

"Functional now," Tarrie finished for him, none too pleased.

"Even seven recruits are going to be well received at Fort," Otto said, for once not trying to sound pompous.

Sorka was frowning, though, an expression unusual enough to her that Tarrie inquired as to its cause.

"I was just thinking. Kit Ping was such a traditionalist . . ." Sorka regarded her husband for a long moment, until he ducked his head, unable to maintain the eye contact. "All right, Sean, you know every symbol in that program. Did Kit Ping introduce a gender discrimination?"

"A what?" Tarrie asked. The other queen riders gathered close, while the young men took discreet backward steps.

"A gender inhibition . . . meaning the queens lay eggs, and the other colors fight!" Sorka was disgusted.

"It may just be that the queens aren't mature enough yet," Sean said, temporizing. "I haven't been able to figure out some of Kit Ping's equations. Maybe the flame production is a mature ability. I don't know why the queens all barfed. We'll have to ask Pol and Bay when we get to Fort. But I tell you what, there's no reason you girls can't use flamethrowers. With wands a bit longer, you wouldn't singe your dragon by mistake."

His suggestion did much to mollify the queen riders for the time being, but Sean hoped fervently that Pol and Bay could give a more acceptable verdict. Seventeen dragons made a more impressive display than seven. And he was determined to impress when the dragonriders flew into Fort Hold. The only burdens dragons should ever carry again were their riders and firestone!

"Actually, Paul," Telgar said, glancing at Ozzie and Cobber, "those photophobes of Wind Blossom's have proved to be extremely useful in subterranean explorations. Their instinct for hidden dangers—pitfalls, in fact, and blind tunnels—is infallible." The geologist gave one of his humorless smiles. "I'd like to keep them now that Wind Blossom has abandoned them, so to speak." Telgar turned to Pol and Bay.

"It's a relief to know they've some use," Pol said, sighing heavily. Both he and his wife had tried to reason with the indignant Wind Blossom when she had been requested to suspend the dragon program. Though she maintained that the emergency transfer from Landing to Fort had damaged many of the eggs in the clutch she had manipulated, Pol and Bay had seen the autopsy reports and knew that claim to be spurious. They had been lucky to hatch six live creatures.

"Once they get to trust you, they're quite harmless," Telgar went on. "Cara adores the latest hatchling, and it won't let her out of its sight unless she leaves the Hold." Again he displayed his mirthless smile. "Keeps watch at her door by night."

"We can't have uncontrolled breeding of those creatures," Paul said quickly.

"We'll see to that, Admiral," Ozzie said solemnly, "but they're right useful little buggers."

"Strong, too. Carry more'n they weigh themselves out of the mines," Cobber added.

"All right, all right. Just limit the breeding."

"Eat anything," Ozzie added for good measure. "Anything. So they keep a place clean."

Paul continued to nod agreement. "I just want any further propagation cleared with Pol and Bay for the biology department."

"We're delighted, I assure you," Bay said. "I didn't approve of them, but I also cannot approve summary termination of any living creature which can be useful."

Telgar rose abruptly, and Bay, wondering if her words had reminded him of Sallah's death, mentally chastised herself for not thinking before she spoke. Ozzie and Cobber sprang to their feet, as well.

"Now that you've finally finished mapping the Fort Hold complex," Paul said, deftly filling the awkward moment, "what are your plans, Telgar?"

A flash of enthusiasm briefly lightened the geologist's face. "The probe reports indicated ore deposits in the Western Range that should be assayed as an alternative to power-costly haulage from Karachi Camp. Best to have resources close to hand." Telgar inclined his head in an abrupt farewell and then strode from the room, Ozzie and Cobber mumbling something suitable as they followed him.

"How that man has changed!" Bay said softly, her round face sad.

Paul observed a respectful silence. "I think we all have, Bay.

Now, is anything to be done about Wind Blossom's intransigence?"

"Nothing until she has an interview with Emily herself," Pol said, his expression neutral. Of necessity, the two scientists had been informed of the governor's true condition, which, twelve days after the accident, remained virtually unchanged.

"I don't know why she won't accept your decision, Paul," Bay said, showing some agitation.

"Tom Patrick says Wind Blossom chooses to distrust the male half of this leadership." Paul grinned. Actually he did find the situation ludicrous, but since Wind Blossom had immured herself in her quarters until she "had a fair hearing," he had grasped the opportunity to transfer personnel to more productive employment. Most of them had been grateful. "You will, of course, continue to monitor the new dragon hatchlings."

"Of course. What's the latest word from Sean and the others?" Pol asked, a trifle anxious. He and Bay had discussed their continued absence, beginning to wonder if it was deliberate. They both knew that Sean resented the dragonriders' messenger status. But what else could he expect? Everyone had to do what he could. Pol and Bay themselves were not exactly inspired by Kwan Marceau's project to monitor the grubs from the grass plot at Calusa, but that was where they could perform a useful service.

"They should be here soon." Paul's voice and expression were neutral. "When does Kwan anticipate a northern trial on those worms of his?"

"More grub than worm," Pol said didactically. "Sufficient have been propagated for a ground test."

"That's good news indeed," Paul said heartily, rising to his feet. "Remember, tomorrow won't be a good day for any kind of test!"

Pol and Bay exchanged looks. "Is it true, Admiral," Pol asked, "that you're not going to fly the full Fall across the mountains?"

"That's right, Pol. We have neither the personnel, the power, nor the sleds to do more than protect the immediate area. So, if those grubs are of any assistance, we will all be grateful to you."

When they had left, Paul sank back down in his chair, swiveling to look out the window at the starlit night. The northern climate was colder than that of the south, but the crisp air made the now-familiar star patterns crystal clear. Sometimes he could almost imagine that he was back in space again. He sighed heavily and picked up the terminal. He had to find some vestige of hope in that depressing inventory Joel had submitted.

If they were extremely careful to use sleds and skimmers on only the most critical errands, they might just last out Pern's current pass through the Oort cloud matter. But when it came around again, what would they do? Paul winced as he remembered the arrogance of Ted Tubberman in preempting the dispatch of the homing device. Had the man known how to activate it properly? Ironic, that! Would it be received? Acted upon? With the help of the technological society they had foresworn, his descendants could survive. Did he want them to? Had they any other choice? With adequate technology, the problem of Thread could possibly be solved. So far, ingenuity and natural resources had failed miserably.

Fire-breathing dragons, indeed! A ridiculous concept, straight out of folk tales. And yet . . .

Resolutely Paul began to scroll out the stark facts and figures of the colony's dwindling supplies.

"Tarrie!" Peter Chernoff came rushing to greet his sister from the cavernous barn set on the east edge of the Seminole Stake headquarters. A tall young man, he was able to look down at the riders who were surrounding him. "Say, you guys, where have you all been?"

"We've been reporting in to Fort everyday," Sean said, surprised.

"I made yesterday's report and even spoke to brother Jake," Tarrie added, her expression anxious. "What's the matter, Petey?"

Reluctant to explain, Peter stamped his feet as he hedged and hawed. "Things are getting tougher. We're not to fly anything anywhere that isn't a priority number one top emergency."

"So that's why we saw so much Thread damage," Otto said, shocked.

Peter nodded solemnly. "And there's Fall at Fort Hold today, and they'll have to sit it out."

"Without any attempt . . ." Dave Catarel was appalled.

"Transporting Landing to the north put too big a strain on sled and power packs." Peter peered down at them, judging their reaction. "And the governor was injured, you know. No one's seen her in weeks."

"Oh, no," Sorka said, leaning into Sean for comfort. Nora Sejby began to weep softly.

Peter gave another of his solemn nods. "It's pretty bad. Pretty bad."

Suddenly everyone was demanding news of his or her own kin, and Peter did his best to answer when he could. "Look, guys, I don't sit on the comm unit all the time. The word is out to sit tight and keep the home stake as clear as possible with ground crews. There's plenty of HNO_3, and it's easy to maintain tanks and wands."

"But not the land," Sean said, raising his voice authoritatively. The babble died abruptly, and his riders looked to him. "There's Thread at Fort today, you said. When?"

"Right now!" Peter replied. "Well, it starts out over the bay—"

"And you have throwers here? Ten of 'em that we could use?" Sean asked eagerly.

"Use? Well, you'd have to ask Cos, and he's not here right now. And what do you need ten throwers for?"

Grinning, Sean turned with a flourish of his hand to indicate the gold riders. "The girls need them to fight Thread! And we've got to work fast to be ready!"

"Whaddya mean?" Peter was dumbfounded. "The Fall's started. You wouldn't even make it out across the sea before it's over. And you're supposed to get in touch with Fort the moment you get here!"

"Peter, be a good lad, don't argue. Show the girls where the throwers are kept and let me see the latest fax of Fort Hold. Or better, the Fort harbor I heard they built. Dragons are a lot faster than that fleet Jim Keroon's shepherding. They haven't passed the Delta West Head yet."

Sean gave Peter no time to think or protest. He sent Otto to run off copies of the installation at the mouth of the Fort Hold River. Tarrie chivvied her brother into showing them where the flamethrowers were kept and helping the girls check out the tanks. In a flurry of golden wings, the queens landed at that storehouse and permitted Sean, Dave, and Shih to secure additional tanks to their backs. Sean shouted directions to Jerry and Peter Semling to check the cargo nets of firestone on the browns and bronzes. Peter Chernoff went from one rider to another, pleading with them to stop. What was he to do? How was he to explain all this? When would they bring all this equipment back? They could not leave Seminole defenseless.

Then all the frenzied preparations were completed, and the bronze and brown dragons had chewed as much firestone as they could swallow.

"Check straps!" Sean roared. He was developing quite a powerful bellow. Of course, he did not need to shout, as all the dragons were listening to Carenath, but it served to release adrenaline into his system, and it helped to encourage those who would soon follow him into danger.

"Checked!" was the prompt response.

"Do we know where we're going?" Setting the example himself, he spread out the fluttering fax for one last long look at the seafront installation with its wharf and the metal unloading

crane that looked like an awkward alien species hunched high over the metal beams that had once been part of a space ship.

"We know!"

"Check your airspace?" He turned his head to the left and the right of Carenath, who was vibrating in his eagerness to jump off.

"Checked!"

"Remember to skip! Let's go!"

Rising up from Carenath's neck as far as the riding straps would permit, Sean raised his arm high, rotated his hand, and then dropped it: the signal to spring.

Seventeen dragons launched themselves skyward, arrowing upward in the bright tropical sky in two V formations. Then, as a bewildered and incredulous Peter Chernoff watched, the Vs disappeared.

Mouth open, Peter stared for one more long moment. Then he turned on his heels, raced to the office, and launched himself at the comm unit. "Fort, this is Seminole. Fort, do you copy? Only you won't."

"Peter, is that you?" his brother Jake asked.

"Tarrie was here, but she left, with a flamethrower."

"Get a hold of yourself, Pete. You're not making any sense."

"They all came. They took our flamethrowers and half the tanks and left. All of them. All at once."

"Peter, calm down and make sense."

"How can I make sense when I don't believe what I saw anyhow!"

"Who was there? Tarrie and who else?"

"Them. The ones who ride dragons. They've gone to Fort. To fight Thread!"

Paul picked up the comm unit. Any occupation was preferable to sitting like a barnacle on a hull in a shuttered room while a voracious organism rained down outside.

"Admiral?" Excitement tingled through Ongola's single word. "We've had word that the dragonriders are on their way here."

"Sean and his group?" Paul wondered why that would excite Ongola. "When did they start?"

"Whenever they started, sir, they're already here." Paul wondered if disappointment had got the better of his imperturbable second-in-command, for he could swear the man was laughing. "The seaport asks should they join the aerial defense of the harbor? And, Admiral, sir, I've got it on visuals! Our dragons are fighting Thread! I'll patch it in to your screen."

Paul watched as the picture cleared and the focus lengthened to show him the unbelievable vision of tiny flying creatures, undeniably spouting flame from their mouths at the silver rain that fell in a dreadful curtain over the harbor. He had that one view before the picture was interrupted by a sheet of Thread. He waited no longer.

Afterward Paul wondered that he had not broken his neck, going down stone steps three at a time. He ran full pelt across the Great Hall and down the metal stairway leading to the garage where the sleds and skimmers were stored. Fulmar and one mechanic were bent over a gyro, and stared in surprise at him.

"You there, get the doors open. Fulmar, you'd better come with me. They may need help." He all but fell into the nearest sled, fumbling with the comm unit. "Ongola, tell Emily and Pol and Bay that their protégés have made it. Record this, by all that's holy, get as much of this on film as you can."

Paul had the sled motor turning over before Fulmar had shut the canopy. He slipped the sled under the door before it was fully open, a maneuver he would have reamed anyone else for attempting, and then, turning on the power, he made an arrow ascent straight up out of the valley. Emerging from the shelter of the cliffs of Fort, he could see the ominous line of Thread.

"Admiral, have you gone mad?" Fulmar asked.

"Use the screen, high magnification. Hell, you don't need it, Fulmar, you can see it with your bare eyeballs!" Paul pointed wildly. "See. Flame. See the bursts. I count fourteen, fifteen emissions. The dragons are fighting Thread!"

It was frightening, Sean thought. It was wonderful! It was the finest moment in his life, and he was scared stiff. They had all emerged right on target, just above the harbor, dragon-lengths ahead of the Fall.

Carenath started flaming instantly, and then skipped as they were about to plow through a second tangle of the stuff.

Are the others all right? Sean anxiously asked Carenath as they slipped back into real space.

Flaming well and skipping properly, Carenath assured him with calm dignity, veering slightly to flame again, turning his head from side to side, searing his way through Thread.

Sean glanced around and saw the rest of his wing following in the step formation they had adopted from Kenjo's sled tactics. That gave them the widest possible range of destruction. Even as Sean looked, he saw Jerry and Manooth wink out and back in again, neatly escaping. Then he and Carenath skipped.

A thousand feet below them, he caught a glimpse of Sorka's wing of five and, following that formation, Tarrie leading the remaining queens.

More! Carenath said imperiously, arrowing upward in a trough between Thread. He turned his head backward, mouth wide open. Sean fumbled for a lump of firestone. This will have to be practiced, he thought. Carenath skipped them out.

Shoth has a wing-score, Carenath announced. *He will continue to fly!*

He'll learn to fly the better for it! Sean retorted.

Then the straps strained at the belt as Carenath seemed to stand on his tail to avoid a stream of Thread which he then followed with flame.

Back in formation! Sean ordered. The last thing they needed was to sear one another. He saw that the others had held their positions as Carenath resumed his.

After that first exhilarating cross of the Threadfall, they all got down to business until flame and evasion became instinctive. Carenath went *between* several times to lose Thread that had wrapped about his wings. Sean locked his jaw against his dragon's pain each time Carenath was scored. By then all the bronzes and browns had received minor injuries. Still they had fought on. The queens constantly encouraged them. Then Faranth reported the arrival of a sled; reported again that ground crews were out in the harbor area, destroying the shells that had made it to the surface. The queen riders had used up the tanks they had taken from Seminole. Sorka was going to get more from the harbor hold.

Faranth asks how long will we fight? Carenath asked.

As long as we have firestone to fight with! Sean replied grimly. He had just taken a faceful of char, and his cheeks stung. In the back of his mind he noted that full face masks would be useful.

Manooth says they have no more firestone! Carenath announced suddenly after a nearly mindless length of fighting time. *Shall they see if there is more at Fort Hold?*

Sean had not realized how far inland their battle had taken them. They were indeed over the imposing ramparts of Fort Hold. He stared in a moment of bewilderment, suddenly very much aware of how he ached from cold and strain. His body felt bruised from the riding straps, his face smarted, and his fingers, toes, and knees were numb.

Tell them to land at Fort! he said. *Thread has moved up into the mountains. We can do no more today!*

Good! Carenath replied with such enthusiasm that Sean forgot his sore cheeks and grinned. He slapped affectionately at his dragon's shoulder as the formation executed a right turn, spiraling down to land.

"Emily!" Pierre burst into his wife's room. "Emily, you'll never believe it!"

"Believe what?" she said in the tired voice that seemed all she could muster since the accident. She turned her head on the cushioned back of the support chair and smiled wanly at him.

"They've come! I heard, but I had to see it to believe it myself. The dragons and their riders have all reached Fort. They reached it in triumph! They've actually fought Thread, just as you dreamed they would, as Kit Ping designed them to do!" He caught the hand she lifted, the one part of her that had not been broken in the crash. "All seventeen brave fine young people. And they cut a real swath in the Fall, Paul says." He found himself smiling broadly, tears in his eyes as he saw color flushing across her cheeks, the lift of her chest, and the flash of interest in her eyes. She raised her head, and he rattled on. "Paul watched them flame Thread from the skies. They didn't stay for the entire Fall, of course, part of it was over the sea anyhow, and the rest will fall in the mountains where it can't do much harm.

"Paul said it was the most magnificent thing he's ever seen. Better than the relief at Cygnus. They have a record of it, too, so you can see it later." Pierre bent to kiss her hand. He had tears in his eyes for Emily, and for the valiant young people who had ridden against so terrible a menace in the skies of their wondrous and frightening new world. "Paul's gone down to greet them. A triumphant arrival. My word, but it puts heart in all of us. Everyone is yelling and cheering, and Pol and Bay were weeping, which is something quite unscientific for that pair. I suppose they feel that the dragonriders are their creations. I suppose they're right, don't you agree?"

Emily struggled in the support chair, her fingers clutching at him. "Help me to the window, Pierre? I must see them. I must see them for myself!"

Most of the inhabitants of Fort Hold turned out to greet them, waving impromptu banners of bright cloth and shouting tumultuously as the dragons backwinged to land on the open field, where here and there ground crews had gotten rid of what Thread had escaped the dragons' fire. The crowd surged forward, mobbing the individual riders, everyone eager to touch a dragon, ignoring at first the riders' strident appeals for something to ease Thread-pierced wings and scored hide.

Gratefully Sean saw a skimmer hovering, and heard the loud-spoken orders to give the dragons room, and let the medics in.

The hubbub subsided a decibel or two. The crowds parted, allowing the medical teams access, giving the dragonriders space to dismount, and whispering sympathetically when the cheering had died down enough so that the dragons could be heard whimpering in pain. Some of those gathered around Carenath eagerly helped Sean doctor him.

Is everyone here to see us? Carenath asked shyly. The bronze turned his left wing so that Sean could reach a particularly wide score and sighed in audible relief as anesthetic cream was slathered on.

"I don't know how we got so lucky," Sean muttered to himself when he was certain that all Carenath's injuries had been attended to. He looked around him, checking to see that all the other dragons had been treated. Sorka gave him a thumbs-up signal and grinned at him, her face smeared with blood and soot. He returned her sign with both fists. "Sheer fluke we got out of that with just sears and scores. We didn't even know what we were doing. Blind luck!" His mind roiled with ways to avoid any sort of scoring and ideas for drills to improve how much Thread a single breath could char. Their fight had been, after all, only the first, brief skirmish in a long, long war.

"Hey, Sean, you need some, too," one of the medics said, pulling off his helmet to anoint his cheeks. "Got to get you looking spruce. The admiral's waiting!"

As if her words were a cue, a murmurous silence fell over the plain. The riders converged together and moved forward to the foot of the ramp where Paul Benden, in the full uniform of a fleet admiral, with Ongola and Ezra Keroon similarly attired flanking him, awaited the seventeen young heroes.

In step, the dragonriders walked forward, past people grinning foolishly in their pride. Sean recognized many faces: Pol and Bay looking about to burst with pride; Telgar, tears streaming down his cheeks, Ozzie and Cobber on either side of him; Cherry Duff upheld by two sons, her black eyes gleaming with joy. He caught sight of the Hanrahans, Mairi holding up his small son to see the pageantry. There was no sign of Governor Emily Boll, and Sean felt his heart contract. What Peter Chernoff had said was true, then. This moment would not be the same without her.

They reached the ramp, and somehow the queen riders had dropped a step behind the others and Sean stood in the center. When they halted, he took a step forward and saluted. It seemed the correct thing to do. Admiral Benden, tears in his eyes, proudly returned the salute.

"Admiral Benden, sir," said Sean, rider of bronze Carenath, "may I present the Dragonriders of Pern?"

About the Author

Born on April 1, Anne McCaffrey has tried to live up to such an auspicious natal day. Her first novel was created in Latin class and might have brought her instant fame, as well as an A, had she attempted to write in the language. Much chastened, she turned to the stage and became a character actress, appearing in the first successful summer music circus at Lambertville, New Jersey. She studied voice for nine years and, during that time, became intensely interested in the stage direction of opera and operetta, ending this phase of her life with the stage direction of the American premiere of Carl Orff's *Ludus De Nato Infante Mirificus*, in which she also played a witch.

By the time the three children of her marriage were comfortably at school most of the day, she had already achieved enough success with short stories to devote full time to writing.

Between her frequent appearances in the United States and England as a lecturer and guest-of-honor at science-fiction conventions, Ms. McCaffrey lives at Dragonhold, in the hills of Wicklow County, Ireland, with two cats, two dogs, and assorted horses. Of herself, Ms. McCaffrey says, "I have green eyes, silver hair, and freckles; the rest changes without notice."

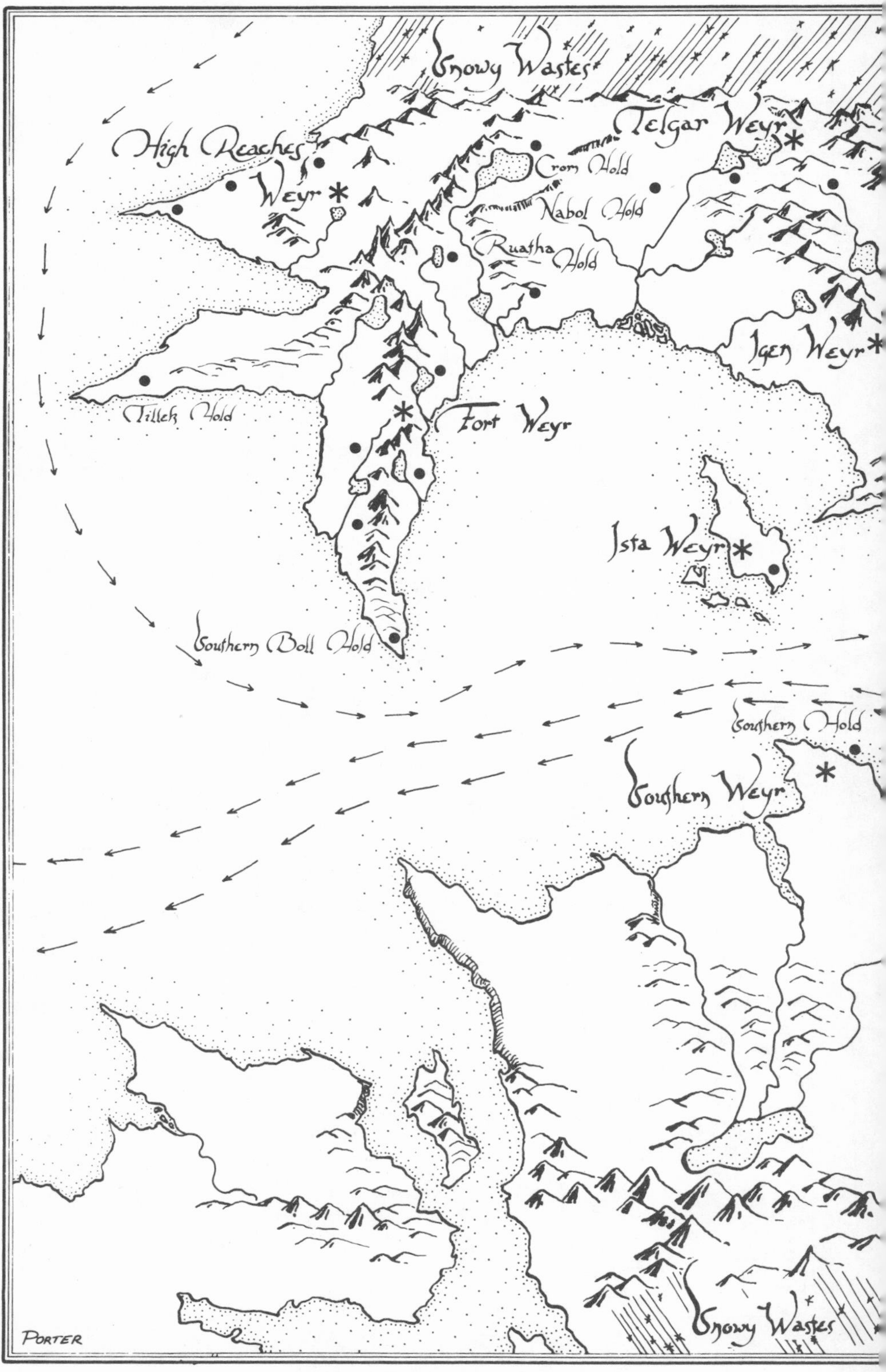
Snowy Wastes
Telgar Weyr
High Reaches Weyr
Crom Hold
Nabol Hold
Ruatha Hold
Igen Weyr
Tillek Hold
Fort Weyr
Ista Weyr
Southern Boll Hold
Southern Hold
Southern Weyr
Snowy Wastes
PORTER